REWRITING THE PAST IN
SCOTTISH LITERATURE, 1350–1550

REWRITING THE PAST IN SCOTTISH LITERATURE, 1350–1550

Kate Ash-Irisarri

D. S. BREWER

© Kate Ash-Irisarri 2025

All Rights Reserved. Except as permitted under current legislation
no part of this work may be photocopied, stored in a retrieval system,
published, performed in public, adapted, broadcast,
transmitted, recorded or reproduced in any form or by any means,
without the prior permission of the copyright owner

The right of Kate Ash-Irisarri to be identified as
the author of this work has been asserted in accordance with
sections 77 and 78 of the Copyright, Designs and Patents Act 1988

First published 2025
D. S. Brewer, Cambridge

ISBN 978 1 84384 677 2

D. S. Brewer is an imprint of Boydell & Brewer Ltd
PO Box 9, Woodbridge, Suffolk IP12 3DF, UK
and of Boydell & Brewer Inc.
668 Mt Hope Avenue, Rochester, NY 14620–2731, USA
website: www.boydellandbrewer.co.uk

Our Authorised Representative for product safety in the EU is Easy Access
System Europe – Mustamäe tee 50, 10621 Tallinn, Estonia,
gpsr.requests@easproject.com

A CIP catalogue record for this book is available
from the British Library

The publisher has no responsibility for the continued existence or accuracy
of URLs for external or third-party internet websites referred to in this book,
and does not guarantee that any content on such websites is, or will remain,
accurate or appropriate

In loving memory
James, Julia, Pepe and Patricia

CONTENTS

List of Figures	viii
Acknowledgements	ix
List of Abbreviations	xi
Introduction	1
1. The North Remembers: Identity and Nation across Scotland's Borders	19
2. Family Ties: The Politics of Scottish Genealogical Memory	50
3. Reassembling Forgotten History: Bower's *Scotichronicon* at Coupar Angus	79
4. Hary's *Wallace* as a Book of Memory	99
5. Memory and Nation in Sir David Lyndsay's *The Dreme* and *The Testament of the Papyngo*	122
6. Sustaining the 'natiue cuntre': Remembering the Past in *The Complaynt of Scotland*	150
Conclusion: Making Stories, Making Memories	172
Bibliography	179
Index	199

FIGURES

1. Genealogical tree with pictorial heads of Scottish kings. University of Edinburgh Library, MS 186, fol. 345r. Reproduced by permission of The University of Edinburgh Heritage Collections.   54

2. The journey of Scota and Gaythelos. Cambridge, Corpus Christi College MS 171A, fol. 14v. Reproduced by permission of The Parker Library, Corpus Christi College, Cambridge.   59

3. The inauguration of Alexander III. Cambridge, Corpus Christi College MS 171B, fol. 206r. Reproduced by permission of The Parker Library, Corpus Christi College, Cambridge.   65

4. The opening page of Hary's *Wallace*. Edinburgh, National Library of Scotland, Adv. MS 19.2.2 (ii), fol. 1r. Reproduced by permission of the National Library of Scotland.   101

ACKNOWLEDGEMENTS

They say it takes a village to raise a child. It is equally true that writing a book is a collective effort, and there are many debts of gratitude that I owe to those who have helped, in various ways, to bring this book to fruition. It goes without saying that the responsibility for any remaining errors and shortcomings is solely my own.

The seeds of my fascination with Older Scots literature were sown by my undergraduate tutor, Sally Mapstone, and potted on by my PhD supervisor, Anke Bernau, whose own interests in memory informed my own. I am thankful to these extraordinary women for their inspiration.

Elements of certain chapters have appeared in earlier incarnations; I would like to thank Palgrave Macmillan, Routledge and Cambridge Scholars Publishing for their permission to include them here. Thanks also to the National Library of Scotland, the Parker Library, University of Cambridge and the University of Edinburgh Heritage Collections for access to their collections and permission to reproduce images. I am grateful for the financial assistance provided by the School of Literatures, Languages and Cultures at the University of Edinburgh for being able to include images. I would like to acknowledge colleagues at Nottingham and Bristol for their encouragement and friendship, especially during the seemingly never-ending tranche of fixed-term contracts. This book was completed at the University of Edinburgh and I am thankful to my colleagues there who have welcomed me and supported this book over the finishing line.

I am fortunate to have been advised and assisted during the writing of this book by numerous colleagues and academic friends; I am grateful to them for sharing their time and knowledge, for their reading of draft chapters, engaging conversations and suggestions for avenues of research. Particular thanks must go to Steve Boardman, Michael Brown, Mark Bruce, Ardis Butterfield, Dermot Cavanagh, Sarah Dunnigan, Elizabeth Ewan, R. James Goldstein, Janet Hadley Williams, Cathy Hume, Robert Irvine, Alasdair MacDonald, Ainsley McIntosh, Gerry McKeever, Pam Lock, Joanna Martin, Roger Mason, David Matthews, Gale Owen-Crocker, David Parkinson, John-Mark Philo, Ros Powell, Rhiannon Purdie, Will Rossiter, Katherine Terrell, Sebastiaan Verweij, Greg Walker, Alice Wickenden and Emily Wingfield.

To Elizabeth Elliott and Lucy Hinnie: thank you for your boundless generosity, insight and friendship. I am a better scholar because of you. To Jenni Hyde, for the breakfast walks and ballad discussions. John McGavin graciously encouraged my work when I was a timid PhD student at her first 'big' conference. I still keep the e-mail as a pep talk and it has been re-read many times during writing this book. I will be forever thankful for the personal and professional friendship shown to me by Nicola Royan, without whose encouragement and guidance I would not still be in academia. Caroline Palmer has been more patient with this book than either of us would care to admit. I offer my thanks to her and the rest of the team at Boydell & Brewer. I am also grateful to my anonymous readers for insightful comments and suggestions.

Thanks to family and friends, who have offered hospitality, childcare and much-needed distraction at the most perfect of times. To Damian, who has been dragged round far too many medieval monuments and listened to more ramblings about medieval Scotland than he would ever have wished for, my deepest appreciation and love. None of this would be possible without you. To Éilis, who makes everything, every day, worthwhile.

It is customary to dedicate first publications to parents. I am indebted to my own, Michael and Sylvia, as well as my sister Connie; without their love, support and encouragement, I would never have made it to university, let alone written a book. I am, however, going to break with tradition and dedicate this book to those who did not get to see its completion: my grandparents, James and Julia Harding, whose retellings of their own histories delighted me as a child; and my parents-in-law, José (Pepe) and Patricia Irisarri, who are remembered always. *Requiem in pace.*

ABBREVIATIONS

AND	*Anglo-Norman Dictionary* (available at anglo-norman.net)
APS	*Acts of the Parliament of Scotland*, ed. by T. Thomson and C. Innes, 12 vols (Edinburgh, 1814–75)
ASLS	The Association for Scottish Literary Studies
BL	British Library
Bruce	*Barbour's Bruce*, ed. by Matthew P. McDiarmid and James A.C. Stevenson, 3 vols, STS 4th ser., 12, 13, 15 (Edinburgh and London: William Blackwood and Sons, 1980–85)
Chron. Bower	Walter Bower, *Scotichronicon*, ed. by D.E.R. Watt et al., 9 vols (Edinburgh and Aberdeen: Aberdeen University Press, 1987–98)
Chron. Fordun	*John of Fordun's Chronicle of the Scottish Nation*, ed. by W.F. Skene, 2 vols (Edinburgh: Edmonston and Douglas, 1871–72)
Chron. Wynt.	Wyntoun, Andrew, *The Original Chronicle of Andrew of Wyntoun Printed on Parallel Pages from the Cottonian and Wemyss MSS., with the Variants of Other Texts*, ed. by F.J. Amours, 6 vols, STS 1st ser., 50, 53, 54, 56, 57, 63 (Edinburgh and London: William Blackwood and Sons, 1903–14).
Compl.	*The Complaynt of Scotland, by Robert Wedderburn*, ed. by A.M. Stewart, STS 4th ser., 11 (Edinburgh: William Blackwood and Sons, 1979)
Dreme	Sir David Lyndsay, *The Dreme of Schir David Lyndsay*, in *The Works of Sir David Lindsay of the Mount*, ed. by D. Hamer, 4 vols, STS 3rd ser., 1, 2, 6, 8 (Edinburgh and London: William Blackwood and Sons, 1931–36)
DOST	*Dictionary of the Older Scottish Tongue* (available at dsl.ac.uk)
EETS	Early English Text Society

EETS	ES Early English Text Society Extra Series
EETS	OS Early English Text Society Original Series
Howl.	Richard Holland, *The Buke of the Howlat*, in *Longer Scottish Poems, vol. 1, 1375–1650*, ed. by Priscilla Bawcutt and Felicity Riddy (Edinburgh: Scottish Academy Press, 1987)
Inchcolm Chrs.	*Charters of the Abbey of Inchcolm*, ed. by D.E. Easson and Angus MacDonald, Scottish History Society, 3rd ser., 32 (Edinburgh: T. and A. Constable for the Scottish History Society, 1938)
MED	*Middle English Dictionary* (available at: https://quod.lib. umich.edu/m/middle-english-dictionary/dictionary)
NLS	National Library of Scotland
ODNB	*Oxford Dictionary of National Biography* (available at: https://www.oxforddnb.com/)
OED	*Oxford English Dictionary* (available at: https://www. oed.com)
Papyngo	Sir David Lyndsay, *The Testament and Complaynt of our Soverane Lordis Papyngo*, in *Sir David Lyndsay: Selected Poems*, ed. by Janet Hadley Williams (Glasgow: ASLS, 2000)
RES	*Review of English Studies*
Rot. Parl.	*Rotuli Parliamentorum*, 6 vols (London, 1767–77)
RPS	*The Records of the Parliament of Scotland to 1707*, ed. by K.M. Brown and others (St Andrews, 2007–) (available at: https://www.rps.ac.uk)
Scal.	*Sir Thomas Gray: Scalacronica (1272–1363)*, ed. and trans. by Andy King, Surtees Society, 209 (Woodbridge: Boydell Press, 2005)
SHR	*Scottish Historical Review*
SLJ	*Scottish Literary Journal*
SSL	*Studies in Scottish Literature*
STS	Scottish Text Society
Wall.	*Hary's Wallace*, ed. by Matthew P. McDiarmid, 2 vols, STS 4th ser., 4, 5 (Edinburgh and London: William Blackwood and Sons, 1968–69)

References to *Scalacronica* and the *Complaynt of Scotland* are given by page number; to *Scotichronicon*, by volume and page; to *Wyntoun* by volume, page and line number; to *The Buke of the Howlat*, the *Dreme* and the *Papyngo* by line number; to *Wallace* and *Bruce* by book and line number.

Quotations from Wyntoun use the Cotton Manuscript unless otherwise stated. I retain yogh (ȝ) and thorn (þ) in quotations but render ß as 'ss'.

Introduction

To make a nation conscious of its identity you must first give it a history[1]

In his 'Scottish' play, Shakespeare imagines a conversation between Macduff and Ross:

> Macduff: 'Stands Scotland where it did?'
> Ross: 'Alas, poor country! Almost afraid to know itself!'[2]

This imagined interaction not only reflects an anxiety about the consequences of Macbeth's tyranny but also suggests that, under that tyranny, Scotland had become unrecognisable from its former glory. The ability for a country to know itself – to self-reflect and recognise its character and singularity – raises some fraught questions. What is, and what was, Scotland? Moreover, how precisely did a kingdom recognise itself as distinct from other realms? These questions inform the subject of this book as they find expression in the literature of Scotland from the late-fourteenth to the mid-sixteenth century. In doing so, they examine the ways in which Scottish and northern English writers of that period signal a particular concern with the affective dimensions of memorialising Scottish history in the articulation of communal identity.

Nearly four hundred years after Shakespeare's imaginary conversation, the Scottish Act of 1998 gave legislative and executive powers to an elected assembly that would have the power to make domestic policy and laws for Scotland. For the first time since 1707, there existed a Scottish Parliament and administration. Devolution was promoted as the political recognition of Scottish national identity as separate from the state identity of the United Kingdom. More than just a constitutional shift in governance, devolution was, for many, a return to Scottish independence from an English nation that had asserted its dominance throughout the British Isles from at least the thirteenth century. Indeed, at the opening of the Scottish Parliament in 1999,

---

[1]   G.W.S. Barrow, *Robert the Bruce and the Community of the Realm of Scotland* (Edinburgh: Edinburgh University Press, 1988), p. 4.

[2]   William Shakespeare, *Macbeth*, ed. by Sandra Clark and Pamela Mason. The Arden Shakespeare, 3rd Ser. (London: Bloomsbury, 2015), 4.3.164–6.

Scotland's then First Minister, Alex Salmond, told the assembly that 'history will judge this day ... as the day when the people reclaimed ownership ... of our country of Scotland'.[3]

For some, the 1998 Act did not go far enough, with devolution seen as a way of preventing Scotland from ever achieving full independence.[4] However, what devolution did achieve was an official crystallisation of a certain kind of Scottishness. Salmond's rhetoric notably emphasises a collective ownership of Scotland by 'the people' of Scotland. This claim to independence is based on a concept of long-standing sovereignty and suggests that being Scottish is rooted in feelings of a shared understanding of difference and separation. In his assessment of the events leading up to Scottish devolution, BBC Scotland's political editor, Brian Taylor, remarked that 'Scottish identity is more than, or perhaps other than, language, culture, sporting links and the rest'. For Taylor, Scottishness is 'vague, imprecise, emotive: an issue which cannot be determined mechanistically or scientifically'.[5] In its imprecision, this idea of Scottishness relies on an identity that stretches back to an immemorial past, but one that everyone agrees is there and is definitive. It is what the 2007 National Outcome Strategy defined as 'the tie that binds people together'; it is 'our sense of *place*, our sense of *history* and our sense of *self*'.[6] This insistence on place, history and self argues for a distinctiveness that is at once definable, but not quite: emotive and, therefore, beyond question. In September 2014, the Scottish Independence Referendum recorded voter turnout at nearly 85 per cent, with 55 per cent voting 'no' to the question, 'should Scotland be an independent country?'[7] The reasons for the failure of the 'Yes Campaign' are many and varied and this is not the book to deal with them. What is striking, however, is how the rhetoric used by leaders and local campaigners

---

[3]   Alex Salmond, Address to the Opening Ceremony of the Scottish Parliament in Parliament Hall, 1 July 1999, https://web.archive.org/web/20081028084301/http://www.scottish.parliament.uk:80/vli/history/firstDays/1999opening2.htm [accessed 28 January 2025].

[4]   The Scottish National Party's position makes clear that, while devolution 'has improved the way in which Scotland is governed', it is 'not the same as independence' because 'under devolution' the Scottish Parliament's 'powers are limited'. https://web.archive.org/web/20080624203841/http://www.snp.org/node/240 [accessed 28 January 2025].

[5]   Brian Taylor, *The Road to the Scottish Parliament* (Edinburgh: Pioneer, 1999; rev. edn, 2002), p. 20.

[6]   The Scottish Government, National Outcome (2007), p. 1, www.scotland.gov.uk/About/scotPerforms/outcomes/natIdentity [my emphasis; accessed 21 June 2014]. This Outcome Strategy is no longer available on the Scottish Government website.

[7]   The local government areas of Dundee City, Glasgow City, North Lanarkshire and West Dunbartonshire recorded a majority 'yes' vote. Scottish Independence Referendum 2014: Analysis of Results. House of Commons Library, Research Paper 14/50 (30 September 2014), p. 4, https://researchbriefings.files.parliament.uk/documents/RP14–50/RP14–50.pdf [accessed 16 May 2019].

INTRODUCTION

on both sides of the campaign once again relied on these ideas of emotion, place, history and identity.[8] This call to sovereignty connected to place and history has a longer tradition, and it is to older expressions that I now turn my attention to explore the ways in which medieval writings about nationhood are often concerned with the emotive potential of history. This affective aspect of national identity is, I contend, related to the uses writers make of memory and their focus on reshaping the past in light of current circumstances. This is not to conflate the past with the present, or to suggest that the same markers of, and motivations for, articulations of nationhood run seamlessly from the fourteenth to the twenty-first century. Notable, though, are the subtle continuities of memory, affect and reshaping history that trace a fundamental way in which societies think about identity, community and what it means to remember the past. Throughout this book, I draw together historical and poetical works that deliberately rely on formalised conceptions of memory and imagination to narrate the nation. For nearly all of the writers discussed, this means returning to the fourteenth-century Wars of Independence as a historical period to be memorialised, reimagined and embedded in the articulation of late-medieval Scottishness.

The Wars of Independence (1296–1323 and 1332–57) were primarily sparked by English attempts to assert feudal authority over Scotland in the wake of Alexander III's death in 1286, which triggered a succession crisis. Alexander's only surviving heir was his grand-daughter, Margaret (the Maid) of Norway (1282/3–90), whose unexpected death on her journey to Scotland led to competing claims (known as the 'Great Cause', 1290–92) to the Scottish throne, with several magnate families vying for power.[9] In reality, the two main contenders were Robert Bruce, fifth lord of Annandale and John Balliol of Galloway and Barnard Castle. In 1291, Edward I (1272–1307) was invited to arbitrate the succession but exploited the opportunity to assert his own claim to overlordship. Edward chose to ignore legal advice that favoured Bruce and judged that Balliol possessed the strongest claim. Balliol became king of Scots in 1292, with the English monarch assuming that the new Scottish king would become his puppet.[10] In December 1292, Balliol acknowledged

---

[8] See, for example, Stuart McAnulla and Andrew Crines, 'The Rhetoric of Alex Salmond and the 2014 Scottish Independence Referendum', *British Politics*, 12 (2017), 473–91.

[9] For a succinct overview of the Wars of Independence, see Michael Brown, *The Wars of Scotland, 1214–1371*, The New Edinburgh History of Scotland, 4 (Edinburgh: Edinburgh University Press, 2004). A comprehensive account of the Second War can be found in Iain A. MacInnes, *Scotland's Second War of Independence, 1332–1357* (Woodbridge: Boydell Press, 2016).

[10] For a detailed account of the Great Cause and its consequences, see A.A.M. Duncan, *The Kingship of the Scots 842–1292: Succession and Independence* (Edinburgh: Edinburgh University Press, 2002), chapters 9–13; Michael A. Penman, '*Diffinicione*

Edward I of England as 'lord superior of the realm of Scotland' and became his 'liegeman for the whole realm of Scotland'.[11] To further his own claims, Edward had letters of enquiry sent to English monasteries seeking information from chronicles and records 'touching in any way our realm and the rule of Scotland'.[12] To support their positions, both the English and the Scots drew on written history, in what R. James Goldstein has called a 'War of Historiography' that persisted through the first War of Independence and Robert the Bruce's reign.[13] By 1294, 'some Scots were working to undermine Edward's lordship' and in 1295 the Scottish parliament convened at Stirling to agree a new treaty with King Philip of France, which popularly became known as the 'auld alliance'.[14] Edward I's subsequent retaliation – the sacking of Berwick in 1296, and the defeat of the Scots at the Battle of Dunbar – can be regarded as the beginning of the military conflict. Edward deposed Balliol and placed Scotland under English rule. Led by figures such as William Wallace and Andrew Moray, the Scots rebelled against English occupation and their victory at the Battle of Stirling Bridge (1297) was a significant early success. Wallace became Guardian of Scotland but was defeated at the Battle of Falkirk in 1298. Betrayed by Sir John Menteith, a Scottish nobleman who at the time was the keeper of Dumbarton Castle, Wallace was captured and executed in London in 1305. After killing his rival, John Comyn, in 1306, Robert the Bruce, earl of Carrick (and Annandale's grandson), was crowned as Robert I. Bruce faced early defeats, but secured key victories, notably at the Battle of Bannockburn (1314). The Treaty of Edinburgh-Northampton (1328) recognised Scotland's sovereignty and ended the First War of Independence. The peace was short lived. Following the death of Robert I (1329), Thomas Randolph,

---

successionis ad regnum Scottorum: Royal Succession in Scotland in the Later Middle Ages', in *Making and Breaking the Rules: Succession in Medieval Europe, c. 1000–c. 1600*, ed. by F. Lachaud and Michael A. Penman (Turnhout: Brepols, 2008), pp. 43–59.

[11] E.L.G. Stones (ed. and trans.), *Anglo-Scottish Relations, 1174–1328: Some Selected Documents* (Oxford: Oxford University Press, 1965), pp. 127.

[12] 'regnum nostrum et regimen Scocie qualitercumque contingencia': Grant G. Simpson and E.L.G. Stones, ed., *Edward I and the Throne of Scotland: An Edition of the Record Sources for the Great Cause*, 2 vols (Oxford: Oxford University Press, 1978), i, 139.

[13] R. James Goldstein, *The Matter of Scotland: Historical Narrative in Medieval Scotland* (Lincoln and London: University of Nebraska Press, 1993), p. 7; see also, pp. 57–103. Andy King and Michael Penman also note the diplomatic and historiographic 'war of words' that underwrote military action between England and Scotland: 'Introduction: Anglo-Scottish Relations in the Fourteenth Century – An Overview of Recent Research', in *England and Scotland in the Fourteenth Century: New Perspectives*, ed. by Andy King and Michael A. Penman (Woodbridge: Boydell Press, 2007), pp. 1–14 (2–3).

[14] Brown, *Wars of Scotland*, p. 173.

INTRODUCTION 5

earl of Moray, became regent for the six-year-old David II (1329–71). In 1332, Edward Balliol (1332–56), John Balliol's son, invaded Scotland, supported by the Disinherited (Anglo-Scottish nobles who had opposed Bruce and were dispossessed of their lands following Bannockburn) and, covertly, by the English king, Edward III. Edward Balliol defeated the Scots at the Battle of Dupplin Moor and briefly seized the crown. David II was forced into exile in France but returned in 1341. Captured at the Battle of Neville's Cross (1346), he was held prisoner in England for eleven years. The Treaty of Berwick (1357) secured David's release and recognition of Scotland's sovereignty, effectively ending the Wars of Independence.[15] As Elizabeth Ewan notes, the Wars of Independence have popularly been seen as 'the crucible' in which 'the concept of nationhood was forged',[16] but *national* feeling was in existence well before the onset of Anglo-Scottish hostilities at the end of the thirteenth century, as has been demonstrated in the work of Dauvit Broun and Nicola Royan.[17] Nor did 1357 signal the end of Anglo-Scottish tensions.[18] It is notable that between the late thirteenth century and the end of Henry IV's reign (1399–1413), every English king sought to press their rights to Scotland through military force.

Alongside the fact that the Scottish historiographical tradition shows that the Scots were conceiving of themselves in 'national' terms much earlier than the early fourteenth century, I want to return to Ewan's important point about the Wars of Independence being retrospectively understood as the point at which the Scottish nation came into being. What Ewan points to here are the ways in which the reception of history is shaped by its representation and, while that might be

[15] Michael Penman discusses the international dimensions of the conflict and its influence on European politics in *David II, 1329–71: The Bruce Dynasty in Scotland* (Edinburgh: Birlinn, 2005).

[16] Elizabeth Ewan, 'Late Medieval Scotland: A Study in Contrasts', in *A Companion to Scottish Poetry*, ed. by Janet Hadley Williams and Priscilla Bawcutt (Cambridge: D.S. Brewer, 2006), pp. 19–33 (32).

[17] Dauvit Broun, 'Becoming a Nation: Scotland in the Twelfth and Thirteenth Centuries', in *Nations in Medieval Britain*, ed. by H. Tsurushima (Donington: Shaun Tyas, 2010), pp. 86–103; Broun, 'The Creation of Scotland', in *Why Scottish History Still Matters*, ed. by E.J. Cowan (Edinburgh: Saltire Society, 2012), pp. 11–23; Broun, *The Irish Identity of the Kingdom of the Scots in the Twelfth and Thirteenth Centuries* (Woodbridge: Boydell Press, 1999); Broun, 'Rethinking Scottish Origins', in *Barbour's Bruce and Its Cultural Contexts: Politics, Chivalry and Literature in Late Medieval Scotland*, ed. by Steve Boardman and Susan Foran (Cambridge: D.S. Brewer, 2015), pp. 163–90; Nicola Royan with Dauvit Broun, 'Versions of Scottish Nationhood, *c.* 850–1707', in *The Edinburgh History of Scottish Literature, Volume 1: From Columba to the Union (until 1707)*, ed. by Thomas Owen Clancy and Murray Pittock (Edinburgh: Edinburgh University Press, 2007), pp. 167–83; Nicola Royan, 'Hector Boece and the Question of Veremund', *Innes Review*, 52 (2001), 42–62.

[18] See MacInnes, *Scotland's Second War of Independence*.

said of all history, it is an element that often gets neglected precisely *because* it is something that is taken for granted. In focusing on the processes by which the past is rewritten, I suggest that, from the fourteenth to the sixteenth century, the Wars of Independence became an influential point of national remembrance. The period from *c.* 1350 to *c.* 1550 witnessed a strengthening in articulations of Scottishness that sought to draw on the memory of the Anglo-Scottish wars as a scaffold with which to shore up collective identity. In *The Matter of Scotland*, R. James Goldstein argues that a feature of Scottish medieval historiography is the insistent desire to align Robert I's kingship with Scottish freedom. This ideological project, Goldstein proposes, was part of a broader approach to shape Scotland's identity as vulnerable so that it could only be strengthened through absolute loyalty to Bruce.[19] The wars represented a pre-Stewart era, but one in which the origin of the Stewarts' dynastic power was established. In the later Middle Ages, then, this particular moment of Scottish history became a potent symbol of identity that could be invoked in meaningful ways. And invoked it was. The Wars of Independence feature heavily in the literary productions of the fourteenth to sixteenth century explored in this study; nearly all of them look back repeatedly and insistently to this earlier period of Scottish history. This suggests that, while contemporaneous tensions might be a catalyst for the peaks and troughs of 'nationalist' literature, remembering past hostilities offered a potent way of imagining the nation, both in the present and for the future. With the exception of Sir Thomas Gray's *Scalacronica*, written in the mid-fourteenth century and which I regard as a 'border' text, all of the other texts I examine were written between *c.* 1440 and *c.* 1550, during the often-turbulent reigns of the Stewart royal dynasty. These texts might be considered partial in their invocations of history, but in ways that develop the inherent partiality of writing about the past. Texts such as Richard Holland's *Buke of the Howlat* (*c.* 1455), Hary's *Wallace* (*c.* 1475), and *The Complaynt of Scotland* (*c.* 1550) memorialise and imagine both the kingdom and its rulers; in doing so, they demonstrate an ideological project that situates vulnerability at the heart of the national imagination. If we read these texts according to this organising principle, it suggests that Goldstein's model of Brucean ideology persists through the literary productions of Stewart Scotland. The writing of Scotland's past becomes, then, deeply engaged in a project of shaping collective memories of a realm and its monarch under permanent threat and in need of protection.

The texts that I examine in this book are the products of a culture that recognised the importance of history and memory to the changing emphases that nationhood assumed over the course of the late fourteenth to the mid-sixteenth century. These imaginative endeavours sought to offer a coherent and collective shape to what they determined should be remembered within various textual

---

[19] Goldstein, *Matter of Scotland*, esp. p. 79.

INTRODUCTION

communities within Scotland. The practice of national memory becomes, then, a mode of selective reconstruction and appropriation that responds specifically to the needs of the circumstances of composition. This is not to say that Scottish writers view nation as always emerging; indeed, they assume that national identity or distinctiveness is – and always has been – there. Rather, all of the writers of this study show a deft awareness of the uses to which the past can be put, drawing specifically on the possibilities that memory and forgetting offer for subtly shifting the emphasis of thinking the nation at any given point.

Nations and Identities

In his seminal essay of 1882, Ernst Renan asked 'Qu'est-ce-qu'une nation?' – What is a nation?[20] This is a question to which there is no simple, or single, answer. In trying to ascertain the meaning of 'nacioun' in late medieval Scotland, the extant evidence presents some challenges. The *Dictionary of the Older Scottish Tongue* (*DOST*), rather vaguely, gives the primary meaning of 'natioun' as 'a nation, in usual uses'.[21] What the 'usual uses' are for *DOST* might be solved by referring to the primary meaning of 'nation' in contemporary definition, which, according to the *Oxford English Dictionary*, is 'a large aggregate of communities and individuals united by factors such as common descent, language, culture, history, or occupation of the same territory, so as to form a distinct people. Now also: such a people forming a political state'.[22] Susan Reynolds preferred the term 'regnal' over 'national' in medieval contexts to avoid the overly simplistic conflation of the nation with the political state. She suggested that 'the idea of the permanent and objectively real nation ... closely resembles the medieval idea of the kingdom as comprising a people with a similarly permanent and objective reality'.[23] However, the term 'nacioun' was used in late medieval Scotland and this is the term I adopt throughout this study and its examination of the memorial processes at work in articulating its meaning.

Several theories of nationhood stress its emergence as a modern phenomenon, seeing the rise of modern nationalism as a reaction against the pre-modern

---

[20] Ernst Renan, '"Qu'est-ce-qu'une nation?" – What is a nation?', trans. by M. Thom in *Nation and Narration*, ed. by Homi K. Bhabha (London: Routledge, 1990; repr. 2003), pp. 8–22.

[21] *DOST*, Natioun, Nacioun, *n.* 1.

[22] *OED*, nation, *n.* 1.1.a.

[23] Susan Reynolds, *Kingdoms and Communities in Western Europe, 900–1300*, 2nd edn (Oxford: Oxford University Press, 1997), p. 252.

world.[24] Yet, as Orest Ranum articulates, the problem of thinking about pre-modern national identity is 'not one of determining whether these identities existed, but of determining what [the] components and functions were at various times'.[25] Perhaps the most influential proponent of the modern nation has been Benedict Anderson, who contends, in his highly influential *Imagined Communities*, that the 'astonishing power of the papacy' during the medieval period meant that any notion of collective identity could be understood only in religious (rather than regnal) terms.[26] Moreover, Anderson suggests, this sense of identity was *unselfconscious*: not thought about, constructed or performed in any way, but understood as a given.[27] Thinking the nation, for Anderson, became possible only with the exploration of the non-European world, the decline of Latin as the language of clerical power and the rise of print culture.[28] Anderson has become rather a straw man for pre-modern scholars, yet his contention that nationalism should be regarded as belonging with other concepts such as religion and kinship offers an understanding of the nation as a cultural belief that is not incompatible with the evidence we find for national discourse in medieval literature. The processes through which communities are imagined – how and why – speaks productively to this study of how late medieval Scottish writers sought to reshape the past in varying political and cultural conditions. While Anderson argues that 'simultaneity-along-time' – referring to the medieval practice of simultaneously situating events in the past, present and future – prevented the nation being imagined as a unit, I would argue that it is precisely this idea of simultaneity that allows for medieval expressions of nationhood which see continuity and synchronicity as constituent parts of thinking the nation.

The *idea* of the nation, specifically because of its vagueness, acquires a potent imaginative potential that requires the individual to feel themselves part of a collective and to associate certain attributes or characteristics with that identity. It is what Broun has suggestively called 'a phenomenon of mind'.[29] The function of national discourse is what Patricia Ingham, among others,

---

[24] See, for example, Anthony D. Smith, *National Identity* (London: Penguin, 1991); Eric Hobsbawm, *Nations and Nationalism since 1780* (Cambridge: Cambridge University Press, 1990); Ernest Gellner, *Encounters with Nationalism* (Oxford: Blackwell, 1994).

[25] Orest Ranum, 'Introduction', in *National Consciousness, History and Political Culture in Early Modern Europe*, ed. by Orest Ranum (Baltimore and London: Johns Hopkins University Press, 1975), pp. 1–9 (6).

[26] Benedict Anderson, *Imagined Communities: Reflections on the Origins and Spread of Nationalism* (London: Verso, 1983; repr. 1991), p. 15.

[27] Anderson, *Imagined Communities*, p. 16.

[28] Anderson, *Imagined Communities*, pp. 16–19.

[29] Broun, 'Rethinking Scottish Origins', p. 164.

INTRODUCTION

has termed 'national fantasy', approximating to a communality that, as Kathy Lavezzo argues, 'speaks to impossible and sometimes contradictory' desires to invoke 'ever shifting bundle[s] of collective quasi-mythic national traits'.[30] In these desires, Thorlac Turville-Petre contends that nationality becomes a powerful identity that seemingly has the least to justify itself.[31] The concept of 'the nation' could be reworked and shaped to fit certain ideologies and frameworks of inclusivity – and exclusivity – in ways that other identities were unable to do. For example, in the mid-fifteenth century, Scottish chronicler Walter Bower used religious identity to establish markers of national difference between the English and the Scots. In Book 3 of *Scotichronicon*, Bower narrates the story of how Pope Gregory sent Augustine to Britain to 'preach the Word of God to the Angles who were blinded by heathen superstition' (*Chron. Bower* 2. 89). Augustine converts the English to Christianity but, in attempting to preach to the West Saxons in Dorset, he is reviled and abused. Bower recalls how, in an act of divine retribution, 'God smote' the Saxons 'in their hinder parts, giving them everlasting shame so that in the private parts both of themselves and their descendants all alike were born with a tail' (*Chron. Bower* 2. 91). The English as a national group are marked by difference that is both somatically and religiously racial. Common religion was no guarantee of shared identity in other respects; the double conversion of the English marks religion as a unit by which difference, rather than unity, could be asserted, as it simultaneously makes English religious history constitutive of Scottish collective identity.

It was not only religion that could constitute national difference in the Middle Ages. The root of 'nation' in *natio*, connoting birth, race or stock, meant that lineage constituted an understanding of differences between peoples. Clearly, nation is more than – or at least not restricted to – a single set of conditions; the shifting contexts of politics, power and social organisation necessitate that what a nation means at any point in time is contingent on a number of interdependent factors. As Geraldine Heng's work demonstrates, from the thirteenth century there emerged a grammar of 'racial classification and hierarchy', which sought to theorise 'a taxonomy of essential differences among peoples'.[32] At the same time Heng suggests, one of the 'distinguishing properties of the medieval nation' is that it is 'always a community

---

[30] Patricia Ingham, *Sovereign Fantasies: Arthurian Romances and the Making of Britain* (Philadelphia: University of Pennsylvania Press, 2001), p. 10; Kathy Lavezzo, *Angels on the Edge of the World: Geography, Literature, and English Community, 1000–1534* (Ithaca and London: Cornell University Press, 2006), p. 9.

[31] Thorlac Turville-Petre, *England the Nation: Language, Literature, and National Identity, 1290–1340* (Oxford: Clarendon Press, 1996), p. 10.

[32] Geraldine Heng, *Empire of Magic: Medieval Romance and the Politics of Cultural Fantasy* (New York: Columbia University Press, 2003), pp. 5, 70. See also,

of the realm, *communitas regni*', in which the 'symbolizing potentials of the king' enable 'an expressive vocabulary' of unity, cohesion, and stability to be imagined.[33] The figure of the king as a locus of nation building is often crucial to understanding expressions of nationhood in medieval texts and it is a key feature, in various ways, in all of the texts that form the subject of this study. This regnal focus allows a king's subjects to understand themselves as a unified community defined by their relationship to the crown as well as each other. This seemingly 'leveling discourse', as Heng terms it, brings into medieval consciousness the 'horizontal comradeship' that is so important to Anderson's view of national beginnings.[34] In this regard, late medieval Scotland offers an important perspective.

Following the death of Alexander III, the 'great men ... the bishops, abbots and priors, the earl and barons' of Scotland 'assembled at Scone' to swear their loyalty to Margaret of Norway. At this 'parliament', six Guardians (*custodes*) were appointed, 'styl[ing] themselves as "appointed by common counsel" or "elected by the community of the realm"'.[35] In G.W.S. Barrow's assessment of Scottish political thought, 'Nothing and no one could be an adequate substitute for the king'; the vacant throne necessitated that the kingdom could '*only* resolve itself into a collective entity, into the universality of its freemen, or, in thirteenth-century language, into the "community of the realm of Scotland"'.[36] This suggests that Scottish practice saw the *communitas regni Scotie* as something that sat beyond the monarch, although intimately connected to it. As Barrow, clarifies:

> Of course, there was such a 'community' even when the king was on the throne, but in normal times, with an adult and vigorous rulers, the community would fade into the background. The king would take the initiative, would act or give orders as he thought best. In serious matters he would naturally take the advice of his council; but this council, in the theory of the time, was no other than a representation of the wider community.[37]

In my examination of late medieval Scottish Latin and vernacular texts, my aim is not to establish whether there was a sense of Scottishness in the fourteenth and fifteenth centuries. That has been established by many scholars; rather I seek to demonstrate *how* that identity was imagined and articulated in texts

---

Geraldine Heng, *The Invention of Race in the European Middle Ages* (Cambridge: Cambridge University Press, 2018).

33 Heng, *Empire of Magic*, p. 72.
34 Heng, *Empire of Magic*, p. 72; Anderson, *Imagined Communities*, p. 7.
35 Barrow, *Robert Bruce*, p. 17.
36 Barrow, *Robert Bruce*, p. 16.
37 Barrow, *Robert Bruce*, p. 16.

INTRODUCTION 11

that draw specifically on memories of Anglo-Scottish conflict to articulate national distinctiveness in relation to the king and the community.

My study concentrates on the commemorative aspects of Scottish historiography to argue that a memorial dimension assumes centrality in the national project of a number of cultural productions written in Scotland from *c.* 1350 to *c.* 1550.[38] In doing so, I explore how specifically chosen recollections were crafted to shape a collective social imaginary. I argue for a deeply reaching impact of the Wars of Independence on the national memory, effectively generating a cycle of trauma that passed through the subsequent generations of Scottish literary production. The texts that I examine demonstrate how the cumulative effects of Anglo-Scottish conflict were woven through the cultural fabric of late medieval Scotland, punctuating the literary expression of both national self-confidence and national self-doubt. The dominant model of trauma, the abreactive model, asserts that traumatic experience generates a 'temporal gap' that results in the unrepresentability of that trauma as a result of the brain's inability to process the event.[39] Conceptualisations of intergenerational trauma, however, think about personal loss – loss experienced by the individual – and historical absence, which is loss experienced by ancestors as a collective.[40] In this model, present identity can be affected (and effected) by historical trauma through a shared heritage. Through rewriting the past and relying on recollections of the Wars of Independence, the texts I examine suggest that a collective memory of inherited experience was instrumental in raising questions about national identity from the fourteenth to the sixteenth century. In doing so, I also contend that these texts rely specifically on medieval understandings of memory and memorial images to articulate the nation.

Medieval Memories

Memory plays a key role in the creation of national character, providing a sense of what it means to participate in a collective enterprise that actively reshapes itself. The texts that form the basis of my study draw on a number of conceptions of memory as their writers engage in reshaping historical narrative. Mary Carruthers points out in her seminal work, *The Book of Memory*, that medieval

---

[38] I use the term 'written in' here to include Gray's *Scalacronica*, which was, in part, produced in Scotland, although Gray, himself, was English.

[39] See Cathy Caruth, *Unclaimed Experience: Trauma, Narrative, and History* (Baltimore and London: Johns Hopkins University Press, 1996), p. 17.

[40] See, for example, the work of Dominick LaCapra, *Writing History, Writing Trauma* (Baltimore and London: Johns Hopkins University Press, 2001).

culture was 'fundamentally memorial'[41] and understood the importance of a well-trained memory to the development of the ethical self. The centrality of memory to the human experience is clear, but what memory was and how it might be described took a variety of forms. The entries for 'memorie' in both *MED* and *DOST* indicate that the term was used to refer to a wide range of concepts, including the faculty of memory, recollection, fame (or reputation), memorial and observance, and the written record.[42] In the Middle Ages, memory provided a foundation for active contemplation and composition; memory made knowledge useful and, combined with intellect (imagination), resulted in the creative recombination of material stored in the mind. This understanding of memory prompted Carruthers to declare that 'the choice to train one's memory or not ... was not a choice dictated by convenience: it was a matter of ethics'; for medieval thinkers a 'person without a memory, if such a thing could be, would be a person without a moral character and, in a basic sense, without humanity'.[43] The traditions of Aristotle (384–322 BCE), Galen (129–216 CE) and Ibn Sina [Avicenna] (*c.* 980–1037) treat memory as the final process in sensory perception which began with the stimulation of the five senses, which were then worked on by intellect (or reason) to become knowledge that might then be stored away.[44] According to medieval faculty psychology, then, memory was a natural function of the body but, in order to work most effectively, memory needed to be trained.[45]

A system of training the memory by making images in the mind was reiterated in treatises such as the *Rhetorica ad Herennium* (86–82 BCE), which gives the fullest and most influential account of *memoria*, as well as in Aristotle's *De memoria et reminiscentia*, Augustine's *Confessions*, and Thomas Aquinas' *Summa Theologiae* (*c.* 1267), to name a few examples from the vast corpus of work on memory produced during the classical period and the Middle Ages.[46]

---

[41] Mary Carruthers, *The Book of Memory: A Study of Memory in Medieval Culture*, 2nd edn (Cambridge: Cambridge University Press, 2008), p. 9.

[42] *MED* and *DOST*, memory, *n*.

[43] Carruthers, *Book of Memory*, p. 14.

[44] See Aristotle, *On Memory*, translated with interpretative essays and commentary by R. Sorabji (Providence, RI: Brown University Press, 1972); Ibn Sina [Avicenna, Latinus], *Liber de anima seu sextus de naturalibus*, ed. by S. van Reit, 2 vols (Leiden: Brill, 1968–72); on Galen, see Ricardo Julião, 'Galen on the Anatomy of Memory', *Medicina nei Secoli*, 34.1 (2022), 55–75.

[45] For an extensive analysis of medieval faculty psychology, see Robert Folger, *Images in Mind: Lovesickness, Spanish Sentimental Fiction and 'Don Quijote'* (Chapel Hill: University of North Carolina Press, 2002), pp. 15–81. See also, Elizabeth Elliott, *Remembering Boethius: Writing Aristocratic Identity in Late Medieval French and English Literatures* (Farnham: Ashgate, 2012), pp. 138–40.

[46] For comprehensive studies see Janet Coleman, *Ancient and Medieval Memories: Studies in the Reconstruction of the Past* (Cambridge: Cambridge University Press,

INTRODUCTION 13

In *De anima*, Aristotle writes that 'the soul never thinks without an image', and, in almost all ancient and medieval works concerning memory training, the emphasis on the visual is paramount.[47] The memory is described as a mental picture, or *phantasm*, that is inscribed or imprinted physically upon the part of the body that constitutes memory: 'the structure of memory, like a wax tablet, employs places [*loci*] and in these gathers together [*collocat*] images'.[48] The *Ad Herennium* describes the formation of loci as the most important part of the development of artificial memory and states that these loci are 'like wax tablets which remain when what is written on them has been effaced and are ready to be written on again'.[49] The conception of the memory as a wax tablet ready to receive and store imprinted sense data was so pervasive throughout ancient and medieval theories of memory that Max Black has termed it a 'cognitive archetype'.[50] Importantly, this is an image that conceptualises the malleability of memory, which can be reworked and reinscribed.

Nevertheless, the image of the memory as a wax tablet does not explain or provide the structures for *ordering* memory. The content and organisation of memory had to be developed from this, for the systematic arrangement of the memory enabled clarity of knowledge. In order to compartmentalise and structure the memory to render it most useful, ancient and medieval theorists often referred to architectural schema. Augustine, for instance, calls the memory a storehouse (*thesaurus*), and the metaphor of the storehouse took on variant forms: of 'storage room', 'treasury' and 'strongbox', *cella* and *arca*.[51] Richard de Bury (1287–1345) writes of reading and remembering as a form of architectural journey, describing how perception passes through the eyes to the 'vestibule of common sense and the atriums of imagination', where it 'enters the chamber of intellect, taking its place in the couch of memory,

---

1992); Carruthers, *Book of Memory*; Frances A. Yates, *The Art of Memory* (1966, London: Pimlico, 1992); Mary Carruthers and Jan Ziolkowski, *The Medieval Craft of Memory: An Anthology of Texts and Pictures* (Philadelphia: University of Pennsylvania Press, 2002).

[47] Aristotle, *De anima*, translated by J.A. Smith from Ross's edition, in *The Complete Works of Aristotle: The Revised Oxford Translation*, ed. by J. Barnes, 2 vols (Princeton, NJ: Princeton University Press, 1984), i. 685.

[48] Cicero, *Partitiones oratoriae*, cited in Carruthers, *Book of Memory*, p. 18.

[49] Yates, *Art of Memory*, p. 23.

[50] Max Black, *Models and Metaphors: Studies in Language and Philosophy* (Ithaca, NY: Cornell University Press, 1962), pp. 219–43.

[51] Augustine, *Confessions*, trans. by R.S. Pine-Coffin (London: Penguin, 1961), pp. 214–17. In her analysis of the symbolic use of buildings in religious and secular texts, Christiania Whitehead discusses how writers used architecture to represent the psychological faculties, particularly memory; *Castles of the Mind: A Study of Medieval Architectural Allegory* (Cardiff: University of Wales Press, 2003), esp. pp. 29–38.

where it engenders the eternal truth of the mind'.[52] In the twelfth-century *De tribus maximis circumstantiis gestorum*, Hugh of St Victor (*c.* 1096–1141) used the image of the money pouch (*sacculus*) as a metaphor for the organised memory. He describes how the internal structure of the bag allowed coins to be sorted according to shape and size. Hugh advised that 'each single thing' should be 'Dispose[d] and separate[d]' into 'its own place ... so that you may know what has been placed here and what there', for 'Confusion is the mother of ignorance and forgetfulness, but orderly arrangement illuminates the intelligence and secures memory'.[53] Images of money bags and cells of memory appear often in vernacular writings; in the fourteenth century, for example, François Villon used the rhymed association of memory (*memoir*) and the closet (*aumoiry*) in his *Lais*.[54] These literary references to architectural memory schemes point to the fact that such devices for training the memory were known and understood beyond scholastic and monastic circles. They also attest to an established practice of referring to the memory as a physical storage space that, if it was well organised, could be opened at will and the most appropriate memory easily selected.

Memory in the Middle Ages, then, was not understood in terms of storing and recalling the past for its own sake but, rather, as a means to enable imagination and composition, usually with a moral aim. Composition, therefore, was both a way of remembering and a way of providing future generations with a memory aid. As Carruthers points out, the contents of medieval treasuries or book-chests 'are valued for their richness in terms of their present usefulness, not their "accuracy" or their certification of "what really happened"'.[55] Consequently, training the memory was not a simple means of increasing the capacity or orderliness of the storage facility. As Elizabeth Elliott notes in her study of the role of Boethian models of consolation in shaping aristocratic identity, composition

> is conceived as an act of memory, dependent upon the collation and reformulation of materials held in the composer's mental inventory. In this context, the process of textual composition could almost be entirely memorial.[56]

---

[52] Richard de Bury, *Philobiblon*, ed. and trans. by E.C. Thomas (London: Kegan Paul, 1888), p. 11.

[53] Hugh of St Victor, 'Three Best Memory Aids', in Carruthers and Ziolkowski, *Craft of Memory*, p. 33.

[54] François Villon, *Oeuvres*, ed. by Louis Thuasne (Geneva: Slaktine Reprints, 1967), pp. 164, 172.

[55] Carruthers, *Book of Memory*, p. 38.

[56] Elliott, *Remembering Boethius*, p. 12; see also Carruthers, *Book of Memory*, pp. 240–57.

INTRODUCTION

While, therefore, all historical writing serves a mnemonic function, the texts that I examine in this study either draw particular attention to metaphors for that memory or explicitly emphasise how formal memory training connects writing about the past to the guidance of ethical behaviour in the present, usually to the benefit of the community of the realm.

What evidence do we have that such theories of memory were current in Scotland from the fourteenth to the sixteenth century? John Higgitt has observed that the 'triumph of reformed protestantism was much more thoroughgoing in Scotland than in England', the result being that the extant material once held by monastic houses is scarce.[57] He also points out that while the books held in royal libraries were 'largely unaffected' by the Reformation, they were 'repeatedly exposed to destruction and dispersal' by the 'crises of the Scottish monarchy in the 16th cent., the abdication of Mary Queen of Scots in 1567, and the departure in 1603 of James VI from Scotland to take up the English crown'.[58] The result is that most of the remaining catalogues and booklists date from after the 1430s and there is very little sense of what might have been owned by Scottish monarchs before Mary's reign (1542–87). From the inventories and booklists that do survive, however, it is possible to see that university and cathedral libraries – as well as the royal collections – contained the stock university texts, and it is not unlikely that many of them circulated in Scotland before the 1430s. Among a wide variety of Latin and vernacular texts were Augustine's *De Civitate Dei* and *Confessiones*, Thomas Aquinas' *Summa Theologiae*, John of Salisbury's twelfth-century *Policraticus*, and the *Ad Herennium*.[59] The libraries of Scotland thus contained many of the political and philosophical works considered crucial by medieval scholars and which were concerned with themes such as kingship, governance and memory. These works point to a nexus of materials that writers could utilise and reliably expect their audiences to have some knowledge of. In this way, the training of the individual memory transforms, in the act of composition, to the shaping of collective memories.

Collective memory, Daniel Poirion suggests, is the 'communion of a group of individual memories around the same themes and models'.[60] For Poirion, writing is 'indeed, rewriting, not only through the trick of borrowing, copying, and imitating, but through the very nature of a spiritual activity that is simultaneously resurgence, reflection, and reminiscence'.[61] To this, I would add that

---

[57] John Higgitt, *Scottish Libraries*, Corpus of British Library Catalogues, 12 (London: British Library, 2006), xxxi–xxxii.

[58] Higgitt, *Scottish Libraries*, xxxii.

[59] Higgitt, *Scottish Libraries*, pp. 2–29.

[60] Daniel Poirion, 'Literature as Memory: "Wo die Zeit wird Raum"', trans. by Gretchen V. Angelo, *Yale French Studies*, 95 (1999), 33–46 (38).

[61] Poirion, 'Literature as Memory', 38.

collective memory focuses on communal acceptance of specific remembrances as authentic and representative. This involves a specific group's intention to select and arrange representations of the past in a way that encourages individuals to adopt these memories as their own. In this way, I broadly work along the lines established by Maurice Halbwachs, who proposed that collective memory selectively appropriates and reconstructs aspects of the past to respond to the needs of the present.[62]

This does not negate the *ars memoria*, which asserted that the purpose of a well-ordered memory was to be able to recall information selectively in order to reorganise it and compose something new. All the texts that I consider are selective in what memories they choose to appropriate and *how* they recombine them. Authors such as Wyntoun, Holland, Bower, Hary, Lyndsay and Wedderburn all write about the nature of Scottishness as it is shaped by remembrance of the past. In doing so, they testify to a desire to select and organise the past in new and imaginative ways, performing collective memory work in the production of new texts. But who comprises these groups, and how they overlap, differs between time and place. Who is doing the remembering (or forgetting) and for what purpose becomes a defining feature of the material they present and is what enables diverse memories of the nation to take shape. All the texts that I consider are selective in what they choose to include and what they choose to omit, and this is dependent on the conditions in which those histories are being written. As a result, Scottish history is reshaped through memory as practice.[63] For, while expressions of national identity in medieval Scottish literature have been discussed in recent years, most recently by Katherine Terrell, the role played by memory as a process in narrating national sentiment has received relatively little attention.[64]

In the first chapter, I argue that borders – textual, geographic and cultural – became a focus for articulations of national memory. The chapter focuses on Sir Thomas Gray's French-of-England *Scalacronica* (*c*. 1355), Andrew of Wyntoun's

---

[62] Maurice Halbwachs, *On Collective Memory*, ed. and trans. by Lewis A. Coser (Chicago: University of Chicago Press, 1992). See also Anne Whitehead on the historically conditioned nature of memory: *Memory* (Abingdon: Routledge, 2008), esp. p. 4.

[63] I am indebted here to Pierre Bourdieu's concept of the *habitus* and also to Monique Scheer's work on 'emotions as a kind of practice', which stresses the historically situated nature of emotion. See Pierre Bourdieu, *Outline of a Theory of Practice*, trans. by Richard Nice (Cambridge: Cambridge University Press, 1977); Monique Scheer, 'Are Emotions a Kind of Practice (and Is That What Makes Them Have a History)? A Bourdieuian Approach to Understanding Emotion', *History and Theory*, 51.2 (2012), 193–220.

[64] Katherine Terrell, *Scripting the Nation: Court Poetry and the Authority of History in Late Medieval Scotland* (Columbus: Ohio State University Press, 2021).

INTRODUCTION

Original Chronicle (*c*. 1424) and Holland's *Buke of the Howlat* (1450s) to consider how borders – often arbitrary in their divisions – are narratively represented and invested with meaning about belonging and identity. In thinking about the presence of the Anglo-Scottish border and Scotland's northern internal divisions in both actuality and cultural memory, I propose that all three writers draw connections between memory and the signification of both familial and national identities. This connection between the family and the nation is explored in Chapter 2 with specific regard to how origin myths and royal genealogy were utilised to shape the ways in which the Scottish realm was imagined. I take as my focus Walter Bower's fifteenth-century *Scotichronicon* to argue that the recreation and remembrance of national beginnings were fundamental to Bower's conception of Scottishness. In the reworking and reordering of mythical origins, royal genealogies and recent dynastic marriages, *Scotichronicon*'s genealogies serve a mnemonic function, becoming a commemorative strategy that generates cohesion and community. If, however, history can be reimagined in historiography, then it supposes that material can not only be rearranged but also redacted or supplemented. What a reshaped history leaves out might be as significant as what it includes. This chapter concludes with a discussion of an event at Robert I's inauguration that occurs in Gray's *Scalacronica* but, crucially, is not mentioned in Scottish historical narratives. In this way, I examine how communities are shaped not only by memory but also by forgetting.

Anxieties around failures of memory, or deliberate forgetting, form the basis of Chapter 3's consideration of the prologue to an abridged version of *Scotichronicon* compiled for the abbey at Coupar Angus. In acknowledging John of Fordun's role in national historiography, Bower invents a memory of the circumstances of the chronicler's endeavours: Edward I's strategy of enforced forgetting through his seizure and destruction of written Scottish historical materials. Bower uses the destruction of the material objects of memory to forge another origin story of the narrative historiographical tradition, and it is one that is rooted in patriotic idealism. Where Bower deals with the loss of archive – physical memory – in Hary's *Wallace*, the poet grapples with anxieties about social amnesia in the late fifteenth century. Written in light of contemporary politics and a foreign policy that Hary presents as dangerously pro-English, the poem uses memory to secure national sovereignty. The *Wallace* deliberately focuses on violence as a way of remembering Anglo-Scottish relations of the late thirteenth and early fourteenth centuries, deliberately drawing on the Wars of Independence as a foundational principle of Scottishness. In doing so, Hary directs his audience to see how the past should (or *must*) be remembered, as poetic truth rather than verifiable fact.

The final two chapters of this study sit across what we might think of as another border in Scottish terms: the Battle of Flodden (1513). I suggest that, post-Flodden, writing about Scottish nationhood changes in emphasis. Where the texts of the fifteenth century look back to the Wars of Independence and anti-English sentiment as a memorial cue for Scottish identity, the early poetry of Sir David Lyndsay and Robert Wedderburn's *Complaynt of Scotland* articulate national thinking in increasingly insular terms. To do so, both writers locate Scottishness as it is represented and enacted by the king and the commonweal. Chapter 5 looks in detail at two of Lyndsay's poems from the early majority of James V: the *Dreme* and the *Testament of the Papyngo*. Both of these poems, I argue, draw on memory as an ethical foundation of character, taking the cardinal virtue of Prudence as a crucial component of governing or working in the national interest. My study concludes with a discussion of Wedderburn's *Complaynt of Scotland* in Chapter 6. Where Lyndsay had personified memory as a guiding figure in the *Dreme*, in the *Complaynt* Wedderburn personifies Scotland as a mother with unruly sons. I suggest that Wedderburn's concerns with Scottish sovereignty and identity in the wake of James V's premature death prompt a recollection of the past glories of Scotland that can be used as a point of comparison for its present condition.

At the end of this study, we come back to the beginning as Wedderburn pulls at the thread of memory of the Wars of Independence to resist contemporary calls to Anglo-Scottish union. However, his focus is far more on the culpability of the Scots in their own demise rather than solely the imperial ambitions of the English. In reshaping the narrative, then, Wedderburn emphasises Scottish collective enterprise as a way of ensuring sovereignty. What it meant to be Scottish in the sixteenth century relies on the same memories as the previous century did, but it assumes a different emphasis. This study therefore considers writing about the past in new ways to show how *memoria*, so fundamental to medieval comprehensions of humanity, played a central role in the ways Scottish writers approached their task of shaping the nation through its past.

1

The North Remembers: Identity and Nation across Scotland's Borders[1]

For a little over one hundred miles, the Anglo-Scottish border wends its way west to east from the head of the Solway Firth to just north of the River Tweed. This line roughly follows the one that was legally fixed in 1237 when Alexander II of Scotland (1214–49) and his brother-in-law, Henry III of England (1216–72), signed the Treaty of York. Its process of becoming and what it has symbolised is rather more complicated. In the eleventh century, the kingdom of Alba expanded south, acquiring Lothian and Strathclyde; in the twelfth century, Galloway became part of the kingdom; in the eleventh and twelfth centuries, several attempts were made to fix a definite boundary between the two kingdoms. G.W.S. Barrow has suggested that by 1092, the 'new castle of Carlisle ... paralleling the New Castle upon Tyne of 1080, constituted the essence of the Border' from the Norman perspective, with the actual border delimited along a line between the Solway and the Esk.[2] David I (1124–53) took Carlisle in 1136 and agreed with King Stephen (1135–54) at Durham to restore the border to the Rere Cross at Stainmore, which had served as a boundary marker between the two kingdoms in the mid-tenth century. The Scots held Carlisle for two decades, before Henry II (1154–89) compelled Máel Coluim IV (1153–65) to surrender the city, along with Cumberland and Westmorland, in 1157. The late twelfth century saw the Scottish kings seeking to assert claims over Northumberland and other territories, and, in 1174, William I (the Lion, 1165–1214) was captured at the Battle of Alnwick during a French-backed invasion of northern England. Following his capture, William was forced to

---

[1] Parts of this chapter have appeared in earlier versions: Kate Ash, 'Friend or Foe? Negotiating the Anglo-Scottish Border in Sir Thomas Gray's *Scalacronica* and Richard Holland's *Buke of the Howlat*', in *The Anglo-Scottish Border and the Shaping of Identity, 1300–1600*, ed. by Mark P. Bruce and Katherine H. Terrell (New York, NY: Palgrave Macmillan, 2012), pp. 51–67; Kate Ash, 'Terrifying Proximity: The Anglo-Scottish Border in Sir Thomas Gray's *Scalacronica*', in *Boundaries*, ed. by Jenni Ramone and Gemma Twitchen (Newcastle: Cambridge Scholars, 2007), pp. 30–44.

[2] G.W.S. Barrow, *The Kingdom of the Scots: Government, Church and Society from the Eleventh to the Fourteenth Century*, 2nd edn (Edinburgh: Edinburgh University Press, 2003), p. 118.

20   REWRITING THE PAST IN SCOTTISH LITERATURE, 1350–1550

sign the Treaty of Falaise, which compelled him to acknowledge Henry II as his feudal overlord. The *Chronicle of Melrose* (produced between 1173 and the early fourteenth century) records the nullification of the Treaty of Falaise, stating that, in 1190, William 'gave ten thousand marks of gold and silver' to Richard I (1189–99) so that he 'might recover his dignities, liberties, and honours, which he had possessed' and 'obtain possession of Berwick and Roxburgh, which king Henry' had 'detained from him by violence for sixteen years'.[3] By the time of Alexander II's succession in 1214, Scotland appeared to be consolidating its territories and, Dauvit Broun notes, from the first quarter of the thirteenth century 'Scocia' was used consistently at Melrose to refer to all of the kingdom's territory rather than to denote the central region 'bounded by the Forth, the central highlands and Moray'.[4]

G.W.S. Barrow argues that prior to the Treaty of York, the Marches constituted a 'boundary in its fullest sense' between Scotland and England, and Michael Brown notes that the 'long state of formal war which existed between the two kingdoms from 1333 to 1474, though it was interspersed by frequent truces, made the borderlands of the two realms into regions of special sensitivity'.[5] To some extent, this reflected the division of the Anglian kingdom of Northumbria between the English and the Scots, such that the border line reflected a political but not a cultural boundary.[6] For much of the thirteenth century, cross-border landholding was a significant feature of Anglo-Scottish relations, and the later Wars of Independence were not disputes over the location of the border itself, even if it became a significant ideological presence in writings concerned with those wars. In 1249, the Laws of the Marches were codified; aimed at providing a process of settling cross-border disputes between kingdoms with entirely separate legal jurisdictions, Cynthia Neville suggests that, in their written form, the laws 'became part of the collective memory of the borderers' as they 'follow[ed] contemporary fashion' in setting down 'in comprehensive and definitive form the customs which had prevailed in the region' in various ways from 'as early as the first half of the eleventh century'.[7] The March Laws instituted a separate jurisdiction that required separate administration. From 1295, raids, the taking of prisoners and ransom negotiations increased, and Andy King notes that from this point to 1323,

---

3   *The Chronicle of Melrose*, ed. by Joseph Stevenson, facsimile reprint (Lampeter: Llanerch Press, 1991), pp. 26–7.

4   Broun, *Irish Identity*, p. 198. C.f. Barrow, *Kingdom of the Scots*, p. 129.

5   Michael Brown, 'The Scottish March Wardenships (*c.* 1340–*c.* 1480), in *England and Scotland at War, c. 1296–c. 1513*, ed. by Andy King and David Simpkin (Leiden: Brill, 2012), pp. 203–29 (203).

6   At its peak, the Anglian kingdom of Northumbria extended as far north as the Firth of Forth.

7   C.J. Neville, *Violence, Custom and Law: The Anglo-Scottish Border Lands in the Later Middle Ages* (Edinburgh: Edinburgh University Press, 1998), pp. 1–2.

IDENTITY AND NATION ACROSS SCOTLAND'S BORDERS

cross-border landholding all but disappeared.[8] After 1296, the English crown instituted March wardens: northern magnates appointed to defend the English Marches against the threat of Scottish invasion. That a large area of the Scottish borders came under English lordship during the fourteenth century meant that cross-border ties were further strained, and March Law was revived during the late 1340s when March wardens assumed a judicial as well as a military role. It was at this point that March wardenships developed in Scotland, where the East, Middle and West Marches reflected the existing territorial interests of powerful border magnates, notably dominated by branches of the Douglas family until 1455, when the Black Douglases' spectacular fall from power saw James, ninth earl of Douglas, exiled to England.[9] Following English victories at Halidon Hill (1333) and Neville's Cross (1346), English administration in Berwickshire, Roxburghshire and Dumfriesshire – which had been ejected by Robert Bruce in the 1310s – was reinstated. It was not until later in the fourteenth century that Roxburgh and Berwick came back under Scottish control. This situation would lead the Anonymous Contributor in Andrew of Wyntoun's *Original Chronicle* to comment specifically on the end of Robert II's reign (1371–90) as the point at which the completeness of the realm was re-established.[10] Throughout the fourteenth century, then, it is possible to see a strengthening of the view that the term 'Scotia', which before the Treaty of York had ostensibly referred to the central regions of the kingdom, now had a broader frame of reference: the *regnum Scottorum*.

While the territories of the Marches gave rise to continued debate between the Scots and the English throughout the later Middle Ages and into the sixteenth century, they also provided space for assimilation. Neville further suggests that 'the impulse to codify custom' in 1249 'was a determined statement of regional identity' that differentiated the border lands from the Scots and the English.[11] This chimes with Andy King's assessment that, by the time of Edward I's sacking of Berwick (1296), the English and Scottish Marchers were 'already thoroughly and comprehensively acculturised' even as the border itself was 'sharply defined'.[12] The geographic Anglo-Scottish border existed as a very real source of influence and inspiration for Scottish

---

[8] Andy King, 'Best of Enemies: Were the Fourteenth-century Anglo-Scottish Marches a "Frontier Society"?', in *England and Scotland in the Fourteenth Century*, pp. 116–35 (118).

[9] See Neville, *Violence, Custom and Law*, pp. 27–45; Brown, 'Scottish March Wardenships'. On the fall of the Douglases, see Michael Brown, *The Black Douglases: War and Lordship in Late Medieval Scotland, 1300–1455* (Edinburgh: John Donald, 2007), pp. 283–311.

[10] See *Chron. Wyntoun* VI.357.1104–10. I discuss this later in the chapter.

[11] Neville, *Violence, Custom and Law*, p. 3.

[12] King, 'Best of Enemies', p. 131. Jackson W. Armstrong provides an important study for thinking about the Anglo-Scottish border; *England's Northern Frontier:*

and English writers throughout the Middle Ages. By the mid-fifteenth century, the chronicler Walter Bower was not only referring to an area called the *confinibus marchiarum* (neighbourhood of the borders; *Chron. Bower* 6. 311) but also identified the people who occupied that land as *marchiani* (Borderers; *Chron. Bower* 7. 283). Rather than a division of land separating the Scots and the English, this demarcation of the Marches suggested ideological, cultural and symbolic divisions that assumed a third identity, that of the border inhabitant, even if this Marcher identity, as Andy King has argued, always assumed a subordinate position to the borderers conceiving of themselves as primarily English or Scottish.[13] This suggestion of a liminal identity finds resonance in Gloria Anzaldúa's argument that boundaries accrue creative potential through the merging of different cultures, even while, as Jeffrey Jerome Cohen maintains, the hybridity that influences texts such as Gray's *Scalacronica* did 'not indicate some peaceful melding of two communities'.[14] The border, therefore, opens up possibilities for identity formation in unique ways as it simultaneously presents uneasy negotiations; it acts as a site of potential anxiety about the multiple identities for which the border makes space. While Barrow has argued for the relative stability of the Anglo-Scottish border, King's suggestion that border raids were of significant economic value to the area indicates that the border inhabitants lived within a systemised structure of violence that had the potential to impact not only individual but also collective identity.[15] As King notes, points of contact such as 'ransom negotiations' and their associated 'chivalric niceties', informed 'prolonged and less formal' cross-border interactions.[16] Sir Thomas Gray's *Scalacronica* points to mounting tensions between England and Scotland as a result of Edward I of England's intention to manipulate the precarious positions of the Bruce and Balliol factions in their pursuit of the Scottish throne following the death of Alexander III in 1286. Here, the ideological division of the border assumes a greater significance for those whose identities were affected by its presence. One way in which this manifests is in Gray's depiction of Scottish

---

Conflict and Local Society in the Fifteenth-Century Scottish Marches (Cambridge: Cambridge University Press, 2020), esp. pp. 49–73.

[13] King, 'Best of Enemies', pp. 134–5.

[14] Gloria Anzaldúa, *Borderlands/La Frontera = The New Mestiza* (San Francisco: Aunt Lute Books, 1987). On the idea of the third space, see also Homi K. Bhabha, *The Location of Culture* (London: Routledge, 1990); Jeffrey Jerome Cohen, *Hybridity, Identity and Monstrosity in Medieval Britain: On Difficult Middles* (Basingstoke: Palgrave Macmillan, 2006), p. 5.

[15] See Barrow, *Kingdom of the Scots*, p. 114; Andy King, '"According to the Custom used in French and Scottish Wars": Prisoners and Casualties in the Scottish Marches in the Fourteenth Century', *Journal of Medieval History*, 28 (2002), 263–90.

[16] See King, 'Best of Enemies', pp. 118–19.

IDENTITY AND NATION ACROSS SCOTLAND'S BORDERS

brutality during the First War of Independence. In his account of the murder of Hugh de Cressingham – Edward I's treasurer in Scotland – Gray recalls that 'it was said that the Scots had him skinned, and had thongs made from his skin, out of spite' (*Scal.* 41). *Scalacronica*, here, chimes with the fourteenth-century chronicles of Guisborough and Lanercost, and supports the creation of a memory of the Scots as barbarians whose glory came, in part, from taking mementos made from their victims' bodies: a war trophy par excellence in which violence functions as a mnemotechnical principle.[17] This violence runs through multiple narratives in *Scalacronica*. For example, Gray's version of the Scottish foundation myth recounts that, having arrived in Spain after fleeing from Egypt, the ancestors of the Scots 'lived by ravaging the peasants of the region' (*Scal.* 19).[18] The implication is that it is in the Scots' nature to be brutal and cruel, which, for Gray, delineates their difference from the English, whose defining characteristic is chivalric behaviour, demonstrated by figures such as his father, another Sir Thomas Gray. In his account of his father's speech to Sir Alexander Mowbray, Gray has his father address his Scottish enemy as a 'knight errant' who had come to perform 'chivalric deeds' (*Scal.* 83). Sir Thomas mocks his enemy, demonstrating both his own chivalric identity and the lack of those knightly qualities in the Scot to whom he speaks. Of course, these narratives are being produced against a backdrop of cross-border conflict, but they become potent memories of Anglo-Scottish interaction. It is possible, however, to discern an identity in *Scalacronica* that is very specifically located in the Marches, as is particularly evident in the critique of Edward III's policies in relation to the Marches in the 1340s, which Gray presumably comments on from direct involvement. In recording these experiences, Gray details how the Marches are continually left to defend themselves and the English garrisons in the north while Edward pursues his interests on the Continent.

In his account of Edward III's pursuit of his claim to the French throne, Gray recalls that it was only when the king had 'lost all the castles and towns in Scotland which he had strengthened' that he turned his eyes to France (*Scal.* 123). Gray intimates that Edward suspends the Anglo-Scottish stalemate to pursue a bigger honour; with the prospect of the prize of France, the Scottish conflict becomes unimportant to the king whose power base in the south was less materially affected by this change of direction. For Gray, however, and for others living in the Marches, the priorities of the king seem misguided. This perception, and the feelings it generates, achieve their greatest expression in Gray's account of how, while Edward was 'leading a high life' encamped

---

[17] See *Chronicle of Walter of Guisborough*, ed. by Harry Rothwell, Camden Society, 3rd Ser., 89 (London: Royal Historical Society, 1957), p. 303; *Chronicon de Lanercost*, ed. by Joseph Stevenson, Bannatyne Club, 65 (Edinburgh, 1839), p. 190.

[18] I discuss the Scottish origin myth in more detail in Chapter 2.

24   REWRITING THE PAST IN SCOTTISH LITERATURE, 1350–1550

in Antwerp, 'the English Marchers were defeated at Pressen' (*Scal*. 127).[19] The English Marchers who, in Gray's recollection, had been instrumental in guarding the border, were now being abandoned for frivolity, and this narrative expresses an understanding of the liminality of the Marchers themselves in English understanding. For Gray, the Marches was a discrete regional society that had a complex relationship to the English crown, and his critique often betrays anxieties of abandonment and isolation.[20] Throughout *Scalacronica*, Gray articulates an ambivalence about the border which recognises the performative nature of identity as well as the interdependence of divergent narratives that recreate historical experience.

The Anglo-Scottish border, although it marked a definitive separation of two kingdoms, is not the only boundary that might be considered significant in later medieval Scotland. At the time of Alexander III's death, Barrow suggests, the 'primary divisions of [the kingdom] were four in number': the 'largest was Scotland north of the Forth', while the other three lay south of the Forth. By 1286, these other regions, 'which had never been known by any single name', were

> understood to comprise the larger Lothian, Clydesdale, Tweeddale and Teviotdale, and also – though their inclusion was more gradual – Cunningham, Kyle and Dumfriesshire. This left, also well to the south of the Forth, [the] third primary division, Galloway, with which [must be included] Carrick, together forming a region which was both geographically and culturally distinct from the rest of southern Scotland. Finally there were the Isles, from the Calf of Man to Sula Sgeir and North Rona, fifty miles north of Cape Wrath.[21]

Scotland's northern and western regions are another important consideration, looking as they did to other borders with Scandinavia and Ireland. Parts of the western and northern territories of Scotland, particularly the Hebrides, Orkney and the Shetland Islands, were under Norse control for much of the period under discussion here. The Treaty of Perth (1266), following the Battle

---

[19] Presson is near Wark, Northumberland.

[20] I address how Gray deals with the Anglo-Scottish border as a geographical and ideological divide in more detail in two chapters: Kate Ash, 'Friend or Foe? Negotiating the Anglo-Scottish Border in Sir Thomas Gray's *Scalacronica* and Richard Holland's *Buke of the Howlat*', in *The Anglo-Scottish Border and the Shaping of Identity, 1300–1600*, ed. by Mark P. Bruce and Katherine H. Terrell (New York, NY: Palgrave Macmillan, 2012), pp. 51–67 (esp. 52–7); Kate Ash, 'Terrifying Proximity: The Anglo-Scottish Border in Sir Thomas Gray's *Scalacronica*', in *Boundaries*, ed. by Jenni Ramone and Gemma Twitchen (Newcastle: Cambridge Scholars, 2007), pp. 30–44 (esp. 34–42).

[21] Barrow, *Kingdom of the Scots*, p. 335.

of Largs, saw Norway cede the Hebrides and Isle of Man to Scotland, while Scotland recognised Norwegian sovereignty over Orkney and Shetland. These territories were not acquired by the Scots until 1468 as part of the marriage settlement between James III and Margaret of Denmark.[22] The lordship of the Isles has often been seen as the thorn in the side – or 'the Celtic Dirk at [the] back' – of Scottish kings.[23] This unfair assessment masks the often cooperative relationship between the king and the lordship.[24] Nevertheless, among several of the Stewart kings there was suspicion of the power of the lordship, and both James II and James III sought to curtail its power and consolidate centralised government, but this was part of a broader project of the Stewart kings to 'create a state in which the king and his central administration gained control of the localities' and reduced magnate power.[25]

Rather than functioning around a highly developed central government, Scotland was split into regional and local power bases. Despite these tensions between the crown and magnates, we should not assume that the regions of Scotland pulled its sense of cohesion apart. The king relied on nobles' power over their estates, and appointed local lords from throughout the realm – lowlands and highlands – to their councils, indicating that they were conscious of the cultural diversity of the kingdom. At the same time, magnates were rewarded for service. The interdependence of crown and magnate meant that cooperation was fundamental. By the end of the fourteenth century, John Barbour was describing 'ye land' of Scotland as extending 'Fra Weik anent Orknay / To Mullyr snwk in Gallaway' (*Bruce* 1.184–8). Barbour's sense here is that Scotland as an imagined community – a phenomenon of the mind – encompassed various linguistic and administrative regions under a broad understanding of a regnal community that stretched from Wick in

---

[22] See Barbara E. Crawford, *The Northern Earldoms: Orkney and Caithness from AD 870 to 1470* (Edinburgh: Birlinn, 2013). On the problems faced by the Scottish crown in relation to Orkney and Shetland, see Ian Peter Grohse, 'The Lost Cause: Kings, the Council, and the Question of Orkney and Shetland, 1468–1536', *Scandinavian Journal of History*, 45.3 (2020), 286–308; Alison Cathcart, '"O wretched king!": Ireland, Denmark-Norway, and Kingship in the Reign of James V', in *Rethinking the Renaissance and Reformation in Scotland: Essays in Honour of Roger A. Mason*, ed. by Steven J. Reid (Woodbridge: Boydell Press, 2024), pp. 118–39, esp. pp. 120–5.

[23] Richard Oram, 'Introduction: A Celtic Dirk at Scotland's Back? The Lordship of the Isles in Mainstream Scottish Historiography since 1828', in *The Lordship of the Isles*, ed. by Richard Oram (Leiden: Brill, 2014), pp. 1–39 (1).

[24] Steve Boardman, 'The Gaelic World and the Early Stewart Court', in *Miorun mór nan Gall, 'The Great Ill-Will of the Lowlander'? Lowland Perceptions of the Highlands, Medieval and Modern*, ed. by Dauvit Broun and Martin MacGregor (Glasgow: Centre for Scottish and Celtic Studies, University of Glasgow, 2009), pp. 83–109.

[25] Sonja Cameron, '"Contumaciously Absent"? The Lords of the Isles and the Scottish Crown', in *The Lordship of the Isles*, pp. 146–75 (172).

the north to the Mull of Galloway in the south-west. This, however, did not prevent perceived cultural and behavioural differences between lowland and highland Scots from provoking comment. For example, in recounting a battle in Strathnaver (1431) between Angus Dubh and Angus de Moray, Bower comments that

> our fellow-Scots across the mountains, living as they do on the border or boundary of the world, experience little of the scorching heat ... by which the blood as a friend of nature might be dried up: it is for this reason that, compared with other nations of the world, they have been found to be naturally more stout-hearted. (*Chron. Bower* 8. 267)

Steve Boardman notes that *Scotichronicon* is 'littered with indications of [Bower's] profound personal dislike of the culture and society of Gaelic Scotland and Ireland', and while that does not mean we should take the chronicler's views as wholly representative of the populace, he is drawing on a popular trope of northern barbarity.[26]

English and Scottish writers' consciousness of various borders – geographical, cultural, linguistic – and what they signified helped to shape their conceptions of individual, regional and national identities. Proximity to a border could also significantly influence responses to it. Based in Norham, Sir Thomas Gray situates himself not only as English but as a Borderer, and his *Scalacronica* often betrays the tensions of identity construction in the historical narrative that he shapes. For Gray, the Anglo-Scottish Marches are not necessarily a positive space in which to construct an identity; the border becomes a site of anxiety about the multiple identities coexisting in the region. The Orkneyman Richard Holland was writing in Moray and, therefore, reflecting on the Douglas presence on the Anglo-Scottish border at some distance. Wyntoun compiled his *Original Chronicle* in Lochleven, which probably escaped the worst of English raiding but was also far enough north for him to take more of an interest in Scotland's northern regions. Their works expose multiple – and often conflicting – responses to an understanding of what it meant to be Scottish, or not, in the fourteenth and fifteenth centuries. Intimately connected to understanding the importance of geographic

---

[26] Steve Boardman, 'Highland Scots and Anglo-Scottish Warfare, *c.* 1300–1513', in *England and Scotland at War*, pp. 231–53 (231). See also Boardman's comments on Fordun and his response to the highlands, in *The Early Stewart Kings: Robert II and Robert III, 1371–1406* (Edinburgh: John Donald, 1996), p. 86. For a wide-ranging discussion of anti-Gaelic sentiment in Lowland Scottish writing that spans the Middle Ages and into the sixteenth century, see Martin MacGregor, 'Gaelic Barbarity and Scottish Identity in the Later Middle Ages', in *Mìorun mór nan Gall*, ed. by Broun and MacGregor, pp. 7–48.

IDENTITY AND NATION ACROSS SCOTLAND'S BORDERS

and cultural boundaries, Sir Thomas Gray, Richard Holland and Andrew of Wyntoun all emphasise affective memory as distinct markers of identity. For Gray and Holland, in particular, the focus on the Anglo-Scottish border as a locus of identity enables a shift in the perceived importance of locality or regionality as markers of sameness and difference specifically related to ideas of geographic or cultural boundaries. In this chapter, I will explore the textual and cultural borderlands at work in Gray's *Scalacronica*, Holland's *Buke of the Howlat* and Wyntoun's *Original Chronicle* to consider the ways in which family assumed a particular importance to thinking about historiographical and memorial projects of the fourteenth and fifteenth centuries. In articulating the significations of the Anglo-Scottish and Scotland's internal borders, Gray, Holland and Wyntoun all emphasise memory and its effect on articulations of individual identity that might be brought to bear in thinking the nation, or vice versa.

Gray's *Scalacronica*: A Text across the Border

Gray's *Scalacronica* covers the history of the British Isles from the beginnings of the world through to 1363 and was the first vernacular chronicle composed by an English knight. As a constable of Norham castle in north-east England, Sir Thomas Gray lived in close proximity to the Anglo-Scottish border. Edinburgh, where he was held prisoner between 1355 and 1357, was less than sixty miles away. Gray had an active military career: he was appointed sheriff and constable of Norham in 1345, he fought at Neville's Cross (1346) and became keeper of the Marches in 1367. He also spent time in France during the Hundred Years' War. Gray was captured by a Scottish ambush in 1355, and in the prologue to his *Scalacronica* he announces that he began writing the chronicle when he was a 'prisoner, taken in war' and held in 'the citadel of Mount Agneth, formerly Maiden's Castle, now Edinburgh' (*Scal.* 3–5). Gray's capture is recorded in Fordun's *Chronica Gentis Scotorum*, in the section now identified by Dauvit Broun as a free-standing chronicle, the so-called *Gesta Annalia II*, in which Gray is noted as the 'son and heir' of 'the lord Thomas Gray, a noble knight' who was also seized (*Chron. Fordun* 2. 362).[27] That his status as a prisoner of war is one of the first things Gray tells his reader highlights a determination to define his identity in relation to his Scottish captors. It also suggests that Anglo-Scottish conflict and the genre of prison writing played significant roles in the construction of, at least, a literary identity. Clearly adopting the Boethian persona of the prison

---

[27] Dauvit Broun, 'A New Look at *Gesta Annalia* Attributed to John of Fordun', in *Church, Chronicle and Learning in Medieval and Early Renaissance Scotland: Essays Presented to Donald Watt on the Occasion of the Completion of the Publication of Bower's Scotichronicon*, ed. by Barbara E. Crawford (Edinburgh: Mercat, 1999), pp. 9–30.

writer, Gray demonstrates in *Scalacronica* a desire to write himself into history, to be remembered by later readers of *Scalacronica* specifically in relation to his chivalric and military connections.[28] This is most evident in the chronicle's prologue, in which Gray deals not only with his intention to write a universal history of *Graunt Bretaigne* (*Scal.* 2) but also with questions of self-representation and of how communal identities might be negotiated by the individual. For Joanna Summers, there is an 'inherent credibility in writing from prison' that establishes authority through situational suffering, 'petitionary confession and truth-telling'.[29] Drawing on this genre, Gray distinguishes his own identity from – and in relation to – that of the Scots and constructs a set of memories that frame his history as a chivalric narrative of Anglo-Scottish relations in the mid-fourteenth century.

In *Scalacronica*'s prologue, Gray writes that 'he who wrote this chronicle ... does not wish to reveal his name plainly' (*Scal.* 3). However, he circumvents this professed desire for anonymity by composing an alphabetical puzzle which enables the willing and able reader to discover his name. The game involves teasing out letters of the alphabet and rearranging them to arrive at the name of *Thomas Grai*:

> Soun habite sa droit vesture / estoit autre tiel de colour; / com est ly chape du cordeler / teynt en tout tiel maner. / Autre cote auoit afoebler, / lestat de soun ordre agarder, / qe de fieu resemble la colour, / et desus en purturature, / estoit li hardy best quartyner, / du signe teynt de la mere, / enviroun palice vn mure, / de meisme peynt la coloure. / Soit. viij. ioynt apres .xix. / si mettez .xij. apres .xiiij. / vn et .xviij. encountrez, / soun propre noun ensauerez / .vij. a .xvij. y mettez, / le primer vowel au tierce aioignez, / soun droit surnoun entrouerez, / solunc lalphabet. / Le noun propre et surenoun portoit, / qe deuaunt luy soun piere auoit. / Qe plus clerement le voet sauoir, / dautre qe de moy lestat auoir, / sortez iettez et diuinez, / sy ymaginez qe vous poez. (*Scal.* 2–4)

> His garment, his right attire, / Was of some such colour, / As is the cloak of a minoritie friar, / Dyed in just such a manner. / He had another coat he wore, / The status of his order it bore, / Which resembles the colour of fire, / And thereon, in portraiture, / Was the hardy beast, quartered / With the painted device of his mother, / The surrounding boundary, a wall, / Painted of the same colour. / Eight joined after nineteen / If you put twelve after fourteen, / One and

---

[28] For a discussion of the Boethian model of the prison-writer, see Joanna Summers, *Late-medieval Prison Writing and the Politics of Autobiography* (Oxford: Clarendon Press, 2004), esp. pp. 13–18. See also, Elliott, *Remembering Boethius*, esp. pp. 2–3, 123–43.

[29] Summers, *Late-medieval Prison Writing*, p. 4.

eighteen put together, / His personal name you will discover, / The seventh to seventeenth matched, / The first vowel to the third attached, / His correct surname you will uncover, / Following the alphabet. / Whoever would know this more clearly, / Shall have it from someone other than me, / Throw lots and divine it, / If you imagine that you can. (*Scal.* 3–5)

By participating in this mnemonic wordplay, the reader arrives at the identity of *Scalacronica*'s writer; yet, there is more to Gray's textual persona than a name. The puzzle focuses on the writer's coat of arms and the beginning of the game puns on Gray's name such that the 'cloak of a minorite friar' provides the link, *Grey friars*. The reader is then prompted to discover the 'other coat', indicating that a substantial part of this puzzle revolves around the recognition of Gray's knightly status, which is reached by piecing together his heraldic badge.

Coats of arms do not merely identify an individual; they are, usually, an amalgamation of the heraldic symbols of ancestors and, therefore, testify to the composite nature of the self, which emerges from the joining of family lines. These markers of identity, as they represent pedigree and status, are inherently public in their function, serving as visual memorial cues of family associations, allegiances and communities. They show to whom (and how well) one is connected. Through the mnemonic puzzle of the prologue, then, Gray creates a chivalric persona, a knight who 'is of that order which is enlightened by good customs, a support for the old, for maidens and for Holy Church' (*Scal.* 3). Richard Moll characterises Gray's prologue as an elaborate act of self-fashioning, in which he appeals to 'an ideal of courtly behaviour inspired by romance conventions'.[30] Moreover, this courtly brain-teaser indicates that Gray assumes an audience for his text that is well acquainted with the images that he presents, both chivalric and local. This is supported by his decision to write in the French of England rather than Latin or English. Gray assumes a certain type of reader, and the language of his chronicle indicates an implied way of reading quite different from monastic Latin productions.[31] Gray's conscious choice of language, then, situates himself and *Scalacronica* within a specific cultural milieu that is crucial to an understanding of the ideas about identity that the text develops.

The use of the mnemonic gives the impression that the identity of *Scalacronica*'s writer is jointly determined by the text and its readers. Just as

---

[30] Richard J. Moll, *Before Malory: Reading Arthur in Late Medieval England* (Toronto: University of Toronto Press, 2003), pp. 39–40.

[31] See Susan Crane, 'Anglo-Norman Cultures in England, 1066–1460', in *The Cambridge History of Medieval English Literature*, ed. by David Wallace (Cambridge: Cambridge University Press, 1999), pp. 35–60.

30   REWRITING THE PAST IN SCOTTISH LITERATURE, 1350–1550

the shield identifies the knight, particularly in medieval romance, by being written into the text as Gray is in *Scalacronica*, the writer's identity is textually determined.[32] In their expression as memory games within the prologue, then, Gray shows how identities are constructed and how they are performed both on an individual and a collective basis. Gray's textual identity can be brought into being only by a collaborative memorial interplay between writer and audience. The prologue's heraldic game points to the complexity, but also the possibility, of identities that are constructed around certain characteristics, such as knightliness, which are identifiable to the right reader and serve as a mnemonic of socialisation.

The acrostic with which Gray presents his readers is not only an intellectual game: it also points to how memory is put to work in the gap between the text and the reader. The wordplay might obfuscate but it also playfully reveals the importance of a creative reading process that was fundamental to medieval understandings of a well-trained memory.[33] Gray both presents and hides his identity within the text and, when he challenges the reader to '*ymaginez*' (*Scal.* 4), he alludes to the faculty of memory that is both creative and active. Gray's use of the acrostic in *Scalacronica*'s prologue is strikingly similar to that at the beginning of Fernando de Rojas's *La Celestina* (1499), where the first letter of each line taken together reveals the author's name: Fernando de Roias.[34] Julian Weiss argues that de Rojas's example demonstrates 'a poetic way of half-remembering' the writer; that the process mirrors the imaginative literary composition whereby the writer locates himself 'between the extremes of exclusion and willed anonymity'.[35] The active work required by the reader to reveal what the writer has hidden shows memory to be a creative reading process as well as a means of composition. In addition to the use of mnemonics, Gray's inclusion of the Sybil as a guide in *Scalacronica*'s dream vision section of the prologue explicitly points to the memorial function of the acrostic because it was a device with which the Sybil was long associated.[36]

---

[32] On the significance of shields and identity, see Yoïchi Shimazaki, 'L'Amour d'Hector et le motif de l'ecu dans le *Lancelot en prose*', *Études de Langue et Littérature Françaises*, 56 (1990), 1–16.

[33] See Carruthers and Ziolkowski, *Medieval Craft*, p. 13.

[34] See Fernando de Rojas, *La Celestina*, ed. by Francisco Alonso (Madrid: Editorial Burdeos, 1987), p. 39.

[35] Julian Weiss, 'Memory in Creation: The Context of Rojas's Literary Recollection', *Bulletin of Hispanic Studies*, 86.1 (2009), 150–8 (154).

[36] See Patrizia Lendinara, 'The *Verse Sybyllae de die indudicii* in Anglo-Saxon England', in *Apocryphal Texts and Traditions in Anglo-Saxon England*, ed. by Katherine Powell and Donald Scragg (Cambridge: D.S. Brewer, 2003), pp. 85–101; Anke Holdenried, *The Sibyl and Her Scribes: Manuscripts and the Interpretation of the Latin Sybilla Tiburtina, c. 1050–1500* (Aldershot: Ashgate, 2006). On the authority of

IDENTITY AND NATION ACROSS SCOTLAND'S BORDERS

From the acrostic that demands a reader's cognitive engagement, *Scalacronica*'s prologue then transitions to a dream vision in which the Sibyl appears to Gray in a tableau similar to that in Boethius' *Consolation*. In the Boethian text, Lady Philosophy appears to the dreamer wearing a robe embroidered at the bottom hem with the Greek letter Pi, and at the top hem with Theta. Between the two, a 'ladder of steps rose from the lower letter to the higher'.[37] Establishing himself in this Boethian tradition, Gray adapts this image to set out the structure of his own history. In Gray's prologue, it is the Sibyl rather than Philosophy who appears and tells him that 'she [will] show him the way to that which he [has] in mind' (*Scal.* 5). The Sibyl takes Gray to an orchard where,

> against a high wall, on a mounting block, they found a ladder made up of five rungs; and on the mounting block under the ladder, two valuable books and a grey friar holding the ladder up with his right hand. 'My friend', said the aged Sybil, 'here you may seem wisdom and folly; the first book [is] the Bible, the second, *The Deed of Troy*. It wouldn't harm your plans to take a look at them'. (*Scal.* 5)

The Sibyl guides the dreaming Gray to what might be regarded as the cornerstone of the English imagination – the Bible and the narrative of the mythic origins of England's ancestors.[38] By imagining these books equally supporting the base of the ladder that the dreamer and the Sibyl will ascend, Gray posits the two as distanced, complementary and equally important origin points for his historiography. That the Sibyl rather dryly reminds the dreamer that it 'wouldn't harm [his] plans' to take a look at them serves as a reminder to him and the reader of their significance. Gray is then guided up four rungs of the ladder. Stopping at each in turn, the Sibyl leads him 'through the wall' (*Scal.* 5) to various locations where he can observe the previous compilers of world and national histories that the Sibyl deems to be the most important. One by one, Gray is shown the sources for each section of his own chronicle: the histories of Walter, archdeacon of Exeter; Bede; Higden; the vicar of Tillmouth.[39]

Sibylline prophecy, see Maureen Quilligan, *The Allegory of Female Authority: Christine de Pizan's Cite des Dames* (Ithaca, NY: Cornell University Press, 1991), pp. 105–16.

[37] Boethius, *The Consolation of Philosophy*, trans. by Victor Watts, rev. edn (London: Penguin, 1990), p. 4.

[38] The Bible and the story of Troy were fundamental not only to the English imagination in the Middle Ages, but also to other European countries, most notably France. See R.E. Asher, *National Myths in Renaissance France: Francus, Samothes and the Druids* (Edinburgh: Edinburgh University Press, 1993), pp. 9–43.

[39] Andy King argues that the reference to Walter of Exeter should be to Walter of Oxford, the mistake a confusion between the Latin soubriquets *Exonie* (of Exeter) and *Oxonie* (of Oxford), *Scal.* 210–11, n.3. The author of the *Historia Aurea* is usually

32   REWRITING THE PAST IN SCOTTISH LITERATURE, 1350–1550

Through the image of the orchard and the wall, alongside the Sibyl's comments on the sources that Gray is to use for his own chronicle, *Scalacronica* presents the reader with landscaped and architectural structures for this new historical work, all of which draw upon formal memory training. Orchards, for example, appear repeatedly in medieval literature – usually romance – as locations for recreation and contemplation; like memory, orchards are both pleasurable and useful.[40] The image of the ladder is one that suggests a state of transition from one position to another, with each source a border between different presentations of the past that Gray must negotiate. In this way, it connects varying kinds of knowledge. The ladder also recalls the *scala Jacobis*, a common topos in religious writing where the mnemonic function denoted spiritual ascent and the precariousness of that ascent. The *scala Jacobis* refers to part of a dream or vision which Jacob received in Bethel (Gen. 28: 12–13). In the dream, the stairway stands on the earth and reaches up to heaven, with messengers ascending and descending and God standing at the top. Jacob's ladder was also used by Richard de Bury as a mnemonic device specifically connected with books, and which he attributes to Hugh of St Victor. In Richard de Bury's conception, the ladder – which allowed for ascent and descent – resembled the well-ordered memory which could be searched and called upon at will.[41]

The architectural structuring of the foundations of *Scalacronica* draws attention to what is being remembered and by whom: it is Gray who 'had dreamed these dreams' and 'remembered well all the details' and who began his chronicle to record that which he '*wished* to remember' (*il voet rementoyuer*; *Scal.* 7; my emphasis). Through the Sibyl's guidance, and through Gray's own admission that *Scalacronica* emphasises the 'deeds' of Brutus and 'his successors', the prologue reminds readers that historiography is selective; the chronicler chooses what to include and, crucially, what to omit. The intention is to remember some things and not others, and *Scalacronica* relies on the active composition and memory of its author and what he considers worthy of remembering. In using this highly stylised way of acknowledging

---

identified as John of Tynemouth, rather than Tillmouth. See V.H. Galbraith, 'The *Historia Aurea* of John, Vicar of Tynemouth, and the Sources of the St Albans Chronicle, 1327–77', in *Essays in History Presented to Reginald Lane Poole*, ed. by H.W.C. Davis (Oxford: Clarendon Press, 1927; repr. 1969), pp. 379–98.

[40] See Teresa McLean, *Medieval English Gardens* (London: Barrie & Jenkins, 1989); Amy Louise Morgan discusses the role of orchards as liminal spaces in romance in '"To play bi an orchardside": Orchards as Enclosures of Queer Space in *Lanval* and *Sir Orfeo*', in *The Medieval and Early Modern Garden in Britain: Enclosure and Transformation, c. 1200–1750*, ed. by Patricia Skinner and Theresa Tyers (London: Routledge, 2018), pp. 91–101.

[41] Richard de Bury, *Philobiblon*, 1, 27–29; 14–15.

his sources, Gray not only follows a tradition of holding the 'best' sources in high esteem but also seeks to present his own work as a continuation of the tradition of authorising a text through its links and debts to previous works. Gray elevates his own work through such associations, as well as pointing to the writing of history as imaginative reworking, a form of memory. The ascent that Gray and the Sibyl make culminates in the fifth rung of the ladder. The Sibyl prevents the dreaming Gray from ascending the fifth rung because it 'signifies future events' (*Scal.* 7). Continuing the allusion to the great and authoritative histories of England, and drawing on the image of the ladder as a memorial structure, Gray implicitly places his own work as the production symbolised by that fifth rung. It is a new narrative of events fundamentally tied to, and shaped by, the previous supporting histories, and it continues the history of the island of Britain according to the reshaping that Gray determines.

That Gray's *Scalacronica* is the product of the fifth rung of the ladder that leans against the wall of memory-history in the orchard is further signified by the ladder itself and its relation to Gray's identity. The importance of the reader's active engagement with the text is exemplified by John Leland, who prepared an abstract of the *Scalacronica* in the sixteenth century. He comments that it was the ladder, specifically, that enabled him to identify the author of the chronicle:

> I gesse, that one of the Greys of Northumbreland was autor of it by the imagination of the dreame that he showith of a ladder yn the prologue. The Grayes give a ladder in their armes.[42]

For Leland, the Old French *gré* (Middle English *gre*) assumes a particular significance here. Meaning *stair*, it is immediately apparent that the title of Gray's work, *Scalacronica*, derives from the dream vision and is directly connected to Gray's authorship. Indeed it is the Sibyl who tells the dreaming Gray that he should call the finished work Scalacronica (*tu lez doys appeller, Scalacronica*; *Scal.* 6). However, given the wordplay in the chronicle's prologue and readers' assumed attunement to this in identifying the author, the dependence on medieval faculty psychology provides the organisational structure of Gray's work. That the chronicle is called *Scalacronica* – ladder chronicle – points to the importance of memory in the preoccupations of this particular history and this particular author. The ladder and its links to Gray's family identity create a link between past, present and future that,

---

[42] John Leland, *Notable Things translated unto Englisch by John Leylande oute of a booke caullid Scala Cronica*; Appendix 1 in Thomas Gray, *Scalacronica*, ed. by Joseph Stevenson (Edinburgh: The Maitland Club, 1836), pp. 259–315 (259). The portion of *Scalacronica* covering 1340–55 is entirely missing from the extant manuscript. It is through Leland's abstract that details covering this section of the chronicle survive.

despite the seeming linearity imposed by both the passage of time and the ascension of the ladder's rungs, becomes a moment of transition that allows for movement both forward and backward. In doing so, the prologue acts as a mode of passage – a progression to knowledge and vision – at the same time that it acts as a temporal (and textual) borderland, on the other side of which lies history and reshaped memory. Gray's self-representation, and his anxieties about setting down his own identity, inform and shape the chronicle that he writes, and readers are heavily encouraged to perform the memory work of reading the spaces between the narratives in light of *Scalacronica*'s prologue. In this way, it is possible to see connections with another vernacular chronicle: Wyntoun's *Chronicle*, where anxieties about representation again are a distinctive feature of the narrative.

Crossing Borders in Wyntoun's *Original Chronicle*

In the opening years of the fifteenth century, Andrew of Wyntoun (*c.* 1350–*c.* 1422), prior of St Serf's, Lochleven, began writing his *Original Chronicle*, a universal history composed in octosyllabic couplets. His principal patron was the prosperous Fife landowner Sir John Wemyss of Wemyss, who served as constable of St Andrew's Castle from 1383 to 1400. Wyntoun had originally planned for his *Chronicle* to comprise seven books and to end with the death of Alexander III in 1286. In this conception, the *Chronicle* would, in effect, detail and commemorate the Canmore dynasty, whose origin was popularly seen as starting with Máel Coluim III (1057–93) and St Margaret (1070–93). In the end, Wyntoun revised his history at least twice, initially continuing the *Chronicle* up to the end of Robert II's reign (1390), and subsequently compiling nine books covering the death of Robert Stewart, duke of Albany (1420), and ending with an account of the early career of Alexander Stewart (d. 1435). He ascribes the portion of the text covering 1325 to 1390 to an 'Anonymous Contributor'. Wyntoun's work was clearly popular from the fifteenth to the seventeenth century; it survives in nine witnesses, which represent all three redactions.[43] From Book VI, Wyntoun focuses solely on English and Scottish history, and he indicates that he draws upon a now-lost Stewart 'genealogy' (*Chron. Wyntoun* II.153.134) by John Barbour.[44] Steve Boardman has argued that Wemyss's affiliation with Robert Stewart, duke of Albany, accounts for

---

[43] Amours, *Chron. Wyntoun*, vol. 1, lxi–lxvii. On the redactions of Wyntoun's *Chronicle*, see W.A. Craigie, 'Wyntoun's "Original Chronicle"', *The Scottish Review*, 30 (1897). 33–54.

[44] On Barbour's now lost genealogy, see Steve Boardman, 'Late Medieval Scotland and the Matter of Britain', in *Scottish History: The Power of the Past*, ed. by Edward J. Cowan and Richard J. Finlay (Edinburgh: Edinburgh University Press, 2002), pp. 47–72 (esp. pp. 51–4).

the *Chronicle*'s political biases, particularly its enthusiasm for the duke and its disregard of David Stewart, duke of Rothesay (1378–1402).[45] It is possible to see how Wyntoun's political affiliations shaped his narrative and, in numerous episodes, the *Original Chronicle* demonstrates an awareness of how the past is remembered and reimagined.

One of these episodes, which focuses on the parentage of Máel Coluim III, appears to engage with contemporary dynastic politics at the same time as it links those directly to a widespread, albeit inaccurate, memory that posited the marriage of Máel Coluim III and St Margaret as the foundational event of a new Scottish dynasty. Rhiannon Purdie has eloquently demonstrated the chronicler's deft rhetorical skill in her analysis of Wyntoun's reshaping of the narrative of Máel Coluim III's parentage. Purdie focuses on the changes that Wyntoun makes to his sources regarding the legitimacy of Máel Coluim III, to argue that, in fabricating the account of Máel Coluim being an illegitimate son of King Duncan by a miller's daughter, Wyntoun sought to rupture genealogical narrative and present Máel Coluim – and his wife, Margaret, daughter of the exiled Saxon king, Edward – as the founders of a new royal Scottish dynasty.[46] In doing so, Purdie suggests, Wyntoun's focus on illegitimate but 'best fit' ruler repurposed history in the prophetic mode in light of the more recent successions of illegitimate Douglases to the earldoms of both Douglas and Angus. In particular, this 'fit for purpose' approach rested on the military prowess of Archibald 'the Grim' (d. 1400) and his nephew, William, first earl of Douglas, on both of whom Albany was dependent for personal support and national defence.[47] Consequently, Purdie argues, Wyntoun's historical project reshaped the past to 'reflect the desires of a broad contemporary audience'.[48]

As with Gray's *Scalacronica*, Wyntoun's choice of vernacular history might have more to do with the status of his audience than their nationality as it were. Gray's use of the French of England and his heavy focus on chivalric matters supposes a noble lay audience. The same might be said for Wyntoun's *Chronicle*, not least because of the decision also to write in the vernacular rather than Latin – several of his narratives make use of the

---

[45] Boardman, *Early Stewart Kings*, p. 272.

[46] Rhiannon Purdie, 'Malcolm, Margaret, Macbeth, and the Miller: Rhetoric and the Re-Shaping of History in Wyntoun's *Original Chronicle*', *Medievalia et Humanistica*, 41 (2016), 45–63.

[47] Purdie, 'Malcolm, Margaret, Macbeth, and the Miller', esp. 53–59. See also Boardman's assessment that by the end of 1389, in a 'dazzling example of *realpolitik*', the 'earldoms of Douglas and Angus were secured in the hands of bastards whose affinities were politically and militarily loyal or indispensable' to Albany, 'both for the preservation of his personal authority within Scotland and in his wider task of defending the realm': *Early Stewart Kings*, p. 166.

[48] Purdie, 'Malcolm, Margaret, Macbeth, and the Miller', 58.

36   REWRITING THE PAST IN SCOTTISH LITERATURE, 1350–1550

language and style of romance. Wyntoun's professed principal influence for his recent Scottish history was the 'romanys', Barbour's *Bruce*. In his prologue, Wyntoun appropriates Barbour's own appeal to his audience's understanding of the relationship between rhetoric and history, by reusing the opening lines of the *Bruce*: 'storyis to heire ar dilectable, / Suppose þat sum be nocht bot fable' (*Chron. Wyntoun*, Wemyss 2.4.31–2).[49] It is probably safe to assume that Wyntoun expected his audience to recognise the reference and to engage their own memories in making the connections between Barbour's narrative and Wyntoun's. The explication recalls the understanding that history was studied as part of the *trivium* (grammar, logic and rhetoric) and the principles of composition would, therefore, be familiar to anyone who had received a certain level of education. Rhetoric was designed to teach (*docere*), move (*movere*) and please (*delectare*), and this prologue demonstrates how memory was understood as a rhetorical practice. *Memoria* also relied on affect, including pleasure, as an ethical tool of instruction. Indeed, as Wyntoun reminds his reader at the opening of his chronicle:

> As men ar be thare qualiteis
> Inclynit to diuersiteis,
> Mony ʒarnys for till heir
> Off tymes þat before þaim wer,
> Staittis changeit and þe greis;
> Quharfor of sic antiquiteis
> Thai þat set haly þare delite
> Gestis or storyis for to write,
> Outhir in metere or in prose,
> Flurist fairly thare purpose
> With qwaynt and curiouse circumstance,
> For to raise hertis in pleasance,
> And þe heraris till exsite
> Be wit or will to do þare delite. (*Chron. Wyntoun*, Wemyss
>   II.2.1–14)

In his attempt to create a coherent single narrative, Wyntoun demonstrates his knowledge of the skill required of him; the process of redaction was also a craft of memory, in which the writer 'fashion[ed] his materials into something new and fresh' that could serve present circumstances.[50] In doing

---

[49] C.f. 'Storys to rede ar delitabill / Suppos yat yai be nocht bot fabill': *Barbour's Bruce*, 1–2.

[50] Albert C. Baugh, 'Convention and Individuality in Middle English Romance', in *Medieval Literature and Folklore Studies: Essays in Honor of Francis Lee Utley*, ed. by Jerome Mandel and Bruce A. Rosenberg (New Brunswick, NJ: Rutgers University Press, 1970), pp. 123–46 (139).

so, Wyntoun displays his desire to add to a common store of knowledge that enabled the production of ethical behaviour in readers.[51] Both elements rely on the mediation of memory to be effective.

The *Chronicle* is also a text deeply invested in ideas of nation and freedom. The Wemyss text, which ends at the death of Robert II in 1390, prays that God will give Robert III 'grace / For to governe and hald his land / In als gude pleyt as he it fand, / To leif it bettir at his deceis' (*Chron. Wyntoun*, VI.354–6.1102–5). The Cottonian MS, which represents the third recension, praises Robert II as the king who 'gouernyt weil' his realm, 'And fre it helde ilka deil, / And left it fre eftyr his decesse' (*Chron. Wyntoun*, VI.355–57.1101–3). Both versions then include a particularly notable comment on the state of Scottish sovereignty and the territorial completeness of the realm:

> And quhen his fader bereyt weis,
> Off Scotland was na fute of land
> Out of þe Scottis mennis hand,
> Outtane Berwyk, Roxburght, and Iedworth;
> And ȝit of þir sa far war furth
> The Scottis mennis part þat to þe land all
> Was hail þairis vtouth þe wall. (*Chron. Wyntoun*, VI.356.1106–12)

Wyntoun brings together the image of an effective Scottish king, whose good governance recovered territory lost to the English, alongside an articulation of national freedom. The image of the land whole, reunited and 'Scottis', presents a potent reshaping of Robert II's legacy and a tall order for his successor to defend. In his study of the modesty topos in Wyntoun's *Chronicle*, R. James Goldstein has provocatively noted that 'Like generations of Scots before him, Wyntoun finds the act of remembering to be the most fundamental political act'.[52] In an interlude between recounting Bruce's murder of John Comyn and Menteith's betrayal of William Wallace, Book 8, Chapter 19 of the *Chronicle* presents an authorial interjection, headed as 'The auttoris wordis' (*Chron. Wyntoun*, V.367). The Wemyss MS is more explicit, indicating that the chapter

---

[51] Emily Wingfield has noted the key elements of Wyntoun's prologues that imply an instructional impetus to the work. Wingfield argues that Wyntoun's investment in key ideas of kingship and good governance reinforces the *Chronicle*'s foundational position within the Scots Advice to Princes genre, a literary concern that connects much late medieval literature in Latin and Older Scots. 'Kingship and Good Governance in Wyntoun's *Original Chronicle*', in *Pre-Modern Scotland: Literature and Governance, 1420–1587. Essays for Sally Mapstone*, ed. by Joanna Martin and Emily Wingfield (Oxford: Oxford University Press, 2017), pp. 19–30.

[52] R. James Goldstein, '"For he wald vsurpe na fame": Andrew of Wyntoun's Use of the Modesty *Topos* and Literary Culture in Early Fifteenth-Century Scotland', *Scottish Literary Journal*, 14.1 (1987), 5–18 (12).

38   REWRITING THE PAST IN SCOTTISH LITERATURE, 1350–1550

includes how 'Wyntoun him excusis fra wyte / And schawis als quhat he couþ dyte' (*Chron. Wyntoun*, V.366). At this seemingly critical juncture of the Wars of Independence, Wyntoun shifts his dependence on Barbour's *Bruce* to relying on the so-called 'Anonymous Contributor' to narrate the reigns of David Bruce and Robert II. Goldstein notes that this particular interjection in Book 8 is 'crucial' to understanding Wyntoun's own sense of himself as a chronicler who necessarily makes use of source material but who also strives to be remembered for his own rhetorical skill in creatively recombining his selected material.[53] In this way, Wyntoun draws attention to the implicit memory work at play in the writing of history.

By the time the Wemyss MS ends, along with Wyntoun's use of the 'Anonymous Contributor', England and Scotland had secured a truce. The Treaty of Leulingham (1389) effectively signalled the end of Anglo-Scottish conflict – for a few years at least – but Wyntoun's interests in borders and identities continue. To think about this in more detail, I want to consider two episodes that sit side by side in the *Chronicle*: Louis, duke of Orléans' speech during Anglo-Scottish negotiations in 1391, followed by the Glasklune episode, an account of tensions between the Gaelic-speaking regions of the northern Scottish territories. These accounts both attest to the complex set of interactions between nation and memory in the *Chronicle*. According to Wyntoun, during the 1391 negotiations, 'sum said, þat Inglis men, / Þat oure nacion defamyt þen, / And said we, gaderit to oure weris, / Micht noucht al passe thre hundyr speris' (*Chron. Wyntoun*, VI.369.1393–96). This insult regarding the Scots' abilities to muster a large army was 'said in þe presens / Off þe Duk of Orlyens', who had always had a 'special affecion' for the 'Scottis nacion' (*Chron. Wyntoun*, VI.369.1399–1402). Wyntoun follows this with a speech by Orléans, who states that there 'Was neuir realme na region / Worthe mar commendacion' (*Chron. Wyntoun*, VI.369.1409–10). The duke points out to the English 'Þat nacion ȝhe may noucht defame, / Bot gif ȝhe smyt ȝoure awyn wiþe schayme' (*Chron. Wyntoun*, VI.370.1445–6). Within this imagined speech, Wyntoun establishes Scottish sovereignty – recognised internationally – alongside an image of Scottish chivalric identity, demonstrated through the affection of the duke of Orléans, who was renowned as a cultivator of chivalric culture.[54] This potent political reimagining on Wyntoun's part also rests on his distinction between the 'Inglis' and 'oure nacion' as Wyntoun encourages his reader to identify themselves as part of that collective Scottish identity. That the duke refers to the 'Scottis nacion' is particularly interesting in light of the chapter that immediately follows his declaration.

---

[53] Goldstein, '"For he wald vsurpe na fame"', 15–16.

[54] For example, Louis founded the Order of the Porcupine in 1394. See D'Arcy Jonathan Dacre Boulton, *The Knights of the Crown: The Monarchical Orders of Knighthood in Later Medieval Europe* (Woodbridge: Boydell Press, 1987), p. 325.

The Glasklune episode, also known as the Battle of Brerachan, shifts the focus from the Anglo-Scottish border to consider the northerly cultural and linguistic borders within the Scottish kingdom that had contemporary resonance. In Book 9, Chapter 12, Wyntoun recounts how, in early 1392, the sons of Alexander Stewart, earl of Buchan (fourth son of Robert II), were involved in a raid into the lowlands of Angus. The episode recollects how a 'gret hee discorde' occurred between Sir David Lindsay, lord of Glen Esk and the 'Hielande men' (*Chron. Wyntoun*, VI.371.1453, 1455). Having set a time and place for meeting to resolve the dispute, Wyntoun narrates that 'Schir Dauid de Lyndissay, þat was wise, / Trowit noucht in þaim [the Highland men]' and sent a spy into their lands (*Chron. Wyntoun* VI.371.1461–2). However, the 'Hielande men' 'coyme downe al suddandly', about 'Thre hundyr' of them, Wyntoun estimates (*Chron. Wyntoun*, VI. 371.1467–70). The story in the Cotton MS continues: 'Qwhen worde oursprede þan þe cuntre / Þat þe Scottis Hielande men / War nere þe wattyr of Ile þen' (*Chron. Wyntoun*, VI.372.1474–6), the good knight Walter Ogilvy, along with Sir Patrick Gray and Sir David Lindsay, seek to engage the raiders in combat. These men, 'sterne and stowt' of heart 'Pressit þaim fast to skayl þat rowte' (*Chron. Wyntoun*, VI.372.1491–2), but Ogilvy is killed, while Gray and Lindsay are badly wounded. At lines 1493–4, Wyntoun writes that 'In þe Stormonde at Gasklwne / Þat dulful dawwerk þat tyme was done'. Wyntoun gives a rather impressive account of the heroism of Lindsay, who engages in combat such that 'Throw þe body he straik a man / With his spere doune to þe erde' (*Chron. Wyntoun*, VI.373.1500–01). This man, however, presses himself upwards and 'With a swak … of his suerde' (*Chron. Wyntoun*, VI.373.1506) he strikes Lindsay through his boot and through to the 'bane' of his leg, severely wounding him (*Chron. Wyntoun*, VI.373.1509). It is only because Lindsay is sitting on his horse that he is not killed. The episode ends with references to the 'gentillis and ȝomen' killed but whose heroism and loyalty means that they 'bidande' on the field with Ogilvy:

> Off his kyn and his housse alssua
> Walde noucht fra hym passe away;
> Bot bidande in þe feylde þat day
> Slayne al to gedyr þai war,
> Þat bidande war wiþe þe schirray þar.
> (*Chron. Wyntoun*, VI.374.1532–6)

The final two lines pick up line 1494 as Wyntoun concludes: 'All oure lande sare menyt downe / Þat dulful dawerk of Gasklowne' (*Chron. Wyntoun*, VI.374.1537–8). In establishing Ogilvy, Gray and, specifically Lindsay, as the heroes of this routing of the raiders, Wyntoun adopts the romance tropes with which his readers would be familiar and which they must now bring to mind.

Lindsay becomes the 'gud', the knights are 'sterne and stowt' in pressing themselves into the thick of battle. Notably, the other men are loyal, remaining (*bidande*) on the battlefield and being slain 'al to gedyr' in service of the 'schirray' and protecting the land. Wyntoun indulges in some further romancing of the Glen as he imagines the battle as 'dulful dawwerk': a doleful day's work.

Wyntoun's account, then, presents his reader with a potent example of loyalty and disloyalty to the crown: by raiding into Angus, Buchan's sons demonstrated an arrogant failure of loyalty that sought to destabilise further the early reign of Robert III. While the Glasklune episode reflects a long-standing power struggle within the Stewart royal family, Wyntoun's reshaping of the events in the minds of his readers inscribes strong cultural divisions between highland and lowland members of the kingdom. As Steve Boardman notes, one important effect of the Glen Brerachan raid was that 'it allowed [Buchan's] opponents to identify him even more closely with a type of Gaelic lordship which was increasingly seen as wild and lawless'.[55] Nevertheless, the slipperiness of the term 'Scottis' between this episode and the recollection of events in France immediately preceding it is significant, for it demonstrates the ways in which Wyntoun approached his history as well as the ambivalent or contested nature of markers of identity. If readers have just encountered the whole 'nacion' being understood as 'Scottis' from the perspective of the duke of Orléans, what were they to make of the insistence in this passage on the 'Scottis Heilande men', who are clearly understood as different? Who is included and excluded by the term 'Scottis' assumes significance. Wyntoun presents his readers with a memorial challenge between these two episodes, but also within the shaping of the Glasklune episode itself. There is an implicit admiration for the sheer physical capabilities of a man (highland or not) to be able to use the spear with which he has been skewered to lift himself up and strike a blow so fierce that it cuts Lindsay's leg to the bone. At the same time, the level of violence confirms the cultural differences between the highlander and the lowlander in ways that repeat crystallising views of highland violence.[56] Lindsay, in particular, was renowned as a 'gentleman' knight, something that Wyntoun might presume his chivalric audience could recall, not least from his own account of the fight between the Scottish knight and the English Sir John Welles that occurred in London in 1390 (*Chron. Wyntoun* VI.359–62). In this recollection, Wyntoun describes Lindsay as being 'al curtasse' in 'his deid' (VI.361.1202) as he spares the life of the wounded Welles. The reader is therefore encouraged to remember the chivalric identity of the lowland Scots – exemplified in David Lindsay – through the extreme unchivalric violence of the unnamed highlander who nearly kills his opponent. It also creates a memorial cue for the chivalric commendation of the Scots from

---

[55] Boardman, *Early Stewart Kings*, pp. 180–1.
[56] See MacGregor, 'Gaelic Barbarity and Scottish Identity', pp. 7–48.

the duke of Orléans in the previous chapter. By comparing these two episodes it is possible to see how Wyntoun reshapes the past and how, in doing so, he creates specific memorial images that show the process of thinking the nation. It is important that the slipperiness of the use of 'Scottis' remains unresolved at the end of Wyntoun's account because it complicates our assumptions about what late medieval writers in Scotland might conclude about Scottishness.

Both Wyntoun and Gray rely on vivid memorial images to think through authorial and chivalric identity. Those individual identities are shaped by the textual and very real borders that *Scalacronica* and the *Original Chronicle* engage with ideologically. Yet, while both writers appropriate borders as a fundamental marker of identity, they acknowledge that those borders are not hard lines of division but contested and productive spaces of memory and identity, both individual and collective. In the final section of this chapter, I turn to the process of memorialising family identity in the service of the crown through spatial and temporal borders by examining Richard Holland's *Buke of the Howlat*.

Holland's *Howlat* and the Textual Borders of Scottishness

As the only full-scale vernacular account of Scotland's history before Bellenden's 1531 translation of Hector Boece's *Scotorum Historia* (1527), Wyntoun's *Original Chronicle* occupies an important position in the Scottish historiographical tradition. This is compounded by the fact that Wyntoun also presents his chronicle in verse. He is clearly influenced not only by the chronicle tradition but also by Barbour's *Bruce*, on which he relies heavily for material on the Wars of Independence; he quotes regularly from the text and directs his readers to find further material 'in þe Bruss buke' (V.354.2715).[57] It is curious, though, that, despite the use Wyntoun makes of Barbour for details of the Wars, the chronicle is much less responsive to Douglas material than the romance biographer was. Wyntoun makes brief references to 'þe gud Lord Iames þe Dowglase' (*Chron. Wynt.* 5.395.3280) but, on the whole, omits him from the chronicle. He also deliberately ignores the relationship between Bruce and Douglas that Barbour had established in the *Bruce*. However, this connection is picked up around three decades following Wyntoun's compilation of the *Original Chronicle* and exploited in Holland's *Buke of the Howlat*, a poem that presents readers with a distinctive response to the Anglo-Scottish border and the magnates who sought to control its territory. At its core, the *Howlat*

---

[57] For discussions of Wyntoun's use of Barbour, see Rhiannon Purdie, 'Medieval Romance and the Generic Frictions of Barbour's *Bruce*', in *Barbour's Bruce and its Cultural Contexts: Politics, Chivalry and Literature in Late Medieval Scotland*, ed. by Steve Boardman and Susan Foran (Cambridge: D.S. Brewer, 2015), pp. 51–74; Goldstein, '"For he wald vsurpe na fame"', 13–16.

is deeply invested in commemorating the prestige of the Black Douglases, the ancestors of Holland's one-time employer. However, in doing this, the poem is at pains to suggest that the Douglases' pre-eminence resulted from their ability to put aside family ambition in service of the national interest or, at least, to align personal and national interest effectively. In doing so, the *Howlat* reshapes dynastic ambition as a memory of national benefit.

A native of Orkney, Richard Holland first appears in the records in 1441 as *clericus cathaniensis*. By 1453 he was precentor of Moray cathedral. The panegyric stanza at the end of the *Howlat* associates Holland with the household of Archibald Douglas, earl of Moray, and his wife, Elizabeth Dunbar; the reference to 'ane dow of Dunbar' (*Howl.* 989) has been taken to mean that Holland composed the poem for Elizabeth.[58] Archibald was the third son of James the Gross, seventh earl of Douglas, and therefore the great-grandson of the 'Good Sir James' through James's illegitimate son, Archibald the Grim (third earl). The 'Black' Douglases had achieved fame with their role in Robert the Bruce's coup of 1306 and were one of the most powerful aristocratic families in fourteenth-century Scotland. Their supremacy, Michael Brown argues, rested on 'the rule or misrule of the family over its tenants and neighbours', and they maintained dominance 'by fear and force', which only ended after a 'bloody conflict' with James II following the murder of William, the eighth earl, in 1452.[59] The death of earl William forced the Douglases into outright rebellion, which led to the death of several members of the Douglas kin, including Holland's patron at the Battle of Arkinholm (1455). Following the downfall of the family, Holland seems to have retreated back to Orkney – he is recorded as priest and canon of Kirkwall in 1457 – before following James Douglas, brother of Archibald and now ninth earl of Douglas, into exile in England in 1467. Holland's *Howlat* looks back to the lauded image of the Black Douglases presented in such texts as Barbour's *Bruce*, in which loyal service to the crown characterised the family. In responding to Barbour's depiction of the 'gud schyr Iames' (*Bruce* 1.29), Holland centralises and expands a brief episode from Book 20 of the *Bruce*, in which Douglas carries Bruce's heart on crusade. In doing so, Holland inventively reimagines the past to centralise Douglas power and loyalty.

Dating the poem has been a matter of much critical enquiry, with Felicity Riddy arguing for a composition date of 1448, where Marion Stewart's

---

[58] See, for example, Sally Mapstone, 'Older Scots Literature and the Court', in *The Edinburgh History of Scottish Literature, 1: From Columba to the Union (until 1707)*, ed. by Thomas Clancy and Murray Pittock (Edinburgh: Edinburgh University Press, 2007), pp. 273–85; Nicola Royan, '"Mark your meroure be me": Richard Holland's *Buke of the Howlat*', in *A Companion to Medieval Scottish Poetry*, ed. by Priscilla Bawcutt and Janet Hadley Williams (Cambridge: D.S. Brewer, 2006), pp. 49–62.

[59] Brown, *The Black Douglases*, p. 1.

IDENTITY AND NATION ACROSS SCOTLAND'S BORDERS

suggestion of a direct connection to the political demise of the Livingston family indicates a date of 1450.[60] More recently, Alasdair A. MacDonald has revisited this issue, putting forward an argument for evidence of a two-stage composition evident in the poem that demonstrates how Holland revised the poem in circumstances quite different from those of its original composition.[61] In his analysis of the *Howlat*, its language and its imagined topography, MacDonald proposes that Holland's poem, in its extant version, should be regarded as most likely being composed in the 1440s but with post-1455 revisions (i.e., after the death of his patron, Archibald, and the fall of the Douglases). The place names in the *Howlat*, MacDonald argues, indicate a particularly northern focus for the poem, which would correspond with Holland's own retreat back to Orkney.[62] Read in this way, MacDonald suggests, the *Howlat* becomes a consolatory poem, but also one in which the 'unrestrained dynastic glorification' of the Douglases might safely still be written.[63] If MacDonald is correct, several memorial aspects of Holland's work sit more immediately below the text's surface. But, almost regardless of its dating, it is clear that Holland directly uses and shapes the past to comment on the present, although the praising of past Douglas glory serves different memorial functions in the 1440s when the poem was originally composed, and the mid-1450s when the Douglases had firmly fallen from power and when a 1455 context might suggest a melancholic perspective of how the past could be narrated. I will focus on two sections of the poem. Firstly, I will examine what has become known as the 'heraldic core' of the *Howlat*

[60] Felicity Riddy, 'Dating the *Buke of the Howlat*', *Review of English Studies*, 37 (1986), 1–10; Marion Stewart, 'Holland's "Howlat" and the Fall of the Livingstones', *Innes Review*, 26 (1975), 67–79. Ralph Hanna seems to concur with Riddy on the date of the poem, noting that the fall of the Livingstones occurred 'in 1449, shortly after Holland composed the poem'; *Howl.*, 31.

[61] Alasdair A. MacDonald, 'Richard Holland and the *Buke of the Howlat*: Remembrance of Things Past', *Medium Ævum*, 86.1 (2017), 108–22 (108).

[62] This rests on MacDonald's reinterpretation of lines 895–7 ('That no bird was him lyke / Fro Burone to Berwike / Wnder þe bewes'). Where Amours had identified 'Burone' with Burrion (the most northerly point of North Ronaldsay and, therefore, the northern tip of the Orkney islands), he identified 'Beriwke' as Berwick-upon-Tweed. The lines thus intimate that the Owl in his borrowed plumage is the finest creature in the whole of Scotland (notwithstanding that Berwick was at this point in English hands). MacDonald argues that the 'Burone' reference is correct but that 'Berwike' should be understood as a reference to the hamlet of Burwick, the most southerly tip of the Orkney islands. In this case, the howlat is imagined as the finest bird in the Orkneys alone. See MacDonald, 'Richard Holland and *The Buke of the Howlat*', 115–16.

[63] As MacDonald notes, by retreating to Orkney, Holland 'had put himself beyond the dangerous clutches of James II, for until 1468–9 Orkney and Shetland still belonged to Denmark-Norway'. MacDonald, 'Richard Holland and *The Buke of the Howlat*', 118.

44 REWRITING THE PAST IN SCOTTISH LITERATURE, 1350–1550

and its representation of sempiternal honour of the Douglases as the supreme
Scottish magnate dynasty. Secondly, I consider the representation of highland
culture as it is depicted in the bird-fable section of the poem. Both of these
sections demonstrate that Holland uses heraldic imagery and memories of
past heroism to situate the fifteenth-century Douglases as the defenders of
Scotland's borders against its 'fais force' (*Howl.* 383).

The *Howlat* incorporates a frame narrative in which the narrator stumbles
upon an owl making 'ane petuos appele with ane pur mane' (*Howl.* 41). The
poem then presents a bird fable in which the howlat complains of being
'fassonit so foule' (*Howl.* 55) such that the other birds each give him one of
their feathers. On receiving these gifts, however, the howlat becomes so proud
and ambitious that Nature demands the return of his borrowed plumage. The
howlat is returned to his original state and is left lamenting his condition.
At the end of the poem, the narrator comments on the composition of the
poem and identifies himself as one 'Holland' (*Howl.* 1001). In a celebratory
mid-section, which occupies lines 378–624, the *Howlat* describes the coats
of arms associated with specific members of the Douglas family. The moral
instruction of the bird fable – concerning misplaced pride – might serve as
a warning, either in a general advisory context or specifically directed at an
unnamed person. If the *Howlat* were to be read in this way, the poem would
presumably need to be read as a warning to all those who would think to contest
the superiority of the Douglases, which might also include the king, James II.

The envelope pattern of the *Howlat* places the heraldic emblazoning of the
Douglas arms and the Douglases' connections to the Stewarts at the sovereign
mid-point of the poem.[64] Pride of place is given to the Douglases' connections
to the Bruces as Holland recalls how James Douglas 'oft blythit the Bruse
in his distres' (*Howl.* 393). Consequently, Bruce 'blissit that blud' (*Howl.*
394) which was 'lelest' (*Howl.* 433). While the poem concerns itself with the
Douglas dynasty, Holland situates this magnate self-representation in relation
to the national concerns of Scotland memorialised in Bruce's fight for Scottish
independence. In doing so, the *Howlat* testifies to the prominent position that
the Douglases held (or had held) in Scotland's political sphere. It also demonstrates the way in which these border magnates were 'fassonit' as central to
Scottish politics and identity. Following the description of the coats of arms
of the king of Scotland, Holland introduces the Douglases:

> Next the soverane signe was sekerly sene
> That servit his serenite ever servabile,
> The armes of the Dowglas, douchty bedene,

---

[64] The central section of the *Howlat* poetically represents the coats of arms of
the shields of Good Sir James (391–546); Archibald 'the Grim', third earl of Douglas
(547–85); Archibald Douglas, earl of Moray (586–98); the two younger brothers of
Archibald, Hugh Douglas and John Douglas, Lord Balvenie (599–603).

IDENTITY AND NATION ACROSS SCOTLAND'S BORDERS

Knawin throw all Cristindome be conysance able,
Of Scotland the werwall, wit ye but wene,
Our fais force to defend and unfalyeable,
Baith barmekyn and bar to Scottis blud bene,
Our lois and our lyking, that lyne honorable.
That word is so wonder warme, and ever yit was,
    It synkis sone in all part
    Of a trewe Scottis hart,
    Rejosand us inwart
        To heir of Dowglas. (*Howl.* 378–90)

This stanza immediately places the Douglases as *the* pre-eminent magnate family, next in line to the king, and the model of service to the crown in that they are 'ever servabile'. It is for this loyalty, which makes them the 'werwall' of Scotland, that the Douglases are 'Knawin throw all Cristindome'. Inviting the reader to participate in this act of commemoration, Holland forcefully asserts that the 'word' is so wondrous and encouraging as it 'ever yit was' that it immediately penetrates (*synkis*) every part of 'a trewe Scottis hart' such that people rejoice 'inwart' to hear stories of the Douglases. Since the twelfth century, references to learning 'bi herte' (by rote) point to the long association of the heart with memory, stemming from the Latin tradition of the heart (*cor*) being used as a synonym for thought, memory and mind, as well as being the seat of knowledge, character and emotion. As Eric Jager notes, this 'semantic range' was inherited by medieval thinkers, as 'record' (*recordari*) linked the heart with 'memory as well as with writing and books'.[65] The reference to the 'word' that inspires the heart in this stanza of the *Howlat* points to these distinct processes of *memoria* by which stories served as noticeable textual memories, the repetition of which meant that the memory of Douglas supremacy was absorbed (another meaning of *synk*) into every true Scottish heart.[66] The heart, however, assumes a particularly singular importance for the Douglases in their heraldic self-representation. In the description of the arms of the Good Sir James Douglas, Holland reminds the reader that it is because of him that the family bears the 'bludy hart' on their arms (*Howl.* 535). The heart at the centre of the Douglas arms denoted James Douglas's service to Robert the Bruce, and his mission to take Bruce's heart to the Holy Land. The visual incorporation of the heart figures as an unmistakable symbol of crown approval. Moreover, it acts as a visual *aide-mémoire* of the honour that the 'lelest' Douglases carry to 'reskewe' Scotland 'fra scaith' (*Howl.* 433).

---

[65] Eric Jager, *The Book of the Heart* (Chicago and London: University of Chicago Press, 2001), xv. See also Mary Carruthers, 'Reading with Attitude, Remembering the Book', in *The Book and the Body*, ed. by Dolores Warwick Frese and Katherine O'Brien O'Keefe (Notre Dame, IN: University of Notre Dame Press, 1997), pp. 1–33.

[66] *DOST*, 'synk', *v.*3.

Bruce's heart and its visual representation on the arms of Douglas – and as retold in the *Howlat* – stand metonymically for the Douglases' role in securing Scotland's independence. The heart not only signifies the relationship between crown and magnate, but also functions as a remembrance of James Douglas's bravery that, for Holland, becomes the fundamental aspect of Douglas identity, perpetuated in the centrality of the 'hert' set 'heirly and hie' on the Douglas arms (*Howl.* 411). Furthermore, the reminder of Bruce's heart is set against a silver background (the silver 'feld'; *Howl.* 410), which signifies the 'cleir corage' of Douglas (*Howl.* 435). Holland's pun on *cor* and *corage* emphasises the memorial aspect of the coats of arms, utilising heraldry as a visual memory of dynastic reputation. This dynastic posturing can be seen in the literary construction of Douglas genealogy. Holland imagines the 'pursevantis gyde' embroidered 'with ane grene tre' from which cheerful 'branchis' stretch out. Each bough is encircled by a 'bill' (*scroll*) on which is written: 'O Douglas, O Douglas, / Tender and trewe!' (*Howl.* 397–403). By implication, the qualities of the Good Sir James – his caring and his loyalty – are passed through the dynastic line, bringing past glory to the present. The introductory stanzas to the Douglas heraldic line-up thus bring together myriad meanings of the heart to prompt readers' memories of the relationship between courage, loyalty and inheritance through consanguinity.[67] The repeated focus on hearts in the *Howlat* – Bruce's heart in the narrative of James Douglas's pilgrimage and on the shield, and the 'trewe Scottis heart' that is meant to be inspired by the memory invoked by the name of Douglas – links the Bruce, the Douglases and the loyal Scottish reader. Holland indicates that, just as commemoration is at the heart of the *Howlat* – quite literally in its structure – so the memories of reciprocal king and magnate loyalty sit at the heart of Scottish identity.

The second significant memorial image that Holland uses to think about Douglas loyalty signifies another connection between the individual and the nation. Once again, in the introductory stanza to the heraldic core, Holland refers to the Douglases as the 'werwall' of Scotland, that readers should 'wit … but wene'. The Douglases are imagined as the 'unfalyeable' resistance against the enemy, '[b]aith barmekyn and bar to Scottis blud' (*Howl.* 382–84). The Douglases' role as *the* defenders of the Anglo-Scottish border is foregrounded as a signifier of national identity; their dynasty maintains the border that demarcates Scotland's sovereignty and they become the barrier that protects the purity of Scottish blood as well as the 'barmekyn' that shields the Scots from English acts of aggression. Rather than a site of contact and exchange made imaginatively possible in Gray's *Scalacronica*, Holland imagines the Anglo-Scottish border as a frontier, a place of walls and impermeable barriers. This sense of a militarised border also occurs in the bird fable, in which the

---

[67] I discuss the role of genealogy in relation to memory and national identity in more depth in Chapter 2.

IDENTITY AND NATION ACROSS SCOTLAND'S BORDERS

'merlyeonis', who are 'borne bacheleris', are described as being 'bald on the bordouris' (*Howl.* 638–9). The merlins connote both nobility and military force. Here, however, the force is not one of defence (the wall) but of attack (boldness). Holland had asserted this courage in his description of James Douglas as 'bald in assay' (*Howl.* 394), something which he imagined as having 'blythit Bruse in his distress' (*Howl.* 393). The birds of prey in the fable section again intimate a hostile environment in which the only contact across the border is belligerent. Holland's *Howlat*, therefore, memorialises the Anglo-Scottish border as intimately connected with Douglas identity that is founded upon loyalty to the king. A similar use of motto and iconography is deployed by Bérault Stuart d'Aubigny, whose personal banner incorporated two smaller banners: one displaying a shield with three lilies, and a border of buckles; the other presenting the arms of Stuart. Joining these two banners was a scroll containing the motto 'Distantia Jungit' (unites things distant). As Bryony Coombs notes, this motto, along with the image of the buckle, stresses 'the Stuart d'Aubigny's role as the connection, or buckle, that held close Scotland and France' in a political and military union.[68] Coombs suggests that Bérault made use of an older appropriation of the buckle arising from a thirteenth-century marriage between the Stewarts and the Bonkyl family.[69] In doing so, his reuse of the symbol attests to the ways dynastic imagery sought to imaginatively remember the past and reshape its resonance in the present.

Where Gray locates his individual identity most firmly in the prologue to his *Scalacronica* – what we might think of as a textual borderland – Holland's commemoration of the Douglases situates their distinctiveness at the centre of the *Howlat*. Framed by both the bird fable and the narratorial sections, which continually look forward and backward to the centre, the Douglas mid-section situates identity as far from the edges as possible. This focus on centrality not only informs the poem's view of the Douglases as the guardians of Scotland's southern boundary but also turns attention to the northern and western cultural borders of Scotland as the *Howlat* engages with the division between the lowland Scots and the *Gàidhealtachd*. As part of the bird fable, Holland introduces the 'ruke' as a 'bard owt of Irland' (*Howl.* 794–5), whose language is mocked as a 'rerd' of 'rane roch' (*Howl.* 794) as he 'maid' his

---

[68] Bryony J. Coombs, '"Distantia Jungit": Scots Patronage of the Visual Arts in France, *c.* 1445–*c.* 1545', 2 vols (Unpublished PhD thesis, University of Edinburgh, 2013), vol. 1, p. 69.

[69] Coombs, '"Distantia Jungit"' p. 80. See also, Elizabeth Bonner (ed.), *Documents sur Robert Stuart: Seigneur d'Aubigny (1508–1544), Guerrier et courtesan au service de Louis XII et de François Ier* (Paris: Comité des travaux historiques et scientifiques, 2011), p. 41, n. 11. John Stewart of Darnely, Bérault's grandfather, descended from John Stewart who was married to Margaret Bonkyl and who died at the Battle of Falkirk (22 July 1298).

'lesingis' to the company (*Howl*. 807). Holland's inclusion of Gaelic shows a familiarity with the spoken language even as he misrepresents and ridicules it. As with the Anglo-Scottish border, this cultural and linguistic boundary offers an opportunity for ambivalent cross-cultural exchange. The mocking depiction of the rook – as a liar whose 'ryme' (*Howl*. 797) serves as an almost incomprehensible set of ramblings –vilifies the Gael as a barbaric Other opposed to the chivalric ideal of lowland 'Inglis' represented by the Douglases. Gaelic narratives are reduced – and dismissed – because the recitation of the 'Irland kingis of the Irischerye', the poet imagines, can be recited not only by the 'schenachy' and the 'clarschach', but also by the 'ben schene' (*singing woman*), the 'bacllach' (*servant*), the 'crekery' (*reciter*) and the 'corach' (*ritual mourner*) (*Howl*. 801–5). Holland dismisses the king-list as simplistic and of little literary or cultural value, both in the figures it lauds and in the skill of the bard in reciting a genealogy which everyone else can recall from memory with no compositional skill. The inference here is that Gaelic material has no relevance to the lowland Scots of the community and that the bard evidences no proficiency in the craft of memory because his recitation is mere recall rather than imaginative composition. This sets the bard of the bird fable in direct opposition to the feat of *memoria* performed by the *Howlat*'s narrator in the presentation of the Douglas arms, which, according to the poem, imagines genealogy in stylistically more sophisticated ways.

This representation is not unique in Holland, and many lowland texts – both in 'inglis' and in Latin – engage in the denigration of highland culture. Drawing on stereotypes of savagery, cruelty and hostility, writers such as Fordun – and subsequently Bower – distinguish between 'the manners and customs of the Scots', which 'vary with the diversity of their speech' (*Chron. Fordun* 42). Jenny Wormald has suggested that by the end of the fifteenth century, Gaelic was thought of as a 'second-class language'.[70] Another possibility is that lowland Inglis texts such as the *Howlat* might be understood as asserting this distinction as a way of denigrating their literary opposition.[71] This has important implications for thinking the nation, by drawing attention to what is included and excluded by any given text's concept of what Scotland was. In her examination of Dunbar's early sixteenth-century *The Flyting of Dunbar and Kennedy*, Elizabeth Elliott demonstrates that 'the work of thinking nation and national identity is scaffolded by the processes of collaboration, circulation and reception that make thinking nation part of the structure of everyday life'.[72] Elliott argues that in the literary model of flyting, which might

---

[70] Jenny Wormald, *Court, Kirk and Community: Scotland, 1470–1625* (Toronto: University of Toronto Press, 1981), p. 61.

[71] Personal correspondence with Elizabeth Elliott.

[72] Elizabeth Elliott, 'Cognitive Ecology and the Idea of Nation in Late-Medieval Scotland: The Flyting of William Dunbar and Walter Kennedy', in *Distributed Cognition in Medieval and Renaissance Culture*, ed. by Miranda Anderson and Michael Wheeler (Edinburgh: Edinburgh University Press, 2019), pp. 86–98 (98).

be understood as a collaborative literary form, the debate over cultural authenticity between Dunbar's lowland 'inglis' and Kennedy's 'Iersche' allows for cohesive and dynamic understandings of a Scottish identity that encompasses diverse voices and cultures. The productive effects of flyting, however, rely precisely upon opportunities for exchange that arise from trading insults. In the *Howlat*, however, these opportunities are thwarted by the rook's silencing by the 'ravyn' and his victimisation by the 'tuchet' and the 'gukkit golk', who 'fylit him fra the fortope to the fut' (*Howl*. 821–4). The 'barde', who is 'smaddit lyke a smaik smorit in a smedy', is forced to flee the hall in search of 'watter to wesche him' (*Howl*. 825–7), to the amusement of the 'lordis' who 'leuch apon loft' that 'the barde was so bet' (*Howl*. 828–9). The prospect of flyting is denied in Holland's *Howlat* and the chivalric focus of both the bird fable and the heraldic core of the Douglas narrative endeavours to fashion a Scottish identity that sees both English and Gaelic figures as antagonists of the realm. Holland's *Howlat* makes the case for Scottishness as it is exemplified by chivalric honour, filtered through the lens of the memory of James Douglas's service to the Bruce and subsequent generations' loyalty to the crown. In its military stance, the poem suggests that Scotland is continually threatened by the presence of the Anglo-Scottish border that requires the military might of such a powerful family.

Gray's *Scalacronica*, Holland's *Howlat* and Wyntoun's *Chronicle* all engage in reshaping chivalric identity as a *memoria gentis*, intimately connecting family and kingdom in mutually beneficial bonds. Holland's text demonstrates how the signification of the border could bolster a very specific sense of Scottishness that was at once lowland and magnatial, where Gray and Wyntoun express anxieties about cross-border contacts, both across a formal border and with regard to the linguistic and cultural borders of the Scottish kingdom. Robert Bevan sees the border as 'sometimes porous, sometimes solid, but always flexing', simultaneously captor and liberator.[73] Responses to the border depend, to a large extent, on the proximity of the writer to that border, but ideological borders assume a literary potency in memorialising both Anglo-Scottish relations and the internal politics of fourteenth- and fifteenth-century Scotland. All three texts discussed in this chapter demonstrate this flexibility of imagination in reshaping the meaning of ideological and physical borderlands. To do so, they engage in memory-as-practice and underline how integral memory is to the very essence of individual and collective identity.

---

[73] Robert Bevan, *The Destruction of Memory: Architecture at War* (London: Reaktion, 2006), p. 141.

2

Family Ties: The Politics of Scottish Genealogical Memory

In using heraldry to celebrate the Douglases in the *Buke of the Howlat*, I suggested that Richard Holland displays a concern with genealogy as a form of memory. While not a formal memory-training technique, genealogy functions as a commemorative strategy; as Lesley Coote argues, it is a discourse of memory. For Coote, the genealogical text functions both as a 'site of memory' and as 'one of the materials of which memory is made'.[1] Holland is far from alone in demonstrating an interest in the politics of lineage and its applicability to the dynastic affairs of medieval Scotland. Numerous king lists and genealogies in chronicles, literary works and other sources attest to this being a well-established feature of writing about kings and magnate families. In her assessment of the cultural productions of James IV's reign, Katherine Terrell has demonstrated that Scottish chroniclers and court poets favoured the genealogical mode and 'jointly created a multifaceted nationalist discourse founded upon the construction of mythical genealogies'.[2] While it assumed a renewed importance in the early sixteenth century, the connection between genealogy and the kingdom's identity in Scotland can be seen from at least the thirteenth century.[3] Dauvit Broun has shown that John of Fordun synthesised 'diverse sources into a chronologically coherent account of Scottish history'; this included what is known as *Gesta Annalia* I and the 'Scottish Monmouth' compiled by Richard Vairement.[4] Walter Bower's continuation of Fordun develops the genealogical framework as an ideological principle. Written during the reign of James II and at a similar time to Holland's *Howlat*, Bower's *Scotichronicon* demonstrates a concern with the memorial possibilities of genealogy and, while its focus is not on the individual magnate

---

[1] Lesley Coote, 'Prophecy, Genealogy, and History in Medieval English Political Discourse', in *Broken Lines: Genealogical Literature in Medieval Britain and France*, ed. by Raluca L. Radulescu and Edward Donald Kennedy (Turnhout: Brepols, 2008), pp. 24–44 (29).

[2] Terrell, *Scripting the Nation*, p. 10.

[3] Broun, 'Birth of Scottish History', pp. 8–15.

[4] Dauvit Broun, *Scottish Independence and the Idea of Britain* (Edinburgh: Edinburgh University Press, 2007), pp. 236, 258–63.

THE POLITICS OF SCOTTISH GENEALOGICAL MEMORY 51

family so much as on the presentation of Scottish kingship, like Holland's poem the chronicle establishes genealogy as a model of remembering and endorsing Scottish sovereignty and identity.

In the prologue to his own working copy of *Scotichronicon* (Cambridge, Corpus Christi College, MS 171, the 'Corpus MS'; hereafter MS C), Walter Bower, abbot of the Augustinian house of Inchcolm, refers to himself as a 'debtor, not through necessity but compelled by love' (*Debitor sum ... non necessitate sed caritate compulsus*; *Chron. Bower* 9. 3) to copy an older chronicle and to continue this work through to the present time. This confessional beginning to Bower's lengthy chronicle refers to the text's composition in the 1440s at the request of Sir David Stewart of Rosyth, a neighbouring laird of the abbey (*Chron. Bower* 9. 3). The chronicle incorporates and extends Fordun's late fourteenth-century *Chronica Gentis Scotorum*, which covered the history of the Scots from their mythical origin to the death of David I in 1153 as well as incorporating scraps of information covering the next two hundred years to Fordun's own time. Bower supplements Fordun's work and then extends the *Scotichronicon* to deal with Scottish history through to the murder of James I in 1437. Prior to James's death, Bower had occupied a prominent position in Scottish royal administration; for example, in 1433, he was involved in reporting on a debate at a council general to discuss a peace embassy from England.[5] He began his chronicle during James II's tempestuous minority, which witnessed the rise of magnate factionalism in the attempt to control the government of the kingdom. The *Auchinleck Chronicle* (*c.* 1460), the only contemporary chronicle for James II's reign, evidences the violence that defined the opening years of James's kingship and intimates an ongoing struggle between the crown and the Scottish nobility as James sought to assert his authority.[6] While Bower was writing for a specific patron he was doing so in the context of a minority in which government was in the hands of the Black Douglases, as well as the Crichtons and Livingstons who had achieved a sudden rise to power and had fallen just as quickly.[7] Concerns with national cohesion in *Scotichronicon* are therefore not surprising, and in this chapter I explore one of the strategies that Bower employs in this regard: the use of genealogy as a way of memorialising collective identity.

Gabrielle Spiegel has done what is perhaps some of the most important work on medieval genealogies in her work on twelfth- and thirteenth-century France.

---

[5] On Bower's career, see D.E.R. Watt, 'Bower [Bowmaker], Walter (1385–1449), abbot of Inchcolm and Historian', *ODNB* [accessed 3 June 2020].

[6] *The Auchinleck Chronicle, ane schort memorial of the scottis corniklis for addicioun,* ed. by Thomas Thomson (Edinburgh, 1819), esp. pp. 3–5.

[7] See Katie Stevenson, *Power and Propaganda: Scotland, 1306–1488* (Edinburgh: Edinburgh University Press, 2014), esp. pp. 42–4; Brown, *The Black Douglases*, esp. pp. 255–82; Christine McGladdery, *James II* (Edinburgh: John Donald, 2015), pp. 58–64.

52 REWRITING THE PAST IN SCOTTISH LITERATURE, 1350–1550

In designating genealogy as a 'perceptual grid' – a structure 'already residing in the social reality' that limited and controlled the historian's narrative – Spiegel suggests that lineage or, more specifically, written genealogy has distinctly social rather than intellectual origins and therefore presents important ways of thinking about social relationships.[8] Spiegel argues that genealogy becomes a central focus of historical narratives at the same time that agnatic consanguinity became the dominant structural model of European noble societies.[9] These genealogical structures reorder time such that past and present (and, indeed, future) exist simultaneously in the genealogical imagination. Genealogy serves as a memory of the passage of time at the very moment that it assures continuity through inheritance. If genealogy becomes a national practice as well as a personal one, agnatic succession assumes potency for thinking about national identity, for, while it bolstered dynastic powerbases, the model might also be used rhetorically to remind readers of the very real transference of memory through blood from one generation – or monarch – to the next.

Outwith the main text of MS C, several folios contain genealogical items in varying states of completeness. In the prelims, there survives a full-page genealogical tree (fol. 2v) that depicts the interrelationships of the English and Scottish royal families; beginning with Máel Coluim III and his wife, St Margaret, the table ends with James II (*rex modernus*). In MS C there is significant damage to the page, but the tree also appears (and is complete) in three other manuscripts, and a revised version appears in MS E, Edinburgh University Library MS 186, fol. 345r (Fig. 1).[10] Two additions to MS C are also of interest. The first (fol. 370) comprises notes on the succession to the earldoms of Orkney and Caithness, which has led Barbara Crawford to conclude that this is an *aide-mémoire* connected to William Sinclair of Roslin's claims to the earldom of Caithness in the 1430s.[11] The genealogy traces Sinclair's claim and ancestry through a maternal line connected to Malise, earl of Strathearn, who had succeeded to the earldoms of Orkney and Caithness 'by right of lineal descent' (*jure successionis linealiter*; *Chron. Bower* 9. 41). Immediately following this paragraph connected to Sinclair, a genealogical table sets out

---

8 Gabrielle Spiegel, *The Past as Text: The Theory and Practice of Medieval Historiography* (Baltimore, MD: Johns Hopkins University Press, 1997), p. 103.

9 Spiegel, *Past as Text*, p. 104.

10 The three manuscripts are: MS R (BL MS Royal 13 E. X), fol. 26v; MS D (Darnaway Castle, the 'Donibristle MS'), fol. 435; and MS H (BL MS Harleian 712), fol. 276 v. The genealogical table in MS E can be accessed at: https://images.is.ed.ac.uk (image reference: 0001272).

11 James I acquiesced to Sinclair's claim in 1434. B.E. Crawford, 'The Fifteenth-century "Genealogy of the Earls of Orkney" and its Reflection of the Contemporary Political and Cultural Situation in the Earldom', *Mediaeval Scandinavia*, 10 (1977), 156–78 (esp. 158).

THE POLITICS OF SCOTTISH GENEALOGICAL MEMORY 53

the French royal dynasty, beginning with St Louis and ending with both Louis XI, eldest son of Charles VII (and husband of James I's daughter, Margaret) on one side and Henry VI of England on the other. Along with this table are additional notes concerned with the right of succession in France. The writer specifically notes, in stark contrast to the material about Orkney and Caithness, that 'it needs to be understood that', in France, 'a woman does not succeed, nor does a male who is a descendant through the female line' (*Chron. Bower* 9. 44). In commenting specifically on English claims to the French throne, the end of the notes details that 'Edward Windsor king of England was not [related to King Philip VI], for he descended through the female line' (*Chron. Bower* 9. 44). Taken together, these preliminary and additional items point not only to a broader concern with genealogy in Bower's composition of *Scotichronicon* (and his readers' responses to it); they also attest to specific cultural differences in the ways inheritance – traced genealogically – functioned.[12] All of these genealogies indicate an understanding that power, authority and territorial possession rested on remembering and tracing ancestry; they also demonstrate that the ways in which those memories could be deployed were culturally contingent and, therefore, up for debate.

Remembering the Mythical Origins of the Scots

The focus on genealogy within *Scotichronicon* and other Scottish historical and literary works brings to the fore a concern with beginnings. Beginnings are significant because they provide, as Anke Bernau suggests, 'a structure for remembering – an entry point into remembrance'.[13] Bernau further argues that, in terms of national narratives, the origin or beginning 'can be seen to represent quintessentially the act of commemoration that the chronicle narrative represents and performs'; it denotes the very act of remembrance performed by the writing of the chronicle itself.[14] From the outset, then, both historiography and the concern with lineage signify an inherent commemorative function in their inception and expression. The importance of origins to later sections of Bower's text calls readers' minds back to the first books of *Scotichronicon* that deal with the creation of the world and, more specifically, the beginnings of Scotland and the Scots through the foundation myth of the eponymous Scota and her husband, Gaythelos. The lineage of the Scottish

---

[12] Primogentiure had been instituted in Scotland by the mid-thirteenth century; however, it is also the case that female succession (or, certainly, male claims to succession through a female line) was not unheard of. There appears to have been an (albeit not always comfortable) acceptance of matrilineal inheritance in Scotland.

[13] Anke Bernau, 'Beginning with Albina: Remembering the Nation', *Exemplaria*, 21.3 (2009), 247–73 (248).

[14] Bernau, 'Beginning with Albina', 248.

Fig. 1 Genealogical tree with pictorial heads of Scottish kings. University of Edinburgh Library, MS 186, fol. 345r. Reproduced by permission of The University of Edinburgh Heritage Collections.

THE POLITICS OF SCOTTISH GENEALOGICAL MEMORY 55

kings recited in Book 10 traces the Scottish monarchy back to this founding mother and father, thematically directing the text's focus to the beginning of a Scottish community by aligning the hereditary monarchy with the overarching governance of the Scots as a people. Genealogy as memory functions as a way of legitimising Stewart kingship by decisively linking the Stewarts with Scottish authority and sovereignty. In drawing the community into this strategy, genealogy functions as the 'national family' history.

The Scota myth, which recounts the descent of the Scots from an Egyptian refugee princess named Scota, had circulated in the northern part of Britain since at least the twelfth century. The bare bones of the narrative can be found in the Scottish records from the tenth century and the essence of the story survives in the ninth-century *Historia Brittonum* and in the eleventh-century Irish *Lebor Gebála*.[15] Baldred Bisset, the leading Scottish procurator in Rome, made significant use of genealogical strategy and origin myth in disputing Edward I's use of the Brutus narrative as a way of claiming overlordship of Scotland.[16] Bisset's *Processus*, presented to the papal curia in 1301, argued that Scota had overthrown the Picts and taken over their kingdom and, as a result, the Scots and Scotland took their name from her.[17] As such, Bisset proclaims, 'the Scots and Scotland are no concern of the king of England; and the English could have claimed no more of a right to the kingdom of Scotland than the Egyptians' (*Chron. Bower* 6. 183). The earliest surviving extended account of the Scota story in Scotland appears in Fordun's *Chronica Gentis Scotorum*, although, as Broun has demonstrated, this lengthier narrative indicates that Fordun incorporated *Gesta Annalia* into his chronicle rather than creating it himself.[18] This narrative is extended by Bower and, for the purposes of my discussion, deserves to be presented at length.

Fordun and Bower recount how 'In the third age, in the time of Moses there was a certain king of one of the kingdoms of Greece' (*Chron. Bower* 1. 27). This king had a son, Gaythelos, who 'was provoked to anger' as a result of not being 'permitted to hold any position of power in the kingdom' (*Chron. Bower* 1. 27). With the support of 'a large company', he 'inflicted many disasters on his father's kingdom with frightful cruelty', such that 'he was driven out of his native land and sailed off to Egypt' (*Chron. Bower* 1.

[15] See William Matthews, 'The Egyptians in Scotland: The Political History of a Myth', *Viator*, 1 (1970), 289–306 (294). See also, Broun, *Irish Identity*, esp. pp. 12–15.

[16] For a discussion of the Brutus myth, and its connections to English claims of Scottish overlordship, see: Wingfield, *Trojan Legend*, pp. 10–15; Terrell, *Scripting the Nation*, pp. 15–26; Goldstein, *Matter of Scotland*, pp. 64–5.

[17] For more detailed discussion of Bisset's *Processus*, see R. James Goldstein, 'The Scottish Mission to Boniface VIII in 1301: A Reconsideration of the *Instructiones* and *Processus*', *SHR*, 70 (1991), 1–15; Terrell, *Scripting the Nation*, pp. 46–51.

[18] Broun, *Scottish Independence*, pp. 215–34.

27), where he was 'united in marriage with Scota the daughter of the Pharaoh' on account of his being 'outstandingly brave and daring and also of royal descent' (*Chron. Bower* 1. 27). Following the death of the pharaoh, Gaythelos was exiled along with his followers, so that 'all the nobles both Greek and Egyptian alike … were cruelly driven away by peasants enrolled in a servile uprising' (*Chron. Bower* 1. 31). Gaythelos, understanding that 'his return route to Greece was barred to him … firmly decreed that he would either seize a kingdom and territory from other peoples', or he would 'take possession of some uninhabited place for settlement' (*Chron. Bower* 1. 33). The story continues that Gaythelos 'entered Africa' along with his followers and 'settled peacefully' in Numidia, where, for the 'forty years during which the children of Israel lived in the wilderness under the leadership of Moses', Scota and Gaythelos wandered 'through many lands', eventually leaving Africa and sailing 'to the vicinity of the islands of Cadiz in Spain' (*Chron. Bower* 1. 35). This, however, was not a welcome development and the local inhabitants 'rushed together from all sides in resentment of their arrival' (*Chron. Bower* 1. 39). Gaythelos 'pursued the inhabitants and plundered a considerable part of their territory' (*Chron. Bower* 1. 39). Returning to the shore, Gaythelos 'pitched his tents on a small mound on higher ground' and surrounded them 'with a wall' and built a 'very strong tower called Brigantia' (*Chron. Bower* 1. 39). Involved in continual warfare, Gaythelos, whose 'whole mind was intent on the protection of his people, as befits a practical and careful ruler', determined that 'he had brought the hardships … upon himself since he had given up the plan which he had originally decided upon, that is to acquire unoccupied lands and so harm no-one' (*Chron. Bower* 1. 39–41). Determined to 'return to the plan he had formed before he left Egypt', Gaythelos ordered his sailors to 'explore the boundless Ocean in search of uninhabited lands' (*Chron. Bower* 1. 41). Seeing 'an island rising up in the distance', they 'sailed quickly back to Brigantia' to report back. Gaythelos, however, was 'overtaken by sudden death' (*Chron. Bower* 1. 41) and it was left to his sons, Hiber and Hymec, to take possession of the land 'not by force' but because they found it 'empty and completely uninhabited' (*Chron. Bower* 1. 43). They called it Scotia 'after [their] mother's name' (*Chron. Bower* 1. 45). Bower notes that this land is the land of Hibernia (Ireland), while it is the northern part of Britain that is known as Scotia:

> The northern part of the island of Britain is called Scotia because the land is known to have been inhabited by a people originally descended from the Scoti. This is demonstrated by the affinity of both language and culture, of arms and customs right up to the present day.
>
> (*Chron. Bower* 1. 45)

THE POLITICS OF SCOTTISH GENEALOGICAL MEMORY   57

R. James Goldstein has argued that the story Fordun narrates betrays the political attitudes of the fourteenth century, particularly the 'right of a sovereign people to hold their native soil against foreign invaders'.[19] In this, we can see Fordun moulding his history very much in line with the deployment of the Scota narrative during the Great Cause. This issue of territorial sovereignty is still one that concerns Bower in the mid-fifteenth century, but his narrative of Scota and Gaythelos also betrays its own deeply contemporary concerns: ambition and the struggle for power internally and the necessity of good rulership. The Scota myth is simultaneously a migration narrative and a remembrance of the beginnings of a community. Like Moses, Gaythelos and Scota lead an exiled people to a promised land, but the story is also a narrative of the naming of the Scots and their settlement in the northern part of the British Isles in an ancient past. In recollecting and reimagining this story, Bower immediately links the Scottish people with their claim to territory; in doing so, the account enables Bower to claim genealogical and geographical heritage and sovereignty for the Scots at a time when they were trying to reclaim lost border territories, such as Berwick and Roxburgh.

Scota initially appears to be a marginal figure in this story of Scottish origins, granted an appearance only by the fact that her sons honour her by naming land after her. The main focus is on Gaythelos and his Greek ancestry. Indeed, in his account of the inauguration of Alexander III (which I discuss later in this chapter), Bower provides his audience with a lineage that can be traced to Iber, the 'son of Gaythelos ... by Scota' (*Chron. Bower* 5. 295). The stress here seems to be on agnatic consanguinity (relation through male descent or on the father's side), with Scota present as a passive vessel of childbearing. Such a perspective is hardly unique; for example, in the English Brutus myth, Brutus's wife, Ingoge, disappears as soon as she has served the purpose of providing an heir. For Jeffrey Jerome Cohen, this narrative hesitancy stems from the fact that maternal bodies are 'problematic sites of origin', either because they are forced to marry men they do not desire (in the case of Ingoge) or because they are unfaithful (in the cases of women such as Guinevere and Ygerna).[20] For Cohen, this inconstancy and instability reflects the fact that 'no secure place' existed for mothers within the 'narratives of nation building connected to the Trojan diaspora'.[21] Of course, the Scota myth is situated distinctly outside of this Trojan framework and, although Goldstein notes only one example (preserved in Fordun) in which the Scottish migration narrative is seen from Scota's perspective, Bower's text does not register an anxiety about the importance of Scota to an understanding of

---

[19] Goldstein, *Matter of Scotland*, p. 121.

[20] Jeffrey Jerome Cohen, *Of Giants: Sex, Monsters and the Middle Ages* (Minneapolis: University of Minnesota Press, 1999), p. 47.

[21] Cohen, *Of Giants*, p. 47.

Scottish origins.[22] *Scotichronicon*'s narrative stresses that it is Scota who reaches Ireland and settles the land with her sons. As Bower recounts, 'Grosseteste says: "And because their duchess [*ducissa*; female leader], who was the highest in rank of all those that were there, was called Scota, they called that part of the country where they first landed (i.e. Ulster) Scotia"' (*Chron. Bower* 1. 45). Moreover, in the only manuscript image to depict Scota and Gaythelos on their travels, it is Scota who is the focus.

The image (Fig. 2) depicting Scota and Gaythelos in a ship is found in MS C. Despite the apparent emphasis on Gaythelos in the written account, the main figure in the illustration is Scota. She stands in the most prominent position on the poop deck and the open gesture of both her hands indicates that she assumes the role of commanding the raising of the sail and the direction of the ship. Gaythelos is not hidden, but he stands almost obscured. The picture represents the greater importance afforded to Scota that is found in the materials associated with the Great Cause, where Scottish models of inheritance competed with English insistence on agnatic kinship. The relationship between text and image in MS C is therefore not straightforward; it intimates how rewriting – or redrawing – the past inflects historical narrative with current affairs. In Book 11, Bower includes a copy of Bisset's draft letter to the papal curia. He later includes the letter itself (*Chron. Bower* 6. 169–89). This letter details the right of Scotland to be free from subjection to Edward I and argues that Edward's aggression 'disturbed the previous state of Scotland's ancient freedom' (*Chron. Bower* 6. 135). Bisset's letter accuses Edward of having 'omitted to write down the truth ... touching only on what seemed to suit his purpose' (*Chron. Bower* 6. 143). It then suggests that the Scots will 'tell more fully' what Edward 'has not yet put in writing, in order to provide fuller knowledge of the story' (*Chron. Bower* 6. 143). Here *Scotichronicon* points to the ways in which memory and forgetting become a rhetorical tool of debate, a nexus of the politics of national sovereignty. Bower reproduces the letter that contains a potted history of the origin myth and asserts that Scotland was 'named after the woman Scota', the 'lady of the Scots' (*Chron. Bower* 6. 143). An important point for the Scottish argument is that it is Scota's maternity that enables her role as a figurehead.[23] The independence and sovereignty that stems from this assertion of the Scots' distinct lineage from Scota seems to push Gaythelos to the margins of the story.

---

[22] In Book 1, Chapter 13, Fordun narrates how Scota 'went forth in terror out of Egypt' (*Chron. Fordun* 1. 13. 11).

[23] Claire Harrill has argued similarly for the centrality of St Margaret of Scotland's significance as a mother. See 'Sanctity and Motherhood in the *Miracula* of St Margaret', in *Christianity in Scottish Literature*, ed. by John Patrick Pazdziora (Glasgow: Scottish Literature International, 2023), pp. 16–34. For a detailed analysis of Scota's role, see Michelle A. Smith, 'Assessing Gender in the Construction of Scottish Identity, *c.* 1286–*c.* 1586' (Unpublished PhD thesis, University of Auckland, 2010), pp. 80–129.

Fig. 2   The journey of Scota and Gaythelos. Cambridge, Corpus Christi College MS 171A, fol. 14v. Reproduced by permission of The Parker Library, Corpus Christi College, Cambridge.

I do not think that Bower intends to set Scota and Gaythelos in opposition in *Scotichronicon*, however; rather, he puts forward a productive model of cognatic kinship – a system of family relationships based on both maternal and paternal sides of a person's family – where, although succession had become agnatic by the mid-fifteenth century, the partnership of husband and wife demonstrated the prestige and power each brought to the heritage and family line of the Scots. Bower asserts that 'the Scots gain additional lustre from the fact that they are sprung from the stock of the king of Athens' as well as from the matrilineal line of Scota (*Chron. Bower* 5. 295). This lustre stems from Bower's characterisation of the Greeks as being

> A most warlike race, well endowed with the gift of wisdom and knowledge, most eloquent in speech, obedient to the laws, pious, peaceable towards other nations, tranquil in its dealings with [their] own citizens, but implacable and belligerent in the face of injuries inflicted by [their] enemies.
> (*Chron. Bower* 5. 295–7)

Through genealogical continuity, the Scots inherit these qualities, the most important of which is the way in which the Greeks respond to 'injuries inflicted by their enemies'. The clear resonance here with recent Anglo-Scottish tensions suggests that Bower intended to remind the Scots of how their ancestors would have responded to aggression and to prompt a re-enactment of that memory in present and future circumstances, which could be seen as analogous to the past.

The importance of joining two illustrious genealogies is certainly suggested throughout *Scotichronicon* in relation to other dynastic lines. In his depiction of the partnership of Máel Coluim III and St Margaret of Scotland, for example, Bower seeks to keep the idea of family and nation at the forefront of his audience's mind. I have argued elsewhere that the two major vision narratives of Margaret in *Scotichroncion* seek to reimagine her role as both queen and wife in distinctly national terms and that Bower seeks to present the Scottish saint as a mother of a nation determined to resist attempts to challenge its sovereignty.[24] In Book 10 of *Scotichronicon*, Bower narrates how the remains of Margaret and Máel Coluim were translated at Dunfermline abbey in 1250. The translation of Máel Coluim and Margaret occurs in *Scotichronicon* immediately after the recitation of Alexander III's genealogy at his inauguration (which I discuss below); in shaping the narrative in this way, Bower suggests to his audience a memorial thread between the recited genealogy, the Scota–Gaythelos myth and the translation of Alexander's eleventh-century saintly ancestors.

Bower narrates that in 1250, Alexander III had the remains of Margaret translated from the grounds of Dunfermline abbey to the interior of the church. While moving Margaret's remains, the bearers' arms became paralysed once they reach the chancel door close to where Máel Coluim was buried at the north side of the nave (*Chron. Bower* 5. 297). It was one of the bystanders, seemingly speaking through divine inspiration, who confirmed that Margaret's remains could be moved only in conjunction with her husband's. Once again, the emphasis is on seeing Margaret and Máel Coluim as a partnership, each supporting and enhancing the power of the other. Parallels might be drawn between Bower's account and Wyntoun's emphasis on Máel Coluim and Margaret's lineage that combines 'Saxonys ande Scottis blude' (IV.355.407), which, as Boardman points out, suggests Wyntoun's determination to show that the marriage of Máel Coluim and Margaret 'fundamentally altered the nature of the Scottish monarchy'.[25] A similar idea can be seen in the *Liber Extravagans*, which describes Máel Coluim's 'family of Scottish stock mingl[ing] with Saxon blood' (*sanguine mixta*; *Chron. Bower* 9. 73). The partnership is an image that Bower pursues in a later recollection of John

---

[24] See Kate Ash, 'St Margaret and the Literary Politics of Scottish Sainthood', in *Sanctity as Literature in Late Medieval Britain*, ed. by Eva von Contzen and Anke Bernau (Manchester: Manchester University Press, 2015), pp. 18–37, esp. pp. 25–34.

[25] Steve Boardman, 'A People Divided? Language, History and Anglo-Scottish Conflict in the Work of Andrew of Wyntoun', in *Ireland and the English World in the Late Middle Ages: Essays in Honour of Robin Frame*, ed. by Brendan Smith (Basingstoke: Palgrave Macmillan, 2009), pp. 112–29 (122).

THE POLITICS OF SCOTTISH GENEALOGICAL MEMORY 61

Wemyss's vision of St Margaret ahead of the Battle of Largs in 1263 (*Chron. Bower* 5. 337–9). In this dream, Wemyss sees a lady 'of radiant beauty' leading 'a distinguished-looking knight' on her right arm, with three 'noble knights' following her. The image here depicts Margaret, Máel Coluim and their three sons 'hurrying to defend [their] country' from the 'usurper' King Hákon IV of Norway (1217–63), who was 'unjustly trying' to 'subject [Scotland] to his rule' (*Chron. Bower* 5. 337). Of course, this was also the decisive battle which led to the transference of the Hebrides from Norwegian to Scottish authority. Alongside the memory here of Margaret's sanctity, is an expectation that the reader connects this recollection with Scottish territorial expansion. While the defence of the realm against those who would seek to conquer it is the dominant concern, here the familial image of Margaret, Máel Coluim and their sons compels the reader to remember the narrative images of the originary Scottish family which pervade the earlier books of *Scotichronicon* and official documents of the Wars of Independence.[26] Bower's text therefore relies on narrative cues and repetition to embed national memory; the visionary episodes demonstrate how the lineage of Scotland's kings is not only to be seen as chronological – a single trajectory of ancestry and descent – but also that these images of origin and community repeatedly play themselves out within Scottish history.

Genealogical Memory and the Inauguration of Alexander III in Bower's *Scotichronicon*

> *'Mortuus est' ... 'pater illius et quasi non est mortuus; simile enim reliquid sibi post se.'*

> His father has died, and yet in a sense is not dead, for he has left a copy of himself behind. (*Chron. Bower* 5. 291; Ecclesiasticus 30: 4)

On 13 July 1249, Alexander III was crowned as Scotland's new king. His father, Alexander II, the 'renowned king of the Scots' (*Chron. Bower* 5. 191), had died seven days previously, leaving the eight-year-old boy to inherit the throne. The epigram to this section is taken from Walter Bower's depiction of Alexander's inauguration, which is described in Book 10 of *Scotichronicon*. It intimates two central concerns in relation to the succession of kings: continuity and sempiternity. Bower's citation of Ecclesiasticus continues:

> he [the father] has left behind him a defender of his house against his enemies who will repay the kindness of his friends. (*Chron. Bower* 5. 291)

---

[26] See my discussion of this vision in Ash, 'St Margaret and the Literary Politics of Scottish Sainthood', pp. 28–31.

62 REWRITING THE PAST IN SCOTTISH LITERATURE, 1350–1550

While the succession of a minority king must have been a cause of anxiety in 1249, Bower's fifteenth-century chronicle retrospectively paints Alexander III's accession as the beginning of a golden age for Scotland, one that was relatively stable and free from magnate struggles. Later in Book 10, and mostly in Bower's additions to Fordun's material, the chronicle praises Alexander and his reign, remarking that

> Every day in the life of this king the church of Christ flourished, its priests were honoured ... vice withered away, deceit disappeared, injustice ceased, virtue thrived, truth grew strong, justice reigned ... Thus he could rightly be called a king on the merits of his integrity and his even-handed justice, because he ruled himself and his people rightly.
>
> (*Chron. Bower* 5. 421–3)

To a certain extent, this is not a wild exaggeration on Bower's part; as Keith Stringer has argued, during Alexander's reign the 'unified Scottish polity envisaged by David I finally emerged' and 'royal power was unprecedentedly penetrating and all-encompassing', to the point that 'regnal cohesion was fortified by clearly defined frontiers, unitary legal and administrative frameworks, a "national" Church, and the unmistakable imprint of a single sovereign authority'.[27] Given that Bower was writing with hindsight of the aftermath of Alexander III's untimely death, the succession crisis and consequent Anglo-Scottish conflict it engendered, it is understandable that Bower sought to codify this king's reign as a distinctive moment in Scottish history. It is also a portrait that mirrors Bower's assessment of Alexander II, whom he describes as a 'renowned king', who 'always hated wrong doing and loved equity and justice', who 'Like the morning star ... grew into the light and sunshine until the fulness of day' (*Chron. Bower* 5. 191). For Bower, Alexander II 'proved to be a source of strength to his fellow-soldiers, appreciative to religious, humble before priests ... generous to those in need ... sober with the arrogant, alarming to malefactors and merciful towards the defeated' (*Chron. Bower* 5. 191–3).

The inclusion of *truth* in the description of Alexander III is particularly powerful, carrying with it notions of faithfulness, loyalty, allegiance and confidence as well as integrity. Alexander is depicted as a king who possesses all of these qualities and inspires these characteristics in his subjects. Alexander is thus a 'copy' of his father just as his Scottish subjects, Bower imagines, emulate him in his loyalty to Scotland and Scottish interests. The reference to Ecclesiasticus and the image of Alexander II leaving behind an image of himself exemplifies what Ernst Kantorowicz has famously called the 'mystic

---

[27] Keith Stringer, 'The Emergence of a Nation State, 1100–1300', in *Scotland: A History*, ed. by Jenny Wormald (Oxford: Oxford University Press, 2005), pp. 39–76 (73).

THE POLITICS OF SCOTTISH GENEALOGICAL MEMORY   63

function' of the 'King's Two Bodies', the body natural and the body politic, which exist together in the figure of the monarch.[28] Alexander II had left behind a body natural image of himself in the form of his biological son and namesake; he had also bequeathed a body politic image of the king of Scots in siring an heir for the kingdom. Biological and political continuity are thus embodied within the king (and King) of Alexander III. This sense of harmony and continuity through dynastic history manifests in Bower's *Scotichronicon* in the recitation of the King's genealogy at Alexander's inauguration. In doing so, Bower uses this historical moment not only as a recollection of an individual's claim to power but also as a commemorative assertion of the independent identity of the Scots under the political sovereignty of the king.

Bower narrates that after the *solemnitatem regie coronacionis*, and 'In accordance with the custom which had grown up in the kingdom from antiquity', Alexander III was taken from the church at Scone and was 'With due reverence ... installed ... on the royal seat' [the stone of Scone] (*Chron. Bower* 5 .293). The use of *coronacionis* is a misnomer here, for Scottish kings were inaugurated and did not, as such, have a coronation, but the slippage is interesting for thinking about the relationship of the king to the Scots as a nation, for the term 'coronation' reminds the reader that Alexander was being crowned (*coronare*) as the head of the nation (*natio*). Bower plays with these associations of *coronacionis*, which suggests that, for him, the inauguration was a symbolic connection between the king and people, nation and identity. Bower then recalls that a 'venerable, grey-haired figure, an elderly Scot' (*Scotus*) appeared at the inauguration and, although a 'wild highlander' (*silvester et montanus*), 'was honourably attired after his own fashion' (*Chron. Bower* 5. 295). This highlander greets the new king 'in a scrupulously correct manner' and 'in his mother tongue' (*materna lingua*, i.e., Gaelic) (*Chron. Bower* 5. 295). He then proceeds to recite the *genealogiam* of the king of Scots, 'linking up each person with the next, until he came to the first Scot, that is Hiber the Scot', son of Gaythelos and Scota (*Chron. Bower* 5. 295). The investiture reveals an act of *memoria* through the ritual of inauguration: the recitation of the monarch's genealogy becomes a memorial act that generates (as it performs) a commemorative narrative. The recitation of the king's lineage ends powerfully with a return to origins (Scota), drawing the reader's attention back to Scotland's mythic foundation, which, through the process of ritualised remembrance, is directly linked with the foundational moment of Alexander's own reign. The ceremony demonstrates how national memory is heavily inflected with notions of memorial practice. Bower remembers Scottish history in such a way as to identify Alexander III not only as his father's heir through his personal body but also as the heir of

---

[28] Ernst H. Kantorowicz, *The King's Two Bodies: A Study in Medieval Political Theology* (Princeton, NJ: Princeton University Press, 1957; repr. 1997), p. 3.

64 REWRITING THE PAST IN SCOTTISH LITERATURE, 1350–1550

Scota through his public body. The genealogy of Alexander's personal and public body demonstrates, then, a preoccupation with foundations that has as much to do with the perception of regnal (or national) continuity as it has to do with the private genealogy of an aristocratic family. King and crown, individual and state, are inextricably knitted together and serve as a model for – and expression of – the community as a whole.

The inauguration of Alexander is depicted in a miniature in MS C (fol. 206r), one of five illustrations in this manuscript – the other four depicting the journey of Scota and Gaythelos (which I have already discussed, see Fig. 2), the meeting between Máel Coluim and Macduff, the funeral of Alexander III and the Battle of Bannockburn. These illustrations depict particularly significant moments in Scottish history and Scottish kingship, with Alexander's reign notably highlighted by two visual narratives: the beginning and end of his kingship. The miniature of the inauguration (Fig. 3) depicts a seated Alexander holding a sceptre, flanked by two nobles, one of whom holds a sword. John Higgitt suggests that these two figures are likely to be Máel Coluim II, earl of Fife, and Malise II, earl of Strathearn.[29] The identification of the earl of Fife would certainly make sense in this instance, given the earl's holding of the right to crown the kings of Scotland.[30] Behind these three figures stands a cross, and to the left of them, a man in significantly different attire *genuflectens* before the king. This man is also in the act of speaking, demonstrated by the scroll coming from his mouth, on which is written: *benach de re albane alex[ander] mak alex[ander]* (God bless the king of Albany, Alexander son of Alexander).[31] The scroll repeats the first spoken words in Bower's account of the inauguration on the same page, but it does so in the highlander's *materna lingua*, Gaelic, which is then translated into Latin by Bower, who notes that the man recites Alexander's lineage back to 'Fergus, first king of the Scots in Albany' (*Chron. Bower* 5. 295).

More than just a visual complement to Bower's text, however, the image of Alexander's inauguration serves several specific functions within *Scotichronicon*.[32] The inclusion of this image as one of only five in the

[29] John Higgitt, 'Decoration and Illustration', *Chron. Bower* 9. 157–85 (174).

[30] Malise's son, Malise III, was the brother-in-law of John Comyn, earl of Buchan, whose wife, Isabel, played a significant role in Robert Bruce's coup of 1306.

[31] *Beannachd* indicates a blessing or benediction, and *beannaich* to bless. Colin B.D. Mark, *The Gaelic–English Dictionary: A Dictionary of Scots Gaelic* (London: Routledge, 2007), bennaich, *v.* 'De' is the genitive of 'Dia' (God). Thanks to Duncan Sneddon and Kate Mathis for their helpful discussions of this phrase with me. See also, John Bannerman, 'The King's Poet and the Inauguration of Alexander III', *SHR*, 68 (1989), 120–49.

[32] Higgitt notes particular differences between the image and Bower's text. See *Chron. Bower* 9. 172.

Fig. 3 The inauguration of Alexander III. Cambridge, Corpus Christi College MS 171B, fol. 206r. Reproduced by permission of The Parker Library, Corpus Christi College, Cambridge.

manuscript points to the importance of this occasion, but the depiction of the highlander and his speech scroll also represents Bower's text as speech made visible (or speech rendered as text by Bower). The speech act – in Bower's text and its visual representation – is at once documentary and performative: documentary in its recording Alexander's inauguration and performative in actively changing Alexander from boy to king (personal to public body) through the remembrance and recitation of his monarchical heritage. Along with Bower's text, the manuscript image re-enacts the past to enable the present and the future; genealogy as performance makes lineage living memory and Alexander a living embodiment of regnal memory. However, the illustration is also an attempt to impose a certain interpretation of the past and to shape the memory of *Scotichronicon*'s audience. While John Bannerman has argued that the description of the poet as a *Scotus montanus* was never intended by Fordun to be understood as a mark of rusticity, the differentiation of the man is significant.[33] The inclusion of the Gaelic text and the description of him as a 'wild highlander' simultaneously denote the man's linguistic and social otherness. The translation of his Gaelic speech – as confirmed by the scroll – into Latin subsumes his cultural difference by appropriating his role as a keeper of monarchical memory, and suggests that he is seen as part of the Scottish realm where, at other points in *Scotichronicon*, Bower demonstrates an ambivalence to this collective national imagining. At the same time, his inclusion in the account and the illustration acknowledges his necessary role in confirming the legitimacy of the Scottish king. He is at once a figure central and marginal.

One immediately noticeable part of the image is the highlander's hands, both drawn in pointing positions. While Higgitt has suggested that these hands indicate merely that the highlander is speaking to the king, I propose that they more specifically denote him pointing and that the gesture is for the benefit of *Scotichronicon*'s audience as well as for the imagined participants of the original scene in 1249.[34] Like the *nota* manicules that appear so often in the margins of medieval manuscripts, the pointing finger indicates an object of importance, something to be taken notice of: something worthy of being remembered. At first glance, it would seem that the object of interest and importance is Alexander himself, the king who has just been crowned and whose lineage the highlander recites (as Higgitt concludes). That the highlander is depicted in a double-handed gesture also represents a particularly significant gesticulation that points towards more than the body of the young king.[35] The pointing finger of the highlander's left hand appears to touch the pommel of the sword held by one of the two attending nobles. If a straight line is traced from the finger of the highlander's right hand, it points not only at Alexander but also at the crown he is wearing and the tip of the sceptre that he holds. The highlander gestures not only to the boy, then; he draws the audience's attention more specifically to the secular and divine symbols of sempiternal kingship: the sceptre and the crown indicate the divinity of the king, the sword the actual power wielded in the kingdom. The emphasis on

---

[33] Bannerman, 'The King's Poet', 122.

[34] Higgitt comments that 'He [the highlander] looks up to the king and the speaking gestures of his hands show that he is addressing him': 'Decoration and Illustration', *Chron. Bower* 9. 172.

[35] As Gale Owen-Crocker has argued in relation to the gestures of figures in the Bayeux Tapestry: 'a minority of figures have *both* hands free and so are able to make double gestures. They ... are usually significant characters depicted at important occasions'; 'The Interpretation of Gesture in the Bayeux Tapestry', in *Anglo-Norman Studies 26: Proceedings of the Battle Conference 2006*, ed. C.P. Lewis (Woodbridge: Boydell Press, 2007), pp. 145–78 (175). I am particularly grateful to Professor Owen-Crocker for her advice during our discussions about the images in the Corpus Christi MS of *Scotichronicon*.

THE POLITICS OF SCOTTISH GENEALOGICAL MEMORY 67

kingship as a ritualised state of being is more apparent in the image than in Bower's text. It highlights one of the main concerns of *Scotichronicon* as a whole: that of good kingship conferred through royal destiny.

The image of Alexander's inauguration is also reminiscent of late medieval depictions of the Annunciation to the Virgin. Drawing on conventions of Annunciation iconography in which Gabriel is depicted kneeling on the left and the Virgin seated on the right, the salutation of the highlander mirrors that of Gabriel to the Virgin with his initial blessing: *Ave gratia plena Dominus tecum.* Ann van Dijk comments that Gabriel's salutation 'projects straight from his mouth, describing an oblique path directly towards its object, the Virgin'.[36] If the *Scotichronicon*'s illustration deliberately recalls the Annunciation, the emphasis is on heralding a new age: just as the Annunciation signified the incarnation and the beginning of Christ's earthly mission, so Alexander's inauguration heralds a new beginning for Scotland in the reign of its new monarch.[37] This is indicated by the fact that the inauguration image also calls to mind the depictions of Christ holding a sceptre. The illustrator's presentation of Alexander thus conflates and recollects two devotional tropes that emphasise, for the viewer, divinely ordained Scottish sovereignty. The succession of Alexander maintains the unbroken continuity of Scottish kingship and reinforces his predestined position as Scotland's rightful ruler. The reader is directed not only to remember the temporal genealogy of the Scottish royal line but also to understand that lineage as prophetic as that of the line of the biblical David.

The authority and authenticity that genealogy lends to the monarch and to the kingdom in this passage come from its re-enactment of a continuity from antiquity, transmitting tradition through performance and repetition. In setting down the highlander's speech, Bower enables the memory of the ritual to be performed in perpetuity. Transforming the speech act into written record prevents tradition from being lost. Once spoken, the moment of the

---

[36] Ann van Dijk, 'The Angelic Salutation in Early Byzantine and Medieval Annunciation Imagery', *Art Bulletin*, 81.3 (1999), 420–36 (420).

[37] Elizabeth L'Estrange has argued that images of the Annunciation and the Nativity purposely employed the Virgin mother as a model of aristocratic motherhood. *Holy Motherhood: Gender, Dynasty and Visual Culture in the Later Middle Ages* (Manchester: Manchester University Press, 2008), esp. pp. 135–42. Emily Wingfield has written about a similar interplay in the *Trinity Altarpiece*. She notes that the details of the altarpiece, including the parallel depictions of the Stewart trinity (of James III, Margaret of Denmark and the future James IV) and the divine Trinity imagine 'a comparison between Margaret as mother of a future Scottish king, and Mary as mother of the heavenly King'. *Scotland's Royal Women and European Literary Culture, 1424–1587* (Turnhout: Brepols, 2023), p. 178. I am grateful to her for allowing me access to proofs of this book ahead of its publication.

highlander's speech cannot be repeated; it exists only in the memory of the speaker and the hearer. But, through recording the words Bower creates a memory aid, produced almost two hundred years after the event, which recollects the highlander's speech every time a reader comes to that section of the chronicle. In essence, *Scotichronicon* rewrites public memory to focus on this legitimising image of Scottish kingship. The tracing of Alexander's genealogy back to Gaythelos and Scota in the fifteenth-century text commemorates the direct continuity between the mythical Scottish past and the historical present; in doing so, it reminds the Scots that their independence was justified because of its antiquity. Bower also generates a link between the highlander and the ecclesiastical historiographer. As *ollamh ríg Alban* (master poet of the king of Scotland), the highlander becomes a keeper of national – or at least sovereign – memory; Bower asserts his own role as the next in line of a keeper of another kind of national memory by performing the cultural function of master historian, reproducing Fordun's work and adding to it. The genealogies at work in Bower's *Scotichronicon* become what Maurice Halbwachs calls a 'collective framework' of memory, a structure that not only preserves but also forges memory through acts of ritual and commemoration.[38] For Bower, this framework is one that authorises the Scottish royal line at the same time that it encompasses the Scottish community of the realm within its claim to identity and independence.

This seemingly glorious and peaceable transfer of power memorialised by Bower was quite unlike the conditions under which he was writing. James II was a similar age to Alexander III when he came to the throne in 1437, which suggests that in the image of the golden age of Scottish kingship conferred on Alexander – and on James I later in *Scotichronicon* – Bower reveals an anxiety about the minority of the 1440s. As Sally Mapstone notes, the contrast between James I's exemplary kingship in the recent past and 'the chaos of the kingless present' offered 'one of the most forceful statements of the attraction of the ideal of authoritative kingly rule in fifteenth-century Scottish literature'.[39] Bower's use of history as a mirror here exploits the Advice to Princes tradition. At the same time it points to the ways in which history-as-memory could be harnessed: history might not only be reinterpreted in light of current events, but it could also be used to shape them.

Despite the idealised depiction of rightful kingship in *Scotichronicon*, however, Bower describes an incident at Alexander III's inauguration in which there is disagreement among the magnates as to whether the young Alexander should be crowned or simply made a knight at this point. Walter Comyn, earl of Menteith, brings the two opposing sides together, maintaining that 'just as a boat is tossed about among the waves without an oarsman, so a kingdom

---

[38] Halbwachs, *Collective Memory*, p. 39.
[39] Sally Mapstone, 'Bower on Kingship', *Chron. Bower* 9. 323.

THE POLITICS OF SCOTTISH GENEALOGICAL MEMORY 69

without a king or ruler is left in the lurch' (*Chron. Bower* 5. 291–3). The maritime analogy is typical of late medieval thinking about kingship; the ship of state's medieval *locus classicus* is Thomas Aquinas' *De regimine principum* (*c*. 1265), in which he writes:

> We must first explain what is meant by the term, king. When a thing is directed towards an end, and it is possible to go one way or another, someone must indicate the best way to proceed toward the end. For example, a ship that moves in different directions with the shifting winds would never reach its destination if it were not guided to port by the skill of its helmsman.[40]

The analogy is discussed in further detail in Chapter 14 of Aquinas' treatise, and Quintin Shaw's fifteenth-century satire, *The Voyage of Court* ('Suppois the courte yow cheir and tretis'), compares the perils of the court to a tempest-tossed ship.[41] Following this tradition, the reader is encouraged to recall that the stability and safety of the national ship of Scotland could be secured, according to Comyn, only by the succession of the son of the late king and the continuity of the royal line. It might be a stretch to suggest Bower's readers might connect the ship of state to the journey of Scotland's founding mother, but through Comyn's imagined rhetoric and the highlander's recitation, *Scotichronicon* creates a connection between the two that allows for this possibility and sees its fruition in the golden age of Alexander III.

The recitation of the king's genealogy at Alexander's inauguration functions as an individual claim to power that stretched back to antiquity and as an assertion of the independent identity of the Scots. In the context of Bower's mid-fifteenth-century chronicle, these two genealogical objectives combine to reassert the importance of Scottish sovereignty for a contemporary audience. *Scotichronicon* claims the remembered past as a legitimising force in the present, and the narrative of national lineage – inheritance from Scota – uses genealogical epistemology to articulate a history of connection between people and territory. By envisioning geography as well as consanguinity, Scottish genealogy asserts that cultural power, imagined as an intimate relationship between the monarch and his subjects, might be recalled, particularly in that very specific designation of the monarch as king *of Scots* rather than king *of Scotland*. In his very title, the Scottish king's genealogy functioned as an

---

[40] Thomas Aquinas, *St Thomas Aquinas on Politics and Ethics*, trans. Paul E. Sigmund (New York: Norton, 1988), 14. Liber primus: Caput I.

[41] See the *Maitland Folio Manuscript*, ed. by William A. Craigie, 2 vols, STS 2nd ser., 7, 20 (1919–27), 1. 384–5. The Maitland Folio contains an excerpt from *De regimine principum* immediately before an excerpt from Wyntoun's *Original Chronicle* that depicts the duke de Orléans' defence of the Scots. See 1. 115 and 1. 125.

implied genealogical memory of the people (or nation), creating not only a vertical bond through time but also a horizontal bond of community united by sempiternal kingship. In bringing together past and present, *Scotichronicon*'s genealogies function in memorial terms by reordering time, asking readers not only to recall the history that they represent but to see their contemporary resonance and their future potential.

In Book 15 of *Scotichronicon*, Bower once again calls to his readers' minds the image of eternal kingship. Rather than looking to the past this time, Bower propels the reader into the future, expressing the hope that James I's 'kingly exercise of government may be to the kings who follow him like a picture delineated in a mirror, reflecting the warm characteristics of virtue (*Chron. Bower* 8. 147). Thinking of more recent history and the minority of James II, Bower fashions genealogy as the transference of virtues deemed to be part of Scottish kingship and identity. In her consideration of the use of amatory verse in the fifteenth-century political sphere, Joanna Martin notes that genealogy was used as a way of 'supplying models of virtuous kingship' in both chronicle and romance.[42] In this respect, genealogy functioned not only as a legitimising narrative of power structures but also as a way of 'correcting' the king through the remembrance and emulation of his kingly ancestors. Like the traditions of the inauguration, genealogy adopted a ritualistic function that linked the identity of the king and the nation in a single commemorative structure. Through the idea of the king as *rex qui nunquam moritur* (a king that never dies), Bower demonstrates that Alexander III, James I and, by implication, James II were images not just of their fathers but of the king of Scots as an unbroken line stretching into both past and future.

Of course, the greatest test of genealogical memory came as a result of the sudden death of Alexander III. In March 1286, hurrying to meet his new bride (he had married Yolande, daughter of the count of Dreux, in October 1285), Alexander, who had 'spurned' the advice of his companions not to ride 'beyond Inverkeithing that night', fell from his horse and broke his neck (*Chron. Bower* 5. 419–21). Bower laments how the 'losses of times which followed clearly show how sad and harmful his death was for the kingdom of Scotland' (*Chron. Bower* 5. 421), not least because, with no surviving son, there was no 'copy' to assume the throne.[43] What followed was a succession crisis that precipitated not only the outbreak of war with England but also the threat of civil war within Scotland. In 1284, a parliamentary act of entail (*tailzie*) regulating royal succession had stated that, should Alexander III die leaving no legitimate son, the magnates would receive his grand-daughter Margaret,

---

[42] Joanna Martin, *Kingship and Love in Scottish Poetry, 1424–1540* (Aldershot: Ashgate, 2008), p. 88.

[43] The children from Alexander's previous marriage to Margaret of England were all deceased by 1286. David died without issue in 1281, followed by his sister, Margaret, in 1283 and then his brother, Alexander, in 1284.

THE POLITICS OF SCOTTISH GENEALOGICAL MEMORY 71

the Maid of Norway, as 'our lady and rightful heir of our said lord the king of Scotland, of all the kingdom, and of the Isle of Man'.[44] Despite this, in April 1286, six guardians were elected to head the royal government in the belief that the queen, Yolande, was pregnant. By November, it was clear that Margaret of Norway was Alexander's only descendant; nevertheless, the oath of 1284 did not guarantee her acceptance as queen.[45] Negotiations between the guardians and King Eric II of Norway saw Margaret set sail for Scotland in September 1290. She died shortly after she reached the Norwegian territory of Orkney.

Much ink has been spilt on the succession crisis that followed, as I indicated in the Introduction. There is one point, however, that is particularly pertinent to the discussion of genealogy that I would like to focus on: the council of 1284 opened the floodgates for claims to the Scottish throne to be argued through female heredity. From several contenders, two major claimants to the throne emerged. John Balliol and Robert Bruce, Lord of Annandale (Robert I's grandfather), both claimed their right to succeed through their descent from David, earl of Huntingdon, the younger brother of Alexander III's grandfather, William I (1165–1214). To do this, each had to look to their maternal ancestors: David's daughters, Margaret and Isabel. While both Bruce and Balliol fundamentally sought to locate their legitimacy in their descent from William I's brother, this mediation through female ancestry is significant. While Margaret and Isabel might not be women at the beginning – as Scota was – their place within the Great Cause focuses attention on the repeated appearances that women made in Scottish history in relation to family memory.[46] It was also at this point that Edward I of England began to appeal to the memory of mythical origins to press his own claim to Scotland, in turn providing an impetus for a more sustained narrative of the Scota story to be developed.[47] The Great Cause meant that claims for and against Scottish sovereignty generated arguments about history and memory, about foundations and origins, that placed female figures at the centre.

[44] *APS*, 1. 424.

[45] For a more detailed discussion of the events of 1286–87, see Brown, *The Wars of Scotland*, pp. 159–61.

[46] For a discussion of the women of the Wars of Independence, see Nicola Royan, 'Some Conspicuous Women in the *Original Chronicle*, *Scotichronicon* and *Scotorum Historia*', *Innes Review*, 59.2 (2008), 131–44; Elizabeth Ewan, 'The Dangers of Manly Women: Late Medieval Perceptions of Female Heroism in Scotland's Second War of Independence', in *Woman and the Feminine in Medieval and Early Modern Scottish Writing*, ed. by Sarah Dunnigan, C. Marie Harker and Evelyn S. Newlyn (Basingstoke: Palgrave Macmillan, 2004), pp. 3–18.

[47] For more detail on Edward I's reliance on mythical origins, see Michael Prestwich, *Edward I* (Berkeley and Los Angeles: University of California Press, 1988), pp. 356–75; 469–516.

Remembering the Spectacle of the Countess of Buchan in Gray's *Scalacronica*

So far, this chapter has considered the importance of remembering Scottish royal genealogy as a way of inculcating memories of identity and independence that regarded mythical origins as fundamental to the articulation of Scottishness in the fourteenth and fifteenth centuries. In doing so, I have suggested that, in *Scotichronicon*, Bower relies on the memory of the Scota myth to make specific connections between origins, recent history and contemporary identity. The narrative echoes enabled by genealogy preserve ideas of Scottish sovereignty in the minds of Bower's readers. In the final section of this chapter, I want to return to Gray's *Scalacronica* and its account of Bruce's inauguration in 1306. This recollection complements *Scotichronicon*'s recollection of Alexander III's inauguration and demonstrates how narratives of women and origin were remembered and contested in contemporary history.

John of Fordun narrates that in March 1306, 'when a few days had rolled after' the death of Sir John the Red Comyn, Robert Bruce, earl of Carrick, took 'as many men as he could get' and 'hastened to Scone'. On 'being set on the royal throne', Bruce was crowned 'in the manner wherein the kings of Scotland were wont to be invested' (*Chron. Fordun* 2. 333). Bower's *Scotichronicon* recollects this episode almost verbatim and Barbour's *Bruce* describes Robert riding 'to be set / In kingis stole and to be king' (*Bruce* 2. 150–1). The narratives of Bruce's inauguration unsurprisingly depict the episode as a hurried affair, carried out with little thought to the sense of occasion, such as that reflected in the account of Alexander III's inauguration, for example. However, in Gray's *Scalacronica*, Bruce's inauguration is depicted slightly differently and in ways which point to the variability of memory and the instability of national remembrance. Gray's narrative of Bruce's inauguration, while still presented as hastily arranged, recounts that Robert 'had himself crowned as King of Scotland at Scone ... by the Countess of Buchan, in the absence of the earl, her son, who was then staying in England at his manor of Whitwick, near Leicester, and to whom the office of coronation of the kings of Scotland belonged in heredity' (*Scal.* 53).[48] The countess of Buchan's role does not appear in the major Scottish chronicles or in Barbour's epic poem. Aside from the episode in *Scalacronica*, the countess is mentioned in connection with Bruce's inauguration in two English texts: the fourteenth-century *Flores Historiarum* – in which she is represented as an adulteress (*adultera*) and the *Passio Scotorum Perjuratorum*, which calls her an 'impious conspirer' (*impia*

---

[48] Gray is incorrect in his account. The office to which he refers belonged to the earl of Fife, who was Isabel's nephew, not her son, although he was in England at the time of Bruce's inauguration. See Michael Brown, *Wars of Scotland*, p. 200.

THE POLITICS OF SCOTTISH GENEALOGICAL MEMORY 73

conjuratrix).[49] Yet, the episode suggests a way of reading Bruce's inauguration as a contemporary foundation myth with imagery that recollects the Scota story and the matrilineal foundations of the Scottish nation.

Gray's account tells how the countess of Buchan takes the place of the absent earl whose right it was to crown the kings of Scotland, but this does not give us the whole picture of the event, nor of the perceived significance of the countess's presence. The office belonged the earl of Fife, the countess's nephew who, at the time, was a ward of Edward I, but the Buchan connection is significant. The countess's husband was John Comyn, earl of Buchan, whose cousin, Sir John the Red Comyn, had been murdered by Bruce in 1306, an act for which Bruce was excommunicated. At this time, then, not only was there growing hostility towards the kingdom itself, but Scotland itself was on the brink of civil war between the Comyn and Bruce factions.[50] Bower writes that 'from the first occurrence of dissension between the noble men Bruce and Balliol over the right to succeed to the kingdom of Scotland' the 'kingdom was split in two', with 'all the Comyns' supporting Balliol (*Chron. Bower* 6. 75). All, apparently, except for the countess of Buchan. As a Comyn, Isabel's husband allied himself with his family – and, ultimately, the English – but the countess fled to Bruce's side, even stealing her husband's best horses and clandestinely travelling to Bruce's inauguration to act as a representative of her (originary) family – the Macduffs of Fife – and to provide the legitimating force for the occasion. Once again, ideas of lineage and memory surface here and what is quite clear is the potential resonance with the past that might be exploited. The countess of Buchan's allegiance is clearly to the hereditary office of the crowning the Scottish sovereign and her fidelity is determined by consanguinity rather than marriage. It is the countess's memory of her blood-kin's allegiances and responsibilities that dominates her actions.

Returning to *Scotichronicon* for a moment, it is possible to see that here Robert the Bruce is being drawn as a 'second Maccabeus', who adopted 'forceful measures in order to free his fellow-countrymen' and 'endured innumerable and unbearable burdens and toils of the heat of the day, cold and hunger by land and sea' (*Chron. Bower* 6. 301). The parallel between the Scots and the Maccabees is one that surfaces regularly in *Scotichronicon* and serves to portray the Scots as a divinely chosen people that must struggle to ensure its survival and independence. It also forms an important part of the

---

[49] See *Flores Historiarum*, ed. by Henry Richards Luard, 3 vols (London: HMSO, 1890), 3. 130; the *Passio Scotorum Perjuratorum*, appears in Marquis of Bute, 'Notice of a Manuscript of the Latter Part of the Fourteenth Century, Entitled *Passio Scotorum Perjuratorum*', *Proceedings of the Society of Antiquaries of Scotland*, 19 (1885), 166–92 (167–84).

[50] See Alan Young, *Robert the Bruce's Rivals: The Comyns, 1212–1314* (East Linton: Tuckwell, 1997), esp. pp. 184–214.

Declaration of Arbroath, in which the community of the realm recounts its liberation 'by our most energetic prince ... who, with the aim of delivering his people and inheritance from ... their enemies, like another Maccabee ... cheerfully suffered toil and fatigue'(*Chron. Bower* 7. 7). The trials and tribulations suffered by Bruce – and by implication the Scots as a whole – certainly mirror those of the Maccabees, but they also call to mind the struggles of the ancient ancestors of the Scots in Egypt and Spain. This intertextual narrative seems to be an important feature of Scottish writing, particularly writing about the Wars of Independence, and it suggests that the process of 'struggle' takes on a particularly significant role for the Scots and their relations with the English. As a careful and practical ruler, Bruce, like Maccabeus and Gaythelos, has the protection of his people at the forefront of his mind. The *Scotichronicon* and the Declaration of Arbroath both prompt their readers to call to mind, to *remember*, not only the story of the Maccabees but also that of the Scots' founding mother and father. As such, Robert is not only another Maccabeus but also another Gaythelos; he is linked directly to Scotland's founding father and this promotes a sense of continuity rooted in both mythological and biblical origins.

In *Scalacronica*, Gray memorialises the countess of Buchan as a female figure instrumental in legitimising Bruce as the new Scottish monarch. In this, she recalls the image of Scota deployed by so many Scottish texts and documents: Isabel assumes the role of a glorious founding mother whose presence at Bruce's inauguration reasserts her own family's hereditary office as it simultaneously invests the scene with a triumphant symbolism that harnesses the legendary sovereignty of the Scots for a markedly contemporary purpose. Read in this way, the countess becomes central to a renewed sense of Scottish independence that finds its expression in the heroic figure of Robert the Bruce. Furthermore, in her position as Comyn's wife, the countess symbolically suggests the greater need for the Scots to put aside their differences, to unite against a common enemy: the English. This need for unity is something that resurfaces in the mid-sixteenth century during calls for an Anglo-Scottish union, which I will discuss in Chapter 6. In *Scalacronica*, then, Bruce's inauguration might be read as a fourteenth-century point of origin, with Scotland emblematically reborn through Bruce and the countess, which takes as its analogy the memory of Scota and her sons. Not only does Robert the Bruce figuratively become the father of the nation, alongside the mother in the person of the countess, but he is also reimagined, as arguably all Scottish monarchs were, as a surrogate son of the familial office of the Macduffs, who claimed the privilege of establishing the new king on the throne.

Gray's narrative draws the reader's attention not only to ideas of loyalty but also to the ways in which memory might function quite practically in certain moments. Evident in Gray's depiction of Isabel is the privileging of certain memories over others: nation over personal polity. In substituting herself for her English-affiliated son (as the text of *Scalacronica* reads), the countess

THE POLITICS OF SCOTTISH GENEALOGICAL MEMORY

of Buchan might have forgotten, or chosen not to remember, her role as a dutiful wife to her husband and his political ambitions, but, in doing so, she remembered her blood family's role in ways that her male relatives seemed unable or unwilling to do. Whereas Scota provided an origin and focus for dynastic and national legitimacy, the countess of Buchan becomes its custodian, a figure of *memoria*. Elisabeth van Houts' work on aristocratic women's roles in the construction of memory is particularly pertinent for thinking about the countess of Buchan. Van Houts argues that, in being expected to become repositories of family memories, aristocratic women were seen as instrumental in the preservation of genealogical remembrance. Moreover, van Houts suggests, a wife would have been expected to shape herself according to the demands of her new family.[51] In Gray's recollection, the countess of Buchan maintains her original familial allegiances. Once again, private and public, family and nation intersect – albeit uneasily – and it becomes possible to discern a suggestion that members of a nation might, in some way, constitute a family unit with its assumed duties and obligations. Reading the episode in this way implies that those members of Scotland who aligned themselves with the English – or with other Scots who did not support Bruce – enacted a forgetting of rightful allegiance. Gray's countess of Buchan seems to feel more keenly her allegiances to Scotland than does her husband.[52] This intersection of family, nation and commemorative practice indicates that for the memory of Bruce's inauguration recorded in *Scalacronica* – as with that of Alexander III's in *Scotichronicon* – the *foci* are legitimacy, power and, fundamentally, a memory of origins.

Both inauguration accounts use memories of origins to signal the importance of identity and belonging and the central role of women in these embodiments of national identity.[53] Gray suggests that the countess of Buchan is a particularly significant figure for what she comes to represent in this episode, and it was a significance not lost on the English who sought to use her image to

---

[51] Elisabeth van Houts, *Memory and Gender in Medieval Europe, 900–1200* (Toronto: University of Toronto Press, 1999), esp. pp. 65–92.

[52] As a comparable figure, see my discussion of the countess of March in Gray's *Scalacronica*, in 'Terrifying Proximity', p. 55.

[53] Emily Wingfield has written about shifts in female identity as a result of marriage. For example, she notes that an inscription on folio 122v of Paris, BnF, MS fr. 958 (a copy of the *Somme le Roi*) 'neatly highlights [Isabella Stewart's] natal identity and the multiple power bases attached to her marital identity' as the wife of François I, duke of Brittany. Focusing on Margaret Tudor, Wingfield suggests that her books of hours 'articulated and commemorated [Margaret's] natal identity as well as (or indeed perhaps more so than) her marital identity, and they acted as memorial volumes through which she was able to maintain ties of family, friendship, and loyalty back to England'; *Scotland's Royal Women*, pp. 105, 234.

create certain memories of their own. Gray records that in the same year as Bruce's inauguration, the countess was captured by the English after the Battle of Methven and 'brought to Berwick' (*Scal.* 53). At Edward I's command 'she was put in a wooden hut, in one of the towers of Berwick castle, with criss-crossed walls, so that all could watch her for spectacle' (*meruail*; *Scal.* 53). However, Edward I not only displayed the countess in a cage – as he had done with female members of Bruce's family – he also prohibited any Scots man or woman from talking to her.[54]

Gray's description of the countess as a *meruail* (marvel), coupled with the prohibition of her fellow Scots to speak to her, invests Isabel with a symbolic power both for the Scots and the English, although that power might be rendered differently depending on the observer's allegiance. In her discussion of wonder, Caroline Walker Bynum argues that the marvellous is singular, both in 'its significance and its particularity'.[55] This might go some way to explain why Gray includes the countess in *Scalacronica* but not, for example, Bruce's sister, Mary, who suffered the same fate. For Gray to give details of other Scots who were captured and imprisoned by Edward in 1306 would suppress the amazement that the singular figure of Isabel invokes, and this carries a distinctly memorial charge (it is something to which I will return in my discussion of Hary's *Wallace* in Chapter 4). The complex meanings of 'wonder' mean that the countess arrests attention but she might do so in one of two ways, depending on who is looking at her. As Bynum notes, the reaction to wonder 'ranges from terror and disgust' to 'solemn astonishment and playful delight'; attention and memory might therefore be prompted by desire *or* terror.[56] As a *meruail*, the countess of Buchan might be remembered as Bynum's wondrous figure or Cohen's monstrous one – or, indeed, both – and *Scalacronica* resists making its interpretation clear.[57] Like the mythic Scota, the countess represents a site around which memory and identity can converge. Gray plays with these ambiguities of representation and its memorial implications. In her assumption of an official function, Isabel represents Scotland and its resistance to English military action; her role in Bruce's inauguration invests him with the same symbolic power. If, however, we read the countess according to Bynum's concept of 'wonder' in which, she argues, the wondrous

---

[54] 'Qe ele ne parle ad nulli ne qe hõme ne fẽme qi soit de la nacion d Escoce': *Documents and Records Illustrating the History of Scotland and the Transactions between the Crowns of Scotland and England, preserved in the Treasury of Her Majesty's Exchequer*, ed. by Francis Palgrave (Record Commission, 1837), p. 358.

[55] Caroline Walker Bynum, *Metamorphosis and Identity* (New York: Zone Books, 2001), p. 73.

[56] Bynum, *Metamorphosis and Identity*, p. 130.

[57] See Jeffrey Jerome Cohen, *Monster Theory: Reading Culture* (Minneapolis: University of Minnesota Press, 1996), esp. p. 7.

THE POLITICS OF SCOTTISH GENEALOGICAL MEMORY 77

is 'a reaction of a particular "us" to an "other"', the textual memory of Isabel as a *meruail* suggests her unusual particularity, and this seems to work against any positive reading.[58] In *Scalacronica*, however, it is only to the English that Isabel appears marvellous, because they cannot comprehend her and what she represents. The implication is that the Scots fully understand her significance and this is why Edward imposes the prohibition on speech. The moment is one in which wonder is staged, deliberately, to evoke reactions of terror, and the imagining of her as a 'spectacle' aims to create a distinctive memory of her in the minds of the English. Gray suggests that in determining to present the countess as marvellous, Edward also seeks to highlight her monstrosity. In doing so, he aims to show and to warn English spectators of the dangers presented by the Scots more broadly.[59] This monstrosity is compounded by the countess appropriating masculine behaviour and by the assumption that the Scots – in recognising Isabel's power – condone this behaviour.

While the countess of Buchan's actions are recalled in *Scalacronica*, they are not preserved in any of the Scottish histories. It perhaps seems strange that an episode with such potential echoes of the Scota myth was not exploited as a political tool by the Scots themselves, especially when they had negotiated narratives of other examples of female heroism during the Wars of Independence.[60] If this account had appeared in Fordun, Bower or even in Barbour's *Bruce*, the ideological imagery and its political resonance would perhaps seem more straightforward. Nicola Royan argues that the Scots engage in acts of strategic forgetting in choosing to write Isabel out of historical memory, deliberately choosing silence because her presence 'would emphasise the abnormality of the event', as well as the 'divided nature of the Scottish nobility'.[61] Royan suggests that the uncertainties of Bruce's accession to the Scottish throne meant that Stewart historiography 'suppress[ed] any episodes that might permit questions regarding the legitimacy of the symbolic act' of Bruce's inauguration.[62] The omission of the Scottish chronicles is just as significant as Gray's remembering, because it demonstrates the ways in which writers of national history impose forgetfulness as part of memorial creativity.

Throughout this chapter, I have argued that origin myths and genealogy function as a form of memory in order to create a sense of community that, at its core, is identified with territorial and political sovereignty. Both *Scotichronicon* and *Scalacronica* raise questions about the uses of the remembered past to

---

[58] Bynum, *Metamorphosis and Identity*, p. 55.

[59] Monsters are named from the verb, *monstrare* (to show), deriving from *monere* (to warn); *OED*, monster, *n.*

[60] See Ewan, 'The Dangers of Manly Women'.

[61] Royan, 'Some Conspicuous Women', 133.

[62] Royan, 'Some Conspicuous Women', 133.

suggest that meaning is created through imaginative rewriting and reinterpretation of historical events. Myths of origin are effective ideological forms but, in order to be so, they cannot remain static. Stories are forced to repeat themselves within contemporary narratives such that they assume the sense of an unbroken line of succession from origin to future. In using mythic figures from a nation's ancient past as parallels or analogues for contemporary (or near-contemporary) figures, both Bower and Gray direct their readers to see the past not as distant and separate, but as fluid and ever present in the destiny of the nation and its identity. As such, memorial knowledge can be useful to a nation's sense of itself only by being continually present. It is the malleability of the past – the ways in which imagined events become the means by which the past is remembered – to which I turn in the next chapter and a consideration of Bower's Coupar Angus version of *Scotichronicon*.

3

Reassembling Forgotten History: Bower's *Scotichronicon* at Coupar Angus

In Chapter 2 I examined how genealogy as a memorial structure was used politically in works such as Walter Bower's *Scotichronicon* to encourage ways of thinking about national independence and identity. I suggested that Bower and other writers conceived of composition as an act of memory; rewriting the past became a crucial element of their process of creating a sense of collective identity in fourteenth- and fifteenth-century northern England and Scotland. While this chapter continues to examine the intersection of memory and historiography, I move away from discussions of genealogy to analyse how Bower remembered English acts of aggression in Scotland. I suggest that these memories were used within a proto-nationalist framework to disseminate a shared history that was understood to be representative of Scotland's struggle for identity and independence. The focus of this discussion is the Coupar Angus *Scotichronicon*, a shorter version of Bower's longer text. I argue that, within the Coupar Angus version of his history, Bower privileges particular moments of Anglo-Scottish conflict by entreating his readers to remember certain events of the Wars of Independence as formative moments of Scottish distinctiveness.

In the Middle Ages, memory, in the form of recollection, was a 'task of composition' rather than simply a means of retention: a creative tool of the mind, providing a basis for active contemplation.[1] This creative aspect of memory – *remembrance* – points to the fact that memories are not only actively made, but that they are open to being repeatedly remade in myriad contexts.[2] Through a close examination of the Coupar Angus Prologue, this process of historical reconstruction becomes distinctly apparent and increasingly political. I suggest that the memories invoked in Bower's prologue are deliberately crafted to evoke emotional responses from his readers, with the specific aim of fostering a sense of Scottish solidarity. In this, Bower strategically employs the *ars memoria*, leveraging its emphasis on emotion as a catalyst for memory, to actively guide and shape his audience's collective remembrance. Through

---

[1] Carruthers and Ziolkowski, *Medieval Craft*, p. 1.
[2] See discussions in previous chapters.

80   REWRITING THE PAST IN SCOTTISH LITERATURE, 1350–1550

Bower's work, then, it is possible to see the intersection of personal cognitive strategies and shared cultural remembrance.

While Mary Carruthers's work focuses primarily on the trained individual memory, she nevertheless argues that texts are the primary medium of the public memory, 'the archival *scrinia* [repository] available to all' from which an individual stores, *ad res* or *ad verba*, 'the chests of his or her own memory'.[3] Carruthers suggests here that the individual memory is often created from a set of pre-existing public memories from which an individual can pick and choose their own set of reminiscences.[4] In my consideration of Bower, however, I propose that a different, and complementary, intersection between individual and collective (public) memories needs to be considered; one which not only understands memory as a socially mediated process but also repositions individual memory as a foundational tool in the service of broader communal narratives. Here, the compilation of individual memories contributes to the formation of a collective memory that is meaningful and representative *because* of its composite nature. In suggesting this approach, I draw on medieval theories of authorship, in which writers drew upon many sources to authenticate their own work. The analogy is not identical, but both the nature of compilation and the appeal to older memories as a legitimating force for the new collective memory being created function in similar ways.[5] In departing from Carruthers's focus on the individual memory, it is possible to see that collective *memoria* not only works to recall past events or people but also intersects with practices of commemoration, memorialisation and remembrance. To train this collective memory, Bower's Coupar Angus prologue demonstrates how writers sought to instruct their audiences to remember certain historical events in precise ways. In this way, Bower – following the medieval mnemonists – appropriates techniques for individual memory training and scales them up to support the training of collective memory. I draw, in part, on Maurice Halbwachs' argument that 'one may say that the individual remembers by placing himself in the perspective of the group, but one may also affirm that the memory of the group relies and

3   Carruthers, *Book of Memory*, p. 234.

4   On the selection of memories for particular purposes see Coleman, *Ancient and Medieval Memories*, p. 52.

5   See A.J. Minnis, *Medieval Theory of Authorship: Scholastic Literary Attitudes in the Later Middle Ages* (London: Scolar Press, 1984), pp. 94–103; Rita Copeland, *Rhetoric, Hermeneutics, and Translation in the Middle Ages* (Cambridge: Cambridge University Press, 1991); Emily Steiner, 'Authority', in *Middle English*, ed. by Paul Strohm (Oxford: Oxford University Press, 2007), pp. 142–59. On political symbolism and the use of authority, see Larry Scanlon, *Narrative, Authority, and Power: The Medieval Exemplum and the Chaucerian Tradition* (Cambridge: Cambridge University Press, 1994).

REASSEMBLING FORGOTTEN HISTORY

manifests itself in individual memories'.[6] The techniques Bower employs in his writing draw heavily on the formal mnemonic preparation for *memoria* that Carruthers discusses; in doing so, Bower demonstrates an awareness of the uses to which the past can be put as well as the ethical principle concerned with creating memories that are useful. My focus, then, is on how these memorial practices might be used in the writing of history, with implications for how the identities of the individual and her place within the community are cultivated.

The Fifteenth-Century Recensions of *Scotichronicon*

Bower completed his sixteen-book *Scotichronicon* around 1445, but this is not the end of the story for this version of Scottish history. While *Scotichronicon* was still being written, Bower was also directing the composition of a shorter form of the chronicle. Sometimes referred to as 'Bower in forty books', the Coupar Angus recension omitted entire chapters of the 'Great Scotichronicon' and shortened others, at the same time as it made additions or rearranged material.[7] Bower himself notes in the prologue to the Coupar Angus recension that he has 'omitted from this shortened *Scotichronicon* various events and notable arguments, digressions and exempla clearly serving different purposes' (*Chron. Bower* 9. 15). Significantly, much of the excised material relates to non-Scottish history, giving the Coupar Angus recension a tighter national focus. The earliest surviving copy of this recension is National Library of Scotland. Adv. MS 35.1.7 (the Coupar Angus MS), which dates from *c.* 1450–88 and, as Watt notes, 'follows a lost exemplar written under Bower's own direction'.[8] Three other extant versions follow the Coupar Angus recension and were copied and reworked between 1480 and 1515. These manuscripts were produced *c.* 1480 in Perth by Patrick Russell (MS P; NLS, Adv. MS 35.6.7), another by notary public Richard Striveling for the bishop of Dunkeld between

---

6 Halbwachs, *Collective Memory*, p. 40.

7 A table in Watt's edition of *Scotichronicon* sets out parallel passages between the Corpus MS (Bower's working copy of *Scotichronicon*) and the Coupar Angus MS; *Chron. Bower* 9. 194–5. Further details of the differences can be found in *Chron. Bower* 9. 211–13.

8 Watt, *Chron. Bower* 9. 212. On the dating of MS CA, see also Roderick J. Lyall, 'Books and Book Owners in Fifteenth-Century Scotland', in *Book Production and Publishing in Britain, 1375–1475*, ed. by Jeremy Griffiths and Derek Pearsall (Cambridge: Cambridge University Press, 1989), pp. 239–56. The Cistercian monastery at Coupar Angus, Perthshire, founded in the 1160s by Máel Coluim IV, was a daughter house of Melrose. Melrose had significant Stewart connections: in the *Bruce*, John Barbour suggests that Bruce's heart was buried there (20. 601–11), and Froissart presents a similar story. See *The Chronicle of Froissart translated out of the French by Sir John Bourchier, Lord Berners, annis 1523–25*, ed. by W.P. Ker (London: D. Nutt, 1901–3), 1. 69–70.

82   REWRITING THE PAST IN SCOTTISH LITERATURE, 1350–1550

1497 and 1515 (MS FE; BL, MS Harleian 4764), and a further one copied in 1509 (MS FF; Aberdeen University Library, SCA MM2/1).[9]

In the late 1450s, after Bower's death, another recension, known as the *Liber Pluscardensis*, was compiled for the abbot of Dunfermline.[10] As with the Coupar Angus recension, this version of *Scotichronicon* abridges the 'Great Scotichronicon' yet adds other material to it.[11] Most significant is the omission of the entirety of Book 7 of the *Scotichronicon*, which, Mapstone argues, 'shows an eschewal of its almost exclusively European content in favour of a Scotland-centred focus'.[12] A further recension, the *Extracta e Variis Cronicis Scocie* (NLS Adv. MS 35.6.13), compiled after 1522, was based on manuscripts in the tradition of the Coupar Angus version and incorporates additional material from elsewhere, including stories from Hary's *Wallace*.[13]

---

[9] A notary public was a legal role in late medieval Scotland. Notaries were responsible for producing legal documents, providing evidence for the courts and for ensuring the authenticity of deeds. Notaries also often compiled literary collections. On the role of notaries, see Hector MacQueen, *Common Law and Feudal Society in Medieval Scotland* (Edinburgh: Edinburgh University Press, 1993), esp. pp. 74–6. On notaries and literary compilations, see Theo van Heijnsbergen, 'The Interaction between Literature and History in Queen Mary's Edinburgh: The Bannatyne Manuscript and Its Prosopographical Context', in *The Renaissance in Scotland: Studies in Literature, Religion, History and Culture Offered to John Durkan*, ed. by Alasdair A. MacDonald, Michael Lynch and Ian B. Cowan (Leiden: Brill, 1994), pp. 183–225 (188); Catherine van Buren, 'John Asloan and His Manuscript: An Edinburgh Notary and Scribe in the Days of James III, IV and V (*c.* 1470–*c.* 1530), in *Stewart Style, 1513–1542: Essays on the Court of James V*, ed. by Janet Hadley Williams (East Linton: Tuckwell, 1996), pp. 15–51 (esp. 15–18).

[10] Five manuscripts of the *Liber Pluscardensis* are extant: Brussels, Bibliothèque Royale de Belgique MS 7396; Edinburgh, NLS Adv. MS 35.5.2; Glasgow, Mitchell Library MS 308876; Glasgow University Library, MS Gen. 333; and Oxford, Bodleian Library MS Fairfax 8.

[11] For a fuller discussion of *Liber Pluscardensis* and its possible authorship, see Sally Mapstone, 'The *Scotichronicon*'s First Readers', in *Church, Chronicle and Learning in Medieval and Early Renaissance Scotland: Essays Presented to Donald Watt on the Occasion of the Completion of the Publication of Bower's Scotichronicon*, ed. by Barbara E. Crawford (Edinburgh: Mercat, 1999), pp. 31–55 (esp. pp. 34–5).

[12] Mapstone, '*Scotichronicon*'s First Readers', p. 39.

[13] Two further MSS of the *Extracta* are extant: NLS Adv. MS 35.4.5 and Oxford, Bodleian Library, MS Lyell 39. See *Extracta e variis cronicis Scocie*, ed. by W.B.D.D. Turnbull, Abbotsford Club (Edinburgh, 1842). For the *Extracta*'s relation to the *Wallace*, see also *Chron. Bower* 6. 241. There is evidence to suggest that Hary had access to, and made use of, the Coupar Angus MS while he was composing the *Wallace*. The dream-vision in Book 7 of Hary's poem, in which Wallace is given a sword by St Andrew, echoes a vision that is found in the Coupar Angus MS but not MS C of *Scotichronicon*. See *Chron. Bower* 6. 287.

A final notable version is a French translation of *Liber Pluscardensis* made *c.* 1519 by Bremond Domat for John Stewart, duke of Albany (Paris, Bibliothèque St-Geneviève, MS 936). On the death of James IV at Flodden in 1513, Albany became heir presumptive, while the young James V's mother, Margaret Tudor, was appointed regent. Margaret forfeited her position when she married Archibald Douglas, sixth earl of Angus, in 1514, and Albany was proclaimed regent. Bryony Coombs has suggested that Albany commissioned a translation of *Liber Pluscardensis* as 'an aid to the education of the newly appointed Regent of Scotland'.[14] Setting out the deeds of Albany's ancestors, the French translation acted as a kind of briefing document and it enabled Albany to 'promot[e] his own powerful position as Regent of Scotland to the influential European nobles with which he was frequently in contact'.[15] Albany's copy of *Liber Pluscardensis*, therefore, signals not only his pride in his new position but also a desire to 'convey to others the integrity and importance of Scotland as a key player on the early 16th century European stage'.[16] The Paris manuscript also contains an illuminated genealogy of the kings of Scotland, beginning with Gaythelos (named Galahel in the manuscript) and Scota; Coombs describes this as an *aide-mémoire* for Albany's position in which the visual images provide 'a distinctive and memorable image ... to serve as an effective mnemonic' with which Albany might recall the most important elements of Scottish history.[17] Domat's French translation for Albany testifies to the perceived authority of the Fordun–Bower historiographical tradition into the early sixteenth century. Each of these versions points to a vibrant practice of engaging with, and reshaping of, Bower's work throughout the fifteenth and sixteenth centuries, either under Bower's own guidance or distinct from it. This engagement, however, is not so unusual; Sally Mapstone has argued that 'a recurrent response' of a 'substantial number' of *Scotichronicon*'s readers was 'to start rewriting it' and, as Dauvit Broun has subsequently shown, this participatory historiography can be seen from at least the work of Fordun.[18] This demonstrates that responses to regnal history not only resulted in close reproduction of textual exemplars but also reveal a 'textual flexibility' that could produce significantly varied versions of material in the Scottish

[14] Bryony Coombs, 'The Artistic Patronage of John Stuart, Duke of Albany 1518–19: The "Discovery" of the Artist and Author, Bremond Domat', *Proceedings of the Society of Antiquaries of Scotland*, 144 (2014), 277–309 (283).

[15] Coombs, 'Artistic Patronage of John Stuart', 283.

[16] Coombs, 'Artistic Patronage of John Stuart', 283.

[17] Coombs, 'Artistic Patronage of John Stuart', 287–8.

[18] Mapstone, '*Scotichronicon*'s First Readers', p. 32; Dauvit Broun, 'Rethinking Medieval Scottish Regnal Historiography in the Light of New Approaches to Texts as Manuscripts', *Cambrian Medieval Celtic Studies*, 83 (2022), 19–47.

historiographical tradition.[19] This dynamic practice was something to which Bower himself was clearly attuned in his reworking of Fordun's material into *Scotichronicon*. In the first five books, he diligently identifies where he is copying Fordun and where he is making additions to this work, while at the end of Book 6, Chapter 23, Bower signals a significant change. He writes:

> So far this has clearly [been the work of] the scribe; the rest [is the responsibility] of the writer.
>
> Assume that John de Fordun is the author so far;
> from here it is the work of the author and of the writer.
> The writer in his turn has added some material
> to the earlier part, which has nevertheless been appropriately identified
> by a marginal note. May Christ protect them both! Amen.
> (*Chron. Bower* 3. 343)

The Coupar Angus recension stands out among revisions of *Scotichronicon* because it is certain that Bower was involved in its compilation. It is possible to see, therefore, the textual – and historical – reshaping taking place under Bower's direction. This is quite different from *Liber Pluscardensis*, which, although a major recension of *Scotichronicon*, establishes a different approach to reworking historiographical material beyond Bower's controlling hand. This certainty of Bower's approval of at least one redaction of the *Scotichronicon* is also importantly different from a text such as Wyntoun's *Original Chronicle*, where, although nine manuscript witnesses are extant, there is no evidence of the role Wyntoun himself played in the construction of any of the three recensions. Bower's own sense of authority and the value of his history are, then, markedly apparent in the work he produces and in the authority that his version of Scottish history subsequently conveys.

There is no mention in the charters of Coupar Angus abbey of the acquisition of Bower's text and there are no extant charters for Inchcolm abbey for this period. However, the Coupar Angus MS bears the inscription *Liber Monasterii S. Marie de Cupro* on a title page dated 1694, indicating that at some point the abbey of Coupar Angus did acquire this copy of the chronicle. In the early eighteenth century, Richard Hay claimed that the manuscript was presented

---

[19] Broun, 'Rethinking Medieval Scottish Regnal Historiography', 21. Broun draws significantly on the work of John Dagenais, Matthew Fisher and Daniel Wakelin here. See John Dagenais, *The Ethics of Reading in Manuscript Culture: Glossing the Libro de Buen Amor* (Princeton, NJ: Princeton University Press, 1994); Matthew Fisher, *Scribal Authorship and the Writing of History in Medieval England* (Columbus: Ohio State University Press, 2012); Daniel Wakelin, *Scribal Correction and Literary Craft: English Manuscripts 1375–1510* (Cambridge: Cambridge University Press, 2014).

REASSEMBLING FORGOTTEN HISTORY

to the abbey at Coupar Angus in 1445 by William, third earl of Orkney and first earl of Caithness (*Willielmo Orcadum et Cataniae Comite*), although, as Watt notes, this date is possibly a mistake, since William Sinclair did not become earl of Caithness until 1455.[20] The Coupar Angus manuscript does have connections to the Sinclairs of Roslin: the opening page of the manuscript (part of which can be seen on the cover of this book) bears the signature 'W Santclair of Roislin knecht'.[21] This signature was identified by H.J. Lawlor as that of Sir William Sinclair of Roslin (d. *c.* 1580–85), the great-grandson of the third earl of Orkney.[22] According to Hay, the book was recovered from Coupar Angus by Sir William in 1560. In 1565, William Sinclair also inherited Patrick Russell's copy of the Coupar Angus recension of *Scotichronicon* (MS P) as well as a copy of the *Extracta* (NLS Adv. MS 35.6.13), on the death of his uncle, Henry Sinclair, bishop of Ross. Sir William annotated these texts with information drawn from other copies of the chronicle as well as from later printed histories, such as those by John Mair, Hector Boece and John Bellenden.[23] As W.F. Skene noted, it is likely that at least five of the extant Fordun manuscripts belonged to the library at Roslin Castle, and a further six (including the Donibristle MS) were, at some point, carefully examined by the Sinclairs.[24] Sir William, then, appears to have been something of a *Scotichronicon* collector and the Sinclairs more broadly had a significant interest in Scottish historiography and literary culture.[25] Alongside the various

---

[20] *Chron. Bower* 9. 193. See also 'Father Hay's Introduction to "The Book of Coupar"', *Inchcolm Chrs.*, pp. 245–8 (246).

[21] Edinburgh, NLS, Adv. MS 35.1.7, p. 1 (note that this manuscript is listed by numbered pages, not folios).

[22] H.J. Lawlor, 'Notes on the Library of the Sinclairs of Rosslyn', *Proceedings of the Society of Antiquaries of Scotland*, 32 (1898), 90–120 (104).

[23] See Ryoko Harikae, 'The Maitland and Sinclair Families: *The Chronicles of Scotland* and its Early Modern Readers', *Textual Cultures*, 7.1 (2012), 97–106 (100). On the Sinclairs as book owners, see also T.A.F. Cherry, 'The Library of Henry Sinclair, Bishop of Ross, 1560–1565', *Bibliotheck*, 4 (1963), 13–24. A list of printed books (but not manuscripts) owned by Henry Sinclair can be found in John Durkan and Anthony Ross, *Early Scottish Libraries* (Glasgow: J.S. Burns & Sons, 1961), pp. 49–60.

[24] Skene notes that on the last page of the Donibristle MS, a later hand has written the following: 'This cronicle is sene oure be Williame Sanclair of Roislin knight and compilyit, augmentit, drawn out of yir cronicles'; *Johannis de Fordun, Chronica Gentis Scotorum*, Historians of Scotland, vol. 1 (Edinburgh: Edmonston and Douglas, 1871), xvi, n.l. Mapstone discusses William Sinclair's annotations in *Scotichronicon* MSS: '*Scotichronicon*'s First Readers', pp. 36–7.

[25] Henry Sinclair, second earl of Caithness (and cousin to Henry, bishop of Ross), was the patron of Gavin Douglas. Douglas describes Sinclair as 'Fader of bukis, protectour to sciens and lair' in the prologue to the first book of the *Eneados*; *The Eneados: Gavin Douglas's Translation of Virgil's Aeneid*, ed. by Priscilla Bawcutt

versions of Fordun and Bower that Sir William inherited from Henry, he also came into possession of his uncle's copy of Wyntoun's *Original Chronicle* (BL MS Lansdowne 197), which bears the signatures of both Henry and William on the upper margin of folio 3.[26].

Each of these witnesses and redactions points to prolonged engagement with the Fordun–Bower narrative of Scottish history; additionally, the various redactions of this historiography – including Bower's continuation of Fordun and Fordun's own process of compilation – are related to the craft of memory in important ways. Albert C. Baugh connects memory-as-practice to the process of redaction: 'while following his source closely in plot and in the sequence of episodes that makes up that plot, [the poet] succeeds in fashioning his materials into something new and fresh'.[27] While Baugh is referring to medieval romance, his sense of the role of the redaction in demonstrating an agile memory is equally applicable to historiography. It is the introduction to the Coupar Angus recension that I am most interested in for the purposes of this chapter, not only because this inflection is distinctively shaped by Bower's portrayal of English hostility towards the Scots, but also because in this prologue it is possible to see this process of redaction as a craft of memory most clearly as an ideological project for Bower.

From Joy to Zeal, and Back Again: The Coupar Angus Prologue

The prologue to the Corpus MS (MS C) situates Bower's historiographical project within the commonplace modesty topos. Here Bower recounts (or imagines) a conversation between 'some men knowledgeable in scholarly matters' who were 'discussing the merits of the compiler' (i.e., Fordun; *Chron. Bower* 9. 3). One of the men describes Fordun as 'an undistinguished man, and not a graduate of any of the schools' (*Chron. Bower* 9. 3). However, another participant in the conversation rebuts this assessment of Fordun, claiming that the chronicle is 'sufficient proof of the quality of his scholarship' because 'he puts into practice what Seneca says', that it 'is not the education of the schools but incessant reading' that is a marker of 'learning' (*Chron. Bower* 9. 3). Bower intriguingly presents an image of a bookish, but not university-educated, Fordun whose achievement is all the more remarkable because, rather than 'boastfully rely[ing] on [his] own feeble intellect', Fordun's wisdom and education comes from 'compar[ing] his own writings with those of a master'

---

with Ian C. Cunningham, 3 vols, STS 5th Ser., 17, 18, 19 (Woodbridge: Boydell Press for the Scottish Text Society, 2020–22), 1 Prol. 85.

[26] Amours notes that this is 'a considerably abridged version of the same class as the Royal MS' of Wyntoun's *Chronicle*; *Chron. Wyntoun* 1. lxvi–lxvii.

[27] Baugh, 'Convention and Individuality in Middle English Romance', p. 139.

and 'imitat[ing] the arrangement' of others' ideas and words.[28] Bower establishes his own historiographical project in this vein, being careful to note that he wishes to 'follow' Fordun's example and imitate his style (*Chron. Bower* 9. 5). Bower elaborates on this idea of style in the preface that follows the prologue to the MS C, writing:

> I shall not aim in my writings at beauty of style with brilliant diction but I shall try to devote my attention to the true riches of different historians and to events known to me otherwise. Indeed the chronicles by themselves are so brilliant, vouched for by the names of the writers that they do not need the lustre of an elaborate style to delight the hearts of readers. In addition to this the artlessness of an uncultivated style has usually removed all suspicion of falsification. For how could anyone who is quite unable to produce a polished style know how to fabricate fiction? (*Chron. Bower* 9. 7–9)

By the end of the prologue and preface to the Corpus *Scotichronicon*, therefore, Bower has established a distinctive style for his work: one that seeks to emulate a learnedness that, like Fordun's, is based on copious reading and the pulling together of various authoritative material while, simultaneously, advocating a plain style that signals authority in its artlessness. Bower's affected modesty eschews rhetorical sophistication for credibility that comes from diligently compiling reputable sources. As is noted in Chapter 2, the prologue to MS C of the *Scotichronicon* establishes Bower's project of copying and continuing Fordun's chronicle as paying a debt to his patron, Sir David Stewart of Rosyth. Bower's depiction of himself as a 'debtor … compelled by love' (*Chron. Bower* 9. 3) performs a peculiarly affective rhetorical function, whereby Stewart's 'urgent requests' that Bower transcribe Fordun's history are reflected back to the reader (including, if not exclusively, Stewart) at the moment that love (*caritas*) is transformed to 'delight the hearts of readers' (*letificandum corda legencium*; *Chron. Bower* 9. 6–7). Joy (*Exultacio*), then, characterises the prologue and preface of MS C. By the time Bower is directing the production to the Coupar Angus recension, this delight has taken on a distinctly national tone.

The unique prologue to the Coupar Angus MS of Bower's *Scotichronicon* immediately confronts its readers with an absence of written historical memory. Bower narrates how

---

[28] As Watt's notes to the prologue explain, in 'the early to mid-14c', a university education for Scots necessitated 'the trouble and expense of years of study at Paris or other universities on the continent' (*Chron. Bower* 9. 10, nn. 29–30). See also, D.E.R. Watt, 'Scottish University Men of the Thirteenth and Fourteenth Centuries', in *Scotland and Europe 1200–1850*, ed. by T.C. Smout (Edinburgh: John Donald, 1986), pp. 1–18.

88 REWRITING THE PAST IN SCOTTISH LITERATURE, 1350–1550

> That ferocious torturer [*Ille truculentus tortor*] the third Edward after
> the last Conquest, the king and tyrant [*tirannus*] of England called
> Longshanks, after the occasion for a dispute arose between the distin-
> guished princes of the Bruce and Balliol families over who had the
> better right of succession to the kingdom, violently appropriated and
> destroyed [*violenter abstulit et delevit*] it [written Scottish history].
> (*Chron. Bower* 9. 12–13)

According to Bower, 'on the pretext' of finding out whether Bruce or Balliol 'could claim the fuller right to the kingdom through a search of ancient writings', Edward had all the Scottish libraries searched for documents. Bower continues:

> after all the libraries of the kingdom had been searched and authentic
> and ancient chronicles of history had been placed in his hands, he took
> some of these away with him to England, and the rest he contemptibly
> consigned to be burned in the flames [*reliquas vero flammis incin-
> erandas despicabiliter commisit*]. (*Chron. Bower* 9. 13)

In Bower's imagination, this act of aggression creates a historiographical void – a memory vacuum – that serves a markedly provocative political function. Through imagining Edward I seizing and destroying Scottish historical narratives in such a violent and contemptible way, Bower presents the English king as a man seeking to control history through one of the primary means by which it could be remembered: the act of writing. In sequestering Scottish chronicles, Edward controls access to certain public loci of Scottish memory-as-history, and in burning the texts that he does not need, or which do not suit his purpose, Edward symbolically destroys the history of Scotland, erasing it from written memory and public record. In doing so, he seeks to scaffold a memory of English overlordship that can be shored up with the historical documents that he has chosen to keep, 'forcibly usurp[ing] the guardianship of' Scotland 'for himself *de facto*' (*Chron. Bower* 9. 13).

This annihilation suggests a process of *organised forgetting* that is being forced on the Scots and, by extension, on their sense of identity through English acts of violence and erasure. As the Czech historian Milan Hübl reportedly told the novelist Milan Kundera, the first step in 'liquidat[ing] a people' is to 'take away' memory:

> You destroy its books, its culture, its history. And then others write
> other books for it, give another culture to it, invent another history for
> it. Then the people slowly begin to forget what it is and what it was.[29]

---

[29] Milan Kundera, *The Book of Laughter and Forgetting*, trans. by Aaron Asher (London: Faber, 1996), p. 218.

This excision or alteration becomes a process of scaffolded forgetting that draws provocative links between culture, history, writing and memory. This can also be seen in Bower's preface as an act of resistance to the English activity, where it is not Bower's individual memory that is under discussion, but a collective memory that existed in the written record that the English sought to suppress. In this prologue, Bower turns to his historiographical predecessor, John of Fordun, presenting him as the saviour of Scottish history. As previously discussed, *Scotichronicon* extends Fordun's fourteenth-century chronicle, and the Coupar Angus introduction creates a specific textual link between Bower's work and the chronicle on which it is based, as well as placing Bower within a wider textual community of historical writing in Scotland.[30] Bower's account of Edward I's destruction of Scottish chronicles imaginatively reconstructs the impetus for Fordun's writing the *Chronica Gentis Scotorum*. While, for Hübl, the writing of 'new history' is left to a victorious occupying force, in Bower's Coupar Angus prologue the Scots are imagined as rewriting – or at least reassembling – their own history as an act of defiance. Bower clearly shows that Fordun responds to English aggression through the act of writing; in Bower's remembrance of Fordun's chronicling activities, the rewriting of history is therefore constructed as an act of partisanship. Following 'the loss of these chronicles', Bower continues, several people attempted to patch together the history that had been destroyed. Among them,

> There emerged a certain venerable priest, sir John Fordun, a Scot by nationality [*Scotus nomine*]. He set his hand to valiant deeds, inspired and on fire with patriotic zeal [*ad forcia manum misit et patrio zelo titillatus efferbuit*]. He never abandoned what he had begun until by laborious studies (for which he scoured England as well as other neighbouring provinces) he made a new collection from what had been lost ... until he put together in adequate chronicle form the volume of five books concerning the agreeable deeds of the Scots.
>
> (*Chron. Bower* 9. 13)

Bower argues that

> The diligence of [Fordun] is to be commended, considering that he himself applied his mind to recording everything for posterity which is shown to be the concern not of man but of the divine will. For that reason he went on foot like an industrious bee throughout the land of Britain and the oratories of Ireland, through cities and towns,

---

[30] See Broun, *Scottish Independence*; Broun, 'A New Perspective on John of Fordun's *Chronica Gentis Scotorum* as a Medieval "National History"', in *Rethinking the Renaissance and Reformation*, pp. 43–60.

universities and colleges, churches and monasteries, holding discussions with historians and visiting chroniclers, examining their books of annals, and conversing and debating knowledgeably with them, making a record of what he wanted on double-leaved writing-tablets. From such exhaustive enquiries he found out what was unknown to him, and he carefully gathered together his findings like combs flowing with honey in the book he carried on his person as if in a beehive. (*Chron. Bower* 9. 15)

This matches the shaping of the Coupar Angus recension as a more clearly Scottish-focused work. The affective representation of Bower's compulsion to write for his patron in MS C is here superseded by Fordun's compulsion to write for the kingdom. Bower's narrative clearly suggests a nationalist impetus to Fordun's work, and his remark about the patriotic feeling that spurs Fordun on in his search is particularly emotive: Fordun's feelings of loyalty towards Scotland are marked by an enthusiasm and fervour that Bower subsequently tries to evoke in his readers. Towards the end of the prologue, a set of verses entreat the reader to 'Direct a careful heart ... to the page' (*Pagine sollicitum ... cor impende*) and to 'apply [their] mind ... to the fluctuations of this kingdom' (*Regni queque fluida huius hic attende*; *Chron. Bower* 9. 15). In doing so, Bower suggests, the reader might 'Reflect on how changeable [Scotland's] fortunes have been', and they might 'show by [their] conduct that [they] are living more cautiously' (*Chron. Bower* 9. 15). Bower draws here on the three basic functions of rhetoric – to teach (*docere*), to move (*movere*) and to please (*delectare*) – to instruct his readers and prompt them to action.

Yet, as much as Fordun is inspired and on fire, his 'laborious studies' (*Chron. Bower* 9. 13) are informed by a methodical working-through of the sources available to him so that the 'new' material he collects is stored properly in the repository of historiographical memory. In Bower's threefold narrative of Fordun's endeavours – collecting the material, rearranging it and then writing a new history – Bower shows his predecessor compiling his *Chronica Gentis Scotorum* according to the standard model of the medieval theory of imagination, in which sense perception (the material) was transferred to the cell of the brain responsible for logic, or reason (Fordun's ordering), which was then committed to memory (Fordun's production of written history).[31] Accordingly, Fordun's reassembled history is not to be seen only as a work motivated by a historical perspective that Bower intimates is nationalist to some degree; it is to be viewed also as an accurate recollection of the history that has been destroyed, despite the fluid historiographical tradition in which

---

[31] See Alastair Minnis, 'Medieval Imagination and Memory', in *The Cambridge History of Literary Criticism, Volume 2: The Middle Ages*, ed. by Alastair Minnis and Ian Johnson (Cambridge: Cambridge University Press, 2005), pp. 239–74.

Bower sets both Fordun and himself. It is at this point that Bower turns to metaphors of the monastic-trained memory in order to explain Fordun's activities not only as a reconstructive process of a physical archive but also as a 'process' of collective memory training.

Bower describes Fordun as an 'industrious bee' (*apis argumentosa*) scouring the archives and gathering together historical material 'like combs, flowing with honey in the book he carried on his person as if in a beehive' (*Chron. Bower* 9. 15). It is important that Fordun searches *Britain* to locate his sources, for it not only authenticates Bower's account of Edward I removing historical texts from Scotland but also lends a legitimacy to Scottish history through the fact that the English see these texts as important and 'worthy' of confiscation. Bower here is at pains to suggest the types of memory and record that Fordun consults, indicating the comprehensiveness of his search in order to write his book. In this way the texts that Fordun searches and copies are consciously a diverse repository of others' memories or histories – stored within chronicles and other books in order that they can be retrieved at a later date. The text into which Fordun puts his findings – his *tabulis* (*Chron. Bower* 9. 14) – becomes a new repository, or memory-store of this type, but his notebook itself also becomes a metaphor for the memories it contains: it is a beehive, abundant and overflowing with the honeycombs of Scottish national history drawn from many sources.[32] The Latin word for the compartments in which bees store their honey is *cellae* (cell), and there is a long-standing metaphor in which the placement of images in a trained memory is likened to the beehive.[33] Furthermore, this metaphor extended also to the study of books and to the keeping of books in orderly cells in a library, attested to in Richard de Bury's fourteenth-century *Philobiblon*.[34] In fact, de Bury's description of the book collector as an 'industrious' bee 'constantly making cells of honey' is remarkably similar to Bower's recollection of Fordun's process of assembling notes for his national history.[35] The structure of the beehive, with its compart-

[32] Cf. Carruthers's description of florilegia, which, she argues, are the 'essential book[s] of memory' because the genre is 'understood to be volumes only of extracts ... memorative in both origin and purpose', providing 'cues for recollecting material read earlier'; *Book of Memory*, p. 219.

[33] Carruthers, *Book of Memory*, p. 45. This metaphor can be found in Longinus (*c.* first century CE), Quintilian (*c.* 35–*c.* 100) and, possibly, Virgil (70 BCE–19 BCE); moreover, Seneca (*c.* 4 BCE–65 CE) uses the metaphor of the bee to denote a reader or an author. I have previously discussed that the *cella* was a metaphor for the memory; see p. 13.

[34] Carruthers, *Book of Memory*, pp. 42–5.

[35] 'Hi sicut formicae continue congregantes in messem et apes argumentosae fabricantes iugiter cellas mellis' (these, like ants, are continually gathering in the harvest, and the industrious bees are continually making hives of honey') cap. 8, 136: Richard de Bury, *Philobiblon*, ed. and trans. by E.C. Thomas (London: Kegan Paul, 1888), p. 76.

ments for storage, is distinctly architectural and, therefore, denotes the ways in which architecture was used as a common metaphor for the trained memory, the *cell* calling to mind images of the storeroom or the treasure house, or the oratory in which Fordun and Bower might have composed their chronicles. In this description, then, Bower adopts a typical image of both memory and scholarship, again recalling a physical structure that houses both memory and history. Like a physical monument, the textual space of historical narrative becomes a place where memories can be stored; mapped onto the space of the page, these recollections take on precise meanings, ideally understood by, accessible to, and retrievable by all. In this way memory, as embodied within the book, is not only abstract and past, but also tangible and present.

Architectural structures do not always need to function allegorically, however; while Bower's Coupar Angus prologue participates in the metaphorical use of architecture in mnemonic practices, the text also points to the destruction of books as physical artefacts. The books that Bower's Edward destroys are important both for what they contain – the memory of Scotland's past – and for what they symbolise: the material culture from which memory takes its meaning and through which it is secured. In his discussion of the status of architecture during times of conflict, Robert Bevan acknowledges that the destruction of the built environment is an 'inevitable part of conducting hostilities', not only in general destruction that results from conflict but also in a deliberate 'war against architecture' where the 'destruction of cultural artefacts of an enemy people or nation' becomes 'a means of dominating, terrorizing, dividing or eradicating it altogether'.[36] Viewed in this way, the Scottish histories that Edward seeks to erase represent a textual architecture of memory, and Bower's analogy draws on an understanding that collective memory can be located outwith the mind. Moreover, books were stored in buildings that were deliberately targeted by Edward I; as a direct consequence, the architectural structure of the memory becomes linked with the concrete reality of the library, and both become strategic targets for destruction.[37] Scotland's history and the memory of its own nationhood are, therefore, located in the textual space of written *memoria* that is invested with a discursive function of remembrance comparable to the built environment that the English sought to destroy.

Cf. Bower: 'tamquam in alveario, inventa, quasi mellifluos favos accurate congessit': *Chron. Bower* 9. 14.

[36] Bevan, *Destruction of Memory*, pp. 7–8.

[37] As David McRoberts argues, 'when monastic buildings were sacked ... it was likely that books were destroyed even if they were not targeted specifically'; 'Material Destruction Caused by the Scottish Reformation', in *Essays on the Scottish Reformation, 1513–1625*, ed. by David McRoberts (Glasgow: J.S. Burns & Sons, 1962), pp. 415–62 (433).

REASSEMBLING FORGOTTEN HISTORY

A similar incident is highlighted by the late fourteenth-century *Anonimalle* chronicler, who records that, during the 1381 rebellion in England, the rebels 'burned registers and chancery rolls'.[38] By way of explanation, Thomas Walsingham notes in his early fifteenth-century *Chronicon Angliae* the rebels' determination that 'court rolls and muniments should be burned so that, the memory of old customs having been rubbed out, their lords would be unable to vindicate their rights over them'.[39] Walsingham and the *Anonimalle* chronicler both imply here that there existed a recognition that written memory could be targeted deliberately in the hope that what it signified might be destroyed and ultimately forgotten. In *Writing and Rebellion*, however, Steven Justice argues that the rebels' limited familiarity with documentary culture made them determined to 'make it theirs': that they sought to control the way in which these texts could be used rather than destroying them completely.[40] Whether the rebels destroyed or appropriated the documents that came into their possession, one thing is clear: books, like the built environment, were understood both symbolically *and* concretely.

In Bower's depiction of Edward I's intervention in the Great Cause in the Coupar Angus prologue, the reader is presented with both of these actions, and it generates an image of Edward as one who, 'on the *pretext* ... of finding out which of [Bruce or Balliol] could claim fuller right to the kingdom' of Scotland, systematically appropriated and destroyed [*abstulit et delevit*] the written memory of Scotland's past in an effort to seize 'the guardianship of the same kingdom for himself' (*Chron. Bower* 9. 11, 13; my emphasis). If, as Justice maintains, there was a 'precise understanding of the forms and procedures of the document and the archive' among both the educated elite and the broader populace in the later Middle Ages, then Bower (and Bower's Edward) demonstrates a recognition that both memory and the written document are biddable or subject to the process of imagination.[41] This textual consciousness allows

---

[38] 'mistrent en feu toutz les livers des registres et rolles de remembrauncez de la chauncellerir illeoqes trovez': *The Anonimalle Chronicle*; cited in Paul Strohm, *Theory and the Premodern Text* (Minneapolis: University of Minnesota Press, 2000), p. 55.

[39] 'statuerunt omnes curiarum rotulos et munimenta veteran dare flammis, ut, obsolete antiquarum rerum memoria, nullum jus omnino ipsorum domini in eos in posterum vendicare valerent': *Chronicon Angliae, ab anno domini 1328 usque ad annum 1388, auctore monacho quodam sancti albani*, ed. by Edward Maunde Thompson, Rolls Series 64 (London, 1874); p. 287; translation from Paul Strohm, *Theory and the Premodern Text*, p. 55.

[40] Steven Justice, *Writing and Rebellion: England in 1381* (Berkeley: University of California Press, 1994), p. 35.

[41] Justice, *Writing and Rebellion*, p. 48. In relation to documentary culture, documents are usually defined as charters, writs and other legal documents, and the emphasis is on brevity and citability. See Emily Steiner, *Documentary Culture and the Making of Medieval English Literature* (Cambridge: Cambridge University Press,

94   REWRITING THE PAST IN SCOTTISH LITERATURE, 1350–1550

Bower to expose Edward's literate mentality; at the same time, the narrative also shows Bower's own awareness of the malleability of the written document by writing his own version of Edward acting as a wolf in sheep's clothing (*sub ovili vellere*; *Chron. Bower* 9. 14) and Fordun's efforts of *rewriting* the Scottish history that has been lost (*ad recolligendum deperditas*; *Chron. Bower* 9. 23). Bower (and Bower's Edward) also demonstrates a clear understanding of the idea that controlling the past enabled the direction of the future. Bower's sense of loss here not only marks a perceived tragedy for public memory in Scotland but also, conversely, prompts the creation of history; for, without this confiscation of the 'old and ancient' chronicles, Bower suggests that Fordun would *not* have been 'inspired and on fire with patriotic zeal' and, therefore, would not have begun the history that precedes and enables Bower's own textual production.

The remembrance of Edward I's attempted annihilation of Scotland's history in the Coupar Angus prologue is, however, problematised by the fact that there is no evidence to suggest that Edward actually did have Scottish chronicles burned.[42] D.E.R. Watt points out that, although 'some of the Scottish royal archives were certainly taken south to England where some of them remained until the twentieth century', in fact, 'most of Edward's historical investigations' during the overlordship debate put before the Pope 'were confined to chronicles and records kept in England'.[43] Thus the reader of the Coupar Angus *Scotichronicon* is confronted, not necessarily with what might have been lost and subject to reconstruction, but with events that might never have occurred. The preface thus presents the reader with an imagined history, in the sense that it is not factually accurate. While there is no evidence that Edward did burn chronicles, Bower relies on the *possibility* of it having occurred, recalling and reminding his readers of those aspects of Scottish culture that Edward did strategically destroy when monastic houses and other buildings were sacked and razed.

The abbey at Coupar Angus is a particularly apt example. In February 1305, its abbot sent a petition to Edward I's parliament seeking compensation for

---

2003), esp. p. 4. For the purposes of my discussion here I propose that written public records (in which I include chronicles) should be considered as documentary.

42 On Edward I's use of historical documents see E.J. Cowan, 'Identity, Freedom and the Declaration of Arbroath', in *Image and Identity: The Making and Re-making of Scotland through the Ages*, ed. by Dauvit Broun, R.J. Finlay and Michael Lynch (Edinburgh: John Donald, 1998), pp. 38–68.

43 D.E.R. Watt, *Guide to the National Archives of Scotland* (Edinburgh: Scottish Record Office, 1996), pp. ix–x; *Chron. Bower* 9. 18. n. 25–7; See also E.L.G. Stones and G.G. Simpson (eds), *Edward I and the Throne of Scotland, 1290–1295: An Edition of the Record Sources for the Great Cause*, 2 vols (Oxford: Oxford University Press, 1978), i. 137–62.

the burning of the abbey's granges and other damages.[44] While this petition is centred on recompense for the economic damage suffered by the monastery, English acts of aggression could also be seen as a deliberate attempt to attack the Scots' sense of identity that was manifested in, or through, their buildings, some of which would have contained written documents.[45] The implication here is that the English did not only seek to destroy the Scots' sense of identity in destroying the built (or written) environment; their acts of sabotage also allowed them to give the *appearance* of winning a war even if there was no evidence to support this. The burning of Scottish property clearly occupied a strong place in the memory of the monastic community at Coupar Angus, and possibly at other monasteries as well. Gwilym Dodd notes the 'predominance of Scottish religious houses' among the supplications to the English parliaments, which indicates that the Coupar Angus petition was not exceptional.[46] At the same time, the petition provides a local example of English hostility and Scottish reaction to it. It is possible that Bower used the fourteenth-century events at Coupar Angus to inflect the preface of the Coupar Angus *Scotichronicon* with concerns with which his immediate audience there could identify. Of course, the notion of maligning enemy nations and individuals is not unique to this particular version of *Scotichronicon* – it occurs repeatedly elsewhere – but this portrait of Edward's annihilation of Scotland's memory that leads to the rewriting of memory-as-history by Fordun and Bower is especially potent in a recension of the chronicle that emphasises English aggression. In his discussion of the Middle English prose *Brut*, Matthew Fisher notes that many manuscripts of that text 'exhibit moments of unique local interest, revisions or emendations of facts, and substantive interpolations, additions, or expansions to make partisan political points'. This, Fisher contends, is unsurprising, given that 'history writing invites participation, and encourages sophisticated readers to go beyond simply reading the text at hand'.[47] In one way, the Coupar Angus prologue captures this local interest;

---

[44] 'Ad petitionem Abbatis de Conventus de Coupre petentium remedium de dampnis quæ sustinuerunt per combustionem grangiarum et aliarum domorum suarum et per aliam hujusmodi destructionem post pacem reformatam': *Records of the Parliament holden at Westminster 28 Feb., 33 Edw. I (1305)*, ed. by F.W. Maitland, Rolls Series 98 (London, 1893), p. 203 (no. 355).

[45] Melrose, the mother house of Coupar Angus, was also subject to English aggression, being looted by the English army in 1322 and burned on the orders of Richard II in 1385. See Ranald Nicolson, *Scotland: The Later Middle Ages*, Edinburgh History of Scotland, vol. 2 (Edinburgh: Mercat, 1974; repr. 1997), pp. 104, 197.

[46] Gwilym Dodd, 'Sovereignty, Diplomacy and Petitioning: Scotland and the English Parliament in the First Half of the Fourteenth Century', in *England and Scotland in the Fourteenth Century*, pp. 172–95 (185).

[47] Fisher, *Scribal Authorship*, p. 188.

at the same time, Edward's destruction of the Scottish archive is broader in scope and assumes a political significance. Bower implies that it is not just written history that is destroyed by Edward, but also the markers of nationhood embedded in these memories-as-histories, and it is these that need to be recovered. In removing the Scots' access to their own history – either by confiscation or by destruction – Edward I aimed in part to erase that aspect of Scottish identity associated with the public memory of written historical narrative. By 'reassembling what had been lost' (*Chron. Bower* 9. 13),[48] Fordun and Bower, along with other Scottish writers engaged in writing 'histories' of Scotland, aimed to restore that sense of identity through the memory of the written document, even if that meant deliberately presenting alternative facts.

There is a perceived, yet vulnerable, permanence to written history, as there is with the built environment, suggesting that the recording of shared experience allows that collective memory to be preserved and re-enacted in subsequent writings and for later audiences. In this way both architecture and the written document provide space with meaning through their embodiment of ideologies, memories and identities.[49] Bower here presents his readers with multiple ways of remembering and forgetting, and himself seeks to remember what had previously been recorded; at the same time, he highlights Fordun's own recreation of historical narrative and the synthesising of the two accounts in *Scotichronicon*. Yet the recollection of the history that had been lost cannot possibly be remembered in the same way, subject as it is to the imposition of the trauma inflicted by its destruction and manipulation at the hands of the English monarch. The Coupar Angus prologue thus articulates an understanding of the precarity of both architecture and textual production, which are subject to targeted destruction as a strategy of war. Bower juxtaposes the 'ferocious torturer' (*truculentus tortor*), Edward, with the violence inflicted by him both on Scottish texts, which are condemned to oblivion through burning, and on the Scottish people and country (*plebes atque patrie*) who endure plagues and afflictions (*plagas et pressuras*) (*Chron. Bower* 9. 12–14). Bower here explicitly suggests that the violence with which Scotland, its people and its cultural productions are treated becomes physically inscribed (or incised) on the memory; they become wounds that cannot be silenced or even fully understood.

---

[48] 'Ad recolligendum deperditas' (*Chron. Bower* 9. 12).

[49] See Barbara A. Hanawalt and Michal Kobialka (eds), *Medieval Practices of Space* (Minneapolis: University of Minnesota Press, 2000), esp. Jody Enders, 'Dramatic Memories and Tortured Spaces in the *Mistere de la Sainte Hostie*', pp. 199–222; Daniel Lord Smail, *Imaginary Cartographies: Possession and Identity in Late-medieval Marseille* (Ithaca, NY: Cornell University Press, 1999), pp. 43–57, 195–203; Pierre Bourdieu, *The Field of Cultural Production*, ed. and trans. by Randal Johnson (New York: Columbia University Press, 1993).

REASSEMBLING FORGOTTEN HISTORY

Cathy Caruth proposes that trauma acts as a 'wound' through which voices become audible, and, as I have argued, it is the destruction of Scottish textual memories that allows this (re)creation and audibility by Fordun and Bower.[50] It is almost as if, Bower indicates, the reliving or remembering the traumatic experience of the previous century gives Fordun and himself a legitimate voice for their history. Bower's remembrance of the late thirteenth-century evisceration of Scottish history from the body of Scotland's cultural production is a belated reliving of this imagined act of English aggression, and this event is registered as traumatic because, although the act of English atrocity is caught in historical time, the trauma that is stored, collated and recalled becomes what Caruth describes as a 'narrative of a belated experience'.[51] It is this narrative that is reimagined as Scottish history precisely because that history is framed by Bower as a reconstruction necessitated by the traumatic ways in which it came to be forgotten. As Bower would have it, in the prefaces to both the *Scotichronicon* and the Coupar Angus recension, his history serves the 'comfort of the king and the kingdom' as well as being 'a warning for the future and for the edification of readers' (*Chron. Bower* 9. 17). Comfort here carries not only the sense of consolation, but also of providing joy and encouragement to his audience; this brings the Coupar Angus prologue back in line with the preface to MS C and Bower's initial rationale for compiling his history.[52] Bower's decision to write *Scotichronicon*, then, is not only a way of consoling James II and the Scots but is also a way of promoting the feelings of *patrius zelus* through the recollection of Scotland's 'lost' history.

In reassembling 'what had been lost', *Scotichronicon*, in its various recensions, is a self-conscious act of memory. At the same time, the work is also a process of creation as representation. This is principally evident in the Coupar Angus introduction, as it is in texts such as Hary's *Wallace* (discussed in the next chapter), and for historical (or pseudo-historical) writing as a whole, for it highlights the very use of representations of the past and their negotiable varieties of accuracy. Bower and Hary present their audiences with what can be thought of as *poetic* memory: a commemorative textual monument that situates itself in cultural memory, which is not about giving testimony of past events as accurately as possible, but about making *meaningful* statements about the past in a given cultural context of the present.[53] Poetic memory thus relies on a *feeling* of accuracy and authenticity that appeals to a collective audience's ideas about what the past *should* be. These problematic national

[50] Caruth, *Unclaimed Experience*, p. 2.

[51] Caruth, *Unclaimed Experience*, p. 7.

[52] *DOST*, comfort, *n*; solace, *n*.

[53] For more on cultural memory, see Peter Burke, 'History as Social Memory', in *Memory: History, Culture and the Mind*, ed. by T. Butler (Oxford: Blackwell, 1989), pp. 97–113.

memories are consciously and continually being shaped, and this reimagining allows national struggle to be read as an effort shared by the community. In the Coupar Angus prologue, this is exemplified by Bower's image of the king and kingdom, which brings the monarch and his people together in a mutual expression of suffering that affects the whole of Scotland. This is reinforced by the narrative of Fordun and Bower working towards the same goal of reassembling Scottish history for national posterity, yet working more than half a century apart. Moreover, Bower signals that the Coupar Angus copy of *Scotichronicon* represents an exceptional version of the work; he discloses having shortened 'various events and notable arguments, digressions and exempla clearly serving different purposes' (*Chron. Bower* 9. 15). Thus, the Coupar Angus readers' understanding of the work is fashioned by what Bower has chosen to include and exclude, by what to emphasise and the purpose of that specific manuscript. This not only connects members of a community within a specific historical moment, but also brings together the past and the present in the way that I argued genealogy also functions in Bower's *Scotichronicon*. The perceived threat to the Scottish historical record – and implicitly to the national memory and identity documented *by* that record – underlies the repeated calls to remembrance in Bower's *Scotichronicon*.

The anxiety about the preservation of memory that is central to Bower's historiographical project indicates that memory is not merely about retrieving and reassembling the past; it is also about actively resisting the erasure of national consciousness and historical continuity. Bower's emphasis on the emotional resonance of memory signals a deeper concern: the fragility of collective memory in the face of time and political upheaval. In the next chapter, I examine how this anxiety is further echoed in Hary's *Wallace*, where the urgency to memorialise represents a form of resistance as well as preservation. Where Bower has underscored the precariousness of memory, Hary draws attention to the ways in which historical narrative becomes a battleground for identity, where the act of remembering is as much about safeguarding the present as it is about reconstructing the past.

4

Hary's *Wallace* as a Book of Memory

On the first folio of the only extant manuscript of Hary's *Wallace* (NLS Adv. MS 19.2.2), a (presumably) sixteenth-century reader has left an enigmatic doodle (Fig. 4).[1] Alongside the opening lines of Hary's poem there exists an image of a tower with what appears to be a ladder leaning against it. We know nothing of the context of the sketch and one explanation is that it represents a scaffold unrelated to the text the manuscript contains.[2] Nevertheless, as I discussed in Chapter 1, the ladder had distinct associations with memory and with the depiction of vices and virtues. It is tempting to speculate that this doodle might demonstrate a direct response to Hary's text. In sketching this ladder alongside Hary's own calls to 'hald in mynde' the 'nobille worthi deid' of 'our antecessowris' (*Wall.* 1. 1–2), did the impromptu illustrator signal their recognition of, or desire to remember, the virtues of the late fourteenth-century Scots and the vices of the 'ald Ennemys' (the English) who sought to 'hald Scotlande at wndyr' (*Wall.* 1. 7, 13)? That, of course, is an impossible question to answer; however, what I want to consider in this chapter are the ways in which the late fifteenth-century poet known to us as Hary seeks to recollect events of the first Scottish War of Independence at a critical moment of Anglo-Scottish relations during the reign of James III. Hary's *Wallace*, composed *c.* 1475 and surviving in a manuscript from 1488, recounts the life and deeds of William Wallace. The poem acts as a commemoration of Wallace as a national hero: a textual memorial to the man whom Hary depicts as the saviour of Scotland. Written almost two centuries after Wallace's execution, Hary's *Wallace* is the only full-length literary treatment of this Scottish hero. Matthew McDiarmid describes the *Wallace* as 'the greatest single work of imagination in early Scots poetry' and, according to Felicity Riddy, the poem 'fixed the figure of William Wallace in the popular imagination'.[3] Despite the scarcity of

---

[1]   It is unclear whether the pencil sketch has been drawn by the same hand that has annotated the copy of the manuscript, which appears to be in a sixteenth-century hand. The manuscript page can be viewed at: https://digital.nls.uk/232641634.

[2]   I am grateful to colleagues at the Older Scots Conference, Rochester, NY (2016) for a discussion of this image and its various meanings.

[3]   *Wall.* i. vi.; Felicity Riddy, 'Unmapping the Territory: Blind Hary's *Wallace*', in *The Wallace Book*, ed. by Edward J. Cowan (Edinburgh: John Donald, 2007), pp. 107–16 (107).

extant manuscripts, it would seem that the *Wallace* was an extremely popular text. It was one of the earliest prints issued by Scotland's first printers, Walter Chepman and Andrew Myller, between 1508 and 1510. Twenty-three editions of the poem appeared between 1510 and 1707, with another forty-seven produced before 1913. It was reprinted at major crisis points in Scottish history, such as the Reformation (1560), the Union of the Crowns (1603), the Restoration (1660) and the Jacobite Rising of 1745, suggesting that Hary's text, and the memory of Wallace, continually appealed to Scottish audiences, notably at times when Anglo-Scottish relations were at the forefront of political life.[4] Indeed, the composition of the *Wallace* during the reign of James III begins this trajectory of the political impetus and resonance of the text.

The *Wallace* is a poem that generates a picture of William Wallace as the substance of legend; it is also a text that invests much of its narrative with ideas of memory, remembering and commemoration. As with the Coupar Angus preface to *Scotichronicon*, these memorial practices revolve around traumatisation that shapes Wallace's life and legacy. The particular events of Book 6 (in which Wallace's *leman* is killed by the English sheriff, Heselrigg), Book 7 (when Wallace's uncle is murdered along with other Scottish nobles in the Barns of Ayr) and Book 12 (when Wallace is executed) pivot around trauma as a site of interchange between the individual motivated by a desire for vengeance (Wallace) and the consigning of English violence to collective memory (the effect of the story on Hary's audience). These episodes in Wallace's story are similar to what Greg Forter calls 'punctual trauma', a once-occurring catastrophic event that dissociates consciousness from itself.[5] Hary's *Wallace*, however, performs the past through narrative not as pathological fragmentation but as the forging of relationships between past and present that focus attention on collective identity and understanding. In this way, they invite what I am calling a participatory trauma that works to facilitate

---

[4]   In comparison, between 1508 and 1800 there were two printings of Barbour's *Bruce*, and only one between 1700 and 1750, during which time twelve editions of the *Wallace* appeared. On the popularity of the *Wallace* and its printings see Edward J. Cowan, 'William Wallace: "The Choice of the Estates"', in *The Wallace Book*, pp. 9–25.

[5]   Greg Forter, 'Freud, Faulkner, Caruth: Trauma and the Politics of Literary Form', *Narrative*, 15.3 (2007), 259–85 (259). Forter uses 'punctual' trauma to refer to the work of trauma studies scholars, such as Cathy Caruth, who suggest that a 'historical moment might be experienced less as an ongoing set of processes that shape and are shaped by those living through them than as a punctual blow to the psyche that overwhelms its functioning, disables its defenses, and absents it from direct contact with the brutalizing event itself' (259).

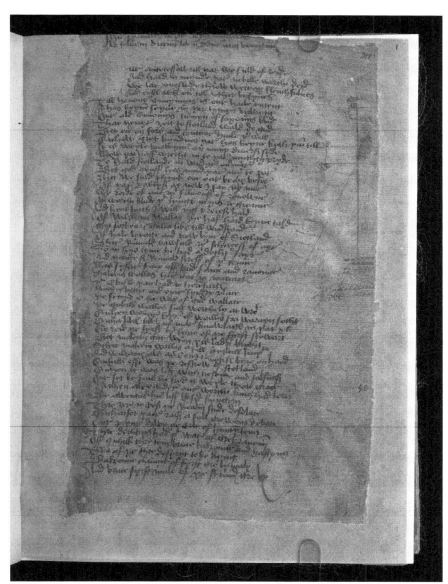

Fig. 4 The opening page of Hary's *Wallace*. Edinburgh, National Library of Scotland, Adv. MS 19.2.2 (ii), fol. 1r. Reproduced by permission of the National Library of Scotland.

102   REWRITING THE PAST IN SCOTTISH LITERATURE, 1350–1550

the integration of the past into the audience's present self-understanding.[6] Hary's rewriting of the past aims not to freeze the past in a timeless state but to create and recreate it in specific moments of recollection. Reconstructions of the past in the *Wallace*, then, become a vehicle for assimilating historical trauma into a late fifteenth-century Scottish cultural identity.

Hary opens and closes the *Wallace* with specific calls to remembrance:

> Our antecessowris that we suld of reide
> And hald in mynde thar nobille worthi deid,
> We lat ourslide throw werray sleuthfulnes,
> And castis ws euir till vthir besynes. (1. 1–4)

> Go nobill buk, fulfillyt off gud sentens,
> ...
> Go worthi buk fullfillit of suthfast deid,
> Bot in langage off help thow has greit neid.
> Quhen gud makaris rang weill in-to Scotland
> Gret harm was it that nane off thaim the fand.
> ӡeit thar is part that can the weill awance.
> Now byd thi tym and be a remembrance. (12. 1449, 1451–6)

Immediately, the reader's attention is drawn to two linked ideas. Firstly, through the use of the present participle 'hald', that they should continue to remember specific moments of the past (the noble deeds of 'our' ancestors) and that Hary's written record should 'byd thi tym' and function as a textual *aide-mémoire*. Secondly, Hary indicates that the memories of Scotland's ancestors are not currently being remembered appropriately because a collective 'we' has been preoccupied with other matters – most likely a reference to the pro-English policies of James's rule. To this, he adds a moral dimension that has implications for the reader; there is a collective action of negligence at work and Hary's suggestion that the Scots have been guilty of 'sleuthfulnes' points to an almost spiritual sin (*acedia*) and certainly a moral responsibility to remember (and resist the king's anglophile project).[7] Hary's solution, then,

---

[6]   My use of the term 'participatory trauma' is informed by the term 'vicarious trauma' coined by Irene Lisa McCann and Laurie Anne Pearlman to describe the process of change resulting from empathetic engagement with trauma survivors. See, 'Vicarious Traumatization: A Framework for Understanding the Psychological Effects of Working With Victims', *Journal of Traumatic Stress*, 3.1 (1990), 131–49. I use 'participatory trauma' to suggest a distinctively cultural version of McCann and Pearlman's concept in which an author's use of literary effects encourages readers to react to specific events in the plot and to participate in characters' experiences.

[7]   Where sloth had been imagined as a spiritual illness (*acedia*) in the early Middle Ages, by the fifteenth century it was viewed more as a sin of the flesh – it denoted

HARY'S *WALLACE* AS A BOOK OF MEMORY

seems to be to improve the health of the nation through the creation of a written memory of one of its most famous protectors. In order to do this, Hary invents a Latin source while failing to mention the *Gesta Annalia*, Wyntoun or Bower as sources and influences for his work. Nevertheless, Hary's *Wallace* shapes its readers' memories through the story it presents, while at the same time Hary notes that his work has itself been shaped by the previous versions of Wallace's story that inflect his own imaginative retelling.

For Hary, these acts of remembrance have a precise purpose: to appeal to a sense of Scottish identity predicated upon hostility towards the men of 'Saxonys blud', who 'neuyr ȝeit to Scotland wald do gud' (*Wall.* 1. 7–8). In this way, he appears to follow writers, such as Bower, whose colophon to *Scotichronicon* – 'Christ he is not a Scot who is not pleased with this book' (*Chron. Bower* 8. 341) – directly appeals to a readership that understands itself to be Scottish.[8] The emotive language of being able to take pleasure in reading a specific text *because* it speaks to Scottish interests and concerns connects historiography and biography in ways that mirror the Coupar Angus' imagining of Fordun's *patrio zelo*; the definition and sustenance of a particularly Scottish – and anti-English – sentiment connects author and audience in complementary acts of commemoration. Both texts equate identity not simply with remembering a particular history, but with the specific ideas of taking *pleasure* in this history. Like Bower's use of genealogy, discussed in Chapter 2, Hary's use of '*our* antecessowris' (my emphasis) is particularly significant in terms of allowing ideas of national sentiment to surface within the text because it manifests feelings of collectivity through its appeal to a shared heritage that Hary's *Wallace* seeks to commemorate. It suggests that those fighting for the Scottish cause become ancestors of the kingdom, as well as of individual families; their 'nobille' deeds adopt a national – as well as a personal – significance in the Scottish fight against the English. It is this struggle, which takes place between the two calls to remembrance at the beginning and end of the *Wallace*, that enables the visibility of Scottish national feeling within Hary's narrative, suggesting – as the Coupar Angus introduction and its emphasis on destruction and reconstruction had done – that trauma, or struggle, is a necessary factor in memory and identity formation.

Trauma in the *Wallace* is both personal (Wallace is an individual) and collective (Hary entreats his audience to use Wallace as an *exemplum* for their sense of Scottishness). The act of cultural genocide that I have suggested

---

laziness in general – and in the later Middle Ages had supplanted avarice as the most reprehensible vice. See my chapter, 'Mnemonic Frameworks in *The Buke of the Chess*', in *The Impact of Latin Culture on Medieval and Early Modern Scottish Writing*, ed. by Alessandra Petrina and Ian Johnson (Kalamazoo, MI: Medieval Institute Publications, 2018), pp. 41–60.

8 'Non Scotus est Christe cui liber non placet iste' (*Chron. Bower* 8. 340).

Bower depicts in the Coupar Angus *Scotichronicon* is mirrored by another act of attempted governmental genocide in Hary's poem. In Book 1 of the *Wallace*, Hary recalls English behaviour in early fourteenth-century Scotland, writing that

> It was weylle knawyn, in the bernys of Ayr
> Xviii score putt to that dispitfull dede!
> Bot god abowyn has send ws sum ramede.
> (*Wall.* 1. 176–8)

That the tale of the Barns of Ayr was 'weylle knawyn' suggests that the story was in general circulation and that Hary's audience could be expected to anticipate the coming events of his narrative. Hary implies a retelling of the story here: a recollection *and* an extension of other, related, Wallace narratives, found in texts such as Bower's *Scotichronicon* and Wyntoun's *Original Chronicle.*[9] Yet, like Bower's depiction of Edward I burning chronicles in the Coupar Angus introduction, this story is Hary's own invention and he exploits the trope of its being well known in order to authenticate the text. But Hary also uses the idea of collective knowledge, or shared memory, to appeal to a sense of Scottish identity that he bases on responses to English hostility and brutality. Once again he implicates trauma, or the memory of violence, as a point of reference for identity construction precisely because of the creative and memorial purposes that it serves.

Hary tells his audience that the 'Remembrance' of the Barns of Ayr and its 'ramede' is 'forthir in the taile' (*Wall.* 1. 178–9), and he turns to the episode in Book 7. The episode concerns the mass murder of the Scottish nobility by the English at a meeting in a barn in Ayrshire. Hary makes clear that the premeditated actions of the English are an attempt to rid Scotland completely of its own governing force and its heritage through the annihilation of its nobility. The meeting is a trap designed to bring the Scottish nobles together and to 'scour out' their 'rychtwys blud' from Scotland (*Wall.* 7. 16). Furthermore, Hary writes that the 'fals Sotheroun' learn from a 'traytour' how 'thai best mycht the Scottis barownis hang' (*Wall.* 7. 23, 14, 24), once again hinting at the internal political divisions within Scotland. The English secure the barn so that 'Nayne mycht pas in bot ay as thai war cald' (*Wall.* 7. 204), and the Scots are made to enter 'Bot ane at anys' (*Wall.* 7. 28). As they do so a 'rynnand cord' is 'slewyt our' their heads and they are 'hangyt ... to ded'

---

9   Barbour's *Bruce* alludes to a Barns of Ayr incident in which 'Crauford als Schyr Ranald wes / And Schyr Bryce als Blar / Hangyt in-till a berne in Ar' (*Bruce* 4. 36–8). The incident is not the same as Hary's, nor is it described in such detail, but it points to the possibility that stories about Scottish nobles being hanged were circulating at least from the late fourteenth century.

(*Wall.* 7. 207–8). As Hary emphasises, 'Mony ʒeid in bot na Scottis com out' (*Wall.* 7. 216). Wallace's uncle is the first person to be hanged by the English as he enters the barn to 'mak fewte for his land' (*Wall.* 7. 205), but Wallace himself is saved by 'Gret grace' (*Wall.* 7. 168), for he is made to ride back to his uncle's holdings at Crosbie – ironically, in order to collect the 'charter off pees' (*Wall.* 7. 159) that needs to be shown to the English.

Like the burning of the Scottish chronicles by Edward I recalled in the Coupar Angus *Scotichronicon*, the Barns of Ayr massacre is a fictional incident imagined by Hary for the purposes of his narrative. This does not mean, however, that there is not an element of 'truth' located within the episode itself, despite its not being historical 'fact'. The episode is deliberately fabricated as an instance of 'punctual' trauma to help Hary's audience recall the past; in doing so it provides Hary with a locus for a collective memory that encourages his audience's participation in the feelings of anger and grief that can be elicited from this empathetic experience with the poem's characters. In telling the reader specifically that 'Xviii score' (*Wall.* 1. 177) men were killed, Hary visualises for the reader large-scale atrocity, creating a more easily remembered event than the slightly more abstract invective that the Scots should know that the English 'neuyr ʒeit to Scotland wald do gud' (1.8). What I suggest here is that, while the specific incident did not itself take place, the Barns of Ayr episode comes to represent, synecdochally (or 'punctually'), the systemic trauma of English atrocity in Scotland. The Barns of Ayr fuses and crystallises myriad events into one single *readable* and *representative* moment that can be stored in the memory because of its violent intensity.[10] In doing so, Hary's 'memory' seemingly follows Augustine's concept of *colligere* – collecting – which Carruthers explains as having 'a specific meaning of gathering together the memories of what one has read and stored in separate places earlier, as well as a general meaning of collecting up earlier experiences of all sorts'.[11] It is through this process of collation and composition, Augustine suggests, that learning and the production of new knowledge occur; moreover, this extended understanding works emotionally, for 'memory also contains ... feelings (*affectiones*), not in the same way as they are present to the mind when it experiences them, but in quite a different way that is in keeping with the special powers of the memory'.[12] In inventing a mnemonic image, Hary also seeks to tag this recollection emotionally, and the scale of the Barns of Ayr episode is particularly appropriate to medieval *memoria*, which often

---

[10] Likewise, Riddy argues that the 'Englishmen's violation of Wallace's wife', in Book 5, is 'a version of their violation of Scotland. Scotland, we come to see, is [Wallace's] mother, wife and daughter'; 'Unmapping the Territory, p. 109.

[11] Augustine, *Confessions*, pp. 218–19; Carruthers, *Book of Memory*, p. 245.

[12] Augustine, *Confessions*, p. 220.

lauded the mnemotechnical possibilities of violence.[13] Moreover, emotional tagging makes this recollection paradoxically personal, encouraging readers to commit the singular, spectacular, event to memory. In this way, Hary's alternative facts act in similar ways to his use of racist language and metonymy that, R. James Goldstein has argued, enable Hary to justify excessive Scottish violence against the English.[14] In order for the episode to embed itself in the memories of his audience, Hary seeks to elicit not only emotions of grief in his description of the Barns of Ayr but, more importantly, feelings of anger directed against the English who, with 'suttelte and wykkit illusione', 'kest all the wayis thai mocht' put the 'worthi Scottis' into 'confusione' (*Wall.* 7. 4–6). There are other moments of English brutality within the *Wallace* and throughout Scottish history, but the Barns of Ayr episode acts as a culmination of horrific violence that brings Hary's protagonist and his audience together into a collective feeling of hatred and a desire for vengeance. As Hary addresses his audience at the end of the episode: 'ʒhe nobill men that ar off Scottis kind, / Thar petous ded ʒhe kepe in-to ʒour mynd / And ws rawenge quhen we are set in thrang' (7.235–7). The Barns of Ayr incident is at once personal and public, individual and collective, past and present. The episode demonstrates Scotland's loss of its nobles and governors at the same time as it represents the individual grief of Wallace for his uncle who has been killed. Just as Wallace can be understood as standing for Scotland throughout the poem, so the Barns of Ayr episode stands for the great number of violent attacks meted out by the English on Scotland and its people.

The Barns of Ayr episode thus becomes what Pierre Nora terms a *lieu de mémoire*: a site of commemoration – at once physical and symbolic – that emerges out of a desire to memorialise the past.[15] It is a specific narrative site to which Hary attaches the memory of Scotland's history. Hary creates a shared memory between the individual members of his audience (and also between text and audience) in order to bring the collective into being, for without shared memory, and a focus for it, collective identity cannot exist. At the same time, as Bower had done with the image of the bee in the Coupar Angus *Scotichronicon*, Hary also draws upon schematic forms for training the memory to suggest how this image might function within a collective imagination. The barn itself is a literal storehouse in the world of the narrative, but it acquires a more politically charged connotation when it becomes a macabre repository for the dead Scottish nobility, whose corpses are 'kest' by the English 'in the nuk' of the barn (*Wall.* 7. 226). The barn, then, is also

---

[13] Carruthers, *Book of Memory*, pp. 75, 167–72.

[14] Goldstein, *Matter of Scotland*, pp. 220–30.

[15] Pierre Nora, *Realms of Memory: Rethinking the French Past*, 3 vols. Volume 1: Conflicts and Divisions, trans. by Arthur Goldhammer (New York: Columbia University Press, 1996), p. 2.

HARY'S *WALLACE* AS A BOOK OF MEMORY   107

mimetic of the nation; in imagining the barn as a *lieu de mémoire*, Hary makes this building a focus for national grief and remembrance in place of myriad memories that it at once encompasses and overshadows. Similarly, Hary's narrative on the page becomes a physical storehouse of memory, just as chronicles – as a distinctive form of written testimony – become the collective receptacles for national memories. The episode thus draws upon the *ars memoria* as a way of fixing the atrocity in the minds of Hary's audience.

While Hary states at the beginning of the episode that the nobles could only enter the barn one at a time, the 'trew woman' (*Wall.* 7. 252) who speaks to Wallace after the incident has taken place recounts that 'Our trew barrouns be twa and twa past In' to the barn (*Wall.* 7. 271). Although the image of the Scottish nobles entering the barn in pairs recalls aristocratic processionals,[16] the image poignantly echoes Noah's Ark into which 'two and two went in' of 'every thing that moveth upon the earth', as 'the Lord had commanded' (Genesis 7: 8–10). Noah's flood was a common episode in the extant English mystery-play cycles, and G.R. Owst notes that it was one of the 'more familiar Biblical narratives' that would have been preached in the vernacular.[17] It is very likely that Scottish audiences would also have recognised its significance in symbolising God's judgment and his promise of salvation. Hary, therefore, harnesses a powerful image that would have been familiar to his audience and one that he could expect them to call to mind, and he combines this with the more learned uses of the image of the Ark in the training of the memory.

The presentation of Noah's Ark as a schema for the trained memory and as *memoria spiritualis* is discussed at length by Hugh of St Victor (*c.* 1078–1141) in *De arca Noe morali*, in which the Ark is depicted as a compartmentalised structure similar to the concept of the memory as a series of organised compartments.[18] Furthermore, Carruthers suggests that Hugh's *arca* (as Noah's Ark and as trained faculty) collapses the multiple objects to which it refers into the 'common metaphor of store-house ... as so many ancient and medieval metaphors of this type also do'.[19] When this idea is related to Hary's *Wallace*, it is possible to see that Hary combines the multiple meanings of the barn as storehouse within this passage. While this vision of Noah's Ark is not as

---

[16] I am grateful to John McGavin for reminding me of this in our conversations about the *Wallace* and memory.

[17] G.R. Owst, *Literature and the Pulpit in Medieval England: Neglected Chapter in the History of English Letters and of the English People* (New York: Barnes & Noble, 1961), p. 114. See also, Brian Murdoch, *The Medieval Popular Bible: Expansions of Genesis in the Middle Ages* (Cambridge: D.S. Brewer, 2003), pp. 96–126.

[18] For example, the twelfth-century Spanish *Beatus super Apocalypsim* held at the John Rylands Library, Manchester, depicts Noah's Ark as a structure with forty-two compartments. See Rylands Latin MS 8, fol. 15r.

[19] Carruthers, *Book of Memory*, p. 55.

108   REWRITING THE PAST IN SCOTTISH LITERATURE, 1350–1550

fully developed in the *Wallace* as it is in Hugh of St Victor's writing – in which the Ark acts as a complete ethical and moral structure allegorically representing the Church and the individual's spiritual progress – it is distinct enough to suggest that the memorial function of the Ark, and the moral impetus of memory, is being deliberately called to mind. This further highlights the importance of memory and knowledge to Hary's narrative, but it also reveals the ways in which the *Wallace* prompts its readers to store the poem's events in their individual memories at the same time as the collective experience of being a community of readers commits the Barns of Ayr episode to the public memory and written record.

Noah's Ark was meant to be a structure of salvation, rather than of destruction, and its recollection by Hary – perhaps purposefully – sits uncomfortably in this respect with the destruction meted out by the English in Ayrshire, in order to imprint itself in the memory. The *Wallace* seems to invert the biblical narrative in which the unworthy die and the worthy are saved; Hary deliberately juxtaposes the sense of salvation associated with the Ark with the cunning barbarity of the English at Ayr, and their conversion of the 'towboth' (*Wall.* 7. 202) into a slaughter-house. The 'towboth' was a public building used for the collection of tolls and customs, which sometimes also housed the prison and was the site of executions. Anne McKim indicates that in Hary's narrative of the Barns of Ayr, the reader is supposed to understand the Barns specifically as a prison, but in the context of Hary's commentary – that 'Sic a towboth sen syne wes neuir seyne' (*Wall.* 7. 202) – I think the broader sense is more likely.[20] Hary cannot believe that a tollbooth which took payment in lives could ever have existed: that a building designed to deal with legal matters has become the place in which such an unlawful act is perpetrated.

Following this image of destruction, the Barns of Ayr episode subsequently shifts to the description of the corpse of Wallace's uncle, whose body is brought from the Barns and which serves as a physical reminder of the destruction of the Scottish nobility. The narrative moves from the collective space of the Barns to the personalised tableau of Wallace's grief as the 'trew woman' tells Wallace that his uncle was 'Out off ʒon bern … born', and 'laid law on cald erd' before her (*Wall.* 7. 277–78). In an almost ritualistic manner, the woman kisses Ranald's 'frosty mouth' and, 'with a claith … couerit his licaym' (*Wall.* 7. 279; 281). The image of Ranald's corpse becomes the final moment of the Barns of Ayr episode, a disturbing and highly visual image conjured to stick in the mind, providing another – deliberately emotive – way in which the audience can remember and recollect the meaning of the Barns and what they represent, both for Wallace and for Hary's audience. Goldstein argues that, in this moment, which he determines to be 'one of the saddest moments of the

---

[20] See *Blind Hary: The Wallace*, ed. by Anne McKim (Edinburgh: Canongate, 2003), p. 17, n. to line 202.

poem', Hary 'constructs a pietà of words' in which the audience is 'invited to participate in the grief of the characters' in ways that late-medieval Passion lyrics invoke vicarious suffering alongside Mary.[21] In the mind's eye, the reader is encouraged to remember the visual scene of the crucified Christ embraced by Mary, but Hary was also writing for an audience who typically prepared corpses of loved ones for burial, which extends the participatory grief from literary and devotional association to Hary leading his audience through their own associative memories.[22] Textually, this pietà echoes – and poignantly reverses – the moment in Book 2 when Ranald meets Wallace, who he assumed was dead. Hurrying to Riccarton, Ranald immediately embraces Wallace and, although he 'mycht nocht spek', he 'kyst him tendirlye' while tears 'bryst fro his eyne two' (*Wall.* 2. 426, 428). Holding him, Ranald 'at the last rycht freindfully said ... / "Welcum, neuo, Welcum, deir sone, to me!"' (*Wall.* 2. 430–1).[23] The image of Ranald's corpse represents not only an individual man mourned by his nephew; Ranald's laid-out body, coupled with the memory of the Barns themselves, becomes symbolic of the state of the nation in relation to English brutality as Hary carefully associates Scotland's suffering at the hands of the tyrannical English with Christ's persecution under Pontius Pilate.

The death of Wallace's wife[24] in Book 6 is the audience's most recent textual memory of Wallace's grief that precedes the Barns of Ayr episode in Book 7, and Hary verbally parallels the two moments.[25] In Book 6, Wallace's wife saves him from English soldiers by providing an exit route to escape with his men. When the English realise that she has helped Wallace to evade them, they 'Put her to dede' (*Wall.* 6. 193). As with the subsequent Barns of Ayr episode, it is a 'trew woman' (*Wall.* 6. 197) who informs Wallace of 'how all this deid was done' (*Wall.* 6. 199). Hary writes that on learning of his wife's death, a 'paynfull wo socht till [Wallace's] hart full sone' (*Wall.* 6. 200) in a reaction that foreshadows his response to hearing of the death of Ranald.

---

[21] Goldstein, *Matter of Scotland*, pp. 229–30.

[22] D.S. Miall and Donad Kuiken term these emotions 'fiction feelings' and 'aesthetic feelings' where events of a story's plot or the aesthetic techniques of the text 'interrupt the reader's automatic processing of language and cue personal memories'; 'A Feeling for Fiction: Becoming What We Behold', *Poetics*, 30 (2002), 222–41 (esp. 223–5).

[23] Both of these incidents also foreshadow Wallace's lament for Sir John Graham following his death at the Battle of Falkirk; *Wall.* 11. 378–404.

[24] Critical scholarship usually refers to Wallace's wife as his *leman*, but she specifically refuses this moniker in Book 5, saying she 'wyll no lemman be' (*Wall.* 5. 693). Following this, I refer to the 'woman in Lanark' as Wallace's wife.

[25] Wallace briefly refers to the deaths of his father and brother in Book 3: 'Than Wallace said, "Her was my fadir slayne, / My brothir als, quhilk dois me mekill payne"' (*Wall.* 3. 111–12).

Hary follows the popular notion of the heart being the site of understanding and feeling as well as memory.[26] But the audience is also told that, were it not for 'schayme' (*Wall.* 6. 201), Wallace would have fallen to the ground, 'For bytter baill [*sorrow/anguish*] that in his breyst was bound' (*Wall.* 6. 202). Concealing ('fenʒeit'; *Wall.* 6. 208) his own feelings, however, Wallace's focus is on redirecting his companions' grief into action, remarking that 'Quhar men may weipe thar curage is the les; / It slakis Ire off wrang thai suld radres' (*Wall.* 6. 223–4).[27] This concealment is markedly different from Wallace's response to hearing of the death of Ranald, where he 'wepyt for gret los off his kyne / That with wnes apon his hors he baid' (*Wall.* 7. 272–3). Two immediate possibilities present themselves for the difference in reaction. The first is that, by the time of the Barns of Ayr, the cumulative effect of two significant deaths overwhelms Wallace. The second is that the death of Ranald, alongside so many other Scottish nobles, assumes a greater political and symbolic meaning. Hary provides little clue as to which meaning his audience should privilege, although Wallace's vision in Monkton church in Book 7, which I discuss later in this chapter, might indicate that the latter interpretation holds more weight. This sits at odds, however, with Wallace's response to the English queen, who asks him why he cannot stay away from 'violent wer' against the English (*Wall.* 8. 1325). Wallace's response begins with an account of Edward I's desire for overlordship in Scotland and a reference to the Barns of Ayr, but it ends with him weeping as he recounts the death of his wife, who 'dulfully was dycht' (*Wall.* 8. 1368). It is this memory that 'Out of [his] mynd … will neuir bid' (*Wall.* 8. 1369). These moments suggest that Hary's Wallace serves as a figure who models and fosters the audience's memorial practice through empathetic response to his sorrow. At various moments throughout the *Wallace*, but especially at the death of Wallace's wife and the Barns of Ayr episode, Hary confronts his audience with loss and mourning. The loss of his wife and his uncle become pivotal moments in Wallace's life and define his relationship with the English, who have perpetrated these crimes. Similarly the large-scale massacre of the Scottish nobility that sits alongside – and encompasses – Ranald's death is a moment of national punctual trauma that elicits collective grief in the *Wallace*'s audience. Here Hary demonstrates how the individual and the collective merge in the *Wallace*; read in this way, the Barns of Ayr can be seen as a collective moment – an abstraction – of mourning. This allows the reader at once to assimilate collective and individual memory

---

[26] Jager, *Book of the Heart*, esp. p. 4.

[27] As Andrew Lynch notes, because medieval emotion is cognitive and embodied, emotion and action are 'inseparable', and emotion is often treated as action; 'Malory and Emotion', in *A New Companion to Malory*, ed. by Megan G. Leitch and Cory James Rushton (Cambridge: D.S. Brewer, 2019), pp. 177–90 (178).

into a meaningful image where Ranald stands in place of many and active grief integrates loss into a new Scottish cultural identity.[28]

Throughout the *Wallace*, Hary prompts his audience to recall their inherited memories of violence in which their ancestors may have suffered, and these individual memories are brought together in the imagined atrocity of the Barns of Ayr, in which they take on national significance. In *Memory, History, Forgetting*, Paul Ricoeur proposes that loss 'constitutes a genuine amputation of oneself to the extent that the relation with the one who has disappeared forms an integral part of one's self-identity'.[29] What Ricoeur argues here is that the mourning that follows loss, which is a process of reconciliation, internalises this sense of severance and 'transforms the physical absence of the lost object into an inner presence': a presence that manifests itself in a creation of identity.[30] Textually, this is what Bower hints at in the Coupar Angus introduction: that the lost history he tries to reassemble becomes a defining feature of his own history. It also becomes a history that is essential for all Scots to keep in mind; it is a crucial part of what makes them Scottish. This concept of mourning is also present in the *Wallace*, in which Hary uses Wallace's personal loss, and the wider implication of the loss of Scotland's nobility, to create a feeling of sorrow within his audience for atrocities that took place nearly two centuries previously. The mourning, then, is not only for the events of the narrative, but also for the memories that Hary suggests were being forgotten in the pro-English policies of the late fifteenth century. Returning to the sentiment of the opening lines of the poem, Hary calls on those 'nobill men that ar off Scottis kind' to 'kepe' 'Thar petous dede ... in to ʒour mynd / And ws rawenge quhen we ar set in thrang (*Wall.* 7. 235–37). The repeated calls to *us* and *we* create a collectivity among Hary's readers – they are of one 'kind' [nature] – with which he aligns himself and Wallace, past and present. Hary uses the loss and mourning of Books 6 and 7 to prescribe and interiorise a Scottish identity formed around the figure of Wallace as a national hero: a man who did *not* forget the brutality of the English because it became part of his identity. At once, Hary appeals both to memory – he asks his readers to 'kepe in ... mynd' his story – and to the history that he is setting down as 'suthfast' (*Wall.* 12. 1451), recognising their complementary functions in identity formation, an identity that emerges from the storehouse of the murdered Scottish nobles. Hary's insistence on memory here notes the power of intergenerational trauma. This is specifically *not* a call to commemorate; by keeping this history in mind here, memory functions as an act of present repetition.

[28] Cf. Anderson's idea of the tomb of the unknown soldier in *Imagined Communities*, p. 4. The idea is similar here, although Ranald is given a name.

[29] Paul Ricoeur, *Memory, History, Forgetting*, trans. by Kathleen Blamey and David Pellauer (Chicago and London: University of Chicago Press, 2004), pp. 359–60.

[30] Ricoeur, *Memory, History, Forgetting*, p. 366.

112   REWRITING THE PAST IN SCOTTISH LITERATURE, 1350–1550

Ricoeur suggests that the 'historiographical operation' – that is, the act of historical reconstruction – can be seen to be the 'scriptural equivalent of the social ritual of entombment, of the act of sepulcher'.[31] He explains that 'Sepulcher ... is not only a place set apart in our cities', the 'place which we call a cemetery and in which we depose the remains of the living who return to dust'. It is 'an *act*, the act of burying'.[32] This is a distinct feature of Hary's *Wallace*, both in terms of providing a sepulchre for Wallace the man in the mind of Hary's audience, and also for Scotland's history as a whole. The reader sees briefly this idea of the act of sepulchre in the description of Wallace's uncle that I have just discussed. The recording of the scene as a moment of history points to Ricoeur's sense of a scriptural monument being created in the act of writing that mirrors the ritual of preparing and burying Ranald's corpse. In its invocation of Crucifixion iconography, the scene also posits Wallace's uncle as a martyr. This deliberate recollection prepares the reader for Wallace's death, which is specifically written to be seen as an act of national martyrdom. In grieving with Wallace for the deaths of his wife and uncle, the audience is finally invited to grieve for Wallace in Book 12.

As with the recalling of significant deaths in earlier books, Hary is reluctant to give the details of Wallace's death. The reader is never permitted to see Wallace-as-corpse – Hary 'will nocht tell' (*Wall.* 12. 1407) – although Hary briefly recounts for his audience what happened to Wallace's body: it was 'dewydyt' into 'v partis and ordand for to pas' (*Wall.* 12. 1407–8).[33] Yet, Hary claims, despite the fact that his body was fragmented, Wallace's 'spreyt by liklynes was weill' (*Wall.* 12. 1409). It is important for Hary that Wallace's spirit remains intact, not only so that it 'can fayr / To lestand blys' (*Wall.* 12. 1405–6), but also because of what Wallace's spirit signifies for a collective identity that revolves around his memory. Wallace's spirit, unlike his dispersed corpse, provides a single focal point for identity formation, another potential sepulchre. This sepulchre is markedly different, however, from the 'tomb' of

---

[31] Ricoeur, *Memory, History, Forgetting*, p. 365. 'To investigate the relation between history and memory, Ricoeur distinguishes three phases in the historiographic operation. The first is what he calls the "documentary phase". It is the phase of the eye-witnessing, indispensable for establishing the archives whose aim is to ground the evidence. This is to say that historiography is archived memory. The second phase is explicatory/comprehensive, where one seeks answers for specific questions of research. The third phase is called representative, this is the phase where one gives form in writing, where the historian declares the intention of representing the past as it happened'; Abdelmajid Hannoum, 'Paul Ricoeur on Memory', *Theory, Culture, and Society*, 22 (2005), 123–7 (127).

[32] Ricoeur, *Memory, History, Forgetting*, p. 366; my emphasis.

[33] Furthering the Christ-like images, the splitting of Wallace's body into five parts mirrors the five wounds of Christ as much as it recalls to mind the punishment for traitors.

HARY'S *WALLACE* AS A BOOK OF MEMORY   113

the Barns of Ayr because, although Wallace's physical body is dead, his spirit (like memory) lives on. Moreover, Hary cannot provide a physical monumental focus within the narrative after Wallace's death because nothing like that exists. Instead Hary's narrative, his 'worthi buk' (*Wall.* 12. 1451), and the very act of writing itself, become Wallace's sepulchre: a physical monument around which it was possible to gather and remember. Hary creates a link between the spirit and the letter; both provide a way of remembering Wallace and his 'nobille worthi deid' (*Wall.* 1. 2). In this way, Hary's *Wallace* exemplifies Ricoeur's conviction that sepulchre is both a place – the cemetery – and an act – the historiographical operation. The *Wallace* as material – and textual – document stands in for the non-existent tomb of Wallace, and so Hary's narrative assumes the role of sepulchre as a 'material place' and 'thus becomes the enduring mark of mourning, the *memory-aid* of the act of sepulcher'.[34] As an *aide-mémoire*, Hary's *Wallace* performs the social ritual of remembrance not only of the dead, but also of what it means to be Scottish.

Throughout the *Wallace*, Scottish integrity is pitted against English deviousness and attempts to wipe out Scottish resistance to their rule. Hary creates the Barns of Ayr (and the *Wallace* as a whole) not only as a sepulchre, but also as a *lieu de mémoire* to function as an abstract and permanent emblem of Scottish suffering that Hary fears was being 'smord' (*forgotten, suppressed, suffocated*) (*Wall.* 12. 1434). That is to say, the possibility of forgetting – forced or not, imagined or not – prompts Hary's rewriting of the past just as it had prompted Fordun and Bower. Nora maintains that, if 'we still dwelled among our memories, there would be no need to consecrate sites embodying them; *Lieux de mémoire* would not exist, because memory would not have been swept away by history'.[35] Hary hints at this historical necrosis in his admonition of the contemporary situation at the very beginning of the *Wallace*. At the same time, he seeks to prompt memory through his reimagining of history as a living story. Having begun his narrative by writing that the keeping alive of the memory of 'Our anteccessowris', and 'thar nobille worthi deid' should be of the greatest importance, Hary qualifies this by saying that 'vthir besynes' has taken precedence and that 'Till honour Ennymyis is our haile entent' (*Wall.* 1. 1–5). Matthew McDiarmid argues that in writing these lines Hary was directly criticising James III's policy of marriage alliances, which had provoked renewed anxiety regarding Scottish independence.[36] James's legacy is as an actively pro-English monarch, and his pursuit in 1474 of a marriage alliance between his son, James, then duke of Rothesay, and Cecily, the youngest daughter of Edward IV, was not popular, particularly among the Scottish magnates in the borders and who sympathised politically with James's brother, Alexander, duke of Albany. According to Norman

---

[34] Ricoeur, *Memory, History, Forgetting*, p. 366.
[35] Nora, *Realms of Memory*, p. 2.
[36] McDiarmid, *Wall.* i. xv.

114 REWRITING THE PAST IN SCOTTISH LITERATURE, 1350–1550

MacDougall, by the late 1470s, Albany had become 'an uncontrollable March Warden wrecking royal foreign policy'.[37] Alongside the 'unpopular and often arbitrary policies' pursued by James, Albany's own political ambitions gained support; the *Wallace*, therefore, can be read as a poem that 'boldly articulated the feelings of those who were opposed to the English alliance of 1474'.[38] Hary situates Scotland's 'ald Ennemys' firmly in England – they 'cummyn of Saxonys blud' (*Wall.* 1. 7) – a country that James was apparently favouring over the will of the Scottish nobility. Hary maintains that, rather than holding 'in mynde' (*Wall.* 1. 2) the memory of the Scots, James preferred to honour those who, as had 'beyne seyne in thir tymys bywent' (*Wall.* 1. 6), were Scotland's enemies. Hary intends his assertions to be read as statements of fact that Scotland's official policy under James III – its 'haile entent' – is 'Till honour Ennymyis' who, as demonstrated in Hary's narrative, desire to obliterate Scotland's sense of its independence, subsuming it into the governance of the English king.

Both Bower's preface to the Coupar Angus *Scotichronicon* (discussed in Chapter 3) and Hary's *Wallace* demonstrate an understanding that their texts function to (re)create what has been lost to the Scottish collective memory; that memories which are no longer lived – or within living memory – must be recollected so that they can be repeated through imaginative composition. To this end, Hary's *Wallace* and Bower's Coupar Angus *Scotichronicon*, as texts and as physical objects, become sites of memory themselves. History is repeated and recalled to Scotland's memory by Bower's account of Fordun's *patrio zelo* that prompted his 'collection' of lost history, and by Hary's account of Wallace's sacrifice for his nation. This sacrifice is narrated with strong religious overtones that align the *Wallace* with the narratives of saints' lives as Hary seeks to present William Wallace as Scotland's 'martyr' (*Wall.* 12. 1307). It is this idea of martyrdom that I now examine, for it indicates the ways in which Hary desired Wallace to be remembered by his Scottish readers.

William Wallace as Hary's Martyr

Hary's *Wallace* commemorates the life and deeds of a historical Scottish hero and, as such, contains written on its pages a remembrance of William Wallace in the form of a historical narrative. The manuscript book-as-object contains memory on a written surface: ink physically inscribed on vellum (or paper in the case of the extant *Wallace* manuscript) that has been stripped and pounded to provide a suitable surface on which to write. In the most fundamental of ways, then, the physical text of Hary's narrative functions as a way of setting down and organising Wallace's life into a memorable poetic and visual structure. In their introduction to *The Book and the Body*, Dolores

---

[37] See Norman MacDougall, *James III* (Edinburgh: John Donald, 2009), p. 534.
[38] MacDougall, *James III*, p. 248.

Warwick Frese and Katherine O'Brien O'Keeffe note the double meaning of *scribere*, meaning both to 'incise' and to 'write',[39] and in his telling of the narrative and his concentration on the violent episodes in Wallace's life, Hary draws on both of these meanings. Hary reminds his audience that the poem is a 'Remembrance' (*Wall.* 1. 179) – a creative composition. The *Wallace* is an act of poetic representation not only because of the historical distance of Hary's audience from the events being recollected, but also because of its historical *inaccuracy*, and it adopts memorial strategies both in its narrative and in its physical form. As a physical object Hary's text also performs and recollects the memorial function of the narrative. Carruthers argues that 'books are themselves memorial cues and aids, and memory is most like a book, a written page or a wax tablet upon which something is written'.[40] Moreover, she suggests, the 'metaphor of memory as a written surface' is 'so ancient' and 'so persistent in all Western cultures' that it must 'be seen as a governing model'.[41] I suggest that the *Wallace* itself acts as a memorial structure in its presence as a physical object (and, therefore, as a physical extension of memory), and in a metaphorical sense of being a structure in which memories can be set down and organised. Viewed in this way, the book itself supports the memorial process of the narrative of the *Wallace*.

Furthermore, Hary's poem is a memorial structure informed by violence, pain and compunction. As Carruthers notes:

> The 'wounding' of the page (in punctuation) and the wounding of memory (in 'compunctio cordis') are symbiotic processes, each a requirement for human cognition to occur at all ... violence seems to be a recurring preoccupation, almost a mnemotechnical principle.[42]

The link between incising and writing signified by *scribere* becomes clear in this description of the violence enacted upon the page as well as the memory. It suggests that violence occurs both in history – in the events taking place – and in the writing of history, through the physical process of creating the material text. Within the *Wallace*, Scottish historical collective memory is incised with the remembrance of English atrocity, but is transformed into a call to memory and identity by the regulated violence of the production of Hary's 'nobill buk, fulfillyt of gud sentens', his 'worthi buk, fullfillit of suthfast deid' (*Wall.* 12. 1449, 1451).

---

[39] Dolores Warwick Frese and Katherine O'Brien O'Keeffe, 'Introduction', in *The Book and the Body*, i–xviii (x).

[40] Carruthers, *Book of Memory*, p. 18.

[41] Carruthers, *Book of Memory*, p. 18.

[42] Carruthers, 'Reading with Attitude', p. 2.

Consequently, the *Wallace* as a physical object acts as a *Liber memorialis*, a book of memory, but one that is concentrated almost solely on William Wallace. *Libri memoriales* were first written in the Carolingian period and registered the names of those who had been the most frequent benefactors of the community.[43] Rosamund McKitterick argues that these *Libri* 'constitute written forms other than historical narratives in which the past was remembered and commemorated', and that the *Libri* 'augment oral modes and memory as a form of communication', functioning symbolically on 'many different social and spiritual levels'.[44] Ultimately, for McKitterick, they demonstrate the 'use of writing in commemoration and the recording of social memory'.[45] Hary adopts the function of the *Libri memoriales* and applies it to a national, rather than a local, context; the manuscript book of the *Wallace* registers the name and actions of one of Scotland's most important benefactors. But the *Wallace* also becomes a *Liber memorialis* for Hary in his own appeals to nationhood in the fifteenth century. Hary prays that his book will serve as a memory not only of Wallace's struggle against the English, of whom he 'slew / ... nocht halff enew' (*Wall.* 12. 1385–6), but also as one that inspires his audience not to forget the sovereignty that Wallace fought for. What I suggest here is that Hary seeks to register his own bequest to the Scottish national community – the preservation of Wallace's story in the public memory, a story and sentiment that he feared would be 'scour[ed] out' (*Wall.* 7. 16) if it was not set down as text.[46] The typical supplication that comes at the end of the poem also suggests this. Hary entreats his audience:

> I ӡow besek of ӡour benevolence
> ...
> For her is said als gudly as I can;
> My spreyt felis na termys of Pernase.
> Now besek god that gyffar is of grace,
> Maide hell and erd and set the hewyn abuff,
> That he ws grant off his der lestand luff.
> (Wall. 12. 1457–64)

---

43 Jacques le Goff notes that the 'custom of saying prayers for the dead became widespread early in the history of the Church', and these *Libri* provided a record of those to be remembered; *History and Memory*, trans. by Steven Rendall and Elizabeth Claman (New York: Columbia University Press, 1992), p. 72. On *Libri memoriales* see also Karl Schmid, 'Zur Problematik von Familie, Sippe und Geschlecht, Haus und Dynastie beim mittelalterlichen Adel: Vorfragen zum Thema "Adel Und Herrschaft im Mittelalter"', *Zeitschrift für die Geschichte des Oberrheins*, 105 (1957), 1–62.

44 Rosamund McKitterick, *History and Memory in the Carolingian World* (Cambridge: Cambridge University Press, 2004), p. 25.

45 McKitterick, *History and Memory*, p. 25.

46 *DOST* smord, *v.*, to smother; suppress, conceal, extinguish.

Similarly, at the end of the *Scotichronicon*, Bower writes: 'reader, in return for their prayers we ask you [to pray] that both authors [Fordun and Bower] may be dwellers in the realm of the sky' (*Chron. Bower* 8. 341). While the use of these tropes is to be expected, I think that they must be read, particularly in Hary's case, as an explicit attempt to register not only the narrative, but also its narrator, in the minds of the texts' audiences.

Libri were particularly associated with remembering martyrs, and Hary is keen to depict Wallace in this way at the end of the narrative; he explicitly tells his audience that 'Rycht suth it is, a martyr was Wallace' (*Wall.* 12. 1307). Wallace is a distinctly national martyr in his refusal to renounce the independence of Scotland and in his determination that the struggle must continue. His final words call out to the Scottish national imagination to remedy Wallace's regret that, for 'part Inglismen I slew / In my quarrell me thocht nocht halff enew' (*Wall.* 12. 1385–6). Far from a defeat of the Scottish cause, Hary seeks to rouse national feeling in his audience and to prompt the contemporary community to action by harnessing the popular tropes of the cults of saints and the dead. Saints' lives were 'absolutely staple and extremely popular reading matter' as well as being, 'arguably, one of the few literary forms to which we know that everyone would have been exposed, in the form of sermons'.[47] The memory of the *Wallace* becomes associational here: Hary deliberately pushes his audience to recall the saints' lives with which they would have been familiar and to transpose the significance of these onto his narrative's hero. Furthermore, in Book 7, Hary had unequivocally connected Wallace to St Andrew, Scotland's 'wowar' (*Wall.* 7. 124).[48] In the dream vision that Hary narrates, and which saves Wallace from being killed at the Barns of Ayr, Wallace sees an 'agit man' (*Wall.* 7. 72) who gives him a 'suerd ... off burly burnist steill', telling him: 'Gud sone ... this brand thou sall bruk weill' (*Wall.* 7. 75–6).[49] While *sone* is perhaps used merely as a friendly greeting here, it does carry with it the suggestion of a familial link. This does not mean that Hary's reader is to regard Wallace as the immediate descendant of this 'agit man'; rather, Wallace is his spiritual heir, and the transference of the sword from this ancient patron of Scotland to the near-contemporary Wallace creates a picture of Wallace as inheritor of a particular kind of Scottish guardianship: patriotic but not royal. The use of the genealogical trope here functions in similar ways to those discussed

[47] Katherine J. Lewis, 'History, Historiography and Re-writing the Past', in *A Companion to Middle English Hagiography*, ed. by Sarah Salih (Cambridge: D.S. Brewer, 2006), pp. 122–40 (123).

[48] *DOST*, vowar, *n.*

[49] A dream vision in which St Andrew presents Wallace with the bloody sword with which to defend Scotland also occurs in the Cupar Angus recension of *Scotichronicon* (*Chron. Bower* 6. 287).

in Chapter 2, highlighting communal relationships between men of 'Scottis kind' (*Wall.* 7. 235), synchronically and diachronically. This is emphasised by the creation of Wallace as guardian in Book 8 and, at the same time, the image legitimises Wallace's position as that guardian. Additionally, the Virgin in the vision 'With a saffyr sanyt [Wallace's] face and eyne' (*Wall.* 7. 94) and, while the reader immediately recalls the cross on which Christ was crucified, Hary's image of the blue sapphire (a sign of 'lestand grace'; *Wall.* 7. 140) also implies here that the Virgin may be making the sign of the saltire of St Andrew, again linking Wallace and Scotland's patron saint. The image of St Andrew gives the dream a particularly nationalist perspective in its location of Wallace as the heir to the Scottish nation: as Guardian, he becomes the *wowar* of Scotland and this is recalled in the monk's vision in Book 12 in which he sees 'Wallace, defendour off Scotland' (*Wall.* 12. 1285), as the man who 'tuk apon hand' Scotland's 'rychtwys wer', and who therefore deserves to be 'lowyt our the lawe' (*Wall.* 12. 1286–7). Using these tropes, Hary's narrative extends from a record of Wallace's deeds to a full *vita* (and even possibly a *passione* at the narrative's closing), establishing Wallace as a Scottish martyr, hero and near-contemporary patron saint. Wallace's martyrdom in Book 12 recollects the vision in Book 7, and Wallace is portrayed as being particularly St Andrew-like. Hary's *Wallace* demonstrates a call to national feeling and an assertion of Scottish independence from England through the very fact that they have their own patron saint and hero willing to fight for their cause.

If the aim of hagiography was to produce an exemplum of Christian life, then the *Wallace* capitalises on this idea. In exploiting the interrelationships between hagiography and historiography, Hary's narrative acts as a national hagiography, promoting Wallace as an exemplum of Scottish national feeling. Wallace is written to 'be a remembrance' (*Wall.* 12. 1456) and to be emulated by Hary's audience.[50] But Hary is not only content to depict Wallace in this way at the end of the poem: he treats him not only as saint-like but also as Christ-like, throughout the narrative.[51] As le Goff notes, if 'Christian memory manifests itself chiefly in the commemoration of Jesus … at a more popular level it focuses particularly on the saints and the dead'.[52] I have already suggested that the depiction of Wallace as a martyr at his execution marks him as both saint-like and Christ-like, but there are other instances in which this link is explicitly made. In Book 4, the woman whom Wallace has been visiting is persuaded to betray him to the English (*Wall.* 4. 718–32). When

---

[50] See Felice Lifshitz, 'Beyond Positivism and Genre: "Hagiographic" Texts as Historical Narrative', *Viator*, 25 (1994), 95–113.

[51] Cf. Joanna Huntington, 'Edward the Celibate, Edward the Saint: Virginity in the Construction of Edward the Confessor', in *Medieval Virginities*, ed. by Anke Bernau, Sarah Salih and Ruth Evans (Cardiff: University of Wales Press, 2003), pp. 327–43.

[52] Le Goff, *History and Memory*, p. 71.

she exposes the plot to Wallace, the woman mourns that she has 'falslye wrocht this trayn. / I haiff ʒou sald' (*Wall.* 4. 759–60). The image of Wallace being sold appears again in Book 12, in which Hary writes of Wallace's being 'sauld' to 'the Sotheroun' by the Scottish magnates.[53] *Sel* means both 'to betray' and 'to sell',[54] and here Hary explicitly associates Wallace's capture with the betrayal and selling of Christ by Judas Iscariot.[55] Conflating Christian and Scottish memory within the image of Wallace, Hary draws attention to his representation of Wallace as a martyr. In asking his book to 'byd thi tym and be a remembrance' (*Wall.* 12. 1458), Hary entreats his audience not only to see his narrative as the physical embodiment – the storehouse or treasure chest – of the memory of Wallace as such a figure, but to use his narrative as a support for their own memories of what being Scottish might mean. It is a national identity predicated on the reading and remembering of Scotland's history and, importantly, Wallace's sacrifice and suffering.

For a narrative that does not hesitate to dwell on violence, Hary is reluctant to provide explicit details of Wallace's execution and he does not allow him to feel pain. Instead Hary emphasises the saintly qualities with which he has invested Wallace throughout the narrative. Death without pain was a common trope of saints' lives; for example, St Cecilia was made to 'stonde in a bathe contynuelly boylynge', but 'felt neuer disese of hete but satte freshely as she had sete in a medw of sote floures'.[56] Likewise, Wallace's 'Gud deuocioun' that had been his 'begynnyng / Conteynd tharwith, and fair was his endyng' (*Wall.* 12. 1403–4). This image of the saintly Wallace further strengthens the link between Wallace and St Andrew that Hary has drawn in Book 7. Moreover, Felice Lifshitz notes that biography – whether of saints or of other figures – appears to have been the most popular form of historical narrative in the Middle Ages and that, between the ninth and eleventh centuries, hagiography and historiography were often indistinguishable. It should come as little surprise, then, that Hary's *Wallace* is simultaneously a historical narrative biography and a story with references to saints' lives in the presentation of Scotland's national hero.[57]

The points at which the *Wallace* makes reference to the book as a physical object are particularly important ones in demonstrating the links between memory and the book. One of the most significant allusions is made during Wallace's execution in Book 12. Hary states that a 'psalter buk Wallace had on him euir, / Fra his childeid fra it wald nocht deseuir' (*Wall.* 12. 1393–4).

---

[53] McDiarmid notes that this is in the manuscript, although he does not include it in his edition. See his note to 12. 1426 (*Wall.* ii. 121).

[54] *DOST*, sel, *v.*

[55] See Matthew 26: 1–16; Mark 14: 10–11; Luke 23: 47–49; John 18: 2–4.

[56] *Gilte Legende*, ed. Richard Hamer, with the assistance of Vida Russell. 2 vols. EETS OS 327, 328 (2006–7), II. 660.

[57] See Lifshitz, 'Beyond Positivism', pp. 95–113.

120   REWRITING THE PAST IN SCOTTISH LITERATURE, 1350–1550

From this the reader learns of the attachment that Wallace feels for the psalter which he has carried with him for the whole of his life, and the reader is made to empathise with Wallace's determination not to be parted from it even when he is 'dispulʒeid off his weid' (*Wall.* 12. 1396). Coupling the images of clothing and the book, Hary implies that Wallace's psalter has become part of his clothing and, by extension, part of the fabric of his identity, suggesting that the psalter has not only been a symbol of his Christian devotion, but also a physical reminder for Wallace of the 'rychtwys wer that he tuk apon hand' (*Wall.* 12. 1286) – a righteous war validated by 'Gud deuocioun (*Wall.* 12. 1403). Wallace asks Lord Clifford to 'lat him haiff his psalter buk in sycht' (*Wall.* 12. 1398) and the book is held 'oppyn befor him' while Wallace 'Stedfast … red, for ocht thai did him thar', until 'thai [the English] till him had done all at thai wauld' (*Wall.* 12. 1399–1401). The psalter here occupies a central place in Wallace's execution. Not only does it emphasise his devoutness – recalling the image of the Virgin choosing Wallace as her 'luf' (*Wall.* 7. 95) – and his belief in the divine sanction of his cause,[58] but it also places the book-as-object in a place of centrality to Wallace's sense of himself, implying the importance with which Hary viewed the material text in relation to Scottish identity and memory that the *Wallace* promotes.

The other important reference to the book as a physical object comes in Book 7, during Wallace's dream vision. After having 'sanyt [Wallace's] face and eyne' with a 'saffyr' (*Wall.* 7. 94), the Virgin presents Wallace with a 'buk' (*Wall.* 7. 105) that 'In iii partis … weill writyn was' (*Wall.* 7. 109). As Wallace attempts to read the book, he awakes. Just as the reader never learns which psalm Wallace is reading at his execution in Book 12, so Hary never tells us what kind of book Wallace is given – the reader learns only that it is split into three parts, each with different coloured letters (brass, gold and silver; *Wall.* 7. 110–11). What is of more importance to Hary here is not necessarily what the book is, but what it *represents*. The clerk interprets the meaning of the book not only for Wallace but also for Hary's reader. Wallace is told that the 'thrynfald buk' is 'bot this brokyn land' (of Scotland) that Wallace 'mon rademe be worthines off hand' (*Wall.* 7. 141–2). The book and its systematic division into three sections acts as a memory-aid for what was at stake in Scotland's struggle against the English. It also reminds the reader of the prophecy that Wallace will save Scotland three times before he dies: 'Off this regioune he sall the Sothroun send, / And Scotland thris he sall bryng to the pes' (*Wall.* 2. 348–9). At the end of Hary's narrative, the audience is able to see that Wallace has indeed been the 'reskew' of Scotland and has passed the cause onto Scotland's rightful king, Robert the Bruce (*Wall.* 12 1142–76).[59]

---

[58]   As he remarks to the English clerk, 'ʒon blyst byschop has hecht I sall haiff blis / And I trow weill at god sall it admyt' (*Wall.* 12. 1364–5).

[59]   As Anne McKim notes, the passage is 'an interesting exercise in propaganda as once again Blind Hary suggest[s] that Wallace fought to make Robert the Bruce's reign possible'; *The Wallace*, pp. 434–5, n. to lines 1164–76.

But I also argue that Hary implicitly draws his audience's memory back to the admonition at the beginning of the *Wallace*, suggesting an anxiety about becoming subject to the English through the contemporary policies of James III. This is also highlighted in Book 2 when Wallace is captured by the English, and the Scots fear him dead. The people lament that without Wallace 'This land is lost ... / Prophesye out, Scotland is lost in cayr' (*Wall.* 2. 169–70). While the lament is specific to the narrative that Hary tells, it is not difficult to see the contemporary resonance: Wallace is no longer alive, Scotland without Hary's retelling of Wallace's story is in danger of forgetting his struggle and sacrifice, and the rapprochement supported by James III increasingly threatened – Hary implies – the independence that Wallace had sought to win.

Throughout this chapter I have argued that, in the recreating and rewriting of history, Hary sought to embody the Scottish nation's historical narratives in a collective memory informed by traumatisation. This provides an insight into the creation of imagined histories that can be used for the purpose of fostering a common identity among the citizens of a nation. As I indicated in Chapter 1, common suffering acts as a unifying force for national sentiment. The sense of lost memory discussed in Chapter 3, along with its subsequent recovery or reassembly, provides the necessary focal point that gives the Scots a common identity through their collective grief. This is also shown in Hary's *Wallace*, in which the imagined histories of the Barns of Ayr, along with Wallace's martyrdom, are inscribed on the national memory and consciousness of the text's Scottish readers. Throughout the *Wallace*, Scotland's trauma becomes the necessary focal point of Scottish identity, reinforcing the vulnerable state of the nation. The book as memory-aid, then, serves to remind Hary's audience that its identity was in danger of being 'scoured out' by the English once more. But alongside these narratives of trauma and enforced forgetting of which Hary writes there comes a way of realising the nation – of bringing national consciousness into being. At once defining the Scots against the English and in relation to acts of violence, Hary begins to suggest that in looking to the 'spirit' of their own countrymen, the Scots might discover what it means to be Scottish. Where *Scotichronicon* potently suggests that it is possible to destroy books, but not memory, the *Wallace* indicates that it is possible to kill the body, but not the spirit. Bower and Hary thus posit the imagining of Scottish identity as a way of looking inward to the state of Scotland itself. This becomes an important way of thinking about Scottish identity in the early sixteenth century, where the national character is imagined as being embodied in the monarch. It is this idea that I examine next in relation to Sir David Lyndsay's early poetry.

5

Memory and Nation in Sir David Lyndsay's *The Dreme* and *The Testament of the Papyngo*[1]

Throughout this study I have argued that, for Scottish writers creatively recollecting the Wars of Independence, the past is crucial in shaping responses to the present situation; that is, rather than these historiographical and literary works being concerned solely with detailing the wars as historical record they recollect the past precisely to affect the present and the future. For example, in Chapter 4 I argued that Hary's *Wallace* creatively reimagines English violence as moments of punctual trauma, revealing a vehement conviction of the dangers posed to Scottish sovereignty and identity by rapprochement with the English. Hary's assessment provides one way of reading, but it is misleading. James III's policies, and his overall approach to governance, were met with opposition that resulted in open rebellion and his death at Sauchieburn in 1488; nevertheless, Alasdair MacDonald tempers the view that he alienated all of his nobility to note that James 'retained the loyalty of important intellectuals and counsellors, such as John Ireland and William Elphinstone'.[2] MacDonald points out that James III's reputation inevitably suffered because he 'had the ironic misfortune to be the father of a son whose reign is generally ... upheld as marking the Golden Age of late medieval Scotland'.[3] James IV's reign (1488–1513) began in the wake of regicide and parricide and ended with the catastrophic defeat at Flodden, following an invasion of England on behalf of the French king, Louis XII (1498–1515), with whom James had maintained

---

[1] Parts of this chapter appeared in an earlier version: '"I beseik thi Maiestie serene": Difficulties of Diplomacy in Sir David Lyndsay's *Dreme*', in *Authority and Diplomacy from Dante to Shakespeare*, ed. by Jason Powell and William T. Rossiter (London: Routledge, 2013), pp. 69–83.

[2] Alasdair A. MacDonald, 'James III: Kinship and Contested Reputation', in *Kings, Lords and Men in Scotland and Britain, 1300–1625: Essays in Honour of Jenny Wormald*, ed. by Steve Boardman and Julian Goodare (Edinburgh: Edinburgh University Press, 2014), pp. 246–64 (263). See also R.J. Lyall, 'The Court as a Cultural Centre', in *Scotland Revisited*, ed. by Jenny Wormald (London: Collins and Brown, 1991), pp. 36–48.

[3] MacDonald, 'Kinship and Contested Reputation', p. 246.

close relations.[4] James IV developed the fiscal practices of his father and 'exploited every device available to him to raise royal revenues ... while successfully retaining the loyalty of his leading subjects'.[5] With regard to Anglo-Scottish relations, James's campaign of 1496 – in support of Perkin Warbeck, the pretender to the English throne – saw the Scottish king flex his military muscles in the borders. In Norman MacDougall's assessment, James saw war as 'a forceful extension of diplomacy', but in 1496 all he achieved was a stalemate with his English counterpart, Henry VII.[6] For all of Hary's objections to rapprochement with the English in the 1470s, it was James IV's marriage to Henry's daughter, Margaret Tudor, in 1503 that brought Scotland and England into an alliance of sorts, although the Treaty of Perpetual Peace was short lived.[7] Most recently, Helen Newsome has demonstrated how Margaret sought to present herself as a mediator between the Scottish and English crowns, most notably when she assumed a brief regency for her son, James V, following James IV's death at Flodden in 1513.[8] In 1514, Margaret negotiated a peace with England, but her regency came to a rather abrupt end in the wake of her marriage to Archibald Douglas, sixth earl of Angus. James was placed into the care of John Stewart, second duke of Albany as Margaret and Douglas fled to England, with Douglas returning to Scotland in late 1515 and Margaret in 1517. From 1525 to 1528, amid a deteriorating marriage, Archibald Douglas took custody of the young king. This period immediately pre- and post-Flodden once again demonstrates the interconnectedness of Scotland's domestic and international relations. For at least one

---

[4]   As Roger Mason notes, 'Thousands of common soldiers died at Flodden', along with 'the king, his bastard son (the archbishop of St Andrews), a bishop, two abbots, nine earls, and fourteen lords of parliament'; Roger A. Mason, 'Renaissance and Reformation: The Sixteenth Century', in *Scotland: A History*, ed. by Jenny Wormald (Oxford: Oxford University Press, 2005), pp. 107–42 (112).

[5]   Mason, 'Renaissance and Reformation', pp. 110–11.

[6]   Norman MacDougall, *James IV* (East Linton: Tuckwell, 1997), p. 140.

[7]   Emily Wingfield briefly discusses the marriage of James and Margaret in *Scotland's Royal Women*, pp. 191–6. See also Sarah Carpenter, '"Gely with tharmys of Scotland and England": Word, Image and Performance at the Marriage of James IV and Margaret Tudor', in *Fresche Fontanis: Studies in the Culture of Medieval and Early Modern Scotland*, ed. by Janet Hadley Williams and Derek McClure (Newcastle: Cambridge Scholars, 2013), pp. 165–77.

[8]   Helen Newsome, 'The Function, Format, and Performances of Margaret Tudor's January 1522 Diplomatic Material', *Renaissance Studies*, 35.3 (2020), 403–24; Newsome, '"sche that schuld be medyatryce (mediatrice) In thyr (these) matars": Performances of Mediation in the Letters of Margaret Tudor, Queen of Scots (1489–1541)' (Unpublished PhD thesis, University of Sheffield, 2018). Newsome's edition of the holograph correspondence of Margaret Tudor is forthcoming with the Royal Historical Society Camden 5th Series.

early sixteenth-century writer, the court also provided a rich imaginative space in which to draw and reshape personal and public memories in the service of the king and the community of the realm.

The early poetry of Sir David Lyndsay subtly shifts the focus of memory and identity from remembering the Wars of Independence to an insular, even court-centred, perspective. In doing so, Lyndsay looks closer to home for the foundation of Scottish identity. In ways similar to, but also quite different from, Bower's interest in the political significance of the *mappa regni* in the *Scotichronicon* that I discussed in Chapter 2, Lyndsay's early poetry concentrates attention on the monarch as the essential locus of communal and national identity. In doing so, Lyndsay suggests that the individual character and behaviour of the monarch reflected and determined the state of the nation as a whole, and that good governance relied on a companionate relationship of regulation of body and kingdom. As J.H. Burns notes, though, early modern kingship was 'more than a matter of bringing personal character and power to bear upon the problems of government'; kingship was 'an institutional role' and the character of the king, 'the virtues (and vices) he possessed and displayed, were matters of great political importance'.[9] The link between sovereignty and morality was, of course, hardly a new idea in sixteenth-century Scotland; as Mapstone has shown, the Advice to Princes tradition is 'one of the most common motifs in the surviving fifteenth-century [Scottish] corpus'.[10] This interest continued into the sixteenth century, assuming a prominent politico-literary position during a prolonged period of minority successions. John Ireland's *Meroure of Wyssdome* was originally written for James III, but was rededicated to his son, James IV, in 1490. In the *Meroure*, Ireland explicitly sets out his educational project for the young monarch who, he insists, 'suld her and ler doctrine and sciens to gowerne eftirwart þe peple' of his kingdom.[11] The perceived failure of the king who rejected counsel and eschewed governing his person well became the focus of Robert Lindsay of Pitscottie's assessment of James IV's defeat and death at Flodden. Pitscottie remarks that the king 'wald vse no counsall for defence of his honour and preserving of his airme bot wssit himself to his awin sensuall plesouris quhilk was the cause of his rwen'.[12] David Lyndsay, therefore, draws on a long tradition of Advice to

---

9   J.H. Burns, *The True Law of Kingship: Concepts of Monarchy in Early Modern Scotland* (Oxford: Clarendon Press, 1996; repr. 2006), p. 2.

10   Sally Mapstone, 'Was there a Court Literature in Fifteenth-century Scotland?' *SSL*, 26 (1991), 410–22 (412).

11   *Johannes de Irlandia's The Meroure of Wyssdome*, vol. 3, ed. by Craig McDonald, STS 4th Ser., 19 (Aberdeen: Aberdeen University Press for the Scottish Text Society, 1990), p. 136.

12   Robert Lindsay of Pitscottie, *The Historie and Cronicles of Scotland*, ed. by Æneas J.G. Mackay, 3 vols, STS 1st ser., 42, 43, 60 (Edinburgh: William Blackwood and Sons, 1899–1911), i.276.

MEMORY AND NATION

Princes literature that assumes a particularly large presence in the cultural memory of late medieval Scotland.

What emerges through the sixteenth-century literature is a refocusing of the concerns of national identity, articulated within a reconsideration of Scotland's own political and cultural milieu during a period marked, as Elizabeth Ewan notes, by 'an unbridled self-confidence as its leaders asserted Scotland's place' as a sovereign state.[13] It is an expression simultaneously troubled by Scotland's internal politics and by the attempt to present to the outside world an image of Scotland as a major European power, a project in which both James IV and James V were particularly invested. Alongside this ambitious national fashioning, the focus on the king as the representative of this confident Scotland meant that a significant portion of late medieval Scottish literature concerned itself with the responsibilities of good governance.[14] The *Dreme of Schir David Lyndesay of the Mont* (1528) and the *Testament and Complaynt of Our Soverane Lordis Papyngo* (1530) focus on the regulation of the monarch's body that directly influences the health of the national body, presented in ethical terms of moral life and the foundation of good character. This moral aspect of nationhood reimagines the ethical foundations of memory and the reshaping of the past to suggest that, in being a good example to his people, the well-ruled – and well-ruling – monarch was therefore responsible, in part, for defining and upholding national character.

'Kepar of the Kingis grace': Sir David Lyndsay and the Court of James V

Little is known of Lyndsay's early life and education; he first appears in the court records during the reign of James IV and it is possible that he was involved in the literary activity of the court as early as 1511, when there is a record of payment made to one 'David Lindesay' for 'ane play coit ... for the play playt in the King and Quenis presence in the Abbay'.[15] He was the eldest son of David Lyndsay (d. *c.* 1524), a middle-ranking landowner, who held lands in the Mount, located just outside Cupar in Fife, and in Garleton near Haddington, East Lothian. Initially usher to the young prince James, in

---

[13] Ewan, 'Late Medieval Scotland', p. 19.

[14] See, for example, James I's *The Kingis Quair* (1424), John of Ireland's *Meroure of Wyssdome* (*c.* 1489), and the late fifteenth-century *The Quare of Jelusy*. On the *Kingis Quair* and the *Quare of Jelusy*, specifically, see Martin, *Kingship and Love*, pp. 19–40.

[15] T. Dickson and Paul J. Balfour (eds), *Accounts of the Lord High Treasurer of Scotland*, 12 vols (Edinburgh, 1877–1916), vol. 4, p. 313. For a more detailed discussion of Lyndsay's political career, see Carol Edington, *Court and Culture in Renaissance Scotland: Sir David Lindsay of the Mount* (Amherst: University of Massachusetts Press, 1994).

1513 Lyndsay found himself 'kepar of the Kingis grace', or 'maister uschar'.[16] Responsible for James V's safety, Lyndsay was thus at the centre of the royal household, at least until 1524, when Archibald Douglas, Margaret Tudor's estranged second husband, took custody of James and Lyndsay was replaced at court. James escaped from his stepfather in 1528, and Lyndsay was reinstated, being appointed herald, an office in which he represented the crown both at home and abroad.[17] In 1530, Lyndsay was appointed Snowdon herald, an office that provided both livery and an annual fee. He was officially appointed Lyon king of arms, the highest heraldic office in Scotland, in October 1542, the same year in which he was knighted.[18]

Lyndsay's literary output, particularly from 1528 to 1530, was thus being produced in the intimate environment of James V's court and the beginnings of his personal rule, something relatively unusual in medieval Scotland, where literature was more likely to come to the court, rather than emanate from it.[19] Moreover, Lyndsay's early poetry is often directly concerned with court life, indicating, as Sarah Carpenter has noted, that Lyndsay sought to influence the young James V by using his 'privileged private involvement in the king's affairs' in his poetry.[20] While Lyndsay's later texts, most notably his *Satyre of the Thrie Estaitis* (1540s), have attracted much critical attention, his earlier work has received far less consideration. Yet it is Lyndsay's earliest poetry that is particularly significant for examining the role of memory in kingly governance and literary patriotism.

Sir David Lyndsay is thought to have composed his *Dreme* around 1528, the year in which James V assumed his majority. Framed by a prologue and an exhortation in which Lyndsay addresses the king directly, the poem is a dream vision allegory of contemporary Scotland in which the dream-narrator falls asleep and is taken on a tour of the earth and the heavenly spheres. Immediately after the narrator has fallen asleep, he sees a lady of 'portatour perfyte' and, demanding her name, learns that she is called 'Dame Remembrance' (*Dreme*, 148, 154). Remembrance leads the narrator on a journey through hell, purgatory, the heavens, the planetary spheres and earth.

---

[16] Treasury records show that from 1512, Lyndsay was in receipt of a royal pension of £40. See Dickson and Balfour (eds), *Accounts of the Lord High Treasurer of Scotland*, vol. 4, pp. 269 and 441.

[17] *RPS* 1528/9/4.

[18] J.K. McGinley, 'Lyndsay [Lindsay], Sir David (1486–1555), writer and herald', *ODNB* [accessed 16 May 2015].

[19] Mapstone, 'Court Literature', esp. pp. 413, 420–2.

[20] Sarah Carpenter, 'David Lindsay and James V: Court Literature as Current Event', in *Vernacular Literature and Current Affairs in the Early Sixteenth Century: France, England and Scotland*, ed. by Jennifer and Richard Britnell (Aldershot: Ashgate, 2000), pp. 135–52 (140).

MEMORY AND NATION   127

She then provides the Dreamer with a description of the 'deuisioun of the Eirth' before showing him 'Paradyce' (*Dreme*, 659–76, 757). This, in turn, prompts the Dreamer to ask his guide to 'schaw' him the 'countre of Scotland' (*Dreme*, 788), at which point the Dreamer cannot comprehend how a country of 'gret commoditeis', with an 'haboundance of fyschis in [the] seis', 'suld nocht ... redound' 'considderand the peple and the ground' (*Dreme*, 81–7, 838–40). In addition to dispensing conventional princely counsel, this visionary journey is systematic, encompassing what would have been considered established knowledge. Through this journey, Lyndsay provides James V with pertinent information about his realm precisely when he most needed it: at the outset of his personal rule. As part of a poem – a story like those with which Lyndsay used to entertain the king in his infancy – this chorographical and histo-riographical material is rendered more readable than, for example Boece's *Scotorum Historiae*. This is not only because the poem is in Scots rather than Latin but because it is presented as a continuation of the material of the story, therefore appealing to the king as entertainment.[21] At this point, the Dreamer and Remembrance enter into a dialogue in which Remembrance seeks to answer the Dreamer's questions about the ways in which Scotland is no longer experiencing a golden age. Remembrance explains that the lack of prosperity in Scotland is not the fault of the 'peple nor the land' (*Dreme*, 845); the 'cause of thir vnhappynes' is 'Wanting of Iustice, polycie, and peace' (*Dreme*, 861). Furthermore, Remembrance makes it clear that she finds the 'falt in to the heid', for 'thay in quhome dois ly our hole relief, / I fynd tham rute and grund of all our greif' (*Dreme*, 878–80). Remembrance concludes:

> The causis principall
> Off all the trubyll of this Natioun
> Ar in to Prencis, in to special,
> The quhilkis hes the Gubernatioun,
> And of the peple Dominatioun,
> Quhose contynewall exersitioun
> Sule be in Iustice Exicutioun. (*Dreme*, 883–9)

Remembrance's final remark several stanzas later provides a bleak outlook, for 'rycht difficill is to mak remeid, / Quhen that the falt is so in to the heid' (*Dreme*, 916–17). This damning tirade, which reminds the reader of the self-interested rulers the Dreamer encounters in the spheres of hell, places responsibility for Scotland's prosperity directly at the feet of the monarch. At this point in the poem the Dreamer and Remembrance are interrupted by a

---

[21] I am grateful to Janet Hadley Williams for this suggestion. It is also worth noting that, at the beginning of the 1530s, James V commissioned John Bellenden to translate Boece's *Scotorum Historiae* into Scots.

'boustius berne' (*Dreme*, 919) who, identifying himself as 'Iohne the comoun weill' (*Dreme*, 931), begins a lament about the plight of Scotland and its lack of good governance that, through the lens of his personal experience, reaffirms everything that Remembrance has just told the Dreamer. It is at this point that Remembrance leads the Dreamer back to the 'cove quhare [he] began to sleip' (*Dreme*, 1017). Before he wakes, the dreamer sees a ship 'spedalye approche' that loosens its sails and 'gan to creip / Towart the land' (*Dreme*, 1019–20). The dreamer experiences 'ane fellown fraye' from the 'cannounis sche leit craik of at onis' and the mariners who 'did so youte and yell' (*Dreme*, 1022–23, 1027), while the ship's assault shakes the 'stremaris frome the topcastell' (*Dreme*, 1024). Here Lyndsay presents a possible future too much like the past that Dame Remembrance has just shown the Dreamer; it is this prospect of division and invasion that 'haistalie' wakens the Dreamer and prompts his hasty return home (*Dreme*, 1028). Removing himself 'in tyll an Oritore', the Dreamer takes his pen and begins the creative composition of setting down 'All the visioun' (*Dreme*, 1031–33) for the king. The prayer that concludes the dream section of the poem exhorts to James the benefit of an opposite kind of future to that presented by the rapidly approaching ship: 'I beseik God for to send the grace / To rewle thy realme in unitie and peace' (*Dreme*, 1035–6). The *Dreme* then ends with an Exhortation to James V, focusing on the young king's responsibilities as Scotland's monarch and urging him to take action to relieve Scotland's troubles.

It is clear from the name of the dreamer's guide – Dame Remembrance – that memory underpins this poem, and this is made explicit in the poem's frame address directly to James V, where it strikes a distinctly personal cadence, requiring the poem's principal reader, the king, to engage in specific acts of memory work. In the 'Epistil' to the *Dreme*, Lyndsay reminds James, the 'Rycht Potent Prince of hie Imperial blude', that

> Sen thy birth, I haue continewalye
> Bene occupyit, and aye to thy pleasoure;
> And, sumtyme, seware, Coppare, Caruoure,
> Thy purs maister, and secreit Thesaurare
> Thy Yschare, aye sen they Natyuitie,
> And of they chalmer cheiffe Cubiculare,
> Qhuilk, to this houre, hes keipit my lawtie. (*Dreme*, 19–25)

Similarly, in the *Complaynt of Schir Dauid Lindesay* (*c.* 1530), Lyndsay asks James to remember how he

> bure thy grace vpon my bak,
> And, sumtymes, strydlingis on my nek,
> dansand with mony bend and bek.
> The first sillabis that thow did mute
> Was *pa, Da Lyn.* (*Comp. Lynd.* 88–92)

MEMORY AND NATION

In both poems, Lyndsay deliberately asks James to remember that, in the unstable environment of the young king's minority, it was Lyndsay who, alongside his other duties at court, was responsible for his safekeeping. And, while Lyndsay suggests a willingness to maintain the role held since James's 'Natyuitie', his use of 'my lawtie' indicates a desire for, or a perceived entitlement to, recompense in light of his former role. Indeed, in his *Complaynt*, Lyndsay teasingly requests that James V grant him a loan of 'ane thousand pound or tway' (462), and in stressing loyal service in the *Complaynt of Bagsche*, the out-of-favour royal hound Bagsche apppeals to 'gude brother Lanceman, Lyndesayis dog, / Quhilk ay hes keipit thy laute' (89–90). The *Dreme*, and these other early works, therefore, petition the new king not to forget the welfare of those who have his best interests at heart.

In detailing his responsibilities within the Stewart household, Lyndsay capitalises on the double meaning of his role as James's 'purs maister and secreit Thesaurare'. These are both financial offices, at least on one level, and the phrase immediately suggests that Lyndsay was the keeper of the king's accounts and private treasury, but there is another layer of meaning here: if Lyndsay was James's private secretary, he was also the keeper of the king's secrets. This has important implications for Lyndsay's self-representation within the royal household and indicates that he was entrusted with James's most intimate affairs.[22] As previously noted, the thesaurus (or storebox) was an important image in medieval memory techniques, providing a way of visualising the mind as a compartmentalised structure in which memories could be organised and stored. Lyndsay thus posits himself as a keeper – and, therefore, also as a recollector – of the king's personal memories. Given the familiar tone of the *Dreme*'s prologue, and the exploitation of Lyndsay's intensely personal memories of James V's childhood, this seems to be a position that the poet does not want to relinquish. From the outset, the reader sees Lyndsay using the memorial function politically and with a view to situating his text and himself within an advisory role.[23]

This advisory stance is reinforced throughout the *Dreme*'s prologue, particularly at the moment where Lyndsay recalls at length the stories that he used to tell the young king: stories of Hector, Arthur, Jason and the 'Prophiseis of Rymour' among others (*Dreme*, 32–46). These tales, all exemplary and easily recognisable as such, provide an interpretive context for the 'storye of the new' that Lyndsay tells the king he is about to narrate. The inclusion of Thomas the Rhymer (*c.* 1220–*c.* 1298), famous for his prophetic writings,

---

[22] On the administrative roles imagined by these lines, see Athol L. Murray (ed.), 'Accounts of the King's Pursemaster, 1539–40', *Miscellany of the Scottish History Society*, 10 (1965), 13–51.

[23] See Janet Hadley Williams, 'David Lyndsay and the Making of James V', in *Stewart Style, 1513–1542: Essays on the Court of James V*, ed. by Janet Hadley Williams (East Linton: Tuckwell, 1996), pp. 201–25.

provides a particularly Scottish context for the dream vision that James is about to hear. James and the rest of Lyndsay's audience must discern that this new story will have an advisory component and should be understood as seeking to provide instruction within a specifically Scottish framework.[24] In this way, Lyndsay portrays himself as having acted not only as James's servant, but also as an educator, one who has tried to teach the young king the arts of good governance through examples from antiquity. At the same time, Lyndsay leverages his knowledge of James's personality to entertain as well as teach and advise the young monarch. In both the *Dreme* and the *Testament of the Papyngo* (discussed later in the chapter), he uses dramatic delivery to amuse and enliven the didactic content. At this point, then, Lyndsay is not only a 'secreit Thesaurare' (a storehouse), but a poet who can create and recreate memory imaginatively and for the situation at hand. What Lyndsay presents next – his 'storye of the new' – is a far more contemporary example, but one which requires its reader to recollect the previous stories that form its advisory framework. The *Dreme*'s Epistil thus pre-empts the role of Dame Remembrance within the dream vision, prompting the reader to see her not only as a guide but also as a mode of interpretation. The Epistil and its partner Exhortation at the end of the poem frame the narrative of the dream-narrator's account of his vision and the events leading up to it, as well as a providing a context for the interpretation of the dream itself.

The dream vision was a well-established form in Scotland by the fifteenth century and it continued to flourish into the sixteenth. I briefly discussed in the previous chapter the use of the dream vision as a form of prophecy in Hary's *Wallace*, and Bower's *Scotichronicon* contains about eighty dream visions, suggesting a political use of the genre in Scotland. But dream visions did not just appear in these epic and historical texts and are made use of throughout the Scots literary corpus. For example, the *Kingis Quair* (*c*. 1424), surviving uniquely in Bodleian Library, MS Arch. Selden. B. 24, is a semi-autobiographical poem attributed to James I, which, although it touches on the Advice to Princes tradition, leans more toward the amatory than the overly political.[25] The form continues in such texts as Robert Henryson's fifteenth-century *Testament of Cresseid*, in William Dunbar's 'Quhen Merche wes with variand windis past' (concerning the marriage of James IV and Margaret Tudor in 1503) and *The Goldyn Targe* (1490s), and in Gavin Douglas's *The Palice of Honour* (1503), although these works do not focus explicitly on advisory concerns. Lyndsay does, however, note his debt to Douglas in particular,

---

24 It is also possible that Lyndsay refers here to 'The Prophesies of Rhymour, Beid, and Marlyng', a poem popular in Scotland and the north of England. See Marcus Merriman, 'Mary, Queen of France', in *Mary, Queen of Three Kingdoms*, ed. by Michael Lynch (Oxford: Blackwell, 1988), pp. 291–9.

25 See Martin, *Kingship and Love*, esp. pp. 19–39.

MEMORY AND NATION

131

whom he regards as having 'prerogative' – superiority – 'abufe' all of his contemporaries 'quhen he wes in to this land on lyue' (*Papyngo*, 27–30). Thus, rather than seeming an outdated genre in late medieval and early modern Scotland, the dream vision was still being used as an authoritative vehicle for the exploration of sensitive political dilemmas. This is not to say that it did not change and evolve in this period; while Douglas Gray argues that later medieval examples of the genre 'cannot match the subtlety of Chaucer or the strange power of Langland', he suggests that the works of Dunbar, Douglas and Skelton 'triumphantly demonstrate the genre's power and possibilities'.[26] Moreover, there seems to be a change in the concerns of the use of the dream vision after Flodden; where the poetry of Dunbar and Douglas revels in the flourishing cultural environment of James IV's court, Lyndsay's writing, despite being influenced and informed by this period, is preoccupied with the uncertainty and instability of another Scottish minority kingship, seeing James IV's court as a lost golden age to be remembered and lamented.

The main section of Lyndsay's *Dreme*, the dream vision itself, begins in a conventional style: Lyndsay's narrator finds himself unable to sleep 'throuch heuy thocht' (*Dreme*, 66). However, instead of picking up a book to read, as the narrators of Chaucer's *Parliament of Fowls* and Henryson's *Testament of Cresseid* do, he wanders through the 'sleit' (*Dreme*, 61) to the sea, where he finds a cave in which to rest, with the purpose of passing the time with 'pen and paper to Register, in ryme, / Sum mery mater of Antiquitie' (*Dreme*, 122–3).[27] Recording how his 'spreit' was 'opprest' with 'sleip' (*Dreme*, 140), the narrator, 'Constranit ... to sleip', 'dremit' 'ane maruellous visioun' (*Dreme*, 145–7). Where the dream visions of Chaucer, Langland, Dunbar and Douglas open with descriptions of springtime, Lyndsay's *Dreme* situates the narrator within the harsher and bleaker winter month of January, in which 'snaw and sleit perturbit all the air' (*Dreme*, 61). While this is reminiscent of Henryson's opening to the *Testament of Cresseid* with its 'doolie sessoun' of Lent in which 'Schouris of haill gart fra the north discend',[28] there are also parallels with John Bellenden's 'Proheme apon the Cosmographie', another political

---

[26] Douglas Gray, 'Gavin Douglas', in *A Companion to Medieval Scottish Poetry*, pp. 149–64 (151).

[27] Geoffrey Chaucer, *The Parliament of Fowls*, in *The Riverside Chaucer*, ed. by Larry D. Benson and F.N. Robinson, 3rd edn (Oxford: Clarendon, 1987), pp. 385–94; Robert Henryson, *The Testament of Cresseid*, in *The Poems and Fables of Robert Henryson*, ed. by H. Harvey Wood (Edinburgh and London: Oliver and Boyd, 1958), pp. 103–26.

[28] Henryson, *Testament of Cresseid*, lines 1–7.

poem from a writer with close connections to the household of James V.[29] The 'Proheme' opens with a wintry astrological scene:

> The frosty nicht wᵗ hir prolixit houris
> hir mantill quhyt spred on the tendir flouris.
> Quhen ardent labour hes addressit me
> Translait the story of oure progenitouris.
> Thair greit manheid wisdom and honouris.
> Quhair we may cleir (as in ane mirror) se
> The furius End sumtyme of tirannye.
> Sumtyme the gloir of prudent gouernouris
> Ilk stait apprysit in thair facultie
> My wery spreit desyring to repress
> My Emptiue pen of frutles besiness
> Awalkit furth to tak the recent are.[30]

In both the *Testament of Cresseid* and the *Dreme*, Henryson and Lyndsay's narrators seek out the distinctly practical way of escaping the 'snaw and sleit' of the Scottish coastal environment by visiting caves on the shoreline. Lyndsay's cave also has distinctly memorial implications and serves as a memory space within the poem. The narrator envisages using the cave as a natural oratory in which to pursue his writing (*Dreme*, 120–3) and, like the storebox, it acts as an analogy for memory itself. As Albertus Magnus observes in his commentary on *De memoria et reminiscentia*:

> Those wishing to reminisce [i.e. wishing to do something more spiritual and intellectual than merely remember] [should] withdraw from the public light ... because in the public light the images of sensible things are scattered and their movement is confused ... This is why Tullius in the *ars memoranda* ... prescribes that we should imagine and seek out dark places having little light.[31]

---

[29] Between August 1515 and August 1522, Bellenden was employed as *clericus expensarum* (clerk of expenses) in James's household. His involvement with the court in many ways mirrors Lyndsay's as both appear to have become casualties of the duke of Albany's regency before being reinstated at the king's assumption of personal rule in 1528. Lyndsay refers to Bellenden's literary activities in *The Testament of the Papyngo*, line 51. See Nicola Royan, 'John Bellenden [Bannatyne], *c*. 1495–1545x8, poet and translator', *ODNB* [accessed 3 November 2021].

[30] John Bellenden, 'The proheme of the croniculs compylit be the famous and Renownit clerk maister Iohine bellentyne', in *The Bannatyne Manuscript Written in Tyme of Pest, 1568 by George Bannatyne*, ed. by William Tod Ritchie, 4 vols, STS 2nd ser., 22, 23, 26; 3rd ser., 5 (Edinburgh and London: William Blackwood and Sons, 1928–34), vol. 2, pp. 9–19, lines 10–21.

[31] Albertus Magnus, *De memoria et reminiscentia, Opera omnia*, ed. by Borgnet, IX, p. 108; cited in Yates, *Art of Memory*, p. 79.

As the narrator's idea is to 'defende' himself from 'Ociositie' (idleness) in the cave (*Dreme*, 121), it is not improbable that his desire to 'Regester, in ryme', involves memory work of the intellectual kind – reminiscence and active composition – that forms the basis of the poem itself. In addition to using the cave as a space in which to conduct memory work, the narrator's disposition also invokes the memorial activity that takes place throughout the poem. The *Dreme*'s opening, with its melancholic narrator unable to sleep because of his 'Remembryng of diuers thyngis gone' (*Dreme*, 67), points to a moment of unorganised recollection that seems to derive from Aristotle's theory that melancholics remember uncontrollably because they are too fluid; the narrator's sleepless state is a consequence of being out of humoral and memorial balance.[32] Yet, Boncompagno (b. *c.* 1170) posits that those suffering from melancholia retain information well due to their hard and dry disposition. Albertus appears to negotiate these two aspects of melancholia and memory and, in discussing the 'type of melancholia which is the temperament of *reminiscibilitas*', he proposes that the 'temperament of reminiscence' is not the dry-cold melancholy that Boncampagno argues allows for good memory, but the 'dry-hot melancholy' that is 'intellectual' and 'inspired'. The *Dreme*'s narrator appears to display all of these attributes at some point throughout the poem, but, in the instance of his seeking shelter in the cave, it would seem that the uncontrollable memory that keeps him awake gives way to the inspired and intellectual reminiscence of the dream itself. Giulio Camillo also uses the cave as one of the grades of his memory structure; in part, this is linked to Saturn, the planet of melancholy, suggesting that Lyndsay's *Dreme* draws on quite specific images of the cave and its connection to memory and melancholia.[33] Coupled with the image of the cave as a space for memory (rather than simply as a practical place of shelter), the beginning of the *Dreme* specifically points to the use and importance of memory within the poem and its fundamental association with individual consciousness that will have a bearing on the state of the nation later in the poem.

On his way to the cave, the *Dreme*'s narrator meets 'dame Flora', 'dissagysit' in 'dule weid', reminiscing that in May she 'wes dulce and delectabyll' (*Dreme*, 78–9). Moreover, the 'small fowlis' make 'great lamentatioun' to Nature, saying 'blyssit be Somer, with his flouris; / And waryit be thow, winter, with thy schouris' (*Dreme*, 85–91). Lyndsay's use of symbolic naturalism here hints at the pessimism of the dream to come, in particular the dialogue section in which the Dreamer comments on the natural fertility of the land of Scotland, which is being misused; this is followed by the complaint of John the Commoun Weill. In stark contrast to, and yet with strong echoes of,

---

[32] Aristotle, *De memoria*, 453a 14. This is an idea I return to in my discussion of *The Complaynt of Scotland* in Chapter 6.

[33] See Yates, *Art of Memory*, pp. 69, 165.

Dunbar's *Goldyn Targe*, in which the narrator sees 'May, of myrthfull monethis quene, / Betuix Aprile and Iune hir sistir schene', Lyndsay's *Dreme* points to the political instability of the 1520s that meant Scotland was experiencing the opposite of the sunny paradise that Dunbar describes.[34] This is not to say that Lyndsay's poem finds no consolation or opportunity for a return to a glorious age like that of James IV's rule; the Exhortation, for all its stern language and demands, reminds the reader of the lessons of the dream and indicates that it is possible to return Scotland to a state of stability and wealth. This, however, must begin from a point of recollection and the use of a good memory to prompt correct action. Lyndsay tells James:

> Faill nocht to prent in thy Remembrance,
> That he [God] wyll nocht excuse thyne Ignorance,
> Geue thow be rekles in thy gouernyng.
> Quharefore, dres the, abone all vther thing,
> Off his lawis to keip the obseruance,
> And thow schaip lang in Ryaltie to ryng. (*Dreme*, 1040–45)

Lyndsay's *Dreme* argues that what is required for a stable nation is the education and good counsel of the king, allowing him to 'Tak Manlie curage, and leif thyne Insolence, / And vse counsale of nobyll dame Prudence' in order to 'Drawe to thy courte Iustice and Temporance; / And to the Commoun weill haue attendance' (*Dreme*, 1064–5, 1067–8). As a cardinal virtue, Prudence was one of the four chief moral virtues, along with justice, temperance and fortitude, to which Lyndsay refers in this advice to James.[35] For Lyndsay, the wisdom and prudence of the king (mastered by ethical self-government), as well as the good advice of his counsellors, provide the way by which Scotland can return from a cold winter to a 'blyssit' summer (*Dreme*, 90). From its outset, then, Lyndsay's *Dreme* serves as an advisory piece, not only for the young king to whom it is specifically addressed, but also implicitly for those would-be advisors and for a wider Scots audience. At its heart, the *Dreme* advocates that the return to a glorious age of Scottish political and cultural identity is achievable through a concerted effort of good governance, which is informed and motivated by memory.

---

[34] William Dunbar, *The Goldyn Targe*, in *The Poems of Willliam Dunbar*, ed. by Priscilla Bawcutt, 2 vols (Glasgow: ASLS, 1998), vol. 1, pp. 184–92, lines 82–3.

[35] Lyndsay also refers to the 'four gret verteous cardinalis'; *The Complaynt of Schir David Lindesay*, in *Sir David Lyndsay: Selected Poems*, ed. by Janet Hadley Williams (Glasgow: ASLS, 2000), pp. 41–57, line 379. He lists them at lines 380–90.

Prudence in Scotland

The *Dreme* is not unique in advocating prudence as central to the remembrance of good governance; it is a concern that appears in Scottish literature from at least the time of John Barbour's *Bruce* and was an idea that the earlier Brucean propaganda machine sought to promote. It is certainly the aspect of kingship that preoccupies the Stewart dynasty, which constantly looked to secure the memory of Bruce as a political and behavioural model. Furthermore, in Book 12 of the *Scotichronicon*, Bower specifically refers to the quality of prudence in relation to King Robert I, recollecting that Bruce was 'very bold, whilst at the same time wary and provident, perspicacious and prudent' (*Chron. Bower* 6. 321). Bower clarifies this by stating that the 'three chief constituent elements of prudence flourished in [Bruce], namely memory, intelligence and foresight, which are chiefly required in a ruler' (*Chron. Bower* 6. 321). That the *Scotichronicon* regards prudence as a quality required by the monarch implicitly suggests that it should be a quality of the Stewart kings that they have inherited from Bruce or, at the very least, they should aspire to the example set by their ancestor. Moreover, Bower states that prudence is depicted with three faces (*trifaciata depingitur*), representing the wise man who is able to consider the past, present and future together (*Chron. Bower* 6. 320). Bower's description of Bruce's prudent nature continues in Book 12, in which he discusses Seneca's views of good counsel, writing that, in his *Four Virtues*, Seneca says that 'it is fitting for the prudent man to weigh up advice and not slide swiftly towards false counsels with easy credulity' (*Chron. Bower* 6. 327). As a prudent ruler, Bruce is able to foresee the consequences of particular events and is able to act upon this knowledge; Bower here creates a relationship between memory, prudence and good counsel that continues into Lyndsay's work of the early sixteenth century.

Memoria was seen as an integral part of the cardinal virtue of Prudence alongside intelligence [*intelligencia*] and foresight [*providencia*], whereby one was enabled to make good decisions concerning future actions. Recollection was thus seen as a way of comprehending the present and contemplating the future, suggesting its pre-emptive role in making good judgements, rather than recalling the past for its own sake. The anonymous *Ad Herennium*, which describes the art of memory 'based upon the building plan of a familiar house', classifies Prudence as 'intelligence capable, by a certain judicious method, of distinguishing good and bad; likewise the knowledge of an art is called Wisdom; and again, a well-furnished memory and experience in diverse matters is termed Wisdom'.[36] Thomas Aquinas later argued for a consideration of Prudence as a moral virtue, 'of the utmost necessity for human life', for

---

[36] [Cicero], *Rhetorica ad Herennium*, ed. and trans. by Harry Caplan (Cambridge, MA: Harvard University Press, 1954), III, 2–3.

136   REWRITING THE PAST IN SCOTTISH LITERATURE, 1350–1550

to 'live well means acting well'.[37] This certainly seems to be the case in Lyndsay's text, which concerns itself with the governance of the king's body as a reflection of the state of the nation: its repeated advice is concerned with how to behave morally and devoutly. Moreover, if memory was believed to be the primary repository of wisdom, then such a reading of Lyndsay's *Dreme* would be entirely appropriate for a text so clearly situating itself within the Advice to Princes genre. In a text that revolves around advising the young James V, and which demonstrates the need for wisdom and good judgement, it is perhaps not surprising that the Dreamer's teacher is the personification of memory precisely because of the association of remembrance with the cardinal virtue of Prudence. Finally Lyndsay's instruction in the Exhortation is that James follow the counsel of 'dame Prudence' (*Dreme*, 1065); thus the poem moves from the recollection of the Dreamer, allegorised as his journey with Lady Remembrance, to the ability to interpret past events that is characterised by Dame Prudence and the memory work with which James is being asked to engage.

The quality of Prudence requires both a knowledge of the past and an ability to interpret and use this knowledge wisely. Lyndsay's *Dreme* provides James with a written record of memory (of his own life and that of Scotland's condition), and the means with which to interpret it by giving him Remembrance as a guide who answers the Dreamer's questions, and through the Exhortation which directs James to the right course of action. In asking James to 'prent' in his 'Remembrance' (*Dreme*, 1040) the fact that God will not excuse immoral behaviour, Lyndsay is not only urging him to see that the king is answerable to an omniscient God, but also to fix in his mind the ways in which James should not allow himself to become, or remain, ignorant – ways in which the *Dreme*, as an advisory poem, seeks to teach him. Lyndsay's use of 'prent' here is also significant. *DOST* defines its primary meaning as 'an impression or imprint on a surface', especially 'one made by a stamp, die, seal, or the like'.[38] Of course, given the date of Lyndsay's text, it is also likely that the *Dreme* here refers to print culture and the printing of letters on paper. Although Lyndsay provides a written memory in the form of his *Dreme*, the insistence to James that he should imprint the lessons within his own memory again recalls the ways in which the memory was thought of as a wax tablet on which memorial impressions were made, and to the ways in which memories or experiences physically altered the body. Here the desire is that the printing of memory within both James's personal and kingly selves will ensure a behaviour that 'embodies' his education. With echoes of Hary's *Wallace*, the *Dreme* indicates

---

[37] Thomas Aquinas, *Summa theologiae*, Blackfriars edition (Latin and English), 61 vols (New York: McGraw-Hill, 1964–81), i–ii, Q.57, art. 5, resp.; cited in Carruthers, *Book of Memory*, p. 82.

[38] *DOST*, prent, *n.* 1.

that it is not only memory that is inscribed on the page; the text also demands that the kingly body be *inscribed* with the memory of the narrative in such a way that it is easily remembered and recalled.

As an Advice to Princes work, Lyndsay's *Dreme* provides a point of reflexive exchange where the king as reader of a literary text and as interpreter of the educative mode are brought face to face. It is a text which requires James to apply the lessons the Dreamer has learnt within the political realm of Scotland. For this reason, the Exhortation entreats James to 'Hait vicious men, and lufe thame that ar gude; / And ilke flattrer thow fleme frome thy presence, / And flas reporte out of thy courte exclude' (*Dreme*, 1070–2). Yet, while the Advice to Princes tradition shaped the king's role as verbal and literary interpreter, Lyndsay does not expect his young king to begin to decipher the *Dreme*'s allegory alone. For if the foundation of good moral character consisted of the combination of action and memory, the Dreamer, on waking, must exchange his vision for action, translating it into a programme for the king to consider. As Joanna Martin observes, Dame Remembrance represents the 'important intellectual power of memory and of learning from the past'; in this way, she acts as a guide for the dream-narrator in the ways similar to Lady Philosophy who guides Boethius, and Beatrice and Virgil who guide Dante.[39] But Remembrance is also very different from these and functions, in some ways, like the Sibyl in *Scalacronica*'s prologue and the Virgin Mary in the *Wallace*'s dream. She does not offer consolation but, rather, points to solutions that might be learnt from applying the lessons of the past to the present. It is Remembrance who is instrumental in teaching the dream-narrator, training his memory to recall and interpret the events of his dream, but it is the responsibility of the Dreamer himself (and, by extension, James V) to translate the text of the dream and apply it to the problems facing Scotland. The poet eventually adopts the role of Dame Remembrance himself, recalling and recounting the vision and all that it encompasses for the benefit of the young king: as Remembrance 'did to [the Dreamer] report' (*Dreme*, 800), so does Lyndsay report to his king. Lyndsay thus posits himself as a guide and figure of good counsel (and memory) for the young King James, and this is further emphasised in Lyndsay's Exhortation at the very end of the *Dreme*. Lyndsay directs James to 'Use counsall of thy prudent Lordis trew' (*Dreme*, 1110), and to 'Wyrk with counsall, so sall thow neuer rew' (*Dreme*,

---

[39] Martin, *Kingship and Love*, p. 166. Memory also acts as one of the guides for the dream-narrator pilgrim in Lydgate's *Pilgrimage of the Life of Man* (1426); see Susan Hagen, *Allegorical Remembrance: A Study of the Pilgrimage of the Life of Man as a Medieval Treatise on Seeing and Remembering* (Athens, GA and London: University of Georgia Press, 1990).

1113), implicitly including himself and his narrative in this selection of good counsellors.[40]

While drawing on the *ars memoria*, Lyndsay's *Dreme* does not mark formal memory training as the only, or even the most important, aspect of *memoria* or prudence. Instead, the *Dreme* looks to the ways in which the recollective aspect of the individual mind might be used effectively in the application of good judgement. Through the call to self-governance and action through interpretation, Lyndsay marks prudence as an ethical structure, appealing to personal experience and addressing questions of how the ability to govern oneself serves as a theoretical model whose application could be universal. Experience was understood as a composite of memories – both individual and communal – generalised and judged, that gave rise to knowledge as the foundation of ethical training and behaviour. Throughout the dream the appeals to James to govern himself correctly are linked to the Dreamer's witnessing of the suffering of Scotland through the misgovernance of the land, suggesting that the self could be seen as a microcosm of the created world. In his warning that God 'wyll not excuse' James 'Geue [he is] rekles in gouernyng' (*Dreme*, 1041–2), Lyndsay refers both to the governance of the king's own body and to the national body of which he has 'the gubernatioun' (*Dreme*, 1056). The land here becomes a reflection of the king's body, and it is the microcosm of the kingly self that directly determines the condition of the macrocosm of Scotland. In drawing a further parallel with the body and earthly society, Lyndsay's text intimates that if James is incapable of governing his own body, then he has little chance of being able to govern the kingdom. In creating this link in the *Dreme*, Lyndsay deals with several networks of memory – historical, personal and cosmological – and these memories become layered within the text as well as in the individual and the national imaginations.

The cultivation of ethical memory based on experience thus forms the basis of Lyndsay's advisory programme, reflecting the widespread belief that prudence was a fundamental characteristic of good moral character. The Epistil, in particular, recreates a personal memory of Lyndsay's that is designed to prompt the same (or a similar) memory within the king's consciousness, providing a catalyst for the dream narrative that forms the main section of the poem. It is also, as Sandra Cairns notes, a section in which pleasure is emphasised through the recollection of happy memories; the way in which Lyndsay cares for the infant 'full tenderlie' (*Dreme*, 9), for example, provides a contrast with the later section of the poem where the reader is to learn from

---

[40] Nicholas Perkins notes that the role of good counsel was 'agreed by medieval commentators to be vital to the health of the body politic, and the problems and benefits of counsel are discussed at length in medieval mirrors for princes'; *Hoccleve's Regiment of Princes: Counsel and Constraint* (Cambridge: D.S. Brewer, 2001), p. 57.

MEMORY AND NATION 139

unhappy recollections.[41] This sense of pleasure and nostalgia is distinctly absent in the Exhortation, where, in light of the dream narrative that the reader has just experienced, the emphasis is placed on the duties and responsibilities of the new king. As such, Cairns argues, the purpose of the poem is to educate the king, transforming him from child to adult.[42] The Exhortation is certainly more public in tone; the nostalgic and intimate references to Lyndsay telling the young James stories are replaced by commands that the king 'Use counsall of thy *prudent* Lordis ... / And se thow nocht presumpteouslie pretend / Thy awin perticulare weill for tyll Ensew' (*Dreme*, 1110–12; my emphasis). The concerns of medieval scholarship – where textual authority is seen as a source of ethical guidance – are imbued with the craft of memory, emphasising the need to convert the wisdom of the *auctores* into private property, by replacing original texts in favour of a version which has been transformed by the reader and tied to networks already connected in the mind. In the case of the *Dreme*, Lyndsay displaces the well-known stories that he used to tell the infant king with a new version of advisory literature and moves from the general descriptions of hell and the heavens to the specific complaints of the commonweal of Scotland. Moreover, Lyndsay uses the memory of the Epistil, as well as the dream narrative, as an associative network that he hopes will strike a chord in James's own memory and will motivate him to practical action.[43] Throughout the *Dreme*, Lyndsay seeks to use personal memories to counsel the king and his audience. These memories are both Lyndsay's own recollections of a politically stable Scotland and his own loyalty to the crown (in which loyalty acts as a personalised form of political stability), and also the memory of the experiences of the Dreamer in his narrative. Lyndsay's continual emphasis is on the way memory (and its relationship to good governance and prudence) acts as the foundation of ethical behaviour and how the king's individual behaviour serves as a model for (and reflection of) the state of his kingdom.

[41] Sandra Cairns, 'Sir David Lyndsay's *Dreme*: Poetry, Propaganda and Encomium in the Scottish Court', in *The Spirit of the Court: Selected Proceedings of the Fourth Congress of the International Courtly Literature Society (Toronto 1983)*, ed. by Glyn S. Burgess and Robert A. Taylor (Cambridge: D.S. Brewer, 1985), pp. 110–19 (110).

[42] Cairns, 'Sir David Lyndsay's *Dreme*', p. 110. Janet Hadley Williams also takes this view, remarking that the 'opening epistle, lightly petitionary, is affectionate panegyric; the concluding epistle is austerely formal counsel'; 'Sir David Lyndsay', in *A Companion to Medieval Scottish Poetry*, pp. 179–91 (187).

[43] On the association between ethics and practical action, rather than speculation, see Dante Alighieri, 'Epistle to Can Grande della Scala', in *Medieval Theory and Criticism, c. 1100–c. 1375: The Commentary Tradition*, ed. by A.J. Minnis and A.B. Scott, rev. edn (Oxford: Clarendon Press, 1988), p. 462.

A Country 'raggit, rewin, & rent': The Consequences of Forgetting Prudence

Lyndsay's *Dreme* encompasses two frame structures that signal interpretive modes of reading. Firstly, the Epistle and Exhortation speak directly to James V, situating him as the main – or at least the most significant – reader of the text. These sections, focusing on the personal relationship between monarch and poet, frame the dream-narrator's story which, in turn, frames the dream vision itself. In a structure that comprises narrative within narrative, the *Dreme* mirrors the journey that the Dreamer takes through the various segments of hell and purgatory, and the order of the planets in the cosmographical section of the poem (*Dreme*, 365–525). While the structure of this section echoes medieval encylopedic texts, it also recalls formal memory-training treatises that suggest the use of mental images of heaven and hell in the construction of artificial memory.[44] Guiding the Dreamer, Dame Remembrance descends 'Doun throw eird' into 'the lawest hell' where 'ȝowting and ȝowling' can be heard from the 'mony cairfull creature[s]' in the 'flame of fyre' (*Dreme*, 162–6). Religious men and those in positions of power attract the greatest condemnation in Lyndsay's hell, as they would do to a greater extent in his later dramatic representation, *Ane Satyre of the Thrie Estaitis*. The images of 'Proude and peruerst Prelattis', 'fals flattrand freris' alongside 'diuers Papis and Empriouris' (*Dreme,* 169–78), act as moral recollections for both the Dreamer and the reader as both are told these figures have been punished for 'Couatyce, Luste, and ambysioun' (*Dreme*, 186–8). Like a mnemonist, Lyndsay's narrator appeals to the human capacity for emotion in order to create a secure impression in the memory; by repeatedly focusing on the consequences of living badly, the poet reminds his audience of the spiritual and civic repercussions of indulging in an immoral life. The repetition of the grotesque image is integral to attempts to shape individual character, such that the reader's memory of the Dreamer's experience aims to influence future behaviour. Memory works negatively within Lyndsay's *Dreme* here, imprinting hideous (and therefore more likely to be remembered) images in the Dreamer's mind – and that of the reader – in order that he should recollect how *not* to behave. The journey through hell brings both the Dreamer and the reader face to face with previous generations; quite literally the present encounters the past. The ability to recollect acts as a way to salvation because, through memory, the individual can strive to fulfil the Christian duty to perfect oneself. But Lyndsay's *Dreme* does not only focus on teaching the king how to behave morally; it also provides him with the means by which to begin this

---

[44] For example, Cosmas Rossellius' *Thesaurus Artificiosae Memoriae* (Venice, 1579) includes woodcuts depicting both heaven and hell as artificial memory models. See Yates, *Art of Memory*, plates 8a and 8b.

MEMORY AND NATION

process. Following the *Secretum Secretorum*, the *Dreme* covers a wide range of topics, including statecraft (good governance), astrology and geography, to provide the knowledge necessary for cultivating the royal virtue of prudence. Working within this framework, Lyndsay's *Dreme* advocates the regulation of the king's personal body as a way of creating a link between the king as an individual and the monarch as an institution.

Having asked to leave hell and purgatory, the Dreamer is taken by Remembrance through the elements of 'Erth, walter, air, and fire' and then 'Upwart' to 'se the Heuynnis' (*Dreme*, 380–2). Here the reader is directly confronted with the relationship between the moral state of the individual and the health of the wider community. Following a journey covering the Ptolemaic cosmos, the Dreamer travels 'Up throuch the Speris of the Planetis sewin' (*Dreme*, 385), mirroring the journey he has previously taken through hell; but here the emphasis on the regulation of the planets in their orbits, the nature of the planets and the relations between the planets presents the reader with a world distinctly ordered, well governed and natural.[45] The structuring and compartmentalising of the astrological images that Lyndsay uses suggests a knowledge of formal memory-training schemes and the ways in which they might be used in an advisory context. Thomas Bradwardine's treatise on how to acquire a trained memory, for example, uses the structure of the twelve signs of the zodiac as an elementary memory design and, in perhaps the most famous example from the sixteenth century, Giulio Camillo constructed a memory theatre in which the zodiac, planets and the cave all form vital components of the trained memory.[46] Lyndsay's tight narrative structure indicates that there is a mnemotechnical dimension to the *Dreme*, which mirrors and complements the journey through the spheres of the planets and hell. The use of the zodiac as an indicator of – or influence on – health also suggests a visual map that enabled the reader to consider the health of the body and the soul in relation to ideas of planetary order. As Michael Camille argues, 'Most medieval people ... saw an inextricable link between heavenly and earthly bodies', and the human body was understood in relation to the cosmos.[47] It was an understanding that created a close association between cosmology, medicine and politics. This relationship was often depicted pictorially with the image of the Zodiac man in which the man was surrounded by signs of the zodiac, which directly

---

[45] Lyndsay's poem precisely follows the Ptolemaic model, which depicted a series of circles radiating out from the earth, through the elements of earth and water, then through the planetary spheres of the Moon, Mercury, Venus, the Sun, Mars, Jupiter, Saturn, the Zodiac, the Crystalline sphere to the Emperean 'Quhare God, in to his holy throne deuyne, / Ryngis' (*Dreme*, 516–17).

[46] On Bradwardine, see Carruthers, *Book of Memory*, p. 163–72; on Camillo, see Yates, *Arts of Memory*, pp. 35–74.

[47] Camille, 'Image and the Self', p. 67.

142   REWRITING THE PAST IN SCOTTISH LITERATURE, 1350–1550

mapped onto the parts of the body which they were thought to govern. The thirteenth century also saw the dissemination of humoral theory into popular literature, usually through short mnemonic verses.[48] Sir Gilbert Hay's *Buik of King Alexander the Conqueror* (*c.* 1460), for example, contains a 'Regiment' of the body section based on the widely read *Secretum secretorum*.[49] This 'Regiment' discusses how the health of the physical body might be affected by the moral well-being of the individual. Mapstone argues that in 'the context of this Scottish romance ... it makes good sense', for the advice on good government is 'entirely in keeping with the presentation of Alexander as an exemplary model for Christian knighthood and kingship'.[50] Lyndsay's *Dreme* reinforces these concerns with its focus on the wrongdoings of the monarchs and prelates who occupy hell, coupled with the repeated references to the zodiac and the cycles of the year at the beginning of the poem.

While the Zodiac man was mainly thought of as a map of the individual body, in Lyndsay's *Dreme* an association between the zodiac and the nation occurs. Nor is Lyndsay alone in thinking of the national body as being governed by astrological forces. The fourteenth-century English astrologer, John Ashenden, comments that Scotland must be governed by the zodiacal sign of Scorpio because, like a scorpion, the Scots are 'cruel, proud, excitable, luxurious, bestial, false, and underhanded, and contemptuous of faith and faithfulness'.[51] For Ashenden, national character is determined by astrological influence but this material also performs memory work, becoming a schema that enables a nation to recall either its own or its neighbour's identity. The schema of mapped associations stress natural order and are comparable to visual representations of the memory, which structure and compartmentalise knowledge. The sense of order that comes through the narrative structure and the descriptions of the spheres further manifests the advisory role that

---

[48] See Sally Mapstone, 'The Scots *Buke of Physnomy* and Sir Gilbert Hay', in *The Renaissance in Scotland: Studies in Literature, Religion, History and Culture, Offered to John Durkan*, ed. by A.A. MacDonald, Michael Lynch and Ian B. Cowan (Leiden: Brill, 1994), pp. 1–44. Mapstone notes that such literature was popular among Scottish readers until at least the early seventeenth century (p. 11).

[49] *The Buik of King Alexander the Conqueror*, ed. by John Cartwright, 2 vols, STS 4th ser., 13, 16 (Aberdeen: Aberdeen University Press for the Scottish Text Society, 1986–90), lines 10, 108–10, 439.

[50] Mapstone, 'Scots *Buke of Physnomy*', p. 4.

[51] 'Et dicit Albumasar istius in libro suo de annorum revolutionibus quod Scorpio preest terre Scotie eo quod homines conveniunt ipsi scorpioni in moribus, sunt ei crudeles, superbi, elati, luxuria et bestialitati, falsi et subdoli, fidem et fidelitatem inflagrentos, et plus mori quam similia cupierit'; John Ashenden, *Pronosticatio coniunctionis Saturni et Martis* [1357]; Oxford, Bodleian Library, MS Digby 176, fol. 34v; cited in Hilary M. Carey, *Courting Disaster: Astrology at the English Court and University in the Later Middle Ages* (New York: St Martin's Press, 1992), p. 88.

the *Dreme* adopts, by urging the need for good order in the kingdom and the essential part it plays in good governance. Reminding the reader of the need for princely self-government as stressed by the Dreamer's journey through hell, the emphasis on a harmonious working together in the image of the planetary spheres demonstrates a causal link between the ethical microcosm and political macrocosm that was the central tenet of medieval political thought, and suggests that politics was to be seen as something 'natural'. Highlighting ideas derived from Aristotle and given expression in influential treatises such as John of Salisbury's *Policraticus* (*c.* 1155) and the *Secretum Secretorum*, the *Dreme* emphasises the relationship between the moral state of the individual (in Lyndsay's case, the monarch) and the health of the body politic that can be traced back to cosmic order.[52] It is national harmony, secured through good governance, that is distinctly absent in the descriptions of Scotland by Remembrance and John the Commoun Weill.

From Dreams to Letters: The Recollections of the King's Parrot

Thus far, this chapter has considered the ways in which formal memory schemes and the poetic recollection of royal childhood memories were deployed by Lyndsay to educate the young James V in the arts of good governance. The emphasis in the *Dreme* is on the regulation of the royal body and the implications this might have for the ways in which the king was deemed fit to rule the national body of Scotland. Axiomatically, national memories – given a voice in John the Commoun Weill – prompt the dream-narrator to counsel the king as to the best way to govern himself and the kingdom, seeing the two as inextricably linked, just as texts such as the *Buke of the Howlat* had memorially connected family and nation. In the final section of this chapter I turn to a text that develops these ideas and which has clear parallels with Holland's bird-fable. Lyndsay's *Testament of the Papyngo* was written in 1530, two years after the *Dreme* and in the year following the *Complaynt*, in which the poet had used his position of familiarity in James V's court to increase his caustic blame of others for Scotland's recent social and political predicament. Even more secure in his position, Lyndsay uses the Papyngo to present a bolder criticism of the courtiers and their role in James V's administration. From the very beginning of the poem, memory becomes a way of consolidating Lyndsay's position as advisor and social critic.

Through the literary models of complaint and epistle, the *Testament of the Papyngo* combines satire and moral instruction as the king's dying parrot doles out advice to both the king and the court. Through her testimony, the

---

[52] See Elizabeth Porter, 'Gower's Ethical Microcosm and Political Macrocosm', in *Gower's Confessio Amantis: Responses and Reassessments*, ed. by A.J. Minnis (Cambridge: D.S. Brewer, 1983), pp. 135–62.

Papyngo attacks the corruption of the Scottish clergy and nobility. The poem tells how the narrator accompanies the king's pet parrot to a lovely garden. Against the narrator's advice, the Papyngo climbs to 'the heychast lytill tender twyste' and sits 'With wyng displayit … full wantounlie' (*Papyngo*, 164–5). Lacking prudence in climbing so high onto a branch that cannot support her, the Papyngo is destined to be blown off the branch as it breaks in 'one blast' from 'Boreas' (*Papyngo*, 166). Mortally wounded by falling upon a 'stob' (stake; *Papyngo*, 169), the Papyngo bewails her ambition, recognising that she should never have frequented the court. She then dictates two epistles to be sent to James V. In the first letter, she urges James to learn to become a good king and to be cognisant of the whims of Lady Fortune. In the second, James is told about the evil to be found in courts and that court life is never governed by constancy or continuity. In the 'Commonyng' between the Papyngo 'and hir Holye Executoris', three wicked birds – magpie, kite and raven – come to offer absolution to the Papyngo in exchange for her worldly goods (*geir*; *Papyngo*, 651). The Papyngo denounces these intruders, bequeathing her possessions to the poor, her heart to the king, her spirit to the queen of faerie and her tripe to the would-be confessors who, in fact, devour her.

The prologue of the *Papyngo* situates Lyndsay's work within a familiar modesty topos. The speaker begins: 'Suppose I had ingyne angelicall, / With sapience more than Salamonicall, / I not quhat mater put in memorie' (*Papyngo*, 1–3). Striving to imitate the divinely inspired wisdom of Solomon, the earthly poet experiences a crisis of confidence and does not know what to commit to memory. These opening lines entice the reader to consider what is worthy of remembering and connect this ability with imagination and knowledge (understanding). The language and tone act as a memorial cue and the reader is directed to expect that the subject matter of the poem will be something worthy of recollecting. In order to get to that subject, the speaker creates a *catena* (chain) of imaginative prowess that stretches from the 'poetis auld' (*Papyngo*, 4) through 'Chawceir, Goweir, and Lidgate', all of whom mastered the 'bell of rethorick' (*Papyngo*, 11–12), the inimitable works of Scottish writers such as 'Kennedie … Dunbar … Rowle … Holland' (*Papyngo*, 16–19) and 'Gawane Dowglas' (*Papyngo*, 27) to the current court of James in which 'schir James Inglis' is known for 'ballatts, farses' and 'plesand playis' (*Papyngo*, 40–1) and where 'Stewart of Lorne wyll carpe rycht curiouslie' (*Papyngo*, 46). In this cacophony of poetic talent, the speaker suggests that 'So thocht I had ingyne (as I have none), / I watt nocht quhat to wryt' (*Papyngo*, 55–6); the field seems saturated, such that there is 'no thyng left bot barrane stok and stone' (*Papyngo*, 58). All that is left, then, is to present the 'complaynt of ane woundit papingo' (*Papyngo*, 63). Such an image, memorable in its bathos, provides the imaginative impetus for the poem's concern with national interests.

MEMORY AND NATION

In the complaint section of the *Papyngo*, the narrator seeks to establish some of the key concerns of the poem, one of which is the idea of the literary example, or mirror. Telling the reader that he 'refuse[d]' 'Prudent counsell' contrary to 'reassoun' (*Papyngo*, 199–200), the narrator suggests that 'Poetis, of me, haith mater to indyte' (*Papyngo*, 203). The narrator recognises the potential for his commemoration as a figure of 'Ambitioun' (*Papyngo*, 201), whose legacy in verse becomes a 'rememberance' by which the reader can 'yow defende frome sic unhappy chance' (*Papyngo*, 218–19). As the narrator recognises his own memorial function, he immediately recalls the failings of his own capacity for memory as represented by prudent behaviour:

> Quhydder that I wes stricken in extasie,
> Or throuch one stark imagynatioun,
> Bot it apperit in myne fantasie
> I hard this dolent lamentatioun. (*Papyngo*, 220–3)

Here Lyndsay accentuates the ways in which emotional – or visionary – states interact with the composition of poetry by invoking the threefold model of the brain as it was conceptualised in medieval faculty psychology. I have discussed this model in relation to Bower's commemoration of Fordun's historiographical enterprise, showing how *imaginativa* facilitated reason and memory. However, here Lyndsay's narrator pinpoints that either 'extasie' or 'one stark imaginatioun' acts as the catalyst for the poetical composition (*fantasie*) of the Papyngo's lament. Drawing on the commonplace of the power of striking visual images, the sight of the 'blude' rushing out of the Papyngo whose 'breist' has 'lychtit' on 'ane stob' (*Papyngo*, 169) has proved potent enough to have an effect on the front cell of the brain (the *phantasia* or *imaginativa*). In a process of reworking this image in the service of instruction, the narrator then imagines that 'this bird did breve … / Hir counsale to the kyng' (*Papyngo*, 225–6). Death therefore becomes a moment of counsel.

Continuing the emphasis on memory's role in good counsel, at the beginning of the first epistle, which follows, the Papyngo commends the king's own 'marciall dedis' as being 'dyng of memorie' (*Papyngo*, 230). Immediately following this, she leaves the king her 'trew unfenyeit hart / To gydder with this cedull subsequent'. In her dealings with the 'gled' (the kite), the Papyngo once again reminds the reader of her 'trew unfenyeit hart' that 'lyis in my memoryall' (*Papyngo*, 767–8) and towards the end of her exchange with 'hir Holye Executouris', she repeats the gift of her heart, asking her executors to 'speid … to the court, but tareyng, / And tak my hart, of perfyte portrature, / And it present onto my soverane kyng' (*Papyngo*, 1117–19). The Papyngo imagines that the king 'wyll clois [her heart] in to one ryng' (*Papyngo*, 1120). Drawing together the written document and the metaphorical seat of *memoria*, the Papyngo situates herself as an object of memory for the king that, so long as he pays attention to her remains, he will be able to 'cancillat out of thy memorie' the 'offciairis' who seek to guide the king in injustice (*Papyngo*, 249–52). Should the king 'excers [his] office prudentlie', the Papyngo suggests, then 'poetis perpetuallie' will 'mak mentioun' of his 'vertew' (*Papyngo*, 262–3). The Papyngo's message is clear: the king is already worthy of memory, but he needs to govern well in order to be commemorated in perpetuity. The image of the prudent king wearing the memory of ambition and pride is particularly striking and it demonstrates James V's own potential as an object of memory work. Not only does the ring symbolise the fate of the Papyngo, but the object on James's person requires cognitive effort by those who view it and who must recall its significance.

The important remembrance for James and the *Papyngo*'s readers is the prudence and good governance that should be enacted in the administration of the kingdom. This is reinforced in the *Papyngo* through the Papyngo's epistle to 'hir Brether of Courte' that they should 'Imprent [her] fall in [their] memoriall' (*Papyngo*, 348). As he had done in the *Dreme*, Lyndsay reuses the idea of stamping memory within the body such that 'preterit tyme may be experience' (*Papyngo*, 364). This recognition that the past operates as a mode of instruction is then treated specifically in lines 409–611, in which the Papyngo highlights the theme of mutability specifically in relation to the court as she imagines that the 'courte cheangeith, sumtyme with sic outrage, / That few or none may makyng resistance, / And sparis nocht the prince more than the paige, / As weill apperith be experience' (*Papyngo*, 409–12). That 'experience' is then set out as a series of stanzas that comment on the relatively recent history of the Stewart kings and their courts. James I is lauded as the 'patroun of prudence / Gem of ingyne' whose 'vertew doith transcende [the Papyngo's] fantasie'; yet he 'wes pietouslie put down' by false conspirators (*Papyngo*, 430–6). The Papyngo describes how her 'hart is peirst with panes for to pance' on James III's court in which 'prudent lordis counsall wes refusit', through which 'Cochrame, with his companye' held James 'quyet, as he had bene inclusit' (*Papyngo*, 449, 455). Thomas Cochrane was a royal favourite of James III who succeeded in turning the king against his brothers Albany and Mar, but who 'clam so heych' that he was 'Stranglit to deith' over 'Lawder bryge' by his enemies (*Papyngo*, 468–70).[53] That these distressing memories generate an emotional response that sorely wounds the Papyngo reminds the reader of the typical use of emotion to stimulate recollection, although here it is memory that evokes the pain that pierces the metaphorical seat of memory.

The problems of James III's reign seem to give the Papyngo the most trouble as she laments, 'Tyll putt in forme that fait infortunat, / And mortall cheange, perturbith myne ingyne' (*Papyngo*, 472–3). In outlining the disruption

---

[53] See Noman Macdougall, 'Thomas [Robert] Cochrane', *ODNB* [accessed 25 October 2022].

to her intellectual faculty (*ingyne*) through writing the past, the Papyngo draws a direct comparison with Scotland's poet-king, James I, whom she has described as the 'Gem of ingyne'. James's *Kingis Quair* (*c*. 1424) had concerned itself with the role of trained memory in the delineation of model kingship, but, where James's intellect and deployment of the *ars memoria* had resulted in a reputation for the exercise of prudent kingship, the Papyngo expresses an anxiety about her own abilities, which appear diminished by literary endeavour.[54] The effects are physical and intellectual as she struggles to reconcile the desire for James to have 'bene ... confortit / With sapience of the prudent Salomone' (*Papyngo*, 479–80) and the recognition that, in this case, the past cannot be reshaped:

> Quhat suld I wys, remedie was thare none:
> At morne, ane king, with sceptour, sweird and croun,
> Att evin, ane dede, deformit carioun. (*Papyngo*, 483–5)

This resignation leads the Papyngo to her final example from James V's family, that of his father, James IV, the 'potent prince' and 'gentyll king' (*Papyngo*, 487). James IV is lauded in the Papyngo's Epistle as the 'myrrour of humylitie, / Lode sterne, and lampe of libiralytie' under whom 'justice did prevaill' (*Papyngo*, 491–3). In eulogising James IV, the Papyngo not only recollects the cultivation of a particular kind of courtly culture that cemented Scotland's 'fame' throughout Europe, but she also thinks about the ways in which the consolidation of monarchical power within Scotland's own borders was achieved, notably through the bringing to heel of the 'savage Iles' who 'Durste nocht rebell' against this king (*Papyngo*, 500, 494, 496). Yet, it is through James's 'awin wylfull mysgovernance', rather than 'the vertew of Inglis ordinance' (*Papyngo*, 512–13), that this golden age is 'Distroyit' on 'Flodoun feilde' (*Papyngo*, 511, 507). The Papyngo refuses 'at lenth it put in memorie' (*Papyngo*, 517), presumably because the proximity of the event to her composition rendered that redundant; the Papyngo could assume that this was in living memory for at least some of her audience. Yet, it is also possible that the event was still too emotionally distressing to be filtered through reason to memory and poetic arrangement. It is at this point that the Parrot demands that her 'brether, marke, in your remembrance, / Ane myrrour of those mutabiliteis' (*Papyngo*, 521–2). Despite having been regarded as a mere parrot at the opening of the poem, the Papyngo's rhetorical skill has reshaped recent Stewart history as a series of vignettes that demonstrate the necessity of good counsel to guide James V's exercise of prudent governance. One of the Papyngo's final exhortations to her fellow courtiers is to 'serve [their] prince with enteir hart trewlie' (*Papyngo*, 602), recalling much earlier

---

[54] See Elliott, *Remembering Boethius*, pp. 123–43.

writers' commendations of those members of the nobility who were able to set aside personal ambition in service of the best interests of the kingdom.

The *Tetsament of the Papyngo* is clearly a text in which Lyndsay demonstrates an interest in national memory and which draws on Scotland's recent past to envisage its future stability. The first half of the poem very much thinks about the usefulness of reshaping that past for a courtly audience who were responsible for the governance of the kingdom, although the second half of the poem, which imagines the discussion between the Papyngo and her 'Holye Executouris' directs its attention to the calls for religious reforms that would loom large through the sixteenth century. In this, there are clear parallels with the *Dreme* in which James V's ability to govern well is directly linked to the ability of those in positions of institutional power more broadly – the court and the church – to act in service to the kingdom rather than fall prey to their own desires and ambitions. These discussions of nation, then, are concerned less with Anglo-Scottish relations of the fourteenth century and more with the internal politics of Scotland as a locus of collective identity, although they are tempered by the recent memory of Flodden. The change in thinking, and understanding, the nation in Lyndsay's early poems seems to move from a memory of violent resistance to the power of moral force, narrated through the body of the monarch and the objects of memory associated with it.

Where the texts that I have examined in previous chapters look back to the Wars of Independence and rely on anti-English feeling as a way of establishing common identity among Scottish audiences, Lyndsay's early poetry seeks to locate Scotland's sense of itself directly in the figure of the king. Through personal address and the exploitation of personal memory, Lyndsay reimagines the recent past as a way of drawing together Scottish history and literary heritage. Through the literary forms of the dream and the complaint, Lyndsay's *Dreme* and *Papyngo* demonstrate the relationship between memory and creativity; both forms offer exaggerated and distorted representations of the past that become powerful memorial images through their vivid recollections. Deploying Remembrance as a guide in the *Dreme* enables Lyndsay to impress the importance of memory to his poetics of prudence, while the legal and epistolary modes of the *Papyngo* signal Lyndsay's own confidence in the young king's abilities to respond to, and learn from, diplomatic practice. For Lyndsay, then, in contrast to the desire for continuity shown by other writers in this study, the pressing practice of national memory is one of change. Sir David Lyndsay's poetry from the 1520s and 1530s was, as Janet Hadley Williams has argued, 'an important influence on the young James V's development and on the ways in which the king was perceived by his realm'.[55] Through works such as the *Dreme* and the *Papyngo*, Lyndsay sought to furnish his

[55] Hadley Williams, 'David Lyndsay and the Making of James V', p. 202.

readers with a constructed memory that imagined the king as a specific locus of communal identity. In the next chapter, my focus shifts to consider *The Complaynt of Scotland*, a translation and reworking of Alain Chartier's early fifteenth-century text, *Le Quadrilogue Invectif*. Written *c.* 1548 and printed in Paris in 1550, the *Complaynt* specifically draws on the craft of memory to express an increased concern with the dangers of forgetting at a point where Scotland's security was once again under threat, not only from the English but also from members of the Scottish community itself.

6

Sustaining the 'natiue cuntre': Remembering the Past in *The Complaynt of Scotland*

Despite the political destabilisation at the beginning of the sixteenth century that resulted from Flodden and the long minority of James V, the king's personal rule during the 1530s quickly sought to re-establish the crown's authority through a course of action that has been represented by Gordon Donaldson as 'something of a reign of terror' that betrayed 'a streak of sadistic cruelty in his nature'.[1] Jamie Cameron points out that it is 'difficult to find the evidence on which Donaldson builds such a damning and influential verdict' of James.[2] For Cameron, while the domestic power struggles of the reign were prolonged – lasting at least until the execution of James Hamilton of Finnart in 1540 – the personal rule of James V was also marked by the effective development of the judicial system and the intention to craft a Scottish imperial monarchy.[3] In Cameron's assessment, James V was no more ruthless and effective than many of his forebears, and his reign was marked by tensions both within and outwith Scotland's borders. While Anglo-Scottish relations were tense during the 1520s, by the mid-1530s they had acquired a religious dimension as anti-clerical factions attempted to persuade the king to emulate Henry VIII's assertion of monarchical supremacy over the Church. Aware of England's isolation in Europe following Henry's break with Rome, James adeptly navigated the political landscape by leveraging a Protestant England against a Catholic Europe. James's marriages, first to Francis I's daughter, Madeleine of Valois (1537), and then to Mary of Guise-Lorraine (1538), demonstrate a strategic use of the marriage market, positioning Scotland as a kingdom oriented towards European alliances and interests as well as obtaining papal securities. Tensions between Henry VIII and James V had bubbled away, but became particularly apparent at this time as England sought to 'persuade' its

---

[1] Gordon Donaldson, *James V–James VII*, The Edinburgh History of Scotland, vol. 3 (Edinburgh: Mercat, 1965), p. 62.

[2] Jamie Cameron, ed. by Norman MacDougall, *James V: The Personal Rule, 1528–1542* (East Linton: Tuckwell, 1998), p. 329.

[3] Cameron, *James V*, esp. pp. 255–85.

northern neighbour of the benefits of religious reform as Henry began to press his interests in Scotland.

By 1542, relations between Henry and James had completely broken down and, at this point, Henry issued his Declaration, in which he carefully raised the spectre of past Anglo-Scottish relations through his deployment of the Galfridian myth of Brutus. In seeking to bring the mythic past to bear on contemporary diplomatic relations, Henry followed Edward I in arguing that Scotland, rather than being a sovereign nation, was a vassal of the English king.[4] In November of that year, Henry launched a major raid into south-west Scotland, defeating the Scots at the Battle of Solway Moss. By December 1542, Scotland once again faced an all-too-familiar situation; two weeks after Solway Moss, James V died, leaving his seven-day-old daughter, Mary – his only heir – now Queen of Scots. The prospect of having such a young successor to the Scottish crown must have struck a chord with those able to remember the succession of Mary's father in 1513, and, as Joanna Martin has noted, by the early sixteenth century, the 'succession of infant, child and adolescent Stewart kings, all of whom had to be carefully raised to the duties of government, stretched back over a century and seems to have had a strong hold on the cultural memory'.[5] John Knox would remark in his anti-Marian *History of the Reformation in Scotland* (1586–87) that, following the death of James V, 'all men lamented that the realm was left without a male to succeed', although, as Jenny Wormald reminds us, 'the mid-sixteenth century saw an astonishing rash of women rulers' that shows Knox's propaganda for what it is.[6] Alongside the youthfulness of James's heir, the added issue of a female ruler might also have carried echoes of the death of Alexander III in 1286 and the ill-fated succession of the Maid of Norway, whose death precipitated the Great Cause and had, in part, led to the beginning of the first Scottish War of Independence. But history did not repeat itself. By the middle of the sixteenth century, the Stewart hold on the Scottish throne meant that there were no immediate internal rivals to Mary's succession. Yet, as Roger Mason notes, the

---

[4]   The full title of Henry's text is *A Declaration, conteyning the iust causes and consyderations of this present warre with the Scottis, wherin also appereth the trewe and right title, that the kinges most royall maiesty hath to the souerayntie of Scotland.* London, 1542.

[5]   Martin, *Kingship and Love*, p. 177.

[6]   John Knox, *The history of the reformation of religion within the realm of Scotland ... Together with the life of the author, and several curious pieces wrote by him ... By the Reverend Mr. John Knnox ... To which is added I. An Admonition to England and Scotland ... by Antoni Gilby II. The first and second books of discipline* (Glasgow, 1761), Bk 1, p. 75. Jenny Wormald, *Mary, Queen of Scots: A Study in Failure* (1988; repr. Edinburgh: John Donald, 2017), p. 35.

152   REWRITING THE PAST IN SCOTTISH LITERATURE, 1350–1550

young Mary's status 'opened up opportunities for other royal families to further their dynastic interests through the promise of Mary's hand in marriage'.[7]

The Battle of Solway Moss precipitated almost a decade of what Lorna Hutson has described as an 'explicitly punitive, deliberately brutal' English campaign to conquer and subdue Scotland.[8] During the early years of Mary's minority, a series of conflicts known as the 'Rough Wooings' (1544–50) saw Henry VIII and, at one point, Francis I of France seek to absorb Scotland into their respective dynastic empires. In a campaign that has been equated to Edward I's invasions of Scotland in the late thirteenth and early fourteenth centuries, Henry VIII sought to coerce the Scottish administration into a betrothal between Henry's son, Edward Prince of Wales (who became King Edward VI in January 1547), and the young Scottish queen. Marcus Merriman notes that this war took place in two stages: the first phase, from November 1543 to June 1546, under Henry VIII, and then a second phase, directed by Edward's Protector, the duke of Somerset, from September 1547 to March 1550.[9] As Edward was Henry's only male heir, the significance of this match cannot be underestimated. Mirroring the short reign of the Maid of Norway, during which Margaret had been betrothed to the then Prince of Wales, the future Edward II, a union of this kind would have meant that any children of the marriage would inherit both kingdoms, presumably with Scotland subordinate to its larger and more aggressive English partner. Henry's campaigns, followed by those of Somerset, devastated Scotland; for example, English reports attest to the violence that saw the inhabitants of Dunbar burnt while they slept, and abbeys and villages 'brent, raced, and cast downe'.[10] William Patten's *The Expedicion into Scotlande* recounts that along the sands of the Firth of Forth following the battle of Pinkie, 'the dead bodyes lay as thik as a man may note cattel grasing in a full replenished pasture. The Ryuer ran al red with blood.'[11]

---

[7]   Roger Mason, 'Dame Scotia and the Commonweal: Vernacular Humanism in *The Complaynt of Scotland* (1550)', *The Mediaeval Journal*, 10.1 (2020), 129–50 (131).

[8]   Lorna Hutson, *England's Insular Imagining: The Elizabethan Erasure of Scotland* (Cambridge: Cambridge University Press, 2023), p. 8. Hutson's book appeared after this book was completed and I have not been able to engage with its arguments as fully as it deserves.

[9]   Marcus Merriman, *The Rough Wooings: Mary Queen of Scots, 1542–1551* (East Linton: Tuckwell Press, 2000), p. 6. Merriman's account provides the fullest discussion of the Rough Wooings.

[10]   *A collection of state papers, relating to affairs in the reigns of King Henry VIII. King Edward VI. Queen Mary, and Queen Elizabeth*, ed. by Samuel Haynes (London, 1740), pp. 52–4. See Hutson's discussion of Edward Seymour's invasion of Scotland; *England's Insular Imagining*, pp. 22–4.

[11]   William Patten, *The Expedicion into Scotla[n]de of the most Woorthely Fortunate Prince Edward, Duke of Soomerset, Vncle Vnto our most Noble Souereign Lord Ye Ki[n]ges Maiestie Edvvard the. VI. Goouernour of Hys Hyghnes Persone,*

'be ane instrument to delyuir vs': Virtue, Inheritance and Voluntary Intellection

In Chapter 10 of the *Complaynt of Scotland*, the Actor states that 'realmes ar nocht conquest be buikes bot rather be bluid' (*Compl.* 64). The rise in what might be classed as a 'war of words' during the Rough Wooings might suggest this was certainly not the case from the English perspective, whereby repeated textual interventions sought to garner ideological support for military action against Scotland. The war of words continued through the second Rough Wooing, most notably with James Henrisoun's *Exhortacion to the Scottes to conforme themselfes to the honourable, Expedient, & godly Union betweene the two realms of Englande & Scotland*, which was printed before the Battle of Pinkie in September 1547, and the duke of Somerset's *Epistle or exhortaction, to unite & peace, sent from the Lorde Protector, & others the kynges most honourable counsaill of England: To the Nobilites, Gentlemen, and Commons, and al others the inhabitauntes of the realme of Scotland*, printed in February 1548. In this, Marcus Merriman notes the fairly widespread circulation of these texts both within Scotland and on the Continent, and the distinctly religious tones that underpin subsequent writings concerned with the matter of an Anglo-Scottish union.[12]

In his Declaration, Henry claimed that the 'present warre hath not proceded of any demaund' of the English 'right of superioritie, which the kings of Scottes haue alwais knowledged by homage and fealtie' but, rather, the current situation 'hath ben prouoked and occasioned vpon present matier of displeasure, present iniury, present wrong mynistred by the Nephieu to the Vncle most vnnaturally' (n.p.). This insistence on the present appears to downplay the appeal to history that characterised much earlier historiography and documentary duelling in Anglo-Scottish relations. However, the Declaration then proceeds to comment at length on the 'fact' of English superiority and Scottish fealty as demonstrated 'fyrst by historie, written … as for confirmation of the trueth in memory', second, by 'instrumentes of homage made by the kynges of Scottes, and dyuers notable personages of Scotlande' and, third, 'by regesters and recordes iudicially and autentiquely made' (n.p.). What follows is a detailed exposition of the centuries-old English claim to sovereignty over Scotland, which essentially rehashes Edward I's argument that Scotland was a dependency of the English crown, proven by the Brutus origin myth but fleshed out with multiple examples of Scottish kings allegedly paying homage to their English superiors. The general tone

---

and Protectour of Hys Graces Realmes, Dominions [and] Subiectes made in the First Yere of His Maiesties most Prosperous Reign, and Set Out by Way of Diarie, by W. Patten Londoner (London, 1548), n.p.

12 See Merriman, *Rough Wooings*, pp. 277–87.

of the Declaration rests on the familial links between the English and Scottish crowns, with Henry making repeated references to James V as his 'Nephieu'. Here Henry appears to exploit the uncle–nephew motif of heroic literature and medieval romance, whereby a special and reciprocal relationship existed: an uncle's duty to love, protect and avenge the nephew was to be mirrored by the nephew's responsibilities to his uncle. This relationship, as presented in medieval romance, usually rested on maternal lineage, whereby the uncle was the mother's brother and the nephew the sister's son.[13] Such was the case between Henry and James.

The Complaynt of Scotland was the single piece of Scottish counter-propaganda to be printed contemporaneously with the situation it addresses. It has been described by its most recent editor, A.M. Stewart, as a 'political propaganda pamphlet in a literary framework' that functions simultaneously as 'a nationalist document and social criticism'.[14] Extant in four printed copies, all survive without a title page that might provide evidence of authorship and place of publication. Stewart identified Robert Wedderburn at the most likely author and suggests that the text was most likely printed in Paris in 1550, and I follow Stewart's assessment of this in my discussion in this chapter.[15] Written in the early years of Mary Stewart's minority and dedicated to her mother, Mary of Guise, who, in 1554, replaced James Hamilton, second earl of Arran, as regent for the young queen, the *Complaynt* uses the literary dream vision to comment on Scotland's relations with England, the failings of the three estates and the need for strong, effective governance within Scotland. The familial aspect that Henry VIII deployed in his dealings with Scotland is one that Wedderburn's *Complaynt* makes distinct use of in depicting Scotland as the mother of her people, something which I will discuss further in this chapter. However, Wedderburn also draws on the recollective power of genealogy in his dedication of the *Complaynt* to Mary of Guise. Although Mary was the queen mother, at the point of Wedderburn's dedication, she was not regent or governor – that privilege belonged to Arran – and the queen had recently been dispatched to France. In choosing to dedicate his text to Mary of Guise, Wedderburn seeks to emphasise the genealogical – or dynastic – concerns of the *Complaynt*. In this way, the dedication shores up Franco-Scottish alliances as much as the text thinks through the shared suffering of France and Scotland at the hands of the English. For those familiar with its source – Chartier's text – the drawing together of collective French and Scottish experiences and memories could not be coincidental.

---

[13] On this motif, see Thomas J. Garbáty, 'The Uncle–Nephew Motif: New Light into Its Origins and Development', *Folklore*, 88.2 (1977), 220–3.

[14] *Compl.* xxxiii.

[15] See *Compl.* viii–xi.

SUSTAINING THE 'NATIUE CUNTRE'

The opening sentence of the dedication immediately sets the tone and focus of Wedderburn's subsequent text, as he refers to 'the precius germe of [Mary's] nobilite' that generates not only 'tendir leyuis of vertu' but also 'hoilsum frute of honour quhilk is ane immortal ande supernatural medicyne' to the kingdom (*Compl.* 1). Here, Wedderburn emphasises the importance of nobility of blood; Mary is 'nobil' not only as a result of her 'verteous verkis' but also through being 'nobil of genolligie, be rason that [she is] discendit of the maist vail3eant princis that ar vndir the cape of hauyn' (*Compl.* 2–3). To consolidate this, Wedderburn spends part of the dedication detailing the virtues of her relatives, including her descent from Godfrey de Bouillon (the pre-eminent leader of the First Crusade) before finally 'rehers[ing]' the 'memor' of Mary's 'nobil ande vail3eant fadir' (*Compl.* 4). He concludes that the 'vail3eant actis of [her] predecessours' and Mary's own 'grit prudens' reveal that she is 'ane rycht nobil, baytht of vertu and of genoligie' (*Compl.* 5). Wedderburn thus undertakes the memory work of connecting past and present while intimately connecting Scottish future security to Scottish links with France, whose perceived nobility sits in stark contrast with the 'rauisant volfis of ingland' (*Compl.* 2). Wedderburn states that fervent devotion compels him to present Mary with 'ane tracteit of the fyrst laubir of [his] pen' (*Compl.* 5), and it is at this point that he refers to his own recollective project, which is the writing of the *Complaynt*. Wedderburn describes how he

> began to reuoule the librarye of [his] vndirstanding, and [he] socht all the secreit corneris of [his] gazophile, ymaginant vitht in the cabinet of [his] interior thochtis, that ther var na mater mair conuenient ande necessaire, for this present dolorus tyme, nor to reherse the cause ande occasione of the onmersiful afflictione of the desolat realme of scotland. (*Compl.* 5)

Prompted by the genealogy of Mary's family that he has 'rehersed', Wedderburn's own memory is characterised by a set of more obviously mnemonic metaphors of the library, the 'gazophile' (a *hapax legomenon* meaning 'treasury') and the cabinet. The images of rummaging in this description demonstrate Wedderburn's memorial agility: he can identify and select the most appropriate memories for the task in hand. Moreover, he can *imagine*; that is, he can creatively assemble his selection of material in order to make memory useful to the present situation. As Wedderburn indicates, his 'war of words' is prompted by the recollected virtues of Mary of Guise, but it is made 'necessaire' by the current situation in Scotland, which he imagines can be remedied by the intellectual virtue of 'prudens' that Mary can choose to remember and exercise.

Textual Memories, Literary Inheritance and Looking Back to the Future

The *Complaynt* draws heavily on Alain Chartier's *Quadrilogue Invectif* (1422) and, as Margaret and Glenn Blayney have demonstrated, on Chartier's less well-known *Le Traité de l'Esperance* (*c*. 1428).[16] It seems that Chartier, who had visited Scotland in 1427 as one of the party negotiating the marriage of James I's daughter, Margaret, to the dauphin (afterwards Louis XI), was familiar in Scotland. *The Porteous of Nobleness*, a Scots version of Chartier's *Le Breviaire de Nobles*, was published *c*. 1508 by Chepman and Myllar. It is likely, therefore, that versions of Chartier's *Quadrilogue* and *Le Traité de l'Esperance* also circulated in Scotland during the first half of the sixteenth century. A copy of 'the werkis of Allane Charter' is listed in the 1578 inventory of the royal library at Edinburgh Castle, which was compiled shortly after the forced resignation of James VI's regent, James Douglas, fourth earl of Morton. Whether this text was acquired during Mary's reign, or during that of either her father or grandfather, cannot be determined.[17] Alongside the clear indebtedness to Chartier, Wedderburn also engages closely with much Scottish estates satire, for example *The Thre Prestis of Peblis* (earliest witness, Asloan Manuscript, *c*. 1515–30) and Lyndsay's contemporaneous first iteration of *Ane Satyre of the Thrie Estaitis* (*c*. 1540) as well as his poetry from the 1520s and 1530s. Rather than taking Chartier's text and rather bluntly translating it, it is evident that Wedderburn engaged in a craft of memory that saw him reshaping his materials into a new narrative that spoke directly to the circumstances of the 1540s in Scotland, just as he had indicated he was doing in the dedication to Mary of Guise. It is a text that sees him simultaneously consider how English military aggression north of the border *and* the internal political situation in Scotland affect the kingdom's prosperity and identity. The *Complaynt*, therefore, sits at a juncture between two traditions of Scottish articulations of nationhood that I have outlined in previous chapters: the outward-looking tradition of defining the nation in comparison with other nations (specifically with regard to Anglo-Scottish relations), and the self-reflective tradition of focusing on Scotland's internal politics as a way of understanding the kingdom's position on the European political stage that could be considered to dominate the post-Flodden era.

Exploring the divisions within the three estates and the threat to Scotland from its English neighbour, the *Complaynt* suggests a simultaneous consideration of insular and broad ways of promoting national identity, which come

---

[16] Margaret S. and Glenn H. Blayney, 'Alain Chartier and *The Complaynt of Scotland*', *RES*, 9 (1958), 8–17; see also William Allen Neilson, 'The Original of *The Complaynt of Scotlande*', *JEGP*, 1 (1897), 411–30.

[17] The item is listed in Higgitt, *Scottish Libraries*, p. 108, item 9.

both from the representation of Scotland as a community with a sense of self and from its wider relations with other countries. The literary models to which Wedderburn is indebted are particularly interesting here, as his text incorporates elements of dream vision, allegory and complaint. Rebecca Marsland has noted in her study of the literary complaint in medieval Scotland that Wedderburn's *Complaynt* must be considered a central text in the sixteenth-century revival of the complaint genre necessitated by the complicated political situation from James IV's death at Flodden through to James VI's majority in 1583. Marsland also notes that Wedderburn's text 'appears to reject the [Scottish] models for complaint established over the fifteenth century'; rather, she suggests, the *Complaynt* is indebted to English 'clamour' literature that became increasingly popular through the fourteenth and early fifteenth centuries and relied on the topics, forms and language of judicial plaint for its validity.[18]

Written in the aftermath of 'Black Sunday' – the Battle of Pinkie Cleugh, 10 September 1547 – and during the most intense period of Anglo-Scottish warfare of the sixteenth century, the *Complaynt* laments the 'grite afflictione quhilk occurit on oure realme in september.m. v.xlvii ȝeris on the feildis besyde mussilburgh' (*Compl.* 17). Little more than three decades since Flodden, Pinkie Cleugh was another humiliating defeat for the Scots, which left thousands dead and saw fifteen hundred Scots taken prisoner.[19] In the dedicatory epistle to the 'excellent, ande illustir Marie queen of Scotlande, the margareit and perle of princessis' (*Compl.* 1), the *Complaynt*'s author makes reference to 'our mortal ald enemeis' – the English – who

> sen the deceis of oure nobil illustir prince kying iames the fyift, ȝour vmquhile faythtful lord ande hisband, tha said rauisant volfis of ingland, hes intendit ane oniust veyr be ane sinister inuentit false titil contrar our realme in hope to deuoir, the vniuersal floc of oure scottis natione, ande to extinct oure generatione furtht of rememorance. (*Compl.* 2)

Composing a nationalist document responding to the events of the 1540s, the *Complaynt*'s author focuses attention here on the threat England posed to its northern neighbour, but does so specifically in memorial terms. Wedderburn employs rhetoric similar to Hary's *Wallace*, in which the 'auld enemeis' come of 'saxonnis blud', and also to the Coupar Angus recension of Bower's *Scotichronicon*, in which Bower imagined Fordun collecting the fragments of

---

[18] Rebecca Marsland, 'Complaint in Scotland, *c.* 1424–*c.* 1500' (Unpublished DPhil thesis, University of Oxford, 2014), p. 57. The term 'literature of clamour' is Wendy Scase's; *Literature and Complaint in England, 1272–1553* (Oxford: Oxford University Press, 2007), p. 3.

[19] See Michael Lynch, *Scotland: A New History* (London: Pimlico, 1991; repr. 1992), pp. 206–7.

158   REWRITING THE PAST IN SCOTTISH LITERATURE, 1350–1550

Scottish history that the English had attempted to extinguish from memory through the destruction of the textual record. The *Complaynt*'s author points to the English desire to strip Scotland once again of its people and its memories, 'to extinct oure generatione furtht of rememorance' (*Compl.* 2). In a striking parallel with the fears of the earlier texts, Wedderburn's concern is about total obliteration rendered in genealogical images and, with the value of hindsight, a reader might draw distinct parallels with Hary's depiction of the Barns of Ayr episode in which he represents the destruction of the Scottish nobility in similar, although more calculated, fashion. Indeed, Wedderburn makes specific reference to Hary's *Wallace* just after the 'Monologue Recreatyue' section of the *Complaynt*, as the principal shepherd's wife seeks to stem her husband's 'prolixt orison' (*Compl.* 49) by suggesting a Boccaccian or Chaucerian model of tale-telling to pass the time (*Compl.* 49–53). The Actor's recollection of the stories told by the shepherds not only provides a comprehensive list of popular literature in the mid-sixteenth century but also reinforces the importance of the textual memory of both Wedderburn's shepherds and his readers.[20] Michael Twomey has argued that the 'Monologue Recreatuye' serves a pedagogical function within the *Complaynt* and that 'the shepherd's role ... is as a teacher, a repository of Scottish culture, a shepherd of souls'.[21] Twomey refers here specifically to the memorial role that the shepherd performs in reminding Wedderburn's readers 'of the pastoral ontology of Scottish civilization in cosmography', and, I suggest, the textual catalogue that follows it reinforces the specifically Scottish context of this memorialisation.[22]

There are five separate references to the 'barns of Ayr' in the *Complaynt*, suggesting this particular incident invented by Hary had become fixed in cultural memory, or, at least, certainly in Wedderburn's. All five references appear in Chapter XI, in which Dame Scotia focuses on refuting the claim of English overlordship of Scotland. In the first mention, Dame Scotia states that any Scot who

---

[20] A.M. Stewart notes that, given Wedderburn's role as chamberlain to the Knights of St John at Torpichen from *c.* 1549 to *c.* 1550, this list 'might well be a note of the reading of the Knights ... possibly even a note of books in Sandilands' library there'; 'The *Complaynt of Scotland*: A Critical Edition', 3 vols (Unpublished PhD thesis, University of Edinburgh, 1973), vol. 3, p. 84. See also Emily Allen, 'The Speculum Vitae: Addendum', *PMLA*, 32 (1917), 133–62.

[21] Michael W. Twomey, 'Pastoral Encyclopedism in *The Complaynt of Scotland*'s "Monologue Recreative"', in *Literature and Religion in Late Medieval and Early Modern Scotland: Essays in Honour of Alasdair A. MacDonald*, ed. by Luuk Houwen (Leuven: Peeters, 2012), pp. 93–112 (112).

[22] Twomey, 'Pastoral Encyclopedism', p. 111.

SUSTAINING THE 'NATIUE CUNTRE' 159

> consentis til his [the English king's] fals conques of ȝour cuntre sal be recompenssit as ȝour forbears var at the blac perliament at the bernis of ayre quehn kyng eduard maid ane conuocatione of al the nobillis of scotland at the toune of ayre, vndir culour of faitht and concord, quha comperit at his instance, nocht heffand suspitione of his tresonabil consait, than thai beand in his subiectione vndir culour of familiarite, he gart hang cruelly and dishonestly to the nummer of sexten scoir of the maist nobillis of the cuntre. Tua and tua ouer ane balk. (*Compl.* 73)

A similar passage occurs towards the end of the chapter, in which Dame Scotia compares those who are 'participant of the cruel inuasione of inglis men contrar their natyue cuntreye' shall suffer the same fate

> as kyng eduard did til scottis men at the blac parlament at the bernis of ayr quhen he gart put the craggis of sexten scoir in faldomis of cordis tua and tua ouer ane balk of the maist principal of them that adherit til hym in his oniust querrel quhen he vrangusle brotht mekil of scotland in his subiectione. (*Compl.* 81)

In between these two lengthier references to English duplicity working against the Scots, Dame Scotia reminds her three sons (and the reader) of this episode in relation to discussions of other examples of violent conquest that are contained in the 'croniklis of al cuntreis' (*Compl.* 73), whereby the destruction that 'kyng eduard did at the bernis of ayre' (*Compl.* 73) becomes the touchstone. The two other references occur when Dame Scotia describes how 'sextus tarquinus vsit his father counsel for he distroyit and sleu al the principal lordis of gabine as kyng eduard did to the lordis of scotland at the bernis of ayre' (*Compl.* 74), and when she comments on how Henry VIII's cruelty to the Irish and the Welsh should act as an example to Scotland because Henry employed the same approach towards Ireland and Wales as 'sextus tarquinus exsecut on the cite of gabine, and as kyng eduard exsecutit on the barrons of scotland at the bernis of ayre' (*Compl.* 74). There are two particularly notable aspects to Wedderburn's use of the Barns of Ayr episode here. The first is that the linguistic parallels between Wedderburn and Hary strongly suggest that the former directly used the latter and that he assumed that his readers would be familiar enough with the *Wallace*, or at least the Barns story, to call to mind the older text.[23] The second is that Wedderburn relies on verbal repetition throughout his own text, with little variance in the description of the Barns of Ayr episode. This duplication is a broader feature of Wedderburn's *Complaynt*, and throughout it acts as a memory aid for the

---

[23] Wedderburn's image of cords aligned 'tua and tua' is strongly reminiscent of Hary's description that I discussed in Chapter 4; see pp. 107–8.

160 REWRITING THE PAST IN SCOTTISH LITERATURE, 1350–1550

reader, forcing them to repeatedly think back and learn by encountering the same text or event multiple times.

As with Hary's *Wallace* and Bower's Coupar Angus prologue, though, the danger posed by the English may not only be a military one. Despite his statement that realms are not conquered by words but by blood, Wedderburn uses the *Complaynt* to consider the importance of textual memory. As mentioned above, the martial violence meted out by the English on the battle-fields of Scotland was supported by a programme of ideological warfare, and the early sixteenth century saw numerous English pamphlets arguing for the union of the English and Scottish crowns (under an English ruler, of course). This campaign, as noted in Chapter 2, had been going on since Geoffrey of Monmouth's *Historia Regum Brittaniae* and throughout the fourteenth-century Wars of Independence, but under Henry VIII, and then the duke of Somerset, it seemed as if this ideological warfare was, once again, gaining ground. The Complayner responds directly to some of these arguments and is quick to counteract any claims by the English to suzerainty; for example, in Chapter 10 he harshly refutes the 'prophesies of merlyne' to which 'the inglismen gifis vane credens' (*Compl.* 64). In noting that the English 'gifis ferme credit' to these prophecies, the Complayner argues that the 'oratours of Ingland … hes set furtht ane buik quhair be thai intende to preue that scotland vas ane colone of ingland quhen it vas fyrst inhabit' (*Compl.* 64). According to the Complayner, these divinations are not the predictive visions of 'ysaye Ezechiel, Ieremie' or 'the euangel' but, rather, the 'prophane propheseis' of a mythical figure and 'vthir ald corruppit vaticinaris' (*Compl.* 65). Wedderburn sought to malign Geoffrey's history at the same time that the writer's legacy and veracity were being debated in England, most notably by Polydore Vergil (1470–1555). However, Wedderburn is also careful not to discredit visions and prophecies per se, and, in attempting to discredit the divinations of Merlin, the Actor 'rehers[es]' the prophecy found in Higden's *Polychronicon* which indicates that England shall conquered by the Danes, Saxons and Normans before finally being 'conquest be the scottis' (*Compl.* 67). Clearly, some visions were more dubious than others, and Wedderburn is cognisant of the memorial possibility of the dream vision throughout the *Complaynt*, where the main structural dream exists almost as an imagistic premonition that enables a reimagining of Scottish identity.

To an extent the *Complaynt*'s view of Scottish nationhood is determined by the inflammatory anti-English invective that appears in texts such as the *Wallace*, but the text also highlights the perceived need for unity (tempered with godliness) among the people of Scotland in order to deflect English aspirations to the Scottish throne, a union of which would be like a marriage between 'scheip and voluis' (*Compl.* 84). Unlike Hary's vehement attack on the English in the *Wallace* and rather more like Lyndsay's *Dreme*, the *Complaynt* makes a case for a self-reflexive resolution to the question of

SUSTAINING THE 'NATIUE CUNTRE'   161

Scottish nationhood, or what A.M. Stewart describes as an 'understanding of patriotism in a Ciceronian moral sense'.[24] In this regard, the Actor understands Scottishness as loyalty to a *concordia ordinum*, a need for unselfishness, concord and unity in defence of the commonweal; such a stance marks the development of a concern about good governance that has a long tradition in medieval Scottish literature.[25] This self-reflexive framework comes to the fore in the framing of the English threat to the Scots and in the anti-unionist stance of Wedderburn's text; the threat of English invasion is not the principal cause of Dame Scotia's plight but, rather, a direct consequence of Scotland's failure to defend and sustain itself. There is no denying that the English have colonial designs on Scotland, as Wedderburn repeatedly reminds his reader, but, according to the *Complaynt*, it is the lack of unity among Scotland's own people that renders the kingdom vulnerable to the power of its 'ald enemeis' (*Compl.* 1). Where Lyndsay's *Dreme* focused on the king as the country's primary stabilising force and the one responsible for the governance of the realm, the *Complaynt* emphasises the responsibilities of the three estates – and by extension the *common weal*, in the sense of being a synonym for all the monarch's subjects – in providing for, and ensuring, Scotland's health and prosperity (its *common weal*) alongside its liberty.[26] In this way, the *common weal* becomes a key organising idea in the *Complaynt* and Wedderburn uses its varied senses as part of a project of creating common understanding among his readers. We might find parallels to this in Lyndsay's political ideas in his later drama, *Ane Satyre of the Thrie Estaitis*, which was performed first in 1540 and then in a significantly revised form in 1552. In *Ane Satyre*, the figure of John the Common Weal – also found in Lyndsay's *Dreme* – once again appears in want of 'warme clais'.[27] John also threatens that, unless the Three Estates put themselves 'in ordour, / ... John the Common-weil man beg on the bordour'.[28] At the end of the play, John has been welcomed into

[24] *Compl.* xxxiv.

[25] Roger Mason's article on the *Complaynt* examines the debate that the text significantly contributed to 'a vigorous Scottish response to contemporary British unionist propaganda'. But Mason also draws attention to the Ciceronian elements of the text and the use that Wedderburn makes of humanist learning in support of the Scottish patriotic cause; 'Dame Scotia and the Commonweal', 129–50 (131).

[26] I am grateful to Roger Mason for discussion of this and for providing me with a copy of his plenary paper: 'The Idea of the *Common Weal* in Sixteenth-century Scotland', 16th International Conference on Medieval and Renaissance Scottish Language and Literature (Tuscaloosa: University of Alabama, 2021). See also Roger A. Mason, *Kingship and the Commonweal: Political Thought in Renaissance and Reformation Scotland* (East Linton: Tuckwell, 1998).

[27] Sir David Lyndsay, *Ane Satyre of the Thrie Estaitis*, in *Medieval Drama: An Anthology*, ed. by Greg Walker (Oxford: Wiley-Blackwell, 2000), pp. 534–623, line 2463.

[28] Lyndsay, *Ane Satyre*, lines 2464–5.

the Parliament; divested of his ragged clothes, he is provided with 'ane gay garmoun' and assumes his place participating in the production of legislation regarded as essential to the reform of the *common weal*.[29]

This focus, alongside other mid sixteenth-century texts that address the same concerns, suggests shifting ways in which Scotland might identify itself as a nation and differing perspectives on who was involved in determining and preserving that identity. Dame Scotia is explicit in her final exhortation to her 'thre sonnis', urging them to

> condiscend in ane faythful accord, than doutles god sal releue ȝou of the grit afflictione that ȝe haue indurit be the incredule seid of ingland, & alse i beleue that he sal mak ȝou ane instrament til extinct that false generatione furth of rememorance. (*Compl.* 147)

The call here is not only to concord, but also to rid Scotland of its memory of division, to engage in an act of selecting memories of Scottish unity against an English aggressor to imagine a future of Scottish prosperity. As has been the case in all the texts discussed in this book, forgetting plays as much a part in the construction of identity as does remembering.

From this discord and lack of good governance, the Actor deduces that the 'diuyne indignatione, hed decretit ane extreme ruuyne on oure realme' (*Compl.* 18). For the Actor, the only way to return to good governance and repel the English, who now occupy a position akin to a plague, is to 'retere fra oure vice, ande alse to be cum vigilant to seik haisty remeide & medycyne at hym quha gyffis al grace ande comfort, to them that ar maist distitute of mennis supple' (*Compl.* 18). In ways similar to Hary's presentation of William Wallace as Scotland's 'ramede', the Actor situates God as the ultimate salvation for a sixteenth-century Scotland in need of reform. The spiritual sickness afflicting the three estates (Dame Scotia's sons) has resulted in a secular punishment of a plague of potential English dominance. The chapters that precede the Actor's dream of Dame Scotia chastising her sons present a sermon-like call to repentance and national self-fashioning through a return to godliness. In particular, Chapter 4 'conferris the passagis of the thrid cheptour of ysaye, vitht the afflictione of scotland' (*Compl.* 22) and highlights passages from Deuteronomy and Leviticus in which God punishes the Children of Israel who turn away from him. The Actor laments that Scotland has 'sauen oure feildis to the behufe of oure enemeis, ve haue fled fast fra oure enemeis … ande alse ve maye persaue that ve haue beene scurgit vitht the plagis that ar contenit in the thrid cheptour of esaye' (*Compl.* 23). This equation of Scotland with Jerusalem and Judea is to be taken quite literally; the Actor argues that the 'passage of the text nedis nocht ane allegoric expositione, for the experiens of that passage is ouer manifest in oure cuntre' (*Compl.* 23).

---

[29] Lyndsay, *Ane Satyre*, line 3794.

Dreaming the Nation

As I have previously indicated, the *Complaynt* draws heavily on Alain Chartier's *Quadrilogue Invectif* (1422) in its use of the dream vision and the female personification of the land, but it also contains striking parallels with the Scottish dream vision tradition and, in particular, with Sir David Lyndsay's *Dreme* of 1528 in which Dame Remembrance guides the Dreamer and shows him the desolate state of Scotland under a badly governing king. The similarities are such that John Leyden (1775–1811) attributed the *Complaynt* to Lyndsay in his 1801 edition.[30] The use of the dream vision by both Lyndsay and Wedderburn attests to its literary form contributing to the ongoing controversy over the nation through the sixteenth century.[31]

In Chapter 6 of the *Complaynt*, the chapter known as the 'Monologue recreatyue', the Actor comments that writing the first five chapters has the effect of making his body 'be cum imbecille and verye' (*Compl.* 29). Here the Actor demonstrates the physical effects of excessive 'mind-work': the Actor's 'rason' becomes 'fatigat' and 'al [his] membris be cum impotent' (*Compl.* 29). The impotence of the 'membris' directly notes how excessive cognition induces tiredness, which has direct repercussions on that same cognitive function. Here the Actor demonstrates familiarity with the general model of cognition, which understood the second cell of the brain (the *vis cogitativa*) as the rational component, which interpreted and made judgements about information received by the first cell (the *sensus communis*).[32] If tiredness meant that the 'membris' could not receive sense perception correctly (they are 'impotent'), and the 'rason' was so fatigued that it could not process perception, the consequence is that the third cell of the brain – memory – could not function correctly either, because there was nothing to be stored, or that the material to be stored was in some way deficient. This feeling of tiredness exists separate from the condition of sleep, during which it was thought that the five senses were shut off completely and the only active part of the brain was imagination. There is also a moral quality to this tiredness, because not only does the body become weary but also too much writing has the effect of producing an emotional response; the Actor comments that his 'spreit be cum sopit in sadnes', understood as sorrowfulness or, possibly, melancholy (*Compl.* 29). This response is partly connected to the broad considerations

---

[30] *The Complaynt of Scotland; Written in 1548, with a Preliminary Dissertation and Glossary*, ed. by John Leyden (Edinburgh: A. Constable, 1801).

[31] Kylie Murray's forthcoming book examines in detail the centrality of the dream-vision to Scotland's literary and intellectual culture. See *The Making of the Scottish Dream Vision*, British Academy Monographs (Oxford: Oxford University Press, forthcoming).

[32] See, for example, Anthony J. Lisska, *Aquinas's Theory of Perception: An Analytic Reconstruction* (Oxford: Oxford University Press, 2016).

of the ethics of sleep in the Middle Ages, which viewed untimely sleep as bad for both physical and spiritual health, and the health of the community.[33]

This untimely sleep occupies the Actor's mind at the point when he recognises the effects of his 'solist and attentiue laubirs' (*Compl.* 29). He seeks to avoid 'the euyl accidentis that succedis fra the onnatural dais sleip' by choosing to get some fresh air, walking to the 'greene hoilsum feildis' to 'resaue the sueit fragrant smel' (*Compl.* 29). This 'glaidful recreatione' (*Compl.* 29) results in the Actor's meeting with the shepherds, who provide a lengthy description of the planetary spheres and then proceed to a story-telling and musical interlude. At the end of this restorative experience, the Actor purposes to 'returne to the toune … to proceid in the compiling of [his] beuk' (*Compl.* 53). As he does so, however, 'morpheus that slepye gode, assailʒeit al [his] membris, ande oppressit [his] dul melancolius nature … quhar for on neid forse i vas constrenʒeit to be his sodiour' (*Compl.* 53).[34] The Actor then, rather comically, 'purposit to preue ane prettic, i closet my een, to see gyf i culd leuk throucht my ee liddis', but his 'experiens vas sune expirit for tua houris lang', during which time he has a 'hauy melancolius dreyme' which 'perturbit the foure quartaris' of his 'dullit brane' (*Compl.* 53–4). At the beginning of the dream itself, a 'lady of excellent extracione ande of anciant genolygie' appears 'makkand ane melancolius cheir' for the 'grite violens, that sche hed sustenit & indurit' (*Compl.* 54). It is immediately clear that this visionary woman is not a guide like the figures encountered by Gray in the prologue to *Scalacronica*, Wallace in Book 7 of Hary's poem, or Dame Remembrance in Lyndsay's *Dreme*. The Actor's description here suggests something altogether more despairing and the strong emotion of the Actor occasions the visionary sleep in which the afflictions of Scotland that the Actor has been writing about – and which have prompted his weariness – are made manifest in the 'melancolius cheir' of the lady.

The lady's hair might be the 'cullour of fine gold', reminiscent of the women in Hary's *Wallace* and Lyndsay's *Dreme*, but it is 'feltrit & trachlit out of ordour' (*Compl.* 54). Her crown, likewise, is 'hingand & brangland' (*shaking*) so that it 'vas lyik to fal doune fra hyr hede to the cald eird' (*Compl.* 54). Her shield is engraved with 'ane rede rampand lyon in ane feild of gold, bordoryt about viht doubil floure delicis' (*Compl.* 54). If the reader had been in any doubt as to the identity of this figure, the description of the Royal Standard of the king of Scots ensures that the lady is to be understood as a

---

[33] See Megan G. Leitch, *Sleep and Its Spaces in Middle English Literature* (Manchester: Manchester University Press, 2021), esp. pp. 91–150. On the relationship between melancholy and sloth in Scottish literature, see Ash-Irisarri, 'Mnemonic Frameworks in *The Buke of the Chess*', pp. 41–60, and pp. 102–3 in this book.

[34] The linguistic parallels to Lyndsay's *Dreme* here are striking: 'Constranit I was to sleip withouttin more' (*Dreme*, 145).

SUSTAINING THE 'NATIUE CUNTRE' 165

personification of the Scottish kingdom.[35] The lion on the shield, however, is not the one that might be recalled as the victorious symbol used to denote the Scottish kingdom but is described as being 'hurt in mony placis of his body' (*Compl.* 54). Like the lady who is subsequently identified as the 'affligit lady, dame scotia' (*Compl.* 56), this injured lion suggests all is not well with Scotland. It pre-empts the description of Scotia's appearance in greater detail. Scotia's 'mantil' is of a 'meruelouse ingenius fassoune' and the Dreamer describes it in some detail:

> the fyrst part quhilk vas the hie bordour of hyr mantil, there vas mony precius stanis, quhar in ther vas grauit, scheildis, speyris, sourdis bayrdit horse harnes ande al vthir sortis of vaupynis ande munitions of veyr. in the middis of that mantil there vas grauit in carrecters beukis ande figuris, diuerse sciensis diuyne ande humain, vitht mony cheretabil actis ande supernatural miraclis. on the thrid part of that mantil i beheld brodrut about al hyr tail, al sortis of cattel ande profitabil beystis, al sortis of cornis eyrbis, plantis, grene treis, schips, marchantdreis, ande mony politic verkmanlumis for mecanyc craftis. (*Compl.* 54–5)

The clothing of Dame Scotia is thus a very literal representation of the three estates who are personified later in the *Complaynt* as Scotia's three sons. As I have suggested is the case with the description of the planetary spheres in Lyndsay's *Dreme*, the sense here is that the ordered mantle depicts the harmonious 'natural' state of an idealised Scottish politics. This is reinforced not only by the shepherd's descriptions of the planetary spheres in the earlier 'Monologue Recreatyue' but also by the Dreamer's account that the 'mantil' had 'bene maid & vrocht in ald tymys, be the prudent predecessours of this foyr said lady' (*Compl.* 55). The recollection of the predecessors of Dame Scotia invites the reader to perform memory work and successfully remember the past prosperity of Scotland by reconstructing a mental image of an intact and clean mantle. This recollection requires a journey into the past intimated by Wedderburn in the *Complaynt* but remains decisively at the general level, such that the text deals in the tropes of memory but never quite articulates specificity beyond the suggestion of Scotland's prosperous sovereignty that can be determined by the powerful tie of the lineage of the Scottish monarchy. The *Complaynt* reminds the reader of the importance of heritage and lineage, and the importance of the moral character of prudence in the good governance of a kingdom. Scotia's mantle is marked not only as a map or a diagram of

---

[35] Since the time of Alexander II (1198–1249), the royal shield had contained 'a ruddy lion ramping in his field of tressured gold'; Charles J. Burnett, 'Outward Signs of Majesty, 1535–1540', in *Stewart Style*, pp. 289–302 (294).

166 REWRITING THE PAST IN SCOTTISH LITERATURE, 1350–1550

a social system, but it is also 'grauit' with Scotland's memories, which are the very fabric of her appearance. The implication is that the audience should be able to read Scotland's collective identity on Dame Scotia's clothing, just as it might read its past through chronicles and other texts. This metaphor is distinctly linked to medieval *memoria*; as Mary Carruthers notes, memorial images were often grouped together, linked by a *catena* or chain. Even the *texta* itself, she suggests, with its literal meaning of 'something woven', demonstrates the connection between these embroidered images' representations of the past and their present significances.[36]

Having established this idealised view of Dame Scotia's intricately constructed mantle, with its representations of social structures and Scotland's heritage, Wedderburn immediately shifts the reader's perspective to the present condition of this social fabric, demonstrating the passage of time which makes remembering the past meaningful. Like the 'rayment' of Lyndsay's Iohn the Common Weill in both the *Dreme* and *Ane Satyre of the Thrie Estaitis*, Dame Scotia's cloth is 'reuyn & raggit in mony placis', so that the Dreamer can only 'skantly … persaue the stories ande figuris that hed bene grauit vrocht ande brodrut in ald tymmis' (*Compl.* 55). Concluding his description of Dame Scotia's apparel, the Actor writes:

> it vas baytht altrit in cullour ande in beaulte, and reuyn in mony placis, hingand doune raggit in pecis, in sic ane sort, that gyf thay hed bene present that vrocht ande maid it in the begynnyng, thai vald haue clair myskend it, be rasone that it vas sa mekil altrit fra the fyrst fassone. (*Compl.* 55)

For the Actor, Scotland is unrecognisable. That Dame Scotia's mantle is so 'altrit' that 'na man culd extract ony profitabil sentens nor gude exempil' from it (*Compl.* 55) implies that, without care and attention, the memories and lessons of history are not clearly visible; through inattentiveness, the historical fabric becomes unreadable and unusable. In a similar way to the excessive writing affecting the Actor's memorial ability, so the excessive neglect of Scotia's clothing results in a failure of memory; this condition negates the ability of prudence to use the past to make judgements about the future.

While the description of Dame Scotia (*Compl.* 54–5) is closely modelled on Chartier's depiction of France, the image of her mantle also recalls Boethius' vision of Lady Philosophy, whose gown is embroidered top and bottom.[37]

---

[36] Carruthers, *Book of Memory*, p. 78.

[37] For Chartier's description of France, see Alain Chartier, *Le Quadrilogue Invectif*, ed, by Florence Bouchet (Paris: Champion, 2011), pp. 10–14. Twomey describes Dame Scotia as 'a nationalist version of Beothius's Lady Philosophy'; 'Pastoral Encyclopedism', p. 97.

SUSTAINING THE 'NATIUE CUNTRE'   167

Unlike Philosophy's clothing, however, Dame Scotia's vestments are quite clearly perishable and she exists as an admonishing, as opposed to a consolatory, figure. Finally allowed to speak, Dame Scotia, with 'lamentabil regrettis' and 'mony salt teyris', contemplates the 'vidthrid barran feildis, quhilkis in vther tymis hed bene fertil in al prosperiteis' (*Compl.* 55). She observes her three sons:

> The eldest of them [the nobility] vas in harness, traland ane halbert, behynd hym, beand al affrayit ande fleyit for dreddour of his lyue. The sycond of hyr sonnis [the clergy] vas sittand in ane chair, beand clethd in ane sydegoune, kepand grite grauite, heffand ane beuk in his hand, the glaspis var fast lokkyt vitht rouste. hyr ʒongest sone vas lyand plat on his syde on the cald eird, ande al his clathis var reuyn ande raggit, makand ane dolorus lamentatione, and ane piteouse complaynt … he vas sa greuouslye ouer set be violens, that it vas nocht possibil til hym, to stand rycht vp. (*Compl.* 55–6)

Seeing her three sons in this 'langorius stait', Dame Scotia reproaches them 'inuectyuely of ther neclegens couuardeis ande ingratitude vsit contrar hyr' (*Compl.* 56). Reinforcing the damning indictment of the chapters before the 'monologue recreatyuve' and the dream, Dame Scotia expounds that the reason why her clothing is unreadable and ineffective is that its fabric has been abandoned by those who should maintain it: Scotia's three sons. The neglected text of Scotia's mantle comes to symbolise the mistreated land of Scotland and the occlusion of memory through the passage of time and negligence of duty. Dame Scotia recalls how she was in 'maist fortunat prosperite', but is now 'inuadit ande affligit be my ald mortal enemeis', by the 'maist extreme assaltis that ther pouuer can exsecute' (*Compl.* 56). These sons, however, have 'schauen them self ingrat dissymilit ande couuardis in the iust deffens of my veil fayr' (*Compl.* 56) and, in doing so, they have allowed Scotland to become an easy target for the English. The Scots need not worry about the English trying to 'scour out' (*Wall.* 7. 16) or 'extinct' (*Compl.* 2) their people and their memories, the *Complaynt* argues: by not taking care of the mantle, the Scots are guilty of this themselves. As Dame Scotia says to her sons: 'ʒe ar the aduerse party of my prosperite' (*Compl.* 58).

That the three estates are represented as Scotia's sons draws parallels with the Scota foundation myth and also with the vision of Margaret of Scotland in Bower's *Scotichronicon* that I discussed in Chapter 2. It suggests a continued tradition of thinking about legitimacy and sovereignty in Scotland that is tied to origins, antiquity and, importantly, family and memory. Moreover, rather than the more usual image of the body politic, here the *Complaynt* presents its readers with a 'family politic' – a mother and her sons as constituent parts of a kingdom – and an image of the social fabric of Scotland. Dame Scotia asks why her sons have no 'pytie of me ʒour natural mother or quhy haue

3e no pytie of 3our selfis?' (*Compl.* 57). She also reminds them that they 'ar sa diuidit amang' themselves that they ensure their 'auen distructione' and the 'miserabil subiectione' of their mother (*Compl.* 58). While Henry VIII's rhetoric employed the uncle–nephew trope to admonish James V, Wedderburn stresses the child's remembering its responsibilities to both its parents and its siblings; the reader is encouraged to extrapolate the domestic image's applicability to the kingdom, whereby Scotland is understood as the mother and the commonweal as the children. Where Lyndsay's *Dreme* had emphasised the good education and counsel of the king as the prerequisite for a stable, prosperous nation, the *Complaynt* prescribes vigilance and hard work for all Scots for the preservation of the community, something to which Lyndsay would turn in the second act of his *Satyre of the Thrie Estaitis*. The *Complaynt* is not an advisory piece as such; rather, it is a clear invective on the failings of its readers, who must necessarily identify themselves as one of Scotia's three sons. Addressed to all Scots, whatever their societal position, the *Complaynt* demonstrates their responsibilities to each other as a national community, a social fabric. In her reproach to her sons, Scotia specifically highlights the importance of memory. She asks: 'quhy remember 3e nocht, that natur hes oblist 3ou, til auance the salute, and deffens of 3our public veil?' (*Compl.* 57). The emphasis on obligation here demonstrates both a legal and a moral duty to play an active part in working for the prosperity of the realm. That this 'natural loue' and responsibility to one's 'natiue cuntre' should be 'inseperablye rutit in [their] hartis' is further confirmed by Scotia's argument that the subject is reliant on the kingdom, just as a child is reliant on its mother:

> 3our lyuis, 3our bodeis, 3our habitatione, 3our frendis, 3our lyuyngis, ande sustentan, 3our hail, 3our pace, 3our refuge, the reste of 3our eild, ande 3our sepulture is in it. (*Compl.* 57)

For Dame Scotia, all aspects of the individual's life are connected to the kingdom; the land provides sustenance and community that confirms a sense of belonging and identity. The consequences of not taking active responsibility for maintaining the land are clear: those who 'hurtis the public veil ... deserue as grite reproche as tha had sellit traisonablye the realme to there enemeis' for the 'proditione of ane realme succedis to the hurt of the public veil' (*Compl.* 57). The suggestion of treasonous behaviour here is further expounded in Dame Scotia's opposition of her enemies and her subjects. She tells her sons that

> my ald enemeis dois me grite domage vitht ane grite armye of men of veyr be see ande be land. bot 3e [her sons] vndir the cullour of frendschip purchessis my final exterminatione for falt of gude reul ande gouuernance. (*Compl.* 58)

The reader is meant to infer that the enemies to which Dame Scotia refers are the English, who hypocritically seek friendship with the Scots only with an eye to Scotland's destruction. The real traitors of Scotland, however, are not only the Scots who lack good self-governance and are therefore careless and apathetic but also those 'assured' Scots who had been bribed or intimidated into giving allegiance to the English king.[38] This destabilises Scotland, which, in turn, 'fulfillit the inglis mennis desyre', with the consequence that the people of Scotland 'helpit to distroye [their] natyue cuntre' (*Compl.* 58). In Chapter 11, Dame Scotia explicitly links the destruction of Scotland to the failure of memory. The threat posed by the English, she suggests, 'suld be occasione' for the Scots to 'expel hatrent diuisione & auaricius lyffing furtht of [their] hartis' (*Compl.* 70). Moreover, it 'suld prouoke [them] to remembir of the nobil actis of ʒour foir fathers & predecessours, quha deffendit this realme be there vailʒeantes', of which their 'may reid in diueresis passis of [their] cronikillis' (*Compl.* 70–1). Recalling the language of the *Complaynt*'s dedication, along with the working of Scotia's mantle, Wedderburn creates a catena throughout his work that is, ultimately, codependent on his readers' own memories and reading practices; the chain that strengthens the *Complaynt*'s own arguments seeks to weave individuals' memories into a collective 'mantil' of Scottish common understanding.

All that is left for the Scots if they choose not to remember their responsibilities is misery and subjection to the English, and their only hope of remedy is to return to the law of God. In Chapter 9 of the *Complaynt*, Dame Scotia exhorts her sons to 'praye to relief ʒou of ʒour afflictione' (*Compl.* 59), but this turn to God must be tempered with putting 'ʒour handis to verk to help ʒour selfis' in order that God 'sal be mersyful to ʒou' (*Compl.* 59). In true Scottish fashion, the *Complaynt* draws on the story of the Maccabees as a chosen people, positing them as an example for the Scots. At this juncture, the use of this particular image is telling. Considering how much nationalist writing in late medieval Scotland aligns the Scots with the Maccabees, it is likely that the parallel would have been familiar to the *Complaynt*'s readers, but Wedderburn inverts the story to suggest that the Scots *could* be like the Maccabees but, to do so, they need to reform. The way to do this, Wedderburn explicates, is for the three estates to 'expel discentione discord, and ald fede that ringis amang ʒou ... and then ʒe sal triumphe contrar ʒour enemeis' (*Compl.* 137). Here the Maccabees do not encode a tradition of violent resistance as they had in the texts of the fourteenth and fifteenth centuries; rather, they act as a memory of national solidarity as a mode of triumph. Dame Scotia thus asks her sons to remember the examples she has given them of 'nobil romans' and how they

---

[38] Amy Blakeway, 'Assured Scots', *ODNB* [accessed 20 December 2023]. See also Marcus Merriman, 'The Assured Scots: Scottish Collaboration with England during the Rough Wooing', *SHR*, 47 (1968), 10–34.

'concurrit to giddir in accord for defens of there natyue cuntre' (*Compl*.140),
hoping that this memory will

> prouoke ȝou to forȝet the hatrent and rancour that mony of ȝou hes
> contrar vthirs, and to gar ȝou tak curage til accord vitht ane consent
> to resist ȝour ald enemies of ingland. (*Compl*. 140)

The use of 'mony of ȝou' implies that the exhortation has moved beyond
Dame Scotia talking to her three sons and the three estates have become fully
realised as Dame Scotia directly address the myriad readers of the *Complaynt*.

The dream vision in Wedderburn's *Complaynt* never finishes; the last words
are with Dame Scotia and her continuing plea to the Scots to see themselves
as a community and to act morally in such a way that Scotland is able to
defend itself against its old enemies. Like Lyndsay's vision of Scotland, the
land can be fertile and Scotland can sustain itself if the Scots govern it well.
For the Actor, however, good governance is not just the responsibility of
the monarch but is the legal and moral duty of every Scot. Moreover, as
Wedderburn's repeated allusions to lineage, family and the chains linking past,
present and future indicate, the health of the nation depends on memory. In
this way, remembering the past not only assumes meaning in the present but
also becomes the therapeutic potential that can direct the future.

Throughout this chapter, I have suggested that Wedderburn's *Complaynt
of Scotland* demonstrates some of the ways in which the continuity and
difference of Scottish writers' use of memory can be traced through the
early to mid-sixteenth century. Far from being ignorant of the long history
of strained Anglo-Scottish relations, Wedderburn utilises the memories of
previous conflict as a way of imagining solutions to the current situation. In this
respect, he continues a tradition of late medieval writing about the legacy of
the Scottish Wars of Independence. However, as can be seen in Lyndsay's early
poetry, Wedderburn shifts the memorial emphasis and is directly concerned
with the moral aptitude of the commonweal as a marker of its success and
identity as a sovereign nation. In the *Complaynt*, Wedderburn looks to the past
and foregrounds the memory of what Scotland once was – a harmonious and
productive land – and in doing so insists on self-reflexive memory as the way
to remind his contemporaneous readers of their responsibilities to the country
and to each other. The shift is from violent resistance to the moral strength of
the three estates to work productively together for the health of the nation. In
doing so, the *Complaynt* seeks to ensure that Scotland's enemies have no allies
north of the border, and here Wedderburn is quite vocal in his anti-English, or
anti-unionist, sentiments. Through his repeated invective and calls to remember
English atrocities encapsulated in such imaginative history as Hary's Barns of
Ayr episode, Wedderburn's *Complaynt* demonstrates that, while through the

sixteenth century the national focus might have shifted towards the character of the Scots' treatment of themselves, English aggression and its military effects were not so easily erased from the Scottish cultural memory.

Conclusion: Making Stories, Making Memories

Throughout this book, I have traced how some of the major Scottish literary productions of the late-fourteenth to the mid-sixteenth century encourage their audiences to draw on the past as an essential component of shaping and reshaping their conceptions of Scottishness. The book set out to examine how late medieval writers of northern England and Scotland sought to engage memory – a fundamental part of European medieval culture – to formulate and articulate expressions of Scottish national identity that was primarily predicated on Anglo-Scottish tension, real or imagined. *Memoria* takes on various forms in these writings, and the texts of this study reveal a multi-faceted relationship between memory and the cultivation of national feeling.

The preceding six chapters have explored a range of texts, from Gray's *Scalacronica* to Wedderburn's *Complaynt of Scotland*. All of these works demonstrate that, between the mid-fourteenth and mid-sixteenth centuries, memory informed, permeated and enhanced textual articulations of Scottish identity at specific moments in the history of the nation. They draw together several modes of memory – genealogy, historiography, invented memory, enforced forgetting, dream vision – to construct a framework of collective national imagining. The memorial modes reach across both Latin and vernacular texts and indicate a sustained engagement with remembering and rewriting the past throughout late medieval Scotland. For texts such as Gray's *Scalacronica*, Holland's *Buke of the Howlat* and Andrew of Wyntoun's *Original Chronicle*, borders – physical and psychological – provide a focus for the cultural production of national memory; a border's presence, and permeability, becomes a distinctive feature of the literary imagination. In quite different ways, Gray and Holland see the Anglo-Scottish border as a dominant marker of identity. For Gray, the possibility of a Marcher identity – complementary to, but never quite more significant than his status as 'English' – prompts a reimagining of personal and literary identity. Gray's negotiations rely on deploying mnemonic games for an audience who must use their own memory to make sense of the literary puzzles Gray foregrounds in his prologue. For Holland, the symbolism of the Anglo-Scottish border becomes a strategy for commemorating his patron's family at a point in time when their favour with the Stewart king, James II, was very

CONCLUSION 173

much on the wane, if not obliterated. Writing at both temporal and geographic distance from the Douglas domination of the Borders, time and space become productive sites of memory for Holland, who also uses the opportunity to look towards contemporary Scottish divisions – primarily linguistic – to interrogate the intersection of personal, local and regnal affiliations. Holland was not the only writer of early to mid-fifteenth-century Scotland to take an interest in articulating the multiple communal identities at play in the kingdom. Andrew of Wyntoun's accounts of tensions among Scottish regions demonstrate that representing a nation assumed a complex negotiation of identities in which the historian's definitions of the linguistic marker 'Scottis' occasionally slips from referring to those who spoke Gaelic to those who would commonly refer to their language as 'Inglis'. Yet, the ideological sense of who can be classed as 'Scottis' has a broader geographical reach when Wyntoun refers to the completeness of Scottish territories at the end of Robert II's reign. Here the sense of 'Scottis' is more capacious than categorising people by linguistic distinction. While the definitive shift from 'Inglis' to 'Scottis' in lowland conceptions of the language is usually tied to Gavin Douglas's quite conscious distinction between the 'langage of the Scottis natioun' and that of 'Inglys', the antecedents of this can be seen in texts such as the *Original Chronicle*, written almost a century before Douglas's translation of Virgil's *Aeneid*, where they signal the many communities that constituted the realm.[1]

Family and national identity are bridged in narratives of national origin, linking the present Scotland with a historical and mythical past as memorial repetition is shaped by different writers to varying political ends. Both king lists and their embellished versions found in Scottish chronicles throughout the medieval period attest to an understanding of genealogy as a form and component of memory. But it is a form that is dynamic; while these familial lines assume continuity, they recognise that malleability of narrative is fundamental to memory's success. In this respect, the varied narratives that are composed in late medieval Scotland demonstrate the rich memorial processes at work in textual productions that seek both to remember and to forget. As a case study in reimagining the Scottish past, Chapter 3 looked at the prologue to the Coupar Angus recension of Bower's *Scotichronicon*, in which an invented memory enacts mnemonic processes as well as being about historical remembering. Drawing on the affective component of memory – the concept that unusual or highly emotive images were more easily stored and remembered – Bower explains the paucity of Scottish historical writing and the reason for Fordun's compilation of the *Chronica Gentis Scotorum* by distilling English aggression into a destruction of written national memory. The act of burning books is, simultaneously, a striking image for Bower's audience and a past event that prompted

[1] Douglas, *Eneados*, I. Prol. 103, 109.

174 REWRITING THE PAST IN SCOTTISH LITERATURE, 1350–1550

Fordun's actions to recover memory. In this way, the moral dimension of the faculty of memory assumes centrality in memorial creativity. The ideological use of memory that came to the fore in the previous three chapters becomes a fundamental feature of Hary's late fifteenth-century poem *The Wallace*, a text that shapes its audience's perceptions of the social amnesia of James III's reign. As in Bower's prologue to the Coupar Angus *Scotichronicon*, Hary betrays a concern with *poetic truth* – imagined events as a way of narrating the past – that draws specifically on the affective potential of memory to prompt present and future action. For Hary, the craft of memory is not conceptual but the principle of how the *Wallace* works to train his audience's recollective processes.

The literature of the first half of the sixteenth century continues to imagine the relationship between literary history, cultural memory and the articulation of Scottishness. While attention shifts away from the Wars of Independence in the early poetry of David Lyndsay, focus on the king and the *common weal* endures. Lyndsay's *Dreme* and the *Testament of the Papyngo* are inflected with the Advice to Princes genre that marks much late medieval Scottish literature and, in seeking to educate the young James V, Lyndsay sustains a commentary on prudence as a virtue and memory's role in the successful execution of that virtue. The *Complaynt of Scotland* not only reimagines the ragged country of Scotland shown to the dreamer by Dame Remembrance in Lyndsay's *Dreme*, it also returns to the concern with forgetting that characterised Bower's Coupar Angus recension of *Scotichronicon* and Hary's *Wallace*. In doing so, it serves as a textual reminder of the dangers of failing to remember what it meant to be a member of the Scottish national community. It is clear that texts produced during the Stewart dynasty are deeply concerned with memory, it uses and the ends to which it can deployed in rewriting the Scottish past. The literary productions discussed throughout this book demonstrate how the practice of memory – as a process of selective and inventive reconstruction – works to reimagine Scotland and its past in the articulation of communal identity.

At the end of this book, I return to its beginning. In *Scalacronica*, Sir Thomas Gray writes that, following the death of Alexander III in 1286, the lords of Scotland, 'sensing the beginnings of an eventual contest for the realm', agreed a strategy with Edward I's council that Edward's son, Edward of Caernarvon, should marry Alexander's granddaughter Margaret, 'so as to have peace' (*Scal.* 13). According to Gray, the English and Scottish councils agreed that prince Edward should

> remain in Scotland while this father lived, and that after his death, he should always remain for one year in one realm, and another year on the other; and that he should always leave his officers and ministers of the one realm at the beginning of the Marches of the other, so that his council should always be of the nation of the realm in which he was staying at the time. (*Scal.* 13)

CONCLUSION 175

This agreement, while uniting the kingdoms of Scotland and England, also divides them. Agreeing that the king's counsellors should always be 'of the nation of the realm' (*nacioun de realme*) in which the king resides reveals an assumption of the insurmountable diversity of peoples that make up the island of Britain. Thus, an imagined 'united nation' in the fourteenth century conceives of a hybrid supranational – or supraregnal – community that maintains a challenging multiplicity. While the settlement posits a pragmatic solution to the issue of one king ruling two kingdoms, the implication is that these two kingdoms are sufficiently different as to be incompatible with each other.

Of course, in 1603 this union of one king and two parliaments became a reality when James VI (1566–1625) succeeded Elizabeth I and became James I of England. The literature of the early union years brings together many of the ideas I have discussed in this study. Beyond 1550, the links between memory and nation continue in the Scottish literary tradition. The union of the kingdoms necessarily raised questions about literary expressions of Scottishness and, while Britain might have taken shape under a Scottish – and a Stewart – monarch, for Scotland, the figurehead of the centre of power became more remote. After thirty-six years of rule in Scotland, James VI 'decamped' to London. James, himself, sought to de-emphasise his Scottishness in England, recollecting his English heritage and reshaping his personal history to focus on what the Scots and the English had in common. In doing so, he looked to create (or recreate) a greater kingdom of Britain. In a commission written at Hampton Court in February 1604, and read to the Scottish parliament in April of the same year, James took pains to insist that the 'singular mercy and benevolence' of God towards the 'old and ancient kingdom of Scotland' had resulted in a union with 'the realm of England, with great joy and applause on the part of all the inhabitants of the entire island of Britain, separated as it is from the rest of the world'.[2] Representing himself as both a 'dutiful father and shepherd', James reminded the Scots that God had 'included the realms of Scotland and England within the ambit of one island, by language, custom, consent and unity of religion, and mutual harmony', conjoining 'these realms into one dominion'.[3] Here James reshapes the memory of the union of the crowns as a 'conscious coupling' destined by God. How successful it was as a project is an entirely different matter, as this act of imagining met with resistance both north and south of the border.

A number of English poems concerned with James's accession seek to establish the legitimacy of his inheritance, representing his succession as a new beginning, a 'returne' of comfort after the long rule of Elizabeth.[4]

---

[2] *RPS*, 1604/4/6 [accessed 9 September 2021].
[3] *RPS*, 1604/4/6.
[4] Samuel Daniel, *A Panegyrike Congratvlatorie delivered to the kings most excellent maiestie at Bvrleigh Harrington in Rvtlanshire* (London, 1603), lines 31–4.

176   REWRITING THE PAST IN SCOTTISH LITERATURE, 1350–1550

For example, Samuel Daniel's *A Panegyrike Congratvlatorie* (1603) sees the emergence of 'great *Brittaine*' (st. 2. 3) out of the union. For Daniel there is:

> No Scot, no English now, nor no debate: No
> Borders but the Ocean, and the Shore, No
> wall of *Adrian* serves to separate
> Our mutuall loue.
>
> (st. 2. 4–7)

The *Panegyrike* seeks to sweep away the Anglo-Scottish divisions that have been apparent in the literature that I have explored throughout this study. The border that was so crucial to Gray and Holland, for example, could now no longer mark such a national distinction. James's statement in 1604 was that England and Scotland 'raging to their very great detriment and to the comfort of their enemies, for many ages past so to speak savaged each others' entrails, and cruelly tore at each other with mutual butchery and a hatred which was insatiable and almost unending'.[5] This statement vividly recollects the long history of Anglo-Scottish conflict which I have suggested a body of late medieval Scottish literature sought to reimagine in the context of national thinking. In the greater Britain imagined by Daniel, however, the only border that now exists is the ocean surrounding the whole island. Furthermore, the poem appears to erase the Scottish and English identities in favour of an overarching British replacement: Scots and English now no longer exist as a result of the 'vnion' that 'makes vs more our selues, sets vs at one' with 'Nature that ordain'd vs to be one' (st. 3. 7–8). Daniel posits the Anglo-Scottish union of 1603 as something natural; a return to order that had been predetermined and always meant to be, but in such a way that subsumes Scotland into an English-centred understanding of what Britain is assumed to be. Where the Anglo-Scottish border in Holland's *Howlat* had been imagined as a militarised space of walls and impermeable boundaries, the poems of James's accession to the English throne use the river as a way of conceiving a more fluid boundary between the two kingdoms. In 'Faire Famous Flood', in which Scotland bids farewell to James as he crosses the Tweed to take up residence in London, Robert Ayton imagines that the river, 'which sometyme did devyde / … now conjoynes two diadems in one'.[6] Ayton reconceptualises the border, visualizing the Tweed as the 'trinchman' of the Scots' 'mone'.[7] The sense here is that the river acts not necessarily as a body of water that enables

---

5   *RPS*, 1604/4/6.

6   Robert Ayton, '24. Sonnet: On the River Tweed', in *The English and Latin Poems of Sir Robert Ayton*, ed. by Charles B. Gullans, STS 4th ser., 1 (Edinburgh: William Blackwood and Sons, 1963), p. 167, lines 1–2.

7   Ayton, 'On the River Tweed', line 4.

CONCLUSION

two-way traffic between Scotland and England; rather, the river becomes a symbol of loss, a geographical reminder of Scotland's incorporation into a broader union that the Scots' sense of identity needed to negotiate.

The Scots poets, therefore, are not always so celebratory, and voice an ambivalence about Scotland's fate in this union. Rather than expressing feelings of joy, desire or passion, Scottish writers emphasise feelings of loss and abandonment. In his poem 'Scotland's Teares', Alexander Craig (*c.* 1567–1627) laments that in losing its monarch to London, Scotland loses its identity:

> What art thou *Scotland* then? no Monarchie allace,
> A oligarchie desolate, with straying and onkow face,
> A maymed bodie now, but shaip some monstrous thing,
> A reconfused chaos now, a countrey, but a King.[8]

Craig suggests that Scotland is 'made Orphane' through the loss of its king (line 9), echoing James's self-presentation as a father figure. The language of loss in 'Scotland's Teares' reflects a mourning that echoes Gray's fears of abandonment by Edward I in *Scalacronica,* and this is coupled with images of chaos and monstrosity that characterise an ungoverned kingdom. In losing its monarch, the kingdom not only has no governor (it is parentless) but its face – its appearance or identity – becomes 'straying and onkow', unrecognisable, unknowable: Scotland without its king has no identity. Craig conceives Scotland as a body which is now 'maymed', shaped into a 'monstrous' entity that recalls both Lyndsay's John the Commonweal, who is 'raggit, rewin, & rent' (*Dreme*, 921) and the *Complaynt of Scotland*'s vision of the dishevelled social fabric of Dame Scotia. This monstrousness, referred to as a 'reconfused chaos', evokes the early Stewart years in Scotland, and 'Scotland's Teares' sees the union not as a joyful occasion but as a political situation that will plunge Scotland back into a state of instability. The anxiety that Craig expresses is that, in remaining in London, the 'sweet Prince', James, will 'forget' his northern subjects (line 58). While only a brief reference, this articulated anxiety about James's forgetfulness in 'Scotland's Teares' signifies that memory was still shaping the literary perspective of Scottish national identity at the beginning of the seventeenth century.

The Union of the Crowns under James VI did not mark the end of Scottish concerns with thinking the nation, but it did prompt discussions about the relationship between James and his Scottish realm, and the relationship between England and Scotland. As Sarah Dunnigan argues, at the Union, poetry in

---

[8] Alexander Craig, 'Scotland's Teares', in *The Poetical Works of Alexander Craig of Rose-Craig, 1604–1631, Now First Collected*, ed. by David Laing (Glasgow: Hunterian Club, 1873), pp. 18–20; no line numbers.

Scotland renewed political purpose, assuming a 'subtle, skillfully manipulated means of quiet dissent'.[9] The literature of the early union years raises questions about the literary articulations of identities that we might term national. As Scotland's focus of power became more remote, the works of Ayton and Craig, among others, seems to reflect this sense of loss and distance, despite the fact that they also moved to London. Whereas James sought to imagine a union of England and Scotland in a bond that was always inevitable, both English and Scottish writers remain more ambivalent about this project of rewriting the past. The immediate Scottish responses to James's accession look back to late medieval Anglo-Scottish relations as a way of responding to the present and, in doing so, they return to Scottish models of shaping the memory of the past. What I have shown through this study is that Scottish writers from the fourteenth to the sixteenth century demonstrate a sophisticated engagement with medieval memorial practices, adapting formal memory-training techniques within Latin and vernacular literature as a medium through which their audiences might begin to see, or remember, themselves as members of a national community. The texts examined here show how *memoria* takes on various forms; in doing so, they reveal a complex relationship between memory and the past in articulating what it meant to be Scottish and, importantly, in how the nation wrote itself.

[9] Sarah Dunnigan, 'Reformation and Renaissance', in *The Cambridge Companion to Scottish Literature*, ed. by Gerard Carruthers (Cambridge: Cambridge University Press, 2012), pp. 41–55 (51).

BIBLIOGRAPHY

Primary Sources

Manuscripts

Aberdeen University Library, SCA MM2/1
BL MS Harleian 712
BL MS Harleian 4764
BL MS Lansdowne 197
BL MS Royal 13 E. X
Brussels, Bibliothèque Royale de Belgique MS 7396
Cambridge, Corpus Christi College MS 133
Cambridge, Corpus Christi College MS 171
Darnaway Castle, the 'Dalhousie' MS
Edinburgh University Library MS 186
Glasgow, Mitchell Library MS 308876
Glasgow University Library, MS Gen. 333
Manchester, John Rylands Library Latin MS 8
NLS Adv. MS 19.2.2
NLS, Adv. MS 35.1.7
NLS Adv. MS 35.4.5
NLS Adv. MS 35.5.2
NLS Adv. MS 35.6.7
NLS Adv, MS 35.6.13
Oxford, Bodleian Library MS Arch. Selden B. 24
Oxford, Bodleian Library MS Fairfax 8
Oxford, Bodleian Library, MS Lyell 39

Printed Primary Sources

A collection of state papers, relating to affairs in the reigns of King Henry VIII. King Edward VI. Queen Mary, and Queen Elizabeth, ed. by Samuel Haynes (London, 1740).

A Declaration, conteyning the iust causes and consyderations of this present warre with the Scottis, wherin also appereth the trewe and right title, that the kinges most royall maiesty hath to the soverayntie of Scotland (London, 1542).

180 BIBLIOGRAPHY

Aristotle, *De anima*, translated by J.A. Smith from Ross's edition, in *The Complete Works of Aristotle*, ed. by J. Barnes, 2 vols. The Revised Oxford Translation (Princeton, NJ: Princeton University Press, 1984).

——, *On Memory*, translated with interpretative essays and commentary by R. Sorabji (Providence, RI: Brown University Press, 1972).

The Auchinleck Chronicle, ane schort memorial of the scottis corniklis for addicioun, ed. by Thomas Thomson (Edinburgh, 1819).

Augustine, *Confessions*, trans. by R.S. Pine-Coffin (London: Penguin, 1961).

Barbour, John, *Barbour's Bruce*, ed. by Matthew P. McDiarmid and James A.C. Stevenson, 3 vols, STS 4th ser., 12, 13, 15 (Edinburgh and London: William Blackwood and Sons, 1980–85).

Bellenden, J., 'The proheme of the croniculs compylit be the famous and Renownit clerk maister Iohine bellentyne', in *The Bannatyne Manuscript Written in Tyme of Pest, 1568 by George Bannatyne*, ed. by William Tod Ritchie, 4 vols, STS 2nd ser., 22, 23, 26; 3rd ser., 5 (Edinburgh and London: William Blackwood and Sons, 1928–34), vol. 2, pp. 9–19.

Boethius, *The Consolation of Philosophy*, trans. by Victor Watts, rev. edn (London: Penguin, 1990).

Bonner, E. (ed.), *Documents sur Robert Stuart: Seigneur d'Aubigny (1508–1544), Guerrier et courtesan au service de Louis XII et de François Ier* (Paris: Comité des travaux historiques et scientifiques, 2011).

Bower, Walter, *Scotichronicon by Walter Bower in Latin and English*, gen. ed. D.E.R. Watt, 9 vols (Aberdeen: Aberdeen University Press, 1989–98).

The Buik of Alexander the Conqueror, ed. by John Cartwright, 2 vols, STS 4th ser., 13, 16 (Aberdeen: Aberdeen University Press for the Scottish Text Society, 1986–90).

Charters of the Abbey of Inchcolm, ed. by D.E. Easson and Angus MacDonald, Scottish History Society, 3rd ser., 32 (Edinburgh: T. and A. Constable for the Scottish History Society, 1938).

Chartier, A., *Le Quadrilogue Invectif*, ed. by Florence Bouchet (Paris: Champion, 2011).

Chaucer, G., *The Parliament of Fowls*, in *The Riverside Chaucer*, ed. by Larry D. Benson and F.N. Robinson, 3rd edn (Oxford: Clarendon, 1987), pp.385–94.

The Chronicle of Froissart translated out of the French by Sir John Bourchier, Lord Berners, annis 1523–25, ed. by W.P. Ker (London: D. Nutt, 1901–3).

The Chronicle of Melrose, ed. by Joseph Stevenson, facsimile reprint (Lampeter: Llanerch Press, 1991).

Chronicle of Walter of Guisborough, ed. by Harry Rothwell, Camden Society, 3rd ser., 89 (London: Royal Historical Society, 1957).

Chronicon Angliae, ab anno domini 1328 usque ad annum 1388, auctore monacho quodam sancti albani, ed. by Edward Maunde Thompson, Rolls Series 64 (London, 1874).

Chronicon de Lanercost, ed. by Joseph Stevenson, Bannatyne Club, 65 (Edinburgh, 1839).

[Cicero], *Rhetorica ad Herennium*, ed. and trans. by Harry Caplan (Cambridge, MA: Harvard University Press, 1954).

BIBLIOGRAPHY   181

The Complaynt of Scotland; Written in 1548, with a Preliminary Dissertation and Glossary, ed. by John Leyden (Edinburgh: A. Constable, 1801).

The Complaynt of Scotland, by Robert Wedderburn, ed. by A.M. Stewart, STS 4th ser., 11 (Edinburgh: William Blackwood and Sons, 1979).

Daniel, S., *A Panegyrike Congratvlatorie delivered to the kings most excellent maiestie at Burleigh Harrington in Rvtlanshire* (London, 1603).

Dickson, T. and Paul J. Balfour (eds), *Accounts of the Lord High Treasurer of Scotland*, 12 vols (Edinburgh, 1877–1916).

Dunbar, William, *The Poems of Willliam Dunbar*, ed. by Priscilla Bawcutt, 2 vols (Glasgow: ASLS, 1998).

The Eneados: Gavin Douglas's Translation of Virgil's Aeneid, ed. by Priscilla Bawcutt, with Ian C. Cunningham, 3 vols, STS 5th Ser., 17, 18, 19 (Woodbridge: Boydell Press for the Scottish Text Society, 2020–22).

Extracta e variis cronici Scocie from the Ancient Manuscript in the Advocates' Library at Edinburgh, ed. by W.B.D.D. Turnbull (Edinburgh: Abbotsford Club, 1842).

Fernando de Rojas, *La Celestina*, ed. by Francisco Alonso (Madrid: Editorial Burdeos, 1987).

Flores Historiarum, ed. by Henry Richards Luard, 3 vols (London: HMSO, 1890).

Fordun, John of, *Johannis de Fordun, Chronica Gentis Scotorum*, ed. by W.F. Skene, Historians of Scotland, 1 (Edinburgh: Edmonston and Douglas, 1871).

——, *John of Fordun's Chronicle of the Scottish Nation*, ed. by W.F. Skene, trans. by Felix Skene, Historians of Scotland, 4 (Edinburgh: Edmonston and Douglas, 1872).

Gilte Legende, ed. Richard Hamer, with the assistance of Vida Russell, 2 vols, EETS OS 327, 328 (2006–7).

Gray, Sir Thomas, *Sir Thomas Gray: Scalacronica (1272–1363)*, ed. and trans. by Andy King, Surtees Society, 209 (Woodbridge: Boydell Press, 2005).

Gullans, Charles B. (ed.), *The English and Latin Poems of Sir Robert Ayton*, STS 4th ser., 1 (Edinburgh: William Blackwood and Sons, 1963).

Hary, *Hary's Wallace (Vita noblissimi defensoris Scotie Wilelmi Wallace militis)*, ed. by M.P. McDiarmid, 2 vols, STS 4th Ser., 4, 5 (Edinburgh: William Blackwood and Sons, 1968–69).

——, *Blind Hary: The Wallace*, ed. by Anne McKim (Edinburgh: Canongate, 2003).

Henryson, Robert, *The Testament of Cresseid*, in *The Poems and Fables of Robert Henryson*, ed. by H. Harvey Wood (Edinburgh and London: Oliver and Boyd, 1958), pp. 103–26.

Holland, Richard, *The Buke of the Howlat*, in *Longer Scottish Poems, vol. 1, 1375–1650*, ed. by Priscilla Bawcutt and Felicity Riddy (Edinburgh: Scottish Academy Press, 1987), pp. 43–84.

Ibn Sina [Avicenna, Latinus], *Liber de anima seu sextus de naturalibus*, ed. by S. van Reit, 2 vols (Leiden: Brill, 1968–72).

Ireland, John, *Johannes de Irlandia's The Meroure of Wyssdome*, ed. by Craig McDonald et al., 3 vols, STS 4th Ser., 19 (Aberdeen: Aberdeen University Press for the Scottish Text Society, 1926–90).

BIBLIOGRAPHY

Knox, J., *The history of the reformation of religion within the realm of Scotland ... Together with the life of the author, and several curious pieces wrote by him ... By the Reverend Mr. John Knox ... To which is added I. An Admonition to England and Scotland ... by Antonui Gilby II. The first and second books of discipline* (Glasgow, 1761).

Kundera, M., *The Book of Laughter and Forgetting*, trans. by Aaron Asher (London: Faber, 1996).

Laing, D. (ed.), *The Poetical Works of Alexander Craig of Rose-Craig, 1604-1631, Now First Collected* (Glasgow: Hunterian Club, 1873).

Leland, John, *Notable Things translated unto Englisch by John Leylande oute of a booke caullid Scala Cronica*; Appendix 1 in Thomas Gray, *Scalacronica*, ed. by Joseph Stevenson (Edinburgh: The Maitland Club, 1836), pp. 259–315.

Lyndsay, Sir David, *Ane Satyre of the Thrie Estaitis*, in *Medieval Drama: An Anthology*, ed. by Greg Walker (Oxford: Blackwell, 2000), pp. 535–623.

——, *Sir David Lyndsay: Selected Poems*, ed. by Janet Hadley Williams (Glasgow: ASLS, 2000).

——, *The Works of Sir David Lindsay of the Mount*, ed. by D. Hamer, 4 vols, STS 3rd ser., 1, 2, 6, 8 (Edinburgh and London: William Blackwood and Sons, 1931–36).

The Maitland Folio Manuscript, ed. by William A. Craigie, 2 vols, STS 2nd ser., 7, 20 (Edinburgh: William Blackwood and Sons, 1919–27).

Maitland, F.W. (ed.), *Records of the Parliament holden at Westminster 28 Feb., 33 Edw. I (1305)*, Rolls Series 98 (London, 1893).

Murray, A.L. (ed.), 'Accounts of the King's Pursemaster, 1539–40', *Miscellany of the Scottish History Society*, 10 (Edinburgh, 1965), 13–51.

Palgrave, F. (ed.), *Documents and Records Illustrating the History of Scotland and the Transactions between the Crowns of Scotland and England, preserved in the Treasury of Her Majesty's Exchequer* (London: Record Commission, 1837).

Passio Scotorum Perjuratorum, in Marquis of Bute, 'Notice of a Manuscript of the Latter Part of the Fourteenth Century, Entitled *Passio Scotorum Perjuratorum*', *Proceedings of the Society of Antiquaries of Scotland*, 19 (1885), 166–92.

Patten, W., *The Expedicion into Scotla[n]de of the most Woorthely Fortunate Prince Edward, Duke of Soomerset, Vncle Vnto our most Noble Souereign Lord Ye Ki[n]ges Maiestie Edvvard the. VI. Goouernour of Hys Hyghnes Persone, and Protectour of Hys Graces Realmes, Dominions [and] Subiectes made in the First Yere of His Maiesties most Prosperous Reign, and Set Out by Way of Diarie, by W. Patten Londoner* (London, 1548).

Pitscottie, Robert Lindsay of, *The Historie and Cronicles of Scotland*, ed. by Æneas J.G. Mackay, 3 vols, STS 1st ser., 42, 43, 60 (Edinburgh: William Blackwood and Sons, 1899–1911).

Richard de Bury, *Philobiblon*, ed. and trans. by E.C. Thomas (London: Kegan Paul, 1888).

Rotuli Parliamentorum, 6 vols (London, 1767–77).

Shakespeare, W., *Macbeth*, ed. by Sandra Clark and Pamela Mason, The Arden Shakespeare, 3rd Ser. (London: Bloomsbury, 2015).

Simpson, Grant G. and E.L.G. Stones (eds), *Edward I and the Throne of Scotland: An Edition of the Record Sources for the Great Cause*, 2 vols (Oxford: Oxford University Press, 1978).

BIBLIOGRAPHY

Thomas Aquinas, *St Thomas Aquinas on Politics and Ethics*, trans. by Paul E. Sigmund (New York: Norton, 1988).

Stones, E.L.G. (ed. and trans.), *Anglo-Scottish Relations, 1174–1328: Some Selected Documents* (Oxford: Oxford University Press, 1965).

Thomason, T. and C. Innes (eds), *Acts of the Parliament of Scotland*, 12 vols (Edinburgh, 1814–75).

Villon, F., *Oeuvres*, ed. by Louis Thuasne (Geneva: Slaktine Reprints, 1967).

Wyntoun, Andrew, *The Original Chronicle of Andrew of Wyntoun Printed on Parallel Pages from the Cottonian and Wemyss MSS., with the Variants of Other Texts*, ed. by F.J. Amours, 6 vols, STS 1st Ser. (Edinburgh and London: William Blackwood and Sons, 1903–14).

——, *The Orygynale Cronykil of Scotland. By Androw of Wyntoun*, ed. by David Laing, 3 vols, The Historians of Scotland, 2, 3, 9 (Edinburgh: Edmonston and Douglas, 1872–79).

Secondary Sources

Allen, E., 'The Speculum Vitae: Addendum', *PMLA*, 32 (1917), 133–62.

Anderson, B., *Imagined Communities: Reflections on the Origins and Spread of Nationalism* (London: Verso, 1983; repr. 1991).

Anderson, M. and Michael Wheeler, *Distributed Cognition in Medieval and Renaissance Culture* (Edinburgh: Edinburgh University Press, 2019).

Anzaldúa, G., *Borderlands/La Frontera = The New Mestiza* (San Francisco, CA: Aunt Lute Books, 1987).

Armstrong, J.W., *England's Northern Frontier: Conflict and Local Society in the Fifteenth-Century Scottish Marches* (Cambridge: Cambridge University Press, 2020).

Ash, K., '"I beseik thi Maiestie serene": Difficulties of Diplomacy in Sir David Lyndsay's *Dreme*', in *Authority and Diplomacy from Dante to Shakespeare*, ed. by Jason Powell and William T. Rossiter (London: Routledge, 2013), pp. 69–83.

——, 'Friend or Foe? Negotiating the Anglo-Scottish Border in Sir Thomas Gray's *Scalacronica* and Richard Holland's *Buke of the Howlat*', in *The Anglo-Scottish Border and the Shaping of Identity, 1300–1600*, ed. by Mark P. Bruce and Katherine H. Terrell (New York, NY: Palgrave Macmillan, 2012), pp. 51–67.

——, 'St Margaret and the Literary Politics of Scottish Sainthood', in *Sanctity as Literature in Late Medieval Britain*, ed. by Eva von Contzen and Anke Bernau (Manchester: Manchester University Press, 2015), pp. 18–37.

——, 'Terrifying Proximity: The Anglo-Scottish Border in Sir Thomas Gray's *Scalacronica*', in *Boundaries*, ed. by Jenni Ramone and Gemma Twitchen (Newcastle: Cambridge Scholars, 2007), pp. 30–44.

Ash-Irisarri, K., 'Mnemonic Frameworks in *The Book of the Chess*', in *The Impact of Latin Culture on Medieval and Early Modern Scottish Writing*, ed. by Alessandra Petrina and Ian Johnson (Kalamazoo: Medieval Institute Publications, 2018), pp. 41–59.

Asher, R.E., *National Myths in Renaissance France: Francus, Samothes and the Druids* (Edinburgh: Edinburgh University Press, 1993).

Bannerman, J., 'The King's Poet and the Inauguration of Alexander III', *SHR*, 68 (1989), 120–49.

Barrow, G.W.S., 'The Anglo-Scottish Border: Growth and Structure in the Middle Ages', in *Grenzen un Grenzregionen/Frontières et regions frontalières/Borders and Border Region*, ed. by Wolfgang Haubrich and Reinhard Schneider (Saarbrücken: Kommissionsverlag, 1993), pp. 197–212.

——, *The Kingdom of the Scots: Government, Church and Society from the Eleventh to the Fourteenth Century*, 2nd edn (Edinburgh: Edinburgh University Press, 2003).

——, *Robert the Bruce and the Community of the Realm of Scotland* (Edinburgh: Edinburgh University Press, 1988).

Baugh, A.C., 'Convention and Individuality in Middle English Romance', in *Medieval Literature and Folklore Studies: Essays in Honour of Francis Lee Utley*, ed. by Jerome Mandel and Bruce A. Rosenberg (New Brunswick, NJ: Rutgers University Press, 1970), pp. 123–46.

Bawcutt, P. and Janet Hadley Williams (eds), *A Companion to Medieval Scottish Poetry* (Cambridge: D. S. Brewer, 2006).

Bernau, A., 'Beginning with Albina: Remembering the Nation', *Exemplaria*, 21.3 (2009), 247–73.

Bernau, A., Sarah Salih and Ruth Evans (eds), *Medieval Virginities* (Cardiff: University of Wales Press, 2003).

Bevan, R., *The Destruction of Memory: Architecture at War* (London: Reaktion, 2006).

Bhabha, H.K., *The Location of Culture* (London: Routledge, 1990).

—— (ed.), *Nation and Narration*, trans. by M. Thom (London: Routledge, 1990; repr. 2003).

Black, M., *Models and Metaphors: Studies in Language and Philosophy* (Ithaca, NY: Cornell University Press, 1962).

Blayney, Margaret S. and G.H. Blayney, 'Alain Chartier and *The Complaynt of Scotland*', *RES*, 9 (1958), 8–17.

Boardman, S., 'A People Divided? Language, History and Anglo-Scottish Conflict in the Work of Andrew of Wyntoun', in *Ireland and the English World in the Late Middle Ages: Essays in Honour of Robin Frame*, ed. by Brendan Smith (Basingstoke: Palgrave Macmillan, 2009), pp. 112–29.

——, *The Early Stewart Kings: Robert II and Robert III, 1371–1406* (Edinburgh: John Donald, 1996).

——, 'The Gaelic World and the Early Stewart Court', in *Mìorun mór nan Gall, 'The Great Ill-Will of the Lowlander'? Lowland Perceptions of the Highlands, Medieval and Modern*, ed. by Dauvit Broun and Martin MacGregor (Glasgow: Centre for Scottish and Celtic Studies, University of Glasgow, 2009), pp. 83–109.

——, 'Highland Scots and Anglo-Scottish Warfare, *c.* 1300–1513', in *England and Scotland at War, c. 1296–c. 1513*, ed. by Andy King and David Simpkin (Leiden: Brill, 2012), pp. 231–53.

——, 'Late Medieval Scotland and the Matter of Britain', in *Scottish History: The Power of the Past*, ed. by Edward J. Cowan and Richard J. Finlay (Edinburgh: Edinburgh University Press, 2002), pp. 47–72.

Boardman, S. and Susan Foran (eds), *Barbour's Bruce and its Cultural Contexts: Politics, Chivalry and Literature in Late Medieval Scotland* (Cambridge: D.S. Brewer, 2015).

Boardman, S. and Julian Goodare (eds), *Kings, Lords and Men in Scotland and Britain, 1300–1625: Essays in Honour of Jenny Wormald* (Edinburgh: Edinburgh University Press, 2014)

Boulton, D.J.D., *The Knights of the Crown: The Monarchical Orders of Knighthood in Later Medieval Europe* (Woodbridge: Boydell Press, 1987).

Bourdieu, P., *The Field of Cultural Production*, ed. and trans. by Randal Johnson (New York: Columbia University Press, 1993).

——, *Outline of a Theory of Practice*, trans. by Richard Nice (Cambridge: Cambridge University Press, 1977).

Britnell, J. and Richard Britnell (eds), *Vernacular Literature and Current Affairs in the Early Sixteenth Century: France, England and Scotland* (Aldershot: Ashgate, 2000).

Broun, D., 'Becoming a Nation: Scotland in the Twelfth and Thirteenth Centuries', in *Nations in Medieval Britain*, ed. by H. Tsurushima (Donington: Shaun Tyas, 2010), pp. 86–103.

——, 'The Creation of Scotland', in *Why Scottish History Still Matters*, ed. by E.J. Cowan (Edinburgh: Saltire Society, 2012), pp. 11–23.

——, *The Irish Identity of the Kingdom of the Scots in the Twelfth and Thirteenth Centuries* (Woodbridge: Boydell Press, 1999).

——, 'A New Look at *Gesta Annalia* Attributed to John of Fordun', in *Church, Chronicle and Learning in Medieval and Early Renaissance Scotland: Essays Presented to Donald Watt on the Occasion of the Completion of the Publication of Bower's Scotichronicon*, ed. by Barbara E. Crawford (Edinburgh: Mercat, 1999), pp. 9–30.

——, 'A New Perspective on John of Fordun's *Chronica Gentis Scotorum* as a Medieval "National History"', in *Rethinking the Renaissance and Reformation in Scotland: Essays in Honour of Roger A. Mason*, ed. by Steven J. Reid (Woodbridge: Boydell Press, 2024), pp. 43–60.

——, 'Rethinking Medieval Scottish Regnal Historiography in the Light of New Approaches to Texts as Manuscripts', *Cambrian Medieval Celtic Studies*, 83, 19–47.

——, 'Rethinking Scottish Origins', in *Barbour's Bruce and its Cultural Contexts: Politics, Chivalry and Literature in Late Medieval Scotland*, ed. by Steve Boardman and Susan Foran (Cambridge: D.S. Brewer, 2015), pp. 163–90.

——, *Scottish Independence and the Idea of Britain* (Edinburgh: Edinburgh University Press, 2007).

Broun, D. and Martin MacGregor (eds), *Miorun mór nan Gall, 'The Great Ill-Will of the Lowlander'? Lowland Perceptions of the Highlands, Medieval and Modern* (Glasgow: Centre for Scottish and Celtic Studies, University of Glasgow, 2009).

Broun, D., R.J. Finlay and Michael Lynch (eds), *Image and Identity: The Making and Re-Making of Scotland through the Ages* (Edinburgh: John Donald, 1998).

Brown, M., *The Black Douglases: War and Lordship in Late Medieval Scotland, 1300–1455* (Edinburgh: John Donald, 2007).

—, 'The Scottish March Wardenships (*c.* 1340–*c.* 1480), in *England and Scotland at War, c. 1296–c. 1513*, ed. by Andy King and David Simpkin (Leiden: Brill, 2012), pp. 203–29.

—, *The Wars of Scotland, 1214–1371*, The New Edinburgh History of Scotland, 4 (Edinburgh: Edinburgh University Press, 2004).

Bruce, M.P. and Katherine H. Terrell (eds), *The Anglo-Scottish Border and the Shaping of Identity, 1300–1600* (New York, NY: Palgrave Macmillan, 2012).

Burgess, G.S. and Robert A. Taylor (eds), *The Spirit of the Court: Selected Proceedings of the Fourth Congress of the International Courtly Literature Society (Toronto 1983)* (Cambridge: D.S. Brewer, 1985).

Burke, P., 'History as Social Memory', in *Memory: History, Culture and the Mind*, ed. by T. Butler (Oxford: Blackwell, 1989), pp. 97–113.

Burnett, C.J., 'Outward Signs of Majesty, 1535–1540', in *Stewart Style, 1513–1542: Essays on the Court of James V*, ed. by Janet Hadley Williams (East Linton: Tuckwell, 1996), pp. 289–302.

Burns, J.H., *The True Law of Kingship: Concepts of Monarchy in Early Modern Scotland* (Oxford: Clarendon Press, 1996; repr. 2006).

Bynum, C.W., *Metamorphosis and Identity* (New York: Zone Books, 2001).

Cairns, S., 'Sir David Lyndsay's *Dreme*: Poetry, Propaganda and Encomium in the Scottish Court', in *The Spirit of the Court: Selected Proceedings of the Fourth Congress of the International Courtly Literature Society (Toronto 1983)*, ed. by Glyn S. Burgess and Robert A. Taylor (Cambridge: D.S. Brewer, 1985), pp. 110–19.

Cameron, J., ed. by Norman MacDougall, *James V: The Personal Rule, 1528–1542* (East Linton: Tuckwell, 1998).

Cameron, S., '"Contumaciously Absent"? The Lords of the Isles and the Scottish Crown', in *The Lordship of the Isles*, ed. by Richard Oram (Leiden: Brill, 2014), pp. 146–75.

Carey, H.M., *Courting Disaster: Astrology at the English Court and University in the Later Middle Ages* (New York: St Martin's Press, 1992).

Carpenter, S., 'David Lindsay and James V: Court Literature as Current Event', in *Vernacular Literature and Current Affairs in the Early Sixteenth Century: France, England and Scotland*, ed. by Jennifer and Richard Britnell (Aldershot: Ashgate, 2000), pp. 135–52.

—, '"Gely with tharmys of Scotland and England": Word, Image and Performance at the Marriage of James IV and Margaret Tudor', in *Fresche Fontanis: Studies in the Culture of Medieval and Early Modern Scotland*, ed. by Janet Hadley Williams and Derek McClure (Newcastle: Cambridge Scholars, 2013), pp. 165–77.

Carruthers, G. (ed.), *The Cambridge Companion to Scottish Literature* (Cambridge: Cambridge University Press, 2012).

Carruthers, M., *The Book of Memory: A Study of Memory in Medieval Culture*, 2nd edn (Cambridge: Cambridge University Press, 2008).

—, 'Reading with Attitude, Remembering the Book', in *The Book and the Body*, ed. by Dolores Warwick Frese and Katherine O'Brien O'Keefe (Notre Dame, IN: University of Notre Dame Press, 1997), pp. 1–33.

BIBLIOGRAPHY

Carruthers, M. and Jan Ziolkowski, *The Medieval Craft of Memory: An Anthology of Texts and Pictures* (Philadelphia: University of Pennsylvania Press, 2002).

Caruth, C., *Unclaimed Experience: Trauma, Narrative, and History* (Baltimore and London: Johns Hopkins University Press, 1996).

Cathcart, A., "'O wretched king!'": Ireland, Denmark-Norway, and Kingship in the Reign of James V', in *Rethinking the Renaissance and Reformation in Scotland: Essays in Honour of Roger A. Mason*, ed. by Steven J. Reid (Woodbridge: Boydell Press, 2024), pp. 118–39.

Cherry, T.A.F., 'The Library of Henry Sinclair, Bishop of Ross, 1560–1565', *Bibliotheck*, 4 (1963), 13–24.

Clancy, T.O. and Murray Pitttock (eds), *The Edinburgh History of Scottish Literature, Volume 1: From Columba to the Union (until 1707)* (Edinburgh: Edinburgh University Press, 2007).

Cohen, J.J., *Hybridity, Identity and Monstrosity in Medieval Britain: On Difficult Middles* (Basingstoke: Palgrave Macmillan, 2006).

——, *Monster Theory: Reading Culture* (Minneapolis: University of Minnesota Press, 1996).

——, *Of Giants: Sex, Monsters and the Middle Ages* (Minneapolis: University of Minnesota Press, 1999).

Coleman, J., *Ancient and Medieval Memories: Studies in the Reconstruction of the Past* (Cambridge: Cambridge University Press, 1992).

Contzen, E. von, and Anke Bernau (eds), *Sanctity as Literature in Late Medieval Britain* (Manchester: Manchester University Press, 2015).

Coombs, B., 'The Artistic Patronage of John Stuart, Duke of Albany 1518–19: The "Discovery" of the Artist and Author, Bremond Domat', *Proceedings of the Society of Antiquaries of Scotland*, 144 (2014), 277–309.

——, '"Distantia Jungit": Scots Patronage of the Visual Arts in France, c. 1445–c. 1545', 2 vols (Unpublished PhD thesis, University of Edinburgh, 2013).

Coote, L., 'Prophecy, Genealogy, and History in Medieval English Political Discourse', in *Broken Lines: Genealogical Literature in Medieval Britain and France*, ed. by Raluca L. Radulescu and Edward Donald Kennedy (Turnhout: Brepols, 2008), pp. 24–44.

Copeland, R., *Rhetoric, Hermeneutics, and Translation in the Middle Ages* (Cambridge: Cambridge University Press, 1991).

Cowan, E.J. 'Identity, Freedom and the Declaration of Arbroath', in *Image and Identity: The Making and Re-Making of Scotland Through the Ages*, ed. by Dauvit Broun, R.J. Finlay and Michael Lynch (Edinburgh: John Donald, 1998), pp. 38–68.

—— (ed.), *The Wallace Book* (Edinburgh: John Donald, 2007).

—— (ed.), *Why Scottish History Matters* (Edinburgh: Saltire Society, 2012).

——, 'William Wallace: "The Choice of the Estates"', in *The Wallace Book*, ed. by Edward J. Cowan (Edinburgh: John Donald, 2007), pp. 9–25.

Craigie, W.A., 'Wyntoun's "Original Chronicle"', *The Scottish Review*, 30 (1897), 33–54.

Crane, S., 'Anglo-Norman Cultures in England, 1066–1460', in *The Cambridge History of Medieval English Literature*, ed. by David Wallace (Cambridge: Cambridge University Press, 1999), pp. 35–60.

Crawford, B.E., 'The Fifteenth-century "Genealogy of the Earls of Orkney" and Its Reflection on the Contemporary Political and Cultural Situation in the Earldom', *Mediaeval Scandinavia*, 10 (1977), 156–78.

—— (ed.), *Church, Chronicle and Learning in Medieval and Early Renaissance Scotland: Essays Presented to Donald Watt on the Occasion of the Completion of the Publication of Bower's Scotichronicon* (Edinburgh: Mercat, 1999).

——, *The Northern Earldoms: Orkney and Caithness from AD 870 to 1470* (Edinburgh: Birlinn, 2013).

Dagenais, J., *The Ethics of Reading in Manuscript Culture: Glossing the Libro de Buen Amor* (Princeton, NJ: Princeton University Press, 1994).

Dijk, A. van, 'The Angelic Salutation in Early Byzantine and Medieval Annunciation Imagery', *Art Bulletin*, 81.3 (1999), 420–36.

Dodd, G., 'Sovereignty, Diplomacy and Petitioning: Scotland and the English Parliament in the First Half of the Fourteenth Century', in *England and Scotland in the Fourteenth Century: New Perspectives*, ed. by Andy King and Michael A. Penman (Woodbridge: Boydell Press, 2007), pp. 172–95.

Donaldson, G., *James V–James VII*, The Edinburgh History of Scotland, vol. 3 (Edinburgh: Mercat, 1965).

Duncan, A.A.M., *The Kingship of the Scots, 842–1292: Succession and Independence* (Edinburgh: Edinburgh University Press, 2002).

Dunnigan, S., 'Reformation and Renaissance', in *The Cambridge Companion to Scottish Literature*, ed. by Gerard Carruthers (Cambridge: Cambridge University Press, 2012), pp. 41–55.

Dunnigan, S., C. Marie Harker and Evelyn S. Newlyn (eds), *Woman and the Feminine in Medieval and Early Modern Scottish Writing* (Basingstoke: Palgrave Macmillan, 2004).

Durkan J. and Anthony Ross *Early Scottish Libraries* (Glasgow: J.S. Burns & Sons, 1961).

Elliott, E., 'Cognitive Ecology and the Idea of Nation in Late-Medieval Scotland: The Flyting of William Dunbar and Walter Kennedy', in *Distributed Cognition in Medieval and Renaissance Culture*, ed. by Miranda Anderson and Michael Wheeler (Edinburgh: Edinburgh University Press, 2019), pp. 86–98.

——, *Remembering Boethius: Writing Aristocratic Identity in Late Medieval French and English Literatures* (Farnham: Ashgate, 2012).

Ewan, E., 'The Dangers of Manly Women: Late Medieval Perceptions of Female Heroism in Scotland's Second War of Independence', in *Woman and the Feminine in Medieval and Early Modern Scottish Writing*, ed. by Sarah Dunnigan, C. Marie Harker and Evelyn S. Newlyn (Basingstoke: Palgrave Macmillan, 2004), pp. 3–18.

——, 'Late Medieval Scotland: A Study in Contrasts', in *A Companion to Scottish Poetry*, ed. by Janet Hadley Williams and Priscilla Bawcutt (Cambridge: D.S. Brewer, 2006), pp. 19–33.

Fisher, M., *Scribal Authorship and the Writing of History in Medieval England* (Columbus: Ohio State University Press, 2012).

Folger, R., *Images in Mind: Lovesickness, Spanish Sentimental Fiction and 'Don Quijote'* (Chapel Hill: University of North Carolina Press, 2002).

BIBLIOGRAPHY 189

Forter, G., 'Freud, Faulkner, Caruth: Trauma and the Politics of Literary Form', *Narrative*, 15.3 (2007), 259–85.

Frese, D.W. and Katherine O'Brien O'Keefe (eds), *The Book and the Body* (Notre Dame, IN: University of Notre Dame Press, 1997).

Galbraith, V.H., 'The *Historia Aurea* of John, Vicar of Tynemouth, and the Sources of the St Albans Chronicle, 1327–77', in *Essays in History Presented to Reginald Lane Poole*, ed. by H.W.C. David (Oxford: Clarendon Press, 1927; rep. 1969), pp. 379–98.

Garbáty, T.J., 'The Uncle–Nephew Motif: New Light into Its Origins and Development', *Folklore*, 88.2 (1977), 220–23.

Gellner, E., *Encounters with Nationalism* (Oxford: Blackwell, 1994).

Goldstein, R.J., '"For he wald vsurpe na fame": Andrew of Wyntoun's Use of the Modesty *Topos* and Literary Culture in Early Fifteenth-Century Scotland', *Scottish Literary Journal*, 14.1 (1987), 5–18.

———, *The Matter of Scotland: Historical Narrative in Medieval Scotland* (Lincoln and London: University of Nebraska Press, 1993).

———, 'The Scottish Mission to Boniface VIII in 1301: A Reconsideration of the *Instructiones* and *Processus*', *SHR*, 70 (1991), 1–15.

Gray, D., 'Gavin Douglas', in *A Companion to Medieval Scottish Poetry*, ed. by Priscilla Bawcutt and Jane Hadley Williams (Cambridge: D.S. Brewer, 2006), pp. 149–64.

Griffiths, J. and Derek Pearsall (eds), *Book Production and Publishing in Britain, 1375–1475* (Cambridge: Cambridge University Press, 1989).

Goff, J. le, *History and Memory*, trans. by Steven Rendall and Elizabeth Claman (New York: Columbia University Press, 1992).

Grohse, I.P., 'The Lost Cause: Kings, the Council, and the Question of Orkney and Shetland, 1468–1536', *Scandinavian Journal of History*, 43.3 (2020), 286–308.

Hadley Williams, J., 'David Lyndsay and the Making of James V', in *Stewart Style, 1513–1542: Essays on the Court of James V*, ed. by Janet Hadley Williams (East Linton: Tuckwell, 1996), pp. 201–25.

———, 'Sir David Lyndsay', in *A Companion to Medieval Scottish Poetry*, ed. by Priscilla Bawcutt and Janet Hadley Williams (Cambridge: D.S. Brewer, 2006), pp. 179–91.

——— (ed.), *Stewart Style, 1513–1542: Essays on the Court of James V* (East Linton: Tuckwell, 1996).

Hadley Williams, J. and Derek McClure (eds), *Fresche Fontanis: Studies in the Culture of Medieval and Early Modern Scotland* (Newcastle: Cambridge Scholars, 2013).

Hagen, S., *Allegorical Remembrance: A Study of the Pilgrimage of the Life of Man as a Medieval Treatise on Seeing and Remembering* (Athens, GA and London: University of Georgia Press, 1990).

Halbwachs, M., *On Collective Memory*, ed. and trans. by Lewis A. Coser (Chicago, IL: University of Chicago Press, 1992).

Hanawalt, B.A. and Michal Kobialka (eds), *Medieval Practices of Space* (Minneapolis: University of Minnesota Press, 2000).

Hannoum, A., 'Paul Ricoeur on Memory', *Theory, Culture, and Society*, 22 (2005), 123–7.

BIBLIOGRAPHY

Harikae, R., 'The Maitland and Sinclair Families: *The Chronicles of Scotland* and its Early Modern Readers', *Textual Cultures*, 7.1 (2012), 97–106.

Harrill, C., 'Sanctity and Motherhood in the *Miracula* of St Margaret', in *Christianity in Scottish Literature*, ed. by John Patrick Pazdziora (Glasgow: Scottish Literature International, 2023), pp. 16–34.

Heng, G., *Empire of Magic: Medieval Romance and the Politics of Cultural Fantasy* (New York: Columbia University Press, 2003).

——, *The Invention of Race in the European Middle Ages* (Cambridge: Cambridge University Press, 2018).

Higgitt, J., *Scottish Libraries*, Corpus of British Library Catalogues, 12 (London: British Library, 2006).

Hobsbawm, E., *Nations and Nationalism since 1780* (Cambridge: Cambridge University Press, 1990).

Holdenried, A., *The Sibyl and Her Scribes: Manuscripts and the Interpretation of the Latin Sybilla Tiburtina, c. 1050–1500* (Aldershot: Ashgate, 2006).

Houts, E. van, *Memory and Gender in Medieval Europe, 900–1200* (Toronto: University of Toronto Press, 1999).

Houwen, L. (ed.), *Literature and Religion in Late Medieval and Early Modern Scotland: Essays in Honour of Alasdair A. MacDonald* (Leuven: Peeters, 2012).

Huntington, J., 'Edward the Celibate, Edward the Saint: Virginity in the Construction of Edward the Confessor', in *Medieval Virginities*, ed. by Anke Bernau, Sarah Salih and Ruth Evans (Cardiff: University of Wales Press, 2003), pp. 327–43.

Hutson, L., *England's Insular Imagining: The Elizabethan Erasure of Scotland* (Cambridge: Cambridge University Press, 2023).

Ingham, P., *Sovereign Fantasies: Arthurian Romances and the Making of Britain* (Philadelphia: University of Pennsylvania Press, 2001).

Jager, E., *The Book of the Heart* (Chicago and London: University of Chicago Press, 2001).

Julião, R., 'Galen on the Anatomy of Memory', *Medicina nei Secoli*, 34.1 (2022), 55–75.

Justice, S., *Writing and Rebellion: England in 1381* (Berkeley: University of California Press, 1994).

Kantorowicz, E.H., *The King's Two Bodies: A Study in Medieval Political Theology* (Princeton, NJ: Princeton University Press, 1957; repr. 1997).

King, A., '"According to the Custom Used in French and Scottish Wars": Prisoners and Casualties in the Scottish Marches in the Fourteenth Century', *Journal of Medieval History*, 28 (2002), 263–90.

——, 'Best of Enemies: Were the Fourteenth-Century Anglo-Scottish Marches a "Frontier Society"?' in *England and Scotland in the Fourteenth Century: New Perspectives*, ed. by Andy King and Michael A. Penman (Woodbridge: Boydell Press, 2007), pp. 116–35.

King, A. and David Simpkin (eds), *England and Scotland at War, c. 1296–c. 1513* (Leiden: Brill, 2012).

King, A. and Michael A. Penman, 'Introduction: Anglo-Scottish Relations in the Fourteenth Century – An Overview of Recent Research', in *England and Scotland in the Fourteenth Century: New Perspectives*, ed. by Andy King and Michael A. Penman (Woodbridge: Boydell Press, 2007), pp. 1–3.

BIBLIOGRAPHY   191

—— (eds), *England and Scotland in the Fourteenth Century: New Perspectives* (Woodbridge: Boydell Press, 2007).

LaCapra, D., *Writing History, Writing Trauma* (Baltimore and London: Johns Hopkins University Press, 2001).

Lachaud, F. and Michael A. Penman (eds), *Making and Breaking the Rules: Succession in Medieval Europe, c. 1000–c. 1600* (Turnhout: Brepols, 2008).

Lavezzo, K., *Angels on the Edge of the World: Geography, Literature, and English Community, 1000–1534* (Ithaca, NY and London: Cornell University Press, 2006).

Lawlor, H.J., 'Notes on the Library of the Sinclairs of Rosslyn', *Proceedings of the Society of Antiquaries of Scotland*, 32 (1898), 90–120.

Leitch, M., *Sleep and Its Spaces in Middle English Literature* (Manchester: Manchester University Press, 2021).

Leitch, M.G. and C.J. Rushton (eds), *A New Companion to Malory* (Cambridge: D.S. Brewer, 2019).

Lendinara, P., 'The *Verse Sybyllae de die indudicii* in Anglo-Saxon England', in *Apocryphal Texts and Traditions in Anglo-Saxon England*, ed. by Katherine Powell and Donald Scragg (Cambridge: D.S. Brewer, 2003), pp. 85–101.

L'Estrange, E., *Holy Motherhood: Gender, Dynasty and Visual Culture in the Later Middle Ages* (Manchester: Manchester University Press, 2008).

Lewis, K.J., 'History, Historiography and Re-writing the Past', in *A Companion to Middle English Hagiography*, ed. by Sarah Salih (Cambridge: D.S. Brewer, 2006), pp. 122–40.

Lifshitz, F., 'Beyond Positivism and Genre: "Hagiographic" Texts as Historical Narrative', *Viator*, 25 (1994), 95–113.

Lisska, A.J., *Aquinas's Theory of Perception: An Analytic Reconstruction* (Oxford: Oxford University Press, 2016).

Lyall, R.J., 'Books and Book Owners in Fifteenth-Century Scotland', in *Book Production and Publishing in Britain, 1375–1475*, ed. by Jeremy Griffiths and Derek Pearsall (Cambridge: Cambridge University Press, 1989), pp. 239–56.

——, 'The Court as a Cultural Centre', in *Scotland Revisited*, ed. by Jenny Wormald (London: Collins and Brown, 1991), pp. 36–48.

Lynch, A., 'Malory and Emotion', in *A New Companion to Malory*, ed. by Megan G. Leitch and Cory James Rushton (Cambridge: D.S. Brewer, 2019), pp. 177–90.

Lynch, M., *Scotland: A New History* (London: Pimlico, 1991; repr. 1992).

MacDonald, A.A., 'James III: Kinship and Contested Reputation', in *Kings, Lords and Men in Scotland and Britain, 1300–1625: Essays in Honour of Jenny Wormald*, ed. by Steve Boardman and Julian Goodare (Edinburgh: Edinburgh University Press, 2014), pp. 246–64.

——, 'Richard Holland and the *Buke of the Howlat*: Remembrance of Things Past', *Medium Ævum*, 86.1 (2017), 108–22.

MacDonald, A.A., Michael Lynch and Ian B. Cowan (eds), *The Renaissance in Scotland: Studies in Literature, Religion, History and Culture Offered to John Durkan* (Leiden: Brill, 1994).

MacDougall, N., *James III* (Edinburgh: John Donald, 2009).

——, *James IV* (East Linton: Tuckwell, 1997).

BIBLIOGRAPHY

MacGregor, M., 'Gaelic Barbarity and Scottish Identity in the Later Middle Ages', in *Mìorun mór nan Gall, 'The Great Ill-Will of the Lowlander'? Lowland Perceptions of the Highlands, Medieval and Modern*, ed. by Dauvit Broun and Martin MacGregor (Glasgow: Centre for Scottish and Celtic Studies, University of Glasgow, 2009), pp. 7–48.

MacInnes, I.A., *Scotland's Second War of Independence, 1332–1357* (Woodbridge: Boydell Press, 2016).

MacQueen, H., *Common Law and Feudal Society in Medieval Scotland* (Edinburgh: Edinburgh University Press, 1993).

Mandel, J. and Bruce A. Rosenberg (eds), *Medieval Literature and Folklore Studies: Essays in Honor of Francis Lee Utley* (New Brunswick, NJ: Rutgers University Press, 1970).

Mapstone, S., 'Older Scots Literature and the Court', in *The Edinburgh History of Scottish Literature, 1: From Columba to the Union (until 1707)*, ed. by Thomas Clancy and Murray Pittock (Edinburgh: Edinburgh University Press, 2007), pp. 273–85.

——, 'The *Scotichronicon*'s First Readers', in *Church, Chronicle and Learning in Medieval and Early Renaissance Scotland: Essays Presented to Donald Watt on the Occasion of the Completion of the Publication of Bower's Scotichronicon*, ed. by Barbara E. Crawford (Edinburgh: Mercat, 1999), pp. 31–55.

——, 'The Scots *Buke of Physnomy* and Sir Gilbert Hay', in *The Renaissance in Scotland: Studies in Literature, Religion, History and Culture, Offered to John Durkan*, ed. by A.A. MacDonald, Michael Lynch and Ian B. Cowan (Leiden: Brill, 1994), pp. 1–44.

——, 'Was there a Court Literature in Fifteenth-Century Scotland?' *SSL*, 26 (1991), 410–22.

Mark, C.B.D., *The Gaelic–English Dictionary: A Dictionary of Scots Gaelic* (London: Routledge, 2007).

Marsland, R., 'Complaint in Scotland, *c.* 1424–*c.* 1500' (Unpublished DPhil thesis, University of Oxford, 2014).

Martin, J., *Kingship and Love in Scottish Poetry, 1424–1540* (Aldershot: Ashgate, 2008).

Martin, J. and Emily Wingfield (eds), *Pre-Modern Scotland: Literature and Governance, 1420–1587. Essays for Sally Mapstone* (Oxford: Oxford University Press, 2017).

Mason, R., 'Dame Scotia and the Commonweal: Vernacular Humanism in *The Complaynt of Scotland* (1550)', *The Mediaeval Journal*, 10.1 (2020), 129–50.

——, *Kingship and the Commonweal: Political Thought in Renaissance and Reformation Scotland* (East Linton: Tuckwell, 1998).

——, 'Renaissance and Reformation: The Sixteenth Century', in *Scotland: A History*, ed. by Jenny Wormald (Oxford: Oxford University Press, 2005), pp. 107–42.

Matthews, W., 'The Egyptians in Scotland: The Political History of a Myth', *Viator*, 1 (1970), 289–306.

McAnulla, S. and Andrew Crines, 'The Rhetoric of Alex Salmond and the 2014 Scottish Independence Referendum', *British Politics*, 12 (2017), 473–91.

McCann, I.L. and Laurie Anne Pearlman, 'Vicarious Traumatization: A Framework

BIBLIOGRAPHY

for Understanding the Psychological Effects of Working With Victims', *Journal of Traumatic Stress*, 3.1 (1990), 131–49.

McGladdery, C., *James II* (Edinburgh: John Donald, 2015).

McKitterick, R., *History and Memory in the Carolingian World* (Cambridge: Cambridge University Press, 2004).

McLean, T., *Medieval English Gardens* (London: Barrie & Jenkins, 1989).

McRoberts, D. (ed.), *Essays on the Scottish Reformation, 1513–1625* (Glasgow: J.S. Burns & Sons, 1962).

——, 'Material Destruction Caused by the Scottish Reformation', in *Essays on the Scottish Reformation, 1513–1625*, ed. by David McRoberts (Glasgow: J.S. Burns & Sons, 1962), pp. 415–62.

Merriman, M., 'The Assured Scots: Scottish Collaboration with England during the Rough Wooing', *SHR*, 47 (1968), 10–34.

——, 'Mary, Queen of France', in *Mary, Queen of Three Kingdoms*, ed. by Michael Lynch (Oxford: Blackwell, 1988), pp. 291–99.

——, *The Rough Wooings: Mary Queen of Scots, 1542–1551* (East Linton: Tuckwell Press, 2000).

Miall, D.S. and Don Kuiken, 'A Feeling for Fiction: Becoming What We Behold', *Poetics*, 30 (2002), 222–41.

Minnis, A.J. (ed.), *Gower's Confessio Amantis: Responses and Reassessments* (Cambridge: D.S. Brewer, 1983).

——, 'Medieval Imagination and Memory', in *The Cambridge History of Literary Criticism, Volume 2: The Middle Ages*, ed. by Alastair Minnis and Ian Johnson (Cambridge: Cambridge University Press, 2005), pp. 239–74.

——, *Medieval Theory of Authorship: Scholastic Literary Attitudes in the Later Middle Ages* (London: Scolar Press, 1984).

Minnis, A.J. and Ian Johnson (eds), *The Cambridge History of Literary Criticism, Volume 2: The Middle Ages* (Cambridge: Cambridge University Press, 2005).

Moll, R.J., *Before Malory: Reading Arthur in Late Medieval England* (Toronto: University of Toronto Press, 2003).

Morgan, A.L., '"To play bi an orchardside": Orchards as Enclosures of Queer Space in *Lanval* and *Sir Orfeo*', in *The Medieval and Early Modern Garden in Britain: Enclosure and Transformation, c. 1200–1750*, ed. by Patricia Skinner and Theresa Tyers (London: Routledge, 2018), pp. 91–101.

Murray, K., *The Making of the Scottish Dream Vision* (Oxford: Oxford University Press, forthcoming).

Neilson, W.A., 'The Original of *The Complaynt of Scotlande*', *JGEP*, 1 (1987), 411–30.

Neville, C.J., *Violence, Custom and Law: The Anglo-Scottish Border Lands in the Later Middle Ages* (Edinburgh: Edinburgh University Press, 1998).

Newsome, H., 'The Function, Format, and Performances of Margaret Tudor's January 1522 Diplomatic Material', *Renaissance Studies*, 35.3 (2020), 403–24.

——, '"sche that schuld be medyatryce (mediatrice) In thyr (these) matars": Performances of Mediation in the Letters of Margaret Tudor, Queen of Scots (1489–1541)' (Unpublished PhD thesis, University of Sheffield, 2018).

Nicolson, R., *Scotland: The Later Middle Ages*, Edinburgh History of Scotland, vol. 2 (Edinburgh: Mercat, 1974; repr. 1997).

Nora, P., *Realms of Memory: Rethinking the French Past*, 3 vols. Volume 1: Conflicts and Divisions, trans. by Arthur Goldhammer (New York: Columbia University Press, 1996).

Oram, R., 'Introduction: A Celtic Dirk at Scotland's Back? The Lordship of the Isles in Mainstream Scottish Historiography since 1828', in *The Lordship of the Isles*, ed. by Richard Oram (Leiden: Brill, 2014), pp. 1–39.

—— (ed.), *The Lordship of the Isles* (Leiden: Brill, 2014).

Owen-Crocker, G., 'The Interpretation of Gesture in the Bayeux Tapestry', in *Anglo-Norman Studies 26: Proceedings of the Battle Conference 2006*, ed. C.P. Lewis (Woodbridge, 2007), pp. 145–78.

Owst, G.R., *Literature and the Pulpit in Medieval England: Neglected Chapter in the History of English Letters and of the English People* (New York: Barnes & Noble, 1961).

Pazdziora, J.P. (ed.), *Christianity in Scottish Literature* (Glasgow: Scottish Literature International, 2023).

Penman, Michael A., *David II, 1329–71: The Bruce Dynasty in Scotland* (Edinburgh: Birlinn, 2005).

——, '*Diffinicione successionis ad regnum Scottorum*: Royal Succession in Scotland in the Later Middle Ages', in *Making and Breaking the Rules: Succession in Medieval Europe, c. 1000–c. 1600*, ed. by F. Lachaud and Michael A. Penman (Turnhout: Brepols, 2008), pp. 43–59.

Perkins, N., *Hoccleve's Regiment of Princes: Counsel and Constraint* (Cambridge: D.S. Brewer, 2001).

Petrina, A. and Ian Johnson (eds), *The Impact of Latin Culture on Medieval and Early Modern Scottish Writing* (Kalamazoo, MI: Medieval Institute Publications, 2018).

Poirion, D., 'Literature as Memory: "Wo die Zeit wird Raum"', trans. by Gretchen V. Angelo, *Yale French Studies*, 95 (1999), 33–46.

Porter, E., 'Gower's Ethical Microcosm and Political Macrocosm', in *Gower's Confessio Amantis: Responses and Reassessments*, ed. by A.J. Minnis (Cambridge: D.S. Brewer, 1983), pp. 135–62.

Powell, J. and William T. Rossiter *Authority and Diplomacy from Dante to Shakespeare* (London: Routledge, 2013).

Prestwich, M., *Edward I* (Berkeley and Los Angeles: University of California Press, 1988).

Purdie, R., 'Malcolm, Margaret, Macbeth, and the Miller: Rhetoric and the Re-shaping of History in Wyntoun's *Original Chronicle*', *Medievalia et Humanistica*, 41 (2016), 45–63.

——, 'Medieval Romance and the Generic Frictions of Barbour's *Bruce*', in *Barbour's Bruce and its Cultural Contexts: Politics, Chivalry and Literature in Late Medieval Scotland*, ed. by Steve Boardman and Susan Foran (Cambridge: D.S. Brewer, 2015), pp. 51–74.

Quilligan, M., *The Allegory of Female Authority: Christine de Pizan's Cite des Dames* (Ithaca, NY: Cornell University Press, 1991).

Radulescu, R. and Edward Donald Kennedy (eds), *Broken Lines: Genealogical Literature in Medieval Britain and France* (Turnhout: Brepols, 2008).

BIBLIOGRAPHY

Ramone, J. and Gemma Twitchen (eds), *Boundaries* (Newcastle: Cambridge Scholars, 2007).

Ranum, O., *National Consciousness, History and Political Culture in Early Modern Europe*, ed. by Orest Ranum (Baltimore and London: Johns Hopkins University Press, 1975).

Reid, S.J. (ed.), *Rethinking the Renaissance and Reformation in Scotland: Essays in Honour of Roger A. Mason* (Woodbridge: Boydell Press, 2024).

Renan, E., '"Qu'est-ce-qu'une nation?" – What is a nation?', trans. by M. Thom in *Nation and Narration*, ed. by Homi K. Bhabha (London: Routledge, 1990; repr. 2003), pp. 8–22.

Reynolds, S., *Kingdoms and Communities in Western Europe, 900–1300*, 2nd edn (Oxford: Oxford University Press, 1997).

Ricoeur, P., *Memory, History, Forgetting*, trans. by Kathleen Blamey and David Pellauer (Chicago and London: University of Chicago Press, 2004).

Riddy, F., 'Dating the *Buke of the Howlat*', *RES*, 37 (1986), 1–10.

——, 'Unmapping the Territory: Blind Hary's *Wallace*', in *The Wallace Book*, ed. by Edward J. Cowan (Edinburgh: John Donald, 2007), pp. 107–16.

Royan, N., 'Hector Boece and the Question of Veremund', *Innes Review*, 52 (2001), 42–62.

——, '"Mark your meroure be me": Richard Holland's *Buke of the Howlat*', in *A Companion to Medieval Scottish Poetry*, ed. by Priscilla Bawcutt and Janet Hadley Williams (Cambridge: D.S. Brewer, 2006), pp. 49–62.

——, 'Some Conspicuous Women in the *Original Chronicle*, *Scotichronicon* and *Scotorum Historia*', *Innes Review*, 59.2 (2008), 131–44.

Royan, N. with Dauvit Broun, 'Versions of Scottish Nationhood, *c.* 850–1707), in *The Edinburgh History of Scottish Literature, Volume 1: From Columba to the Union (until 1707)*, ed. by Thomas Owen Clancy and Murray Pittock (Edinburgh: Edinburgh University Press, 2007), pp. 167–83.

Salih, S. (ed.), *A Companion to Middle English Hagiography* (Cambridge: D.S. Brewer, 2006).

Scanlon, L., *Narrative, Authority, and Power: The Medieval Exemplum and the Chaucerian Tradition* (Cambridge: Cambridge University Press, 1994).

Scase, W., *Literature and Complaint in England, 1272–1553* (Oxford: Oxford University Press, 2007).

Scheer, M., 'Are Emotions a Kind of Practice (and Is That What Makes Them Have a History)? A Bourdieuian Approach to Understanding Emotion', *History and Theory*, 51.2 (2012), 193–220.

Schmid, K., 'Zur Problematik von Familie, Sippe und Geschlecht, Haus und Dynastie beim mittelalterlichen Adel: Vorfragen zum Thema "Adel Und Herrschaft im Mittelalter"', *Zeitschrift für die Geschichte des Oberrheins*, 105 (1957), 1–62.

Shimazaki, Y., 'L'Amour d'Hector et le motif d l'eiu dans le *Lancelot en prose*', *Études de Langue et Littérature Françaises*, 56 (1990), 6–7.

Skinner, P. and Theresa Tyers (eds), *The Medieval and Early Modern Garden in Britain: Enclosure and Transformation, c. 1200–1750* (London: Routledge, 2018).

Smail, D.L., *Imaginary Cartographies: Possession and Identity in Late-medieval Marseille* (Ithaca, NY: Cornell University Press, 1999).

Smith, A., *National Identity* (London: Penguin, 1991).

Smith, B. (ed.), *Ireland and the English World in the Late Middle Ages: Essays in Honour of Robin Frame* (Basingstoke: Palgrave Macmillan, 2009).

Smith, M.A., 'Assessing Gender in the Construction of Scottish Identity, *c.* 1286–*c.* 1586' (Unpublished PhD thesis, University of Auckland, 2010).

Smout, T.C. (ed.), *Scotland and Europe 1200–1850* (Edinburgh: John Donald, 1986).

Spiegel, G., *The Past as Text: The Theory and Practice of Medieval Historiography* (Baltimore, MD: Johns Hopkins University Press, 1997).

Steiner, E., 'Authority', in *Middle English*, ed. by Paul Strohm (Oxford: Oxford University Press, 2007), pp. 142–59.

——, *Documentary Culture and the Making of Medieval English Literature* (Cambridge: Cambridge University Press, 2003).

Stevenson, K., *Power and Propaganda: Scotland, 1306–1488* (Edinburgh: Edinburgh University Press, 2014).

Stringer, K., 'The Emergence of a Nation State, 1100–1300', in *Scotland: A History*, ed. by Jenny Wormald (Oxford: Oxford University Press, 2005), pp. 39–76.

——, 'States, Liberties and Communities in Medieval Britain and Ireland (*c.* 1100–1400)', in *Liberties and Identities in the Medieval British Isles*, ed. by Michael Prestwich (Cambridge: D.S. Brewer, 2008), pp. 5–36.

Stewart, A.M., 'The *Complaynt of Scotland*: A Critical Edition', 3 vols (Unpublished PhD thesis, University of Edinburgh, 1973).

Stewart, M., 'Holland's "Howlat" and the Fall of the Livingstones', *Innes Review*, 26 (1975), 67–79.

Strohm, P. (ed.), *Middle English* (Oxford: Oxford University Press, 2007).

—— (ed.), *Theory and the Premodern Text* (Minneapolis: University of Minnesota Press, 2000).

Summers, J., *Late-medieval Prison Writing and the Politic of Autobiography* (Oxford: Clarendon Press, 2004).

Taylor, B., *The Road to the Scottish Parliament* (Edinburgh: Pioneer, 1999; rev. edn, 2002).

Terrell, K., *Scripting the Nation: Court Poetry and the Authority of History in Late Medieval Scotland* (Columbus: Ohio State University Press, 2021).

Tsurushima, H. (ed.), *Nations in Medieval Britain* (Donington: Shaun Tyas, 2010).

Turville-Petre, T., *England the Nation: Language, Literature, and National Identity, 1290–1340* (Oxford: Clarendon Press, 1996).

Twomey, M.W., 'Pastoral Encyclopedism in *The Complaynt of Scotland's* "Monologue Recreative"', in *Literature and Religion in Late Medieval and Early Modern Scotland: Essays in Honour of Alasdair A. MacDonald*, ed. by Luuk Houwen (Leuven: Peeters, 2012), pp. 93–112.

Van Buren, C., 'John Asloan and his Manuscript: An Edinburgh Notary and Scribe in the Days of James III, IV and V (*c.* 1470–*c.* 1530), in *Stewart Style, 1513–1542: Essays on the Court of James V*, ed. by Janet Hadley Williams (East Linton: Tuckwell, 1996), pp. 15–51.

BIBLIOGRAPHY

Van Heijnsbergen, T., 'The Interaction between Literature and History in Queen Mary's Edinburgh: The Bannatyne Manuscript and its Prosopographical Context', in *The Renaissance in Scotland: Studies in Literature, Religion, History and Culture Offered to John Durkan*, ed. by Alasdair A. MacDonald, Michael Lynch and Ian B. Cowan (Leiden: Brill, 1994), pp.183–225.

Wakelin, D., *Scribal Correction and Literary Craft: English Manuscripts 1375–1510* (Cambridge: Cambridge University Press, 2014).

Wallace, D. (ed.), *The Cambridge History of Medieval English Literature* (Cambridge: Cambridge University Press, 1999).

Watt, D.E.R., *Guide to the National Archives of Scotland* (Edinburgh: Scottish Record Office, 1996).

——, 'Scottish University Men of the Thirteenth and Fourteenth Centuries', in *Scotland and Europe 1200–1850*, ed. by T.C. Smout (Edinburgh: John Donald, 1986), pp. 1–18.

Weiss, J., 'Memory in Creation: The Context of Rojas's Literary Recollection', *Bulletin of Hispanic Studies*, 86.1 (2009), 150–7.

Whitehead, A., *Memory* (Abingdon: Routledge, 2008).

Whitehead, C., *Castles of the Mind: A Study of Medieval Architectural Allegory* (Cardiff: University of Wales Press, 2003).

Wingfield, E., 'Kingship and Good Governance in Wyntoun's *Original Chronicle*', in *Pre-Modern Scotland: Literature and Governance, 1420–1587. Essays for Sally Mapstone*, ed. by Joanna Martin and Emily Wingfield (Oxford: Oxford University Press, 2017), pp. 19–30.

——, *Scotland's Royal Women and European Literary Culture, 1424–1487* (Turnhout: Brepols, 2023).

——, *The Trojan Legend in Medieval Scottish Literature* (Cambridge: D.S. Brewer, 2014)

Wormald, J., *Court, Kirk and Community: Scotland, 1470–1625* (Toronto: University of Toronto Press, 1981).

——, *Mary, Queen of Scots: A Study in Failure* (1988; repr. Edinburgh: John Donald, 2017).

—— (ed.), *Scotland: A History* (Oxford: Oxford University Press, 2005).

——, *Scotland Revisited* (London: Collins and Brown, 1991).

Yates, F., *The Art of Memory* (1966, London: Pimlico, 1992).

Young, A., *Robert the Bruce's Rivals: The Comyns, 1212–1314* (East Linton: Tuckwell, 1997).

Web-based sources

The Anglo-Norman Dictionary, anglo-norman.net

The Dictionary of the Older Scottish Tongue, www.dsl.ac.uk

The Middle English Dictionary, ed. by Robert E. Lewis, et al. (Ann Arbor: University of Michigan Press, 1952–2001), Online edition in *Middle English Compendium*, ed. by Frances McSparran, et al. (Ann Arbor: University of Michigan Library, 2006–2018), http://quod.lib.umich.edu/m/middle-english-dictionary/

The Oxford Dictionary of National Biography, https://oxforddnb.com

The Records of the Parliament of Scotland to 1707, ed. by K.M. Brown et al. (St Andrews, 2007–13), http://www.rps.ac.uk

Salmond, A., 'Address' to the Opening Ceremony of the Scottish Parliament in Parliament Hall, 1 July 1999, https://web.archive.org/web/20081028084301/http://www.scottish.parliament.uk:80/vli/history/firstDays/1999opening2.htm

The Scottish Government, National Outcome (2007), http://www.scotland.gov.uk/About/scotPerforms/outcomes/natIdentity

Scottish National Party, https://web.archive.org/web/20080624203841/http://www.snp.org/node/240

INDEX

Advice to Princes literature   37 n.51, 68,
  124–5, 130, 136, 137, 174
Albertus Magnus   132
Alexander II, of Scotland   19, 20, 61,
  62–3, 165 n.35
Alexander III, King of Scots   3, 10, 22,
  24, 34, 57, 60, 63, 72
  death   70–1, 151, 174
  inauguration   61–2, 63, 64–5, 68–70,
    75
Alnwick, Battle of   19
Anderson, Benedict   8, 10
Anglo-Scottish border   19, 21–2, 24,
  26–7, 39, 41, 46–7, 48, 49, 172–3,
  176–7
  the Marches, and   20–2, 23–4, 26,
    27, 174
Annunciation   67
Anonimalle Chronicle   93
Anzaldúa, Gloria   22
Aquinas, Thomas   135–6, 163 n.32
  Summa Theologiae   12, 15, 135–6
  De regimine principum   69
Aristotle   12, 143
  De anima   13
  De memoria et reminiscentia   133
  on visual memory   13
Arkinholm, battle of   42
Ashenden, John   142
The Auchinleck Chronicle   51
Augustine, St (of Canterbury)   9
Augustine, St (of Hippo)   13, 105
  Confessions   12, 15, 105
  De Civitate Dei   15
Ayton, Robert   176, 178
  'Faire Famous Flood'   176–7

Balliol, Edward   5
  the Disinherited, and   5
Balliol, John   3–4, 5, 22, 71, 73, 88, 93
Bannerman, John   65

Bannockburn, battle of   4, 5, 64
Barbour, John   25, 34
  The Bruce   25, 36, 38, 41, 42, 72, 77,
    135
Barrow, G.W.S   10, 19, 20, 22, 24
Baugh, Albert C.   86
Bede   31
Bellenden, John   85, 132 n.29
  Chronicles of Scotland   41
  'Proheme apon the
    Cosmographie'   131–2
Bernau, Anke   53
Berwick, Treaty of   5
Bevan, Robert   49, 92
Bisset, Baldred   55, 58
  Processus   55
Black, Max   13
Blayney, Glenn   156
Blayney, Margaret   156
Boardman, Stephen   26, 34, 40, 60
Boece, Hector   85
  Scotorum Historia   41, 127
Boethius   14, 137
  Consolation of Philosophy   31, 137,
    166
  imprisonment, and   27, 31
Boncompagno   133
Bonkyl family   47
Bower, Walter   9, 22, 50, 51
  See also Scotichronicon
Bradwardine, Thomas   141
Broun, Dauvit   5, 8, 20, 27, 50, 55, 83
Brown, Michael   20, 42
The Bruce
  See under Barbour
Bruce, Mary   76
Bruce, Robert, 5th Lord of Annandale, the
  Competitor   3, 71
Brut chronicles   95
Brutus   32, 55, 57, 151, 153

INDEX

The Buke of the Howlat   6, 17, 27, 41–9, 50, 143, 172, 176
   Bruce's heart   45–6
   frame narrative   44, 47–8
   heraldic core   43–6
   representation of Gaelic   47–9
Burns, J.H.   124
Bynum, Caroline Walker   76

Cairns, Sandra   138, 139
Cameron, Jamie   150
Camille, Michael   141
Camillo, Giulio   133, 141
Carlisle   19
Carpenter, Sarah   126
Carruthers, Mary   11–12, 14, 80, 81, 105, 107, 115, 166
Caruth, Cathy   97
Cecilia, St   119
Charles VII, King of France   53
Chartier, Alain   156
   Le Breviaire de Nobles   156
   Le Quadrilogue Invectif   149, 154, 156, 163, 166
   Le Traité de l'Esperance   156
Chaucer, Geoffrey   131
   The Parliament of Fowls   131
Chepman, Walter   100, 156
Chronicle of Melrose   20
Chronicon de Lanercost   23
Cochrane, Thomas   146
Cohen, Jeffrey Jerome   22, 57, 76
Complaynt of Scotland   149, 150–71, 172
   Barns of Ayr   158–60
   clothing, in   164–7, 177
   Dame Scotia   158–9, 161, 162, 165, 167–9, 170
   dangers of forgetting   162, 174
   popular stories in   158
   tiredness and melancholy, in   163–4
Comyn, John, earl of Buchan   73
Comyn, Sir John, Lord of Badenoch ('the Red')   4, 37, 72, 73
Comyn, Walter, earl of Menteith   68–9
Coombs, Bryony   47, 83
Coote, Lesley   50
Coupar Angus, abbey   17, 84–5, 94–5
Craig, Alexander   177, 178
   'Scotland's Teares'   177
Crawford, Barbara   52
Crichton family   51

Daniel, Samuel   176
   A Panegyrike Congratvlatorie   175–6
David, earl of Huntingdon   71
David I, King of Scots   19, 51, 62
David II, King of Scots   5
Declaration of Arbroath   74
Dodd, Gwilym   95
Domat, Bremond   83
Donaldson, Gordon   150
Douglas, Archibald, 3rd earl of Douglas ('the Grim')   35, 44 n.64
Douglas, Archibald, 6th earl of Angus   83, 123, 126
Douglas, Archibald, earl of Moray   42, 43, 44 n.64
Douglas family   35, 43–5, 46–7, 50, 173
   Black Douglases   21, 26, 42, 43, 51
Douglas, Gavin   131, 173
   Eneados   173
   The Palice of Honour   130
Douglas, Sir James (d. 1330)   41, 42, 44, 45, 46, 49
Douglas, James, 7th earl of Douglas   42
Douglas, James, 9th earl of Douglas   42
Douglas, James, earl of Morton   156
Douglas, William, 1st earl of Douglas and earl of Mar   35
Douglas, William, 8th earl of Douglas   42
Dreams   30, 31–3, 61, 117–18, 120, 126–8, 130–1, 133, 134, 136, 137, 138–9, 154, 157, 160, 163–8, 170
The Dreme of Schir David Lyndesay of the Mont   125, 126–43
   John the Commoun Weill   133, 143
Dubh, Angus   26
Dunbar, Battle of   4
Dunbar, Elizabeth   42
Dunbar, William   48–9, 131, 134, 144
   The Flyting of Dunbar and Kennedy   48–9
   The Goldyn Targe   134
   'Quhen Merche wes with variand windis past'   130
Dunnigan, Sarah   177–8
Dupplin Moor, battle of   5

Edinburgh Castle   27, 156
   library   156
Edinburgh-Northampton, Treaty of   4
Edward I, King of England   4, 17, 21, 22, 55, 58, 71, 73, 76, 77, 88, 89, 91,

INDEX

92, 93–4, 96, 104, 105, 110, 151, 152, 153, 174, 177
Edward II, King of England   152, 174
Edward III, King of England   5, 23–4,
Edward IV, King of England   113
    daughter, Cecily   113
Edward VI, King of England   152
Elizabeth I, Queen of England   175
Elliott, Elizabeth   14, 48–9
Eneados
    See under Douglas, Gavin
Erasing memory   88, 92, 96, 171
Eric II, King of Norway   71
Ewan, Elizabeth   5, 125
Extracta e variis cronicis Scocie   82, 85

Faculty psychology   12, 133, 145
Falaise, Treaty of   20
Fisher, Matthew   95
Flodden, battle of   17, 83, 122, 123, 124, 131, 148, 151, 156, 157
Flores Historiarum   72
Fordun, John of   17, 50, 57, 62, 65, 68, 77, 83–4, 85, 86–7, 89–92, 94, 96, 97, 98, 103, 113, 114, 117, 145, 157–8, 173–4
    Chronica Gentis Scotorum   27, 48, 51, 55, 72, 89
Forgetfulness *see also* erasing memory
    and   7, 14, 16, 17, 58, 96, 111, 113, 116, 121, 129, 149, 162, 173, 174, 177
    and intent   17, 75, 77, 88–9, 113, 121, 172
Forter, Greg   100
Francis I, King of France   151, 152
Frese, Dolores Warwick   114–15

Galen   12
Gaythelos   53, 55–6, 57, 58–9, 60, 63, 64, 68, 74, 83
Genealogy   17, 34, 46, 48, 52, 53–5, 60, 63–4, 65, 67–8, 69, 70, 71, 72, 77, 83, 103, 154, 155
    as memorial structure   50–2, 55, 60–70, 77–8, 80, 173
Gesta Annalia   27, 50, 55, 103
Geoffrey of Monmouth   160
    Historia Regum Britanniae   160
Godfrey de Bouillon   155
Goff, Jacques le   118
Goldstein, R. James   4, 6, 37, 38, 57, 106, 108–9

Gower, John   144
Gray, Douglas   131
Gray, Sir Patrick   39
Gray, Sir Thomas   23, 27
Gray, Sir Thomas   26, 27–8
    Scalacronica   6, 16, 17, 22–4, 26, 27–34, 35, 41, 46, 47, 49, 72–7, 137, 164, 172, 174–5, 177
Great Cause   3, 57, 58, 71, 93, 151
Gregory I (Pope)   9
Grief   105–7, 108–11, 121
    and memory   109–10
Guinevere   57
Guisborough, Walter of   23

Hadley Williams, Janet   148
Halbwachs, Maurice   16, 68, 80
Halidon Hill, battle of   21
Hamilton of Finnart, James   150
Hamilton, James, 2nd earl of Arran   154
Hary   16, 104, 105, 106, 113, 116, 117, 120, 121, 159, 174
    See The Wallace
Hay, Sir Gilbert   142
    Buik of King Alexander the Conqueror   142
Hay, Richard   84–5
Heng, Geraldine   9–10
Henrisoun, James   153
    Exhortacion to the Scottes   153
Henry II, King of England   19–20
Henry III, King of England   19
Henry IV, King of England   5
Henry VII, King of England   123
Henry VIII, King of England   150, 152, 154, 159, 160, 168
    Declaration   151, 153–4
Henryson, Robert   130
    The Testament of Cresseid   130, 131–2
Hiber, son of Gaythelos   56, 63
Higden, Ranulf   31, 160
    Polychronicon   160
Higgitt, John   15, 64, 66
Historia Regum Britanniae
    See under Geoffrey of Monmouth
Holland, Richard   16, 26–7, 42–3, 50, 143, 144, 172–3, 176
    See also Buke of the Howlat
Hübl, Milan   88
Hugh de Cressingham   23
Hugh of St Victor   32, 107

202 INDEX

construction of memorial places 14, 107
De arca Noe morali 107–8
De tribus maximis circumstantiis gestorum 14
Hundred Years War 27
Hutson, Lorna 152

Ibn Sina [Avicenna] 12
Ingham, Patricia 8–9
Ingoge, wife of Brutus 57
Inheritance 46, 52, 53, 58, 69, 153, 175
See also genealogy
Ireland, John 122
The Meroure of Wyssdome 124

Jager, Eric 45
James I, King of Scots 51, 53, 68, 70, 146, 147, 156
The Kingis Quair 130, 147
James II, King of Scots 25, 42, 44, 50, 51, 52, 68, 70, 97, 172
James III, King of Scots 25, 99, 100, 113–14, 121, 122, 124, 146, 174
James IV, King of Scots 50, 83, 122–3, 124, 125, 130, 131, 134, 147, 157
as duke of Rothesay 113
James V, King of Scots 18, 83, 123, 125, 126, 127, 128–9, 132, 136, 137, 140, 143, 144, 146, 147, 148, 150–1, 154, 168, 174
James VI/I, King of Scots and England 15, 156, 157, 175, 177–8
John, earl of Carrick
See Robert III
John of Salisbury 15
Policraticus 15, 143
John of Tynemouth 31–2 n.39
Historia Aurea 39
Justice, Steven 93

Kantorowicz, Ernst 62
Kennedy, Walter 144
King, Andy 20, 21, 22
Knox, John 151
History of the Reformation in Scotland 151
Kundera, Milan 88

Largs, battle of 24–5, 61
Lavezzo, Kathy 9
Lawlor, H.J. 85
Lebor Gabála 55

Leland, John 33
Leulingham, Treaty of 38
Leyden, John 163
Liber Extravagans
See under Scotichronicon
Liber Pluscardensis 82–3, 84
Lindsay, Sir David, Lord of Glen Esk 39–40
Lindsay of Pitscottie, Robert 124
Livingston family 43, 51
Louis XI, King of France 53, 156
Louis XII, King of France 122–3
Louis, duke of Orléans 38, 40–1
Louis, St, of France 53
Lyndsay, Sir David 16, 18, 121, 122, 124–6, 129, 130, 131, 148, 174
appointed Lyon king of arms 126
Ane Satyre of the Thrie Estaitis 126, 140, 156, 161, 166, 168
The Complaynt of Bagsche 129
The Complaynt of Schir Dauid Lindesay 128–9
See also The Dreme
See also The Testament of the Papyngo

Maccabees 73–4, 169
Maccabeus, Judas 73
MacDonald, Alasdair M. 43, 122
MacDougall, Norman 113–14, 123
Macduff, Isabel, Countess of Buchan 72–7
capture at battle of Methven 76
imprisonment at Berwick 76
Madeleine of Valois 150
Mair, John 85
Historia majoris Britanniae (*History of Greater Britain*) 85
Máel Coluim II, earl of Fife 64
Máel Coluim (Malcolm) III, King of Alba 34, 35, 52, 60, 61, 64
Máel Coluim (Malcolm) IV, King of Scots 19
Malise II, earl of Strathearn 52, 64
Mapstone, Sally 68, 82, 83, 124, 142
Margaret of Denmark, queen of Scots 25
Margaret, Maid of Norway 3, 10, 70–1, 151, 152
Margaret, St, queen of *Alba* 34, 35, 52, 60–1
Margaret Tudor 83, 123, 126, 130
Marsland, Rebecca 157
Martin, Joanna 70, 137, 151
Mary of Guise 150, 154, 155, 156

INDEX

Mason, Roger 151–2
McDiarmid, Matthew 99, 113
McKim, Anne 108
McKitterick, Rosamund 116
Memory
  as beehive 91–2
  books, and 91–3, 115, 121, 173–4
  cave as metaphor 132–3, 141
  collective memory 11, 15–16, 20, 80,
    89, 91, 92, 96, 98, 100, 105,
    114–15, 121
  emotion, and 45, 79, 98, 105–6, 110,
    140, 145, 146, 147, 163, 164
  excess of 163, 165
  heart as metaphor 45–6, 90, 110,
    145–6
  imagination, and 3, 12, 13, 14, 49, 90,
    93, 106, 138, 144, 163, 172
  ladders, as 32–3, 34, 99
  libri memoriales 116, 117
  melancholy, and 133, 163–4
  money pouch as metaphor 14
  storehouse as metaphor 13, 106–7, 111,
    119, 130
  as wax tablets 13, 115, 136
  as writing surface 45
  See also forgetfulness
Memory training
  Ars memoria 16, 79, 107, 138, 147
  architecture, and 92, 96
  bodily senses, and 13, 12, 90, 163
  ethics, and 12, 36–7, 81, 108, 125,
    138–9
  writing, and 15, 33, 38, 45, 53, 81,
    88–9, 90, 91, 93, 95, 96, 102,
    108, 111–13, 115, 116, 146–7, 172,
    174
  zodiac, and 141–2
Menteith, Sir John 4, 37
Merlin 160
Merriman, Marcus 152, 153
Moll, Richard 29
Moray, Andrew 4
Moray, Angus de 26
Moses 55, 56, 57
Mowbray, Sir Alexander 23
Myllar, Andrew 100, 156

Nennius
  Historia Brittonum, attributed to 55
Neville, Cynthia 20, 21
Neville's Cross, battle of 5, 21, 27
Newsome, Helen 123

Noah's Ark 107–8
Nora, Pierre 106
  Lieu de mémoire 106, 113
Norham (Northumberland) 26, 27

O'Brien O'Keeffe, Katherine 115
Ogilvy, Walter 39
Ollamh rig Alban (master poet of the king
  of Scotland) 68
Original Chronicle, The 17, 21, 26, 27,
  34–41, 84, 86, 104, 172, 173
  Glasklune episode 38–40
  Sir David Lindsay fights Sir John
    Welles 40–1
Owst, G.R. 107

Passio Scotorum Perjuratorum 72–3
Patten, William 152
  The Expedicion into Scotlande 152
Perpetual Peace, Treaty of 123
Perth, Treaty of 24
Philip IV, King of France 4
Pinkie Cleugh, battle of 152, 153, 157
Poirion, Daniel 15
The Porteous of Nobleness 156
Processus
  See under Bisset, Baldred
Prudence 18, 134, 135–9, 141, 144, 146,
  148, 165, 166, 174
Purdie, Rhiannon 35

Randolph, Thomas, earl of Moray 4–5
Ranum, Orest 8
Renan, Ernst 7
Reynolds, Susan 7
Rhetorica ad Herennium 12
Richard I, King of England 20
Richard de Bury 13–14, 32, 91
  Philobiblon 91
Ricoeur, Paul 111, 112, 113
Riddy, Felicity 42, 99
ritual 63, 67, 70, 108, 112
  connection with memory 63, 68, 113
Robert I, the Bruce, King of Scots 4, 5,
  6, 21, 22, 41, 42, 44, 45–6, 49, 71,
  74, 75, 77, 88, 93, 120, 135
  inauguration 72–3, 74, 75–6
  murder of John Comyn 37, 73
Robert II, King of Scots 21, 34, 37, 38,
  39, 173
Robert III, King of Scots 37, 40
  eldest son, David, duke of
    Rothesay 35

INDEX

Rojas, Fernando de   30
   La Celestina   30
Rough Wooings   152, 153
Royan, Nicola   5, 77

Salmond, Alex, First Minister of
   Scotland   2
Sauchieburn, battle of   122
Scota   53, 55–9, 60, 63–4, 68, 69, 71, 72,
   73, 74, 75, 76, 77, 83, 167
Scotichronicon   9, 17, 26, 50, 53–71,
   73–4, 100, 103, 117, 121, 124, 130,
   135, 167
   abridged versions   81–6
   Advice to Princes in   68
   Cambridge, Corpus Christi College,
      MS   51
   Coupar Angus MS (NLS, Adv. MS
      35.1.7)   17, 79–98, 103–4, 105,
      106, 114, 157–8, 173–4
   Declaration of Arboath in   73–4
   illustrations in   58–9, 64–7
   Liber Extravagans   60
Secretum Secretorum   141, 142, 143
Seneca   86, 135
   Four Virtues   135
Seymour, Edward, 1st duke of
   Somerset   152, 160
   Epistle or exhortaction, to unite &
      peace   153
Shakespeare, William   1
   Macbeth   1
Shaw, Quintin   69
   The Voyage of Court   69
Sibyl   31–2, 33, 137
Sinclair, Henry, Bishop of Ross   85
Sinclair, William, 3rd earl of Orkney and
   1st earl of Caithness   52, 85
Sinclair, William (d. 1585)   85
Skene, W.F.   85
Solway Moss, battle of   151, 152
Spiegel, Gabrielle   51–2
Stephen, King of England   19
Stewart, A.M.   154, 161
Stewart, Alexander, earl of Buchan   39
Stewart, Alexander, earl of Mar   34
Stewart, David, duke of Rothesay   35
Stewart, John, duke of Albany   83
Stewart, Marion   42–3
Stewart, Mary, Queen of Scots   15, 151–2,
   154, 156

Stewart, Robert, earl of Fife and duke of
   Albany   34
Stewart of Rosyth, Sir David   51, 87
Stirling Bride, battle of   4
Stringer, Keith   62
Stuart d'Aubigny, Bérault   47

Taylor, Brian   2
Terrell, Katherine   16, 50
The Testament and Complaynt of Our
   Soverane Lordis Papyngo   18, 125,
   130–1, 143–8, 174
Thomas the Rhymer (Thomas of
   Erceldoun)   129–30
The Thre Prestis of Peblis   156
Trauma   11, 96, 97, 100–1, 102, 103–4, 122
   and remembering   103, 104, 105, 110,
   111, 121
Turville-Petre, Thorlac   9
Twomey, Michael   158

Vairement, Richard (Veremundus)   50
Van Dijk, Ann   67
Van Houts, Elisabeth   75
Veremundus, *see* Vairement, Richard
Vergil, Polydore   160
Villon, François   14
Virgin Mary   67, 109, 118, 120, 137

The Wallace   6, 17, 76, 82, 97, 98,
   99–121, 158, 159–60, 162, 164, 174
   anti-English sentiment   103, 105–6,
      111, 113, 114, 157
   Barns of Ayr   100, 104–8, 112–13
   death of Wallace's *leman*   100, 109–10
   manuscript and print   99–100
   Ranald's corpse   108–9, 112
   Wallace's execution   112, 117–20
   Wallace's vision at Monkton   120–1
   See also Hary
Walter of Oxford   31
Walsingham, Thomas   93
   Chronicon Angliae   93
Warbeck, Perkin   123
Wars of Independence   3–6, 11, 17–18, 20,
   38, 41, 61, 74, 77, 79, 122, 124, 148,
   160, 170, 174
Wedderburn, Robert   16, 18, 154, 155,
   156–7, 158, 160, 163, 170
   see also Complaynt of Scotland
Weiss, Julian   30
Wemyss of Wemyss, Sir John   34–5

INDEX

Wallace, William   4, 37, 99–100, 114, 116, 162
Watt, D.E.R.   81, 85, 94
William I, King of Scots   19–20, 71
Wormald, Jenny   48, 151
Wyntoun, Andrew of   16, 26, 27, 34–5, 36–7, 38, 40, 41, 84, 103, 172, 173

the 'Anonymous Contributor'   21, 34, 38
see also Original Chronicle

Ygerna   57
Yolande, queen of Scots   70–1
York, Treaty of (1237)   19